*Sterling Nixon*

**STERLING NIXON**

The final approval for this literary material is granted by the author.
First printing

All characters appearing in this work are fictitious. Any resemblance to real people, living or dead, is purely coincidental.

ISBN: 978-1-951780-34-0 (Trade Paperback)
978-1-951780-35-7 (eBook)
978-1-951780-36-4 (Trade Hardcover)
978-1-951780-37-1 (Audiobook)

Dedicated to Talon, Avelyn, and Janey

## ONE

Acadia—the last human city, a fact every citizen was told from birth. Over two hundred years of war, and yet the Eight Gates still stood, scarred from battle, but unbroken, much like the people living behind them. The massive steel doors looked ominous and foreboding amidst perpetually gray days, standing as a reminder of the death and destruction that lay beyond.

Cojax stared over the defensive ramparts, his eyes barely seeing over the bottom of the wall. He was only in his tenth year— still a Dependent, still a net drain on the city's resources, but that would change soon enough.

This morning he had found himself with more free time than normal, as his schooling was let out early after the exhaustive yearly exams had concluded. He had passed, as always, as was expected from the son of a Numberless. This would be the last year of his secular study, of researching and learning about the histories and cultures of the past—where they went wrong, how democracies formed and fell, and how Acadia removed all inequities and rot from the past.

A breeze picked up, whipping through his black hair, carrying the sounds of the dead land toward him. It was a stoic sight, the land covered in gray dirt and ash, the battlefield of his people. It had once been a rich field for crops, now turned crimson clay with the mix of the blood of his people and *them*.

"There you are," a voice said from behind. "I've been up and down all four hundred stairs looking for you."

Cojax turned, pretended not to be startled. It was Finn, a triplet and one of his best friends.

"Are we even supposed to be here? At the Wall?" Finn asked. "I don't want to have to endure another tongue clamping."

Cojax smiled, a cocky grin spreading across his lips. "If we aren't, I would've gotten in trouble half an hour ago. Besides, tongue clamping is only used when you speak in public to someone of the Tiers before you've earned the right. But where've you been? Where's Brutus and Hadrian?"

"They were waiting to see if we got in trouble first," Finn said. "You know Hadrian would never venture here if there was the slightest chance it was against the rules."

Cojax rolled his eyes, pretending to be more confident than he really was. "What a bunch of Placard-polishers."

No one had expressly told him he could not go to the Wall, and he had heard about plenty of Dependents from other Factions stopping by. The Hellion Faction practically encouraged their Dependents to spend any free time on the Wall and the Prolits often used their young as unofficial spotters.

"And what about the Roaches?" Finn asked. "You're not worried about them?"

Cojax laughed. "The Roaches? Look around, Finn. We've got at least a hundred Validated within fifty yards of us, even more in the levels below." Despite these words, Cojax had rarely taken his eyes off the Killing Fields, and the holes just beyond—the place where the Roaches lived, bred, and feasted on Human flesh. They had both listened to more than one scarred Acadian's tale about the Roaches' uncanny ability to appear where they were not expected, and strike with a power they should not have possessed.

As if responding to his friend's words, Finn looked around, studying the Acadian defenses. They were at the top of a massive wall, one that encircled the entire city—creating a clear line between Humans and the creatures. The Wall was more function than form, standing over one hundred feet and half as wide. It was a peeling gray, made from an advanced form of concrete. On it stood the Validated—the defenders of the city, those that had descended into the Mahghetto and come out again to join the Tiers.

Finn was not fooled—Cojax's words were more bluster than boldness. But he did not call his friend out on it, as Brutus would have, nor did he lecture Cojax as Hadrian would have been apt to do. Instead, he nodded and joined his friend's side, scanning the dead land.

"Have you seen…any?"

"Nah," Cojax answered, his voice solemn.

As they spoke, two Validated walked past them, Blazers on their backs, Arc Blades at their sides. Despite himself, Cojax watched them out of the corner of his eye, a new wariness settling over him. Their helmets were fashioned after the ancient Greek Corinthian style, complete with a raised crest—a prominent, metallic mohawk that ran from the front of the helmet to the back. But these were no ordinary helmets. The surface was sleek and reflective, the color of bronze coupled with an opaque lens over the eyes. As the two Validated moved, the visors on their helmets flickered momentarily, displaying holographic data in the form of scrolling text and shifting maps, a quiet reminder that these warriors were no mere fighters—

What fascinated Cojax most were the glowing circuits that snaked across the armor, like amber veins pulsing with energy beneath the surface. The armor was clearly not only built for physical defense but also enhanced the wearer. It adapted, shifting and reacting to threats in real-time. As one of the Validated approached the Wall, a subtle blue glow emanated from his chest, momentarily illuminating the darkness before fading back into his form, the pulse monitor syncing with the Wall's sensors.

Their weapons—Arc Blades—were far more advanced than any conventional sword. The weapons shimmered with energy, their plasma edges crackling with intensity when charged. Cojax had heard stories about their ability to cut through steel like butter, and the way they hummed with power made his heart race. A combination of ancient craftsmanship and cutting-edge tech, the Arc Blades were deadly tools forged not only for battle but for survival in a world that had long left humanity behind.

Near the center of their right breast was perhaps the most important thing of all—their Sacred Score. It was visible on a small screen and clearly indicated their Tier and how they ranked within it. In a city of ten million Validated, this small interface made it possible to know exactly where and how one stood in the rankings—how much value they provided to society, to Acadia, to the defense of their city.

The warriors walked on, their bronze armored forms becoming silhouettes against the light-streaked horizon. Cojax and Finn exchanged a look—an unspoken acknowledgment of the world they lived in, and the forces that governed it. There were more

Validated sprinkled in twos and fours near them, each set about different tasks, all of them moving with purpose and pride. Not far from where they stood was a large circular ball known as a Gouger. It was a versatile fixture, being able to move where needed and anchoring into the wall once it arrived. Mounted into the side of it were four large Gouger cannons. A Validated was inside, his presence barely seen through the clear ports at the front and back.

"Do you think we'll ever get to wear Static Armor?" Finn whispered, nodding toward the disappearing warriors, awe evident in his voice.

"Of course, when we're older… when we're Validated," Cojax replied, though his tone was more uncertain than he meant to sound. The weight of the armor—the responsibility it carried—was not something that could be earned easily. And in a city built on the foundation of perfect merit, only the Validated, a member of the Tiers, would be allowed to wear it. Cojax couldn't help but feel a mix of envy and fear. The Roaches, with their insidious strength, the Killing Fields, the blood of his people stained across the land—it was all too much to take in.

And then the Horns of Acadia blew, sending a palpable tension through the air.

# TWO

*They had come.*

Finn and Cojax exchanged a poignant look, their minds racing. They both knew what this meant even though neither of them had heard it this close before. The sound was cast from hidden speakers and echoed from the Wall, bouncing off the Corinthian-style buildings made of concrete and sometimes faced with marble.

"Let's get out of here," Finn said, pure panic in his voice.

"Wait," Cojax said simply, his mind too occupied for more words. The Horn of Acadia was a call to arms—a call to battle. An invading force had been spotted somewhere along the Wall, and defenders were responding en masse.

"Come on, Cojax!" Finn said, his voice somehow even more urgent. "You've had your fun."

"Wait," he repeated, his voice so low it was almost carried away in the sound of the assembling warriors. Finn turned around, surprised at the gathering Validated behind him. It had been only mere moments, but already thirty of them had appeared, lining up on the Wall in perfect formation, their armor and weapons streaking with the occasional flash of light—hinting at the shields that protected them. The Wall was so wide it could easily accommodate forty warriors standing front to back, and it would not be much longer before the space was filled—blocking the two young friends from an easy retreat.

Finn gave it one last try. "Cojax, I'm leaving with or without you." He pulled at his friend's arm, but Cojax remained firm, unable to take his eyes from the Killing Field. Finn gave one last desperate tug before giving up completely and fleeing back down the hundreds of stairs that were set in the interior of the Wall.

Cojax was transfixed, his mind taking in the horrific sight. For over two hundred years these creatures had attempted to wipe them out, but they had failed—but perhaps today would be the day that all changed, the day they breached the Wall and flooded through the streets in a wave of carapace and mandibles, turning all to blood and broken bone.

Since the age of six, he'd collected Roach trading cards—each one a glossy window into the enemy's anatomy, strengths, weaknesses, and the strange quirks that set one variant apart from another. His collection was the largest of any that he knew by a large margin, having spent every point he ever earned on them. His mind had been obsessed with the beasts—their sheer size, their individual strengths, and their brutal appendages, each one clinically designed for a single purpose: to kill Acadians, to wipe out the last vestiges of humanity.

But it was one thing seeing a SataniKahn on a playing card, it was something else entirely to see it with your own eyes. Despite the distance, Cojax could pick out the large beasts, their sheer bulk highlighted among the swarming creatures. They stood out among the black carapace, like siege towers of old, their dozens of dagger-like limbs sticking out at odd and asymmetrical locations. They were marbled black and white, their eyes eerily devoid of pupils. Around them, even though Cojax could not see them clearly, were the Reevers, the backbone of the Roach forces. What they lacked in size they made up for in quantity. He knew well that there were dozens of different types, some that exploded upon death while others were covered in thorns that could be shot free from their bodies, but by far the most numerous were the Reever Subjugators, a minor class creature with pincers so strong they could snip through a beam of iron. When they moved, their dozen legs would rub against each other, creating an eerie sound akin to a pair of rusty scissors being opened and closed rapidly.

Despite the distance, Cojax could hear the sound. "It's true. It's all true…" Though he hadn't earned the right to watch the CityScreens, he still knew the creatures were real, knew the danger they posed to Acadia. Yet doubt lingered. He was skeptical by nature, and some part of him always wondered if the threat of the Roaches was merely a lie—another tactic to force obedience. But now that it was all before him, it was undeniable. The creatures existed—and there was no doubt as to their intent.

The air began to hum as HoverBuckets and CargoLifters

passed overhead, each carrying dozens of Validated. The vehicles flew in droves, like swarms of locusts, bursting at the seams with bodies and blades. Twenty yards from the wall, they landed in a flash of dirt and debris, Validated spilling from them with a dire urgency. Within a minute, tens of thousands of Acadians were lining up outside the Wall in exact, boxy formations with incredible efficiency.

*"Why do they form outside the Wall?"* Cojax thought, stunned by the sudden change on the battlefield. *"Why not just hold the Wall?"*

It didn't take long for the Acadians on the ground to transform into a hundred independent Phalanx formations, their lines perfectly aligned with near mechanical precision. They formed a sweeping "V" shape, each column angled just behind the center, which surged slightly ahead like the tip of a spear. Yet it wasn't the formation itself that stunned Cojax—it was how it emerged. No shouted orders. No barked commands. Just silence. Somehow, the commanding Omega had relayed every position with flawless clarity, as if the warriors were linked by instinct. Cojax had always known his people were born for war, forged by battle—but witnessing this unity, this wordless synchronicity, was something else entirely.

Then the battle began.

The Validated opened with a thunderous barrage—blistering volleys launched from the Blazers they had pulled from their backs, while the Gougers stationed along the Wall rained death from above. In response, the Roaches surged forward, overtaken by a sudden, savage frenzy. The black tide of carapace came alive, seething and writhing—creatures crazed with bloodlust, desperate to tear into human flesh.

When the two sides collided, the air detonated with light and sound. Explosions flared. Metal screamed. The earth shook from the sheer violence of the clash. Cojax flinched, instinctively stepping back as the ground shuddered beneath him.

At the vanguard stood the SataniKahns—towering beasts with massive limbs that outpaced the smaller Roaches. They hit the Acadian lines like living battering rams, their hooked mandibles cleaving into the Acadians' collective shields with merciless force. It was a brutal, grinding assault.

Cojax stood unmoving, eyes locked on the chaos before him. Time slipped away, unmeasured and irrelevant. Still, the Acadians held. Their compact Phalanx formations—smaller than the enemy, but disciplined and unyielding—pushed back with ferocious precision, holding the line.

But then—something shifted.

A fracture rippled through the front ranks of the Validated. At first, a few fell. Then a dozen. Then more. The unity of their collective shields had shattered, and now they were each on their own. The Roaches pressed in, sensing the break. Sensing the kill.

Cojax grimaced as the glory of battle dissolved into raw, unfiltered chaos. What had moments before felt like righteous triumph now reeked of blood and ruin. From his vantage point, the carnage was almost unreal—limbs torn, steel shrieking against chitin, the earth itself seeming to cry out beneath the slaughter. A sudden surge of nausea overwhelmed him, his mouth pooling with saliva. He lurched forward, ready to vomit—

—when the wall beside him exploded.

Something the size of a boulder slammed into the stonework with a thunderous crack. It twitched. Twisted. A tangle of serrated limbs unfolded from its body, its spine bent grotesquely at unnatural angles. Cojax froze. His brain refused to comprehend the nightmare that writhed before him.

Then another landed beside it.

This one had a gaping maw that stretched from cheek to cheek, lined with fangs slick with acidic drool. Each drop sizzled on the stone, carving through it like molten metal. These things— whatever they were—had hurled themselves onto the Wall by violently dislocating their spines, turning the whip-crack recoil into biomechanical propulsion.

In seconds, the creatures were everywhere.

Dozens rained down from the sky like a plague, crashing into the ramparts with bone-crunching force. Their limbs flailed, slicing through steel and flesh alike. One turned to him, its gaze devoid of reason, only hunger. In that moment, Cojax knew he was only a breath from death.

Then—light.

In a flash, Arc Blades cleaved through the air, Arc Spears found their mark. The Validated had arrived. Their weapons lit the air with arcs of energy, carving black trails through the creatures' armored hides. One beast screamed—a sound like tearing metal—and toppled back off the Wall, its ichor spraying in a steaming arc.

Cojax snapped back to life, adrenaline flooding his veins. He turned to flee—too late. A clawed limb swung down and grazed his head, knocking him off balance. He crashed hard onto the stone, the breath blasted from his lungs. Another creature barreled into him, but he rolled instinctively, squeezing himself into a narrow crevice between a ruined Gouger and the rear parapet. Just enough space for one terrified boy.

He curled into himself, hands clamped over his ears, eyes slammed shut, trying to block out the screams, the screeches, the dying. Urine stained the front of his pants.

The Wall shook. Another wave crashed against it. The Acadians fought bravely, but they were being overrun. At one point, something enormous struck the Gouger above Cojax's head. It broke free with a metallic groan and tumbled off the parapet, disappearing into the city below like a falling star. Cojax didn't see it. He was too busy praying the monsters wouldn't find him next.

Hours passed. Cojax did not move, hardly daring to breathe, hovering above the pool of vomit that collected under his chin. Slowly, the sounds subsided, the battle noises grew distant and died. Still, he hid, fearful it was some sort of trap.

When Cojax finally crawled from his hiding place, the world had changed.

Smoke drifted through the air like ghostly veils. The sharp scent of burning flesh and ozone filled his lungs. All around him, the Wall had become a graveyard. Shattered stone. Spilled ichor. Torn banners. Blood.

A Validated lay just a few spans away. The man's armor had been split open at the chest, his polished plating peeled back like tin, exposing a deep, mortal wound. Yet his eyes—his eyes still held the horizon. Wide. Unblinking. Cojax froze, thinking him dead, until he noticed the faint rise and fall of the man's chest. Shallow. Strained. But breathing.

And somehow—the dying man was calm. No moans. No pleading. No desperate reaching. Just silence. The soldier stared into the distance as if he could still see some far-off shore beyond the blood and smoke. Then came a final breath—thin and rasping—and he was still.

Cojax knelt beside him, unable to look away. He felt a sudden, sharp ache behind his eyes, a pressure he couldn't name. He hadn't known the man. Didn't even know his name. But at that moment, it didn't matter. He felt a wrenching pity for the man—for the family he was leaving behind.

All around, bodies were strewn like discarded puppets—Roaches cut in half, their limbs twitching in the last echoes of nerve-fire; Validated warriors broken, their weapons still clutched in death grips, their faces still etched with emotion. Some still lived—barely. The dying gasped, choked, reached for comrades who would never rise again.

Cojax staggered to his feet, alone among the wreckage. Whatever glory had existed in the beginning, it had died here—gutted on the Wall, buried beneath bodies and silence. He had no sense of time. He didn't know how many hours he'd stood there, mind blank, lost in the void. Eventually, a single thought drifted through: they had won. The Wall was theirs again. The invaders had been driven back. The attackers had managed to seize a narrow stretch of the ramparts for a few hours—no more than two hundred yards in either direction from where Cojax stood.

Other Validated began to emerge, moving with grim efficiency. Some arrived aboard CargoLifters—massive freighters that descended with a mechanical whine, their undersides lined with magnetic harnesses. The twisted bodies of Roaches were strapped down, their broken carapaces lashed in place before being hauled back over the Wall—returned to the wasteland from which they came, like cursed offerings thrown back into the abyss.

The fallen Validated were handled differently.

Their bodies were lifted with care, but without ceremony, placed onto the backs of Rovers—sleek aerial vehicles with exposed cargo beds. The dead were flown away, toward the Trinity.

No one ever said where.

No rites. No final words. No monuments etched with names. They simply vanished—swallowed by the Trinity. The wounded were treated by the Medicus, their value restored so they could return to duty.

His body retched but nothing came up. He had lost the

contents of his stomach long before. He was largely ignored by the Validated who were busy at work. Occasionally, he was roughly pushed to the side if he got in the way. He felt sick, his mind going through the phases of Battle Shock, his head spinning, his stomach muscles tightening. He came close to retching again but was barely able to keep it at bay. Despite himself, he was drawn to the ramparts again, the place where he first spotted the Roaches. He had to see the aftermath, the devastation that was left behind. His mind needed to see what had become of the ranks of Validated. He had to see how his people had fared. Then he saw it and all breath left his lungs.

The losses were not as great as he had supposed. The Acadians had been pushed hard on the right flank, in the area just below him.

"The Roaches were trying to get close," Cojax said as he reviewed the tactic. He was not the smartest Dependent; he did not have a photographic memory like Hadrian, nor did he receive top marks in his Earth studies, but where he proved talented was in his ability to analyze information. Given time, he could develop new solutions to old, persistent problems.

"They needed to get close enough so the launching creature could reach the Walls," Cojax whispered. The tactic seemed odd, almost naïve. The Roaches had pushed hard, but eventually their flanks paid the price and they were enveloped by Validated from both sides, as evidenced by the mound of dead carapace in the area just in front of him. The tactic was costly and tens of thousands of Roaches paid the price.

*"But why? Just so they could experiment with their new launching Roach? Just to see how effective they were?"*

The more Cojax thought about it, the less it made sense. The logic unraveled as he scanned the battlefield, trying to piece together the fragments of a conclusion he didn't yet understand.

That's when he saw it.

Something was standing in the Killing Field, faintly moving amid the heaps of dead. It walked on two legs—like a Human—but wore no armor, carried no weapon. It was distant, barely more than a shadow against the haze, but Cojax's eyes didn't lie.

Then it vanished, swallowed by the low-lying fog.

A quarter-hour passed before a breeze stirred the mist,

peeling it back like a curtain. The figure reappeared, small and strangely unthreatening. Too benign. Too out of place. It shuffled forward, arms clutched tightly to its chest, pausing every few paces as if exhausted.

Whatever it was, it wasn't a Roach. But what *was* it?

Cojax waited for someone—anyone—to sound the alarm. Surely the Validated had seen it by now. He glanced left. Then right. No reaction. No movement. No raised voices. The soldiers were scanning for larger threats, watching the sky and the ridgelines beyond.

Then it struck him. *"It's too small. They're looking past it. Why aren't the sensors picking it up?"* He should alert someone. *"They need to know."* But he hesitated.

He hadn't earned the right to speak in public. He was still an Innocent—unproven, unrecognized. And in Acadia, speaking without status brought punishments. Harsh ones.

Public humiliation on the CityScreens. Loss of water privileges. Reduced food selection. Solitary confinement. Public lashings. And worst of all—tongue clamping. Just the memory of the cold iron on his tongue made him recoil. But worse than any punishment was the thought of his father's eyes—stern, disappointed.

Still, one voice echoed in his mind: *"Cowardice is the greatest ill of all."*

He breathed deep.

*"I might be disobedient,"* he thought, *"but I'm not a coward."*

Then—an idea.

*"Who says I need to speak?"*

He turned and approached a Validated stationed a few spans away—a tall, broad-shouldered woman in gleaming armor. He tapped her elbow. She turned sharply, expecting a fellow soldier. Instead, her gaze dropped to find Cojax.

Her mouth opened, a reprimand surely forming on her lips, but before she could speak, Cojax pointed toward the Killing Field. At first, she didn't follow his gesture. But when he jabbed more urgently, her eyes narrowed, tracing the line of his finger.

And then she saw it.

Her expression changed in an instant. She lifted her hand to the side of her helmet and spoke rapidly into her Comm-Link, her voice tight, focused. Cojax couldn't hear the words, but he could tell—things were about to change.

Then panic flushed through Cojax, his mind splitting into other possibilities. *"Is this another attack?"*

It was not long before more Validated appeared on the Wall, all of them from the BloodBorne Faction, as indicated by the red symbol in the upper right of their Score Placard. Several of them pointed out the creature while they talked amongst themselves. Cojax felt a little encouraged by the fact that, like him, the warriors had no idea what this creature was. One of the guards triggered the call for battle, which sent a pulse into the right hand of every active Validated Acadian. It was not the highest alert, not like it had been only hours before, and so only those Factions closest to the gate were called.

Once again, the Wall began to swell with Validated.

Cojax's eyes went wide, the horror he had faced returned all at once. He fled for the stairs, careful not to run into any Validated. This nightmare had just started to replay itself, and he wanted no part of it. When he finally reached the ground level, Validated were already in rank and file, their bronze armor reflecting the low-light from the sun, their shields raised and creating an impenetrable wall.

Cojax wished he could melt into the ground—slip between the cracks and vanish. Shame and dread gnawed at his insides. He knew he was in trouble; he just didn't know how much.

Then *he* appeared.

*"Attention! Numberless present!"* came the cry.

It could have been Cojax's salvation—or his damnation. Either way, it was too late to hide. The crowd shifted. Warriors parted like water before a prow, an unseen force pushing them aside. Helmets dipped. Hands snapped into salutes. Silence fell across the parade grounds.

He walked among them like a living myth.

A Numberless—one of the Fifty, a member of the Infinite Council.

Towering nearly half a foot above the tallest soldier, his presence demanded attention. His armor gleamed obsidian— polished to a mirror sheen, etched with thin, amber-lit energy lines that pulsed like veins of living light. A blood-red cape flowed behind him, brushing the stone as he moved. His arms glowed with embedded sensory tech, illuminating the battle tattoos that wound like serpents up his thick limbs.

*Titan.*

Slayer of the Nartic—the twisted monster that had annihilated an entire Quorum at Devil's Gate. Savior of North Crest Ridge. Defender of the Sacred Score. The Omega who stood firm for two days at the Eastern Concave—where blood fell like rain and the ground cracked from the weight of the fallen.

He was legend made flesh.

"Open the gate," Titan commanded, his voice deep and resonant.

For a moment, nothing happened.

Then the ground groaned—a deep, subterranean growl, like some ancient beast awakening beneath their feet. A series of metallic clangs echoed outward as massive gears locked into motion. The great gate shuddered, then began to part, slowly and powerfully. A shaft of diffused light pierced the shaded grounds, widening with every mechanical breath, scattering the shadows. Wind roared through the opening, whipping up a funnel of dust and debris. It spiraled into the air, sweeping through the crowd like a judgment.

Cojax stood frozen, caught in the maelstrom of awe and fear.

Titan had come.

And everything was about to change.

Cojax was so distracted by the gate, he failed to notice the large figure now standing at his side.

"What are you doing here, boy?"

Cojax turned slowly, his stomach twisting into a knot. He recognized the voice instantly. It was a Numberless—a Numberless he knew all too well. Despite every effort, he couldn't bring himself to meet the man's eyes. Instead, he bowed low, pressing his fist to his chest.

"I'm sorry… Father."

"Stay at my side," Titan said, his voice low and thunderous. "Stray from it, and I'll Rift you myself."

Cojax knew full well that Innocents couldn't legally be Rifted—but he also knew Titan never made idle threats. That warning was enough. He saluted and fell into step behind his father without a word.

Titan strode toward the widening gate, his massive form cutting through the crowd like a blade through silk. The Numberless' blood-red cloak snapped in the wind, briefly blotting out Cojax's view.

When the gust subsided, he saw *her.*

A girl. No older than himself. She stood just past the threshold of the gate—thin, trembling, arms locked across her chest. Her clothes were threadbare and colorless, once white but now caked with ash and dirt. Her hair was red—not black and braided like the Acadian girls. Small brown freckles dotted her face, her nose slender, her limbs narrow and malnourished.

But her eyes—her *eyes* were the strangest of all.

*"Blue?"* Cojax blinked. *"How is that possible?"*

He wasn't the only one who noticed. Murmurs sparked through the crowd like embers on dry kindling. Validated hands crept to hilts. Arc Blades flickered to life. Voices rose with mounting hysteria.

"Kill it before it evolves!"

"It's a trap!"

"Cut it down!"

Then one soldier broke ranks and charged, Arc Blade blazing in a streak of light.

*"Hold."*

Titan hadn't shouted. He hadn't even raised his voice. But the effect was instant. The entire parade ground froze.

The Arc Blade-wielding soldier halted mid-lunge, muscles seizing with trained obedience, his weapon flickering down. Every pair of eyes turned.

Titan stepped forward, never looking at the girl.

"Stand down," he said, voice deep and even. "That girl comes with me. Bound in Arc Cuffs. Escorted to the Trinity."

A beat of silence.

Then came a voice—gravel-thick and defiant.

"No."

Titan turned, jaw tightening as he locked eyes with the speaker.

"Atlas."

The other Numberless stepped into view—broader than Titan by half a shoulder, his armor worn and battle-scarred. His dark hair was shaved at the sides, braided tightly down his back in the Screamer tradition. Faded tattoos and deep scars webbed his face, except for one: a fresh crescent curling around his right eye.

The voices fell so only Cojax could hear.

"This is my jurisdiction," Titan said flatly. "My decision."

"It stopped being your decision," Atlas growled, "the moment that thing stepped onto Acadian soil." He pointed a gauntleted finger at the girl beyond the gate.

Titan shook his head once. "She's a child."

"She's not one of us."

"She walks on two legs. She carries no weapon. No armor. She's human—and below the Age of Accountability. That makes her an Innocent." Titan's voice never rose, but its weight was unmistakable. "I've already alerted the Infinite Council. The choice isn't ours anymore."

"You're hesitating," Atlas snapped. "And that hesitation could doom this city."

Titan stepped forward. His voice dropped to a growl.

"And your fear could do the same. Remember your Oath— we don't kill Innocents. We're not Roaches."

Atlas' eyes narrowed. "You're blinded. Look at them."

He gestured to the surrounding soldiers—still at attention, but restless. Hands near hilts. Visors twitching with uncertainty. "They smell weakness."

Titan took another step—closer now, until the two men were a breath apart. "Then let them smell resolve."

Atlas' expression twisted. "This is a mistake."

"This matter goes before the Fifty."

"And if they make the wrong choice?"

Titan didn't flinch. "Then Acadia falls by its own hand," he said softly, "not mine."

"Alongside the god of merit, I also serve the god of necessity. Sometimes necessity outweighs the other—you know this. We all have blood on our hands, but sometimes necessity must dictate our actions."

Titan didn't budge.

Atlas' shoulders fell a fraction. He exhaled sharply, his composure slipping. His next words came low and bitter, thick with venom. "Her presence threatens all of Acadia. And your hesitation may have doomed us all."

## THREE

Titan stood by the entrance, his gaze fixed on Atlas, who now paced the center of the gladiatorial pit like a caged predator. Rage burned behind the man's eyes, his fists clenched so tightly the veins in his forearms stood out like cords of steel. Normally, Titan would have taken this conversation to the upper levels of the Trinity—into the sanctum of the Numberless, where strategy replaced spectacle. There, surrounded by training halls, tactical suites, and the statues of the fallen, cooler heads might have prevailed. But Atlas wasn't in the mood for reason. He had murder on his mind. And Numberless weren't easily talked down from blood.

Instead, they met where the others already were—beneath the vaulted arena, where cheers echoed like ancient thunder and violence was currency.

The stands were packed. Hundreds of First Tiers watched as one of their own units clashed with a legend. In the center of the pit stood Canik, the brute who had broken the Roach line at the Midnight Battle. He wielded a massive blade with casual menace, his every motion a display of calculated brutality. Across from him, three First Tiers shifted nervously. Their armor was battered, shields flickering near exhaustion. It was no longer a fight—it was a countdown.

Their Pulse Beacons, installed before the fight for safety, told the tale: red for danger, yellow for fading, green for strength. Canik's beacon still pulsed green. His opponents were all somewhere in diminishing shades of yellow. The match would end as soon as their shields dipped below the twenty-percent threshold—but no one watching mistook this for mercy.

Titan raised his voice, smooth but commanding, the sound cutting through the din like a blade.

"All First Tiers—out."

The effect was immediate. Canik halted mid-swing. The First

Tiers backed away, breathless, relieved. Around the arena, from the spectating Numberless, a ripple of protest arose. It was considered bad form to interrupt a match—especially one this entertaining.

Titan stepped further into the light. His presence alone drew silence.

He was a mountain in motion—broad-chested, steady-footed, his shoulders squared like sculpted granite. Graying curls crowned his head, evoking an old-world emperor. His eyes were sharp, unreadable. There was no official commander among the Numberless, but Titan carried himself as if forged for it. He didn't ask for authority. He was authority.

Atlas saw it too. And hated him for it.

In the stands, the crowd began to disperse, First Tiers retreating with disciplined silence, backs straight and eyes averted. None dared meet the gaze of the Numberless. These weren't simply warriors—they were the gods of Acadia. They had shed their Sacred Score, transcended the merit scale, and carved their legacy into stone. Their likenesses stood immortal in the Hall of Statues—etched in marble, bronze, obsidian, or steel—witnesses to the glory of their ascension.

The crowd hadn't gathered for bloodsport. They had come to observe greatness. To memorize every movement, every decision, and perhaps glimpse the blueprint of their own rise. But all they had truly witnessed was how thoroughly Canik dismantled his opponents. Blow by blow, the First Tiers were being methodically undone—and Canik wasn't even trying.

Titan spoke again, his voice amplified through his armor's built-in speakers. It boomed like the thunder of a god.

"All First Tiers—out."

This time there was no hesitation. The three combatants bowed deeply before Canik, their feet stirring up clouds of sand as they withdrew. The watching First Tiers had already started to head out, but they quickened their pace—backs bent in reverence, their eyes on the ground as they filed out. Titan's command had become divine decree.

From his side came a voice, old, worn, but confident.

"Sir, do you want me to cancel the summons of the First Tier High Order?" Byron asked. "I assumed, since we were meeting in the

Pit, they would be involved."

Titan turned, only now registering that Byron had been standing beside him. He had joined him at the Wall and remained at his side since.

Byron was the epitome of calculated excellence. His armor gleamed—a polished bronze hue with streaks of pale light coursing across it like frozen lightning, a unique palette given his place on the High Council of the BloodBorne. Typically, that color was utilized by the Armstrong Faction. In a city of ten million, his Placard read Four Hundred and Fifty—an extraordinary feat for a man of forty-two— well past his fighting prime. He hadn't taken a Civil Union, had not raised children to earn subsidized points. Every digit in his Score had been earned the hard way. He had plateaued, however. The upper reaches of the Tiers were a competitive free-for-all—brutal and unrelenting. A few missteps, a single unproductive hour, and one could fall dozens of places overnight.

Titan knew Byron well. Knew the discipline that drove him. He slept four hours a night—if that. In the morning he ate quickly, trained, and volunteered to guard or fight at the Wall before sunrise. He continued on until exhaustion overcame him. Then, without rest, he worked in his Second Stewardship as an Administrator, wielding his mind with the same ruthless precision as his blade. He solved the problems the Numberless ignored. Kept the city turning. Protected its balance.

He had done much for Acadia and even more for the BloodBorne. He was *still* doing much.

But Titan knew, as all the Numberless did, he would never ascend. He would never join the Infinite Council. Never become one of them.

*"How sad,"* he mused.

The thought surprised him. Cold, abstract, but real. He shook it off.

"No," he said at last. "Only the Infinite Council will attend. Lock the doors. Stand guard. Make sure we are not disturbed."

He bowed low, his fist pressed against his chest in salute. The gesture was noble—more noble than he deserved. Then he turned, disappearing with the other First Tiers, his footsteps fading into the sand.

"What's all this?" Canik rumbled, his voice a mixture of mockery and amusement. "Why are you spoiling all my fun, Titan? The great ruiner of all things thrilling and blood-soaked!"

The jab was lighthearted, part of the long-standing banter among the Numberless. But such levity was rare in front of the Validated. The Numberless were legends, not merely warriors. Their deeds were mythologized, their words repeated in training halls and documentaries. If a First Tier dared say anything so irreverent to any of the Fifty, their Score would crater so fast they might as well throw themselves into the Rift.

Titan didn't respond. Not yet. A few First Tiers lingered near the exits, slow to disperse. And Titan—ever the disciple of protocol—held his silence. Where others saw rules, Titan saw religion. In a world where power shifted like sand, order was his last altar.

Instead, he stepped aside—and revealed the girl.

The shift in the room was immediate. The scent of musty clothes and sweat rose from her like smoke. She'd hidden so completely behind Titan's frame that many hadn't even noticed her presence. Now, stepping forward into view, she seemed to materialize from thin air—small, pale, and silent. It was as if Titan had conjured her from his cloak.

A hush fell across the Numberless.

Atlas took his moment. He moved forward, eyes burning with intent. Murder clung to his every motion.

But Titan was faster.

He stepped in front of her, a mountain of muscle and intent, his body a living blockade. Every line in his form radiated righteous defiance—the same indignant power that had made him both feared and respected across Acadia.

The great doors sealed behind them with a thunderous hiss, echoing like a final verdict.

Only the Infinite Council remained—thirty or so Numberless, silent as statues. The rest of their kind, over eight thousand strong, lay dormant in Crono-Stasis, entombed in the high sanctums of the Trinity. Suspended in steel and glass, their bodies locked beyond time, their minds in quiet vigil, waiting for the day Acadia would need gods again.

But these—these were the Awake. The Stewards of the present. The last living deities of a city built on merit and fear. They were called the Fifty, though their numbers rarely reached that. By law, they served fifteen full rotations before being granted the long slumber. Titan had already served sixteen. But with Atlas among their ranks, he could not afford to slumber in Crono-Stasis—not until the brute had learned some sort of control over his rage and lust for dominance.

"She dies," Atlas snarled, hand slipping to the hilt of his blade.

"And you with her," Titan replied, voice like cold iron, mirroring the gesture.

A hush fell like a blade. Not fear—something older. Reverence. Two titans facing off was no scandal. It was sacred spectacle.

Akirian stepped forward.

"What is she?" she asked, her voice low and measured, though danger rippled beneath every syllable. Once, she had been called beautiful. Once, she had been a mother of eight. Once, she was a matron of the BloodLetters Faction. But all that was long buried. What remained was war-forged steel. Her face had become a battlefield of sinew and scar, her left brow split by a pale gash that had never healed. She was known to fight with an Arc Blade in one hand and a Blazer in the other. Her stare could freeze fire.

Titan held her gaze as the girl stood behind him, trembling, as if caught in the eye of a storm.

"She came through the Roach battleline," Titan said. His voice was unamplified, yet every Numberless heard. "Somehow—somewhere—she walked through the breach at the Northern Crest."

"She's not Acadian," Atlas snapped, voicing what they all were thinking.

"Not Acadian," several murmured in disbelief.

"Impossible," Akirian said flatly, stepping forward. Her eyes narrowed. She began to circle the girl slowly, like a predator unsure whether to strike.

The girl looked barely able to stand. Her face was so dirty her features blurred into shadow. She stood still, hands folded across her chest, her wet shirt clinging to her ribs. Her hands trembled—barely perceptible but constant.

"Blood and bile," Akirian muttered. "How did she survive the Killing Fields?" Awe crept into her voice. "She's pitiful. A splash of water could level her." She stepped in and jabbed her finger into the girl's side. The child winced but didn't cry out. Akirian examined her bloodshot eyes.

"Dehydrated. Starved. Alive—but barely." She knelt in the sand before her, still a head taller even when crouched. Her voice softened, if only by degrees. "What's your name, girl?"

Silence.

"Your name?"

"She doesn't understand us," Titan said. "She speaks another tongue—English, maybe Spanish. Whatever it is, it isn't Acadian."

Akirian looked up sharply. "Then how did she survive?"

"That's not the question," came another voice—high, precise, philosophical.

Bacilian.

One of the few Numberless who regularly wore no armor, Bacilian stood with an old-fashioned book cradled in his hands. It looked antique, delicate. Only the Numberless were permitted such eccentricities. His presence was a quiet anomaly among gods built of bronze and fire.

"The question," Bacilian continued, "is what do we do with her now? How many people saw her?"

"Thousands," Titan replied.

"Then there is only one course of action," Atlas said.

He drew his blade with ceremonial flair, the metal whispering death as it cleared its sheath. His eyes darkened, bloodlust boiling beneath the surface.

"She must die. Bag the body. Burn it in the incinerators. Her ashes will dishonor the dead they mix with, but they'll be flushed out soon enough."

"We are all human," Akirian said, her voice sounding tired, as if this were part of an old argument she did not really want to get into at the moment.

"I agree with Atlas—for once," Bacilian said. "I think that is the only way to prevent the rumors from spreading."

"The damage is already done," Akirian said.

"The longer she is alive, the more damage she will do," Atlas said.

"She's just a little girl," Akirian said.

"What are you suggesting? We take her in, drain our resources, allow rumors to spread?"

"This is a city of ten million Validated," Akirian said. "She can hardly eat more than a bird."

"That's not the point!" Atlas exploded. "This is something we have to contain, something we need to put an end to."

The chamber erupted into argument, voices rising like the roar of an oncoming storm. The Numberless split into two camps—one favoring leniency, the other echoing Atlas' call for execution. As the minutes passed, the scales tipped toward blood. Most sided with Atlas. The girl's death seemed inevitable.

But before the vote could be cast, Titan raised a single hand.

The room fell silent.

Atlas spat, fury crawling up his spine. The gesture—so effortless—had stilled the gods of Acadia. And they'd listened. That infuriated him most of all.

Titan scanned the room, locking eyes with each of them. These were his brothers and sisters-in-arms. Every soul here had earned the unearnable. Each had climbed the endless mountain of Tiers, losing blood, kin, and sanity on the ascent. They were the Immortals of Acadia. The Infinite Council.

"All of us have suffered," Titan began, his voice deliberate, raw. "Even those newly appointed bear scars that run deep. Each of us knows what we've been charged with. Each of us has stared down the Roaches and walked away burned."

He paused, letting the silence fill with memory.

"We are the ones who descended into the Mahghetto and emerged again. We left brothers and sisters behind. We climbed, while they fell. And with every step, we lost—children, spouses, comrades. We carry that weight in silence."

Atlas sneered. "What's your point?"

Titan didn't look at him. He spoke instead to the others.

"My point is that it has to *mean* something. Our pain. Our sacrifice. Our city was built atop the ashes of our grief, and it survives because of one sacred law: Merit before all. We are given only what we earn. That is the code by which Acadia lives and dies."

He turned now, facing the girl.

"If we kill her, we betray everything we are. Everything we've bled for. Let her earn her place. Let her rise—or fall—as we did. Let her live and die by her own merit."

For a breathless moment, no one spoke.

Then Canik stepped forward, lips curled in grudging admiration. "Valid point. Had I known you had such talent for oration, I wouldn't have mocked you so much over these last few years."

A ripple of dark chuckles followed.

"If we abandon the Sacred Score," Bacilian stated thoughtfully, "we're no better than the primitives we used to be. *By deeds we rise; by entitlement we fall.*"

"*Merit before all,*" the others intoned in solemn unison.

The room shifted. Heads nodded. The tide turned.

Atlas saw it—and tried one final time to regain control. "Merit is important, yes, but I serve a higher law—one of necessity. I became a Numberless not only by merit, but also in doing what *needed* to be done. We all have. We all are still. Are the lives of the Validated we send to the grave each battle any different? Are they less important than her?"

"She's not Validated," Akirian answered. "So, her life, by law, must be preserved."

Then something in Atlas snapped. With a growl, he charged. His blade arced through the air, a blur of vengeance aimed squarely at the girl's neck.

Titan moved like lightning.

Sparks exploded as their weapons met mid-swing. In the next instant, Titan's pommel slammed into Atlas' face with a sickening crunch. A tooth flew free. Blood sprayed. Atlas staggered backward, stunned but still standing, blade twitching in his grip. His energy shields were up, but without a helmet, his face was unprotected, allowing Titan to capitalize on the weakness.

He lunged again—but a voice cut through the chaos.

"Atlas. Blade down." Akirian's voice was sharp and cold. "The matter is settled. By merit, she will live or die."

Atlas straightened, his lip split, blood trickling down his chin.

"Not if I kill her first," he hissed.

Titan raised his blade and leveled it at Atlas' throat. "If you so much as touch her, not even your Sacred Score will shield you from judgment. *Merit before all.* Defy that, and the Rift will swallow you whole."

"She's not Acadian," Atlas snarled, voice low and venomous. "She's an outsider. Her presence is a cancer. What happens when others see her? When they begin to question the Walls? The Killing Fields? Our entire foundation will crack beneath her footsteps. And you—Titan—you'll have destroyed the very thing you claim to defend. Etch my words into a tablet of gold: she will be the death of all of us—"

"—Enough," Canik interrupted. The humor had left his voice. "Sheath your blade—and your pride. *Merit before all.*"

"*Merit before all,*" several others echoed.

Atlas stood rigid for a moment, then hissed under his breath, "Dimmed fools."

He turned away, stomping across the sand, the storm of his fury trailing in his wake. The doors hissed open as he vanished down the corridor.

All eyes followed him—until a soft gasp broke the tension.

Only Akirian saw the girl collapse.

She darted forward, moving with shocking grace. Her arms caught the child just before the girl hit the ground.

"Quick," Akirian barked. "Summon the First Tiers. This girl needs a Medicus. Now."

# FOUR

These people were so *clean*. Unnaturally so. Their bronze-colored armor gleamed with a persistent sheen, their boots polished to a shine, their hallways sterile and bright. To Jessica, they looked like they'd never known dirt, never survived mud, blood, or hunger. As if disorder itself were a crime and cleanliness their religion.

She didn't understand their language—but she recognized it. Deep, guttural, precise. She had heard it once, perhaps twice, whispered by strangers who wandered the outer roads long ago. But now, surrounded by it, the language felt like thunder made into speech. And for some reason she could not explain, it scraped at her nerves, made her feel trapped and alone.

Everything since crossing the Wall had felt... dreamlike. Not peaceful, but dislocated. Like her mind was no longer inside her body, just hovering somewhere nearby, watching. The *Light City*—as the stories had called it—was real. The gates had opened. The rumors were true.

But none of the stories had prepared her for *this*.

These people weren't just different—they were *impossible*. Taller than anyone she had ever seen. Thicker. Stronger. They walked with the confidence of creatures bred for war, their weapons surreal and legendary. For once, the old women in the village hadn't exaggerated—they had undersold it.

And yet, for the first time in her short, war-ravaged life, Jessica felt something foreign spread through her body. It moved down her spine, into her arms, her fingers, all the way to her toes—a lightness, like exhaling after years of holding her breath. Muscles she didn't know she had began to unclench. It almost felt like... peace.

She might have smiled. She thought she *would* have, had she not been so cold.

*"It's over,"* she told herself. *"The hunger, the pain, the hiding... it's finally over."*

But it wasn't.

Her illusion shattered the moment two of the giants began to argue. Their voices stayed low, but the intensity was impossible to miss. Jessica froze. One of them—a tattooed mountain draped in a black cape—pointed directly between her eyes. His hand alone looked large enough to crush her skull.

She didn't flinch. She couldn't. Her body had turned to ice.

They took her after that—led her gently with firm, unspoken command—into a flying machine unlike anything she had ever seen. Sleek, metallic, humming with quiet menace. She had seen machines like this *once*, in the distance, soaring over a battlefield while her people hid beneath a collapsed roof.

She had thought only the Roaches had machines like that.

Inside, the air was warmer, but not warm. She was placed near the back wall, alone, two soldiers flanking her like statues carved from iron. She shifted against the cold metal, realizing for the first time she was no longer walking freely. *She was not a guest. She was a prisoner.*

But she didn't care.

Even if they were flying her to her death, she would go willingly. There was nowhere else left to run. Nowhere left to go.

That thought—simple and quiet—opened the door in her mind.

*And he was there.*

Blood.

Fire.

The screams.

His hand, reaching for her—and then gone.

Her village had burned in the night. The screaming had torn through the cold like knives. People had fled with nothing but their children on their backs and smoke in their lungs. And she, the smallest and the slowest, had hidden beneath the body of her older brother, his blood drying in her hair as the fire spread.

The memory gripped her so tightly she couldn't breathe. She had thought the Light City would be salvation. But now, locked in silence between two giants, she wasn't sure it would be anything more than *a final ending.*

For a few precious moments, when the gate first groaned

open, her pain had vanished.

It was as if the weight had lifted from her chest and scattered on the wind. But now the memories returned, savage and sharp, carving her open from the inside. They came not like drifting clouds but like infection—spreading, multiplying, poisoning everything they touched. The memory of *him*—ripped from her side by one of the massive creatures—hit like a bolt of lightning to the chest. It sucked the air from her lungs, sent her heart hammering, and forced her to look down, to hide from the unbearable weight of it.

*"I'm alone. There's nothing left. Nothing left because they're all dead. He is dead. I am alone."*

The words spiraled through her mind, tightening with each repetition. Every day they grew louder. More consuming. She had tried to outrun them with silence—holding still, breathing slow, pretending to vanish. Sometimes it worked. This time it didn't. Her chest rose and fell with quick, sharp breaths, each one fueling her dread. Her head throbbed. Her vision blurred. Whether from dehydration, hunger, or sheer exhaustion, she didn't know.

She didn't cry.

She hadn't cried in days.

Tears were water, and water was survival. Grief was a luxury for the well-fed.

Then came the lift—a gentle surge beneath her feet as the aircraft ascended into the sky. Jessica's breath caught. Her gaze snapped to the window and locked there, unblinking, as the world below unfolded into a vision so immense it seemed unreal.

The city did not simply sprawl—it *ascended*, a living monument of light and order stretching to the edge of the horizon. Colossal columns crowned with ornate capitals rose like ivory sentinels above layered terraces, amphitheater-shaped plazas, and forums. Towering structures of alabaster white shimmered beneath the sun, their red-tiled roofs gleaming like a sea of rubies. Roads paved in synthetic stone wound through the city in elegant spirals, and a line of statues stretched from the massive Wall to the heart of the city.

It was Athens reborn—restored to perfection, then fused with a thousand years of technology.

Lines of blue and white light traced the contours of buildings and towers like the veins of a sleeping god. They pulsed with life, with power, whispering through the walls like digital breath. Holographic banners hovered over plazas. Translucent screens flickered with civic information. And above it all, the skies thrummed with movement—vehicles of every shape and speed weaving between spires and domes like birds in a storm of light.

She had never seen so many people—on foot, on balconies, in the air. They moved with mechanical grace, their armor glinting, their faces cold and unreadable. It was as if all of humanity had gathered within this one fortified world—and still, the city stretched beyond the curve of the earth.

Jessica didn't know how to process what she was seeing. It was too big. Too perfect. Too *impossible*.

This wasn't just a city.

It was civilization, perfected.

As the aircraft banked sharply, a shadow rose into view—massive, gleaming, and impossible.

Jessica's breath caught in her throat.

It wasn't a building. It was a monument. A statement. Three towering spires erupted from the earth, fusing at their base like the blades of a trident thrust into the heart of the city. The structure shimmered in the sun, throwing off rays like a polished weapon. It dominated the skyline—colder and more perfect than anything she had imagined. A skyscraping citadel of power and permanence.

*This* was the beacon she had seen from the outskirts. The shining promise that had kept her feet moving when her body had begged to collapse. It had pulled her across the Killing Fields like a lodestar, whispering of refuge, of survival. But now, up close, that promise felt hollow—cruel, even. The closer she came, the less it looked like sanctuary and the more it resembled judgment.

It didn't look constructed. It looked *forged*—poured from molten silver into the shape of dominion. Seamless. Ageless. Unyielding. It gave off the feeling of a god at rest, waiting only to awaken and crush whatever stood beneath its gaze.

This was where they took her.

She would never forget the approach. The heat in her cheeks. The dizzying swirl of movement around her. People—tall, armored, inhumanly poised—gliding through their world with perfect efficiency. Their gazes snapped toward her as she passed. Their voices murmured in clipped syllables she couldn't decipher, but she didn't need translation. She *felt* their meaning in her bones. They were talking about her.

Some curious.

Some confused.

Some full of disdain.

One pointed.

Another scoffed.

Their eyes were sharp—calculating, emotionless, ancient. She stiffened, spine straight not from pride but necessity. Her shirt still clung to her back like a second skin, soaked through with sweat and putrid water. She tried to keep up, to match their stride, to disappear into herself. But each glance, each whisper, each step down the pristine metallic corridors chipped away at her. Her muscles grew heavy. Her limbs numbed. Her breath turned shallow.

She ended up in a sand arena so large it could have fit her whole village in it with room to spare. She stood for what felt like hours, her vision dimming, her muscles knotting in painful spirals, pleading for release.

And then—darkness.

She didn't remember falling. Only waking.

The ceiling above her was sterile white. The light was too clean. The bed beneath her was stiff and foreign. Her skin had been scrubbed raw. Her hair, once matted and tangled, had been brushed and washed. She wore clothes she didn't recognize—gray, soft, tight across her arms. She stared at herself, stunned. For a moment, she didn't feel like *herself*.

Then she saw the metal cup beside the bed.

*Water.*

She lunged.

The first swallow hit her stomach like a fist. She drank again anyway, heedless of the spill that ran down her chin and soaked her shirt. She didn't care. Her tongue rejoiced. Her throat unfurled. It wasn't just water. It was proof she was alive.

Then she noticed the figure standing beside her.

A woman—tall, armored, and silent. Bronze-colored plates clung to her like a second skin, etched with faint lines of light that pulsed softly along the seams. A long sword rested at her side, not ornamental but practical, worn from use. Her face was youthful, but her eyes were not. They carried something hollow. Heavy. Like someone who had seen far too much and dared not speak of any of it.

Jessica would learn her name later—*Halix'Dra*.

The name alone felt like a weapon—strange and sharp, dangerous to say aloud. Jessica didn't dare try. She simply nodded, unsure whether it was expected of her.

Halix'Dra didn't speak. She only turned and gestured to the doorway. Jessica followed.

They descended by lift, deeper into the city's underbelly—into the sub-levels. The brightness above faded, replaced by dim corridors of concrete, steel, and flickering panels. The tunnels hissed with artificial wind, but the air was thin, recycled, and somehow insufficient. It scraped against her lungs. No matter how deeply she breathed, she could never get enough.

She hated it instantly.

This was to be her new home.

The apartment was sparse but functional: a single bedroom, a kitchenette, a narrow dining nook, and a bathroom barely big enough to turn around in. Jessica was given a closet-turned-room, furnished with a thin sleeping mat and a blanket that smelled faintly of sterilization. It was the most comfort she had ever known.

And yet… something inside her twisted.

She was alive. She was safe. She had food. Water. Shelter. But somewhere deep inside her chest, a shadow curled—a pit that widened with every passing hour.

She couldn't name it.

Only feel it.

And that was enough to make her uneasy.

There was something *off* about these people—something dark veiled beneath the splendor and brilliance of their world. Behind their gleaming armor and towering walls, a shadow lingered. It wasn't in what they said or did, but in what they didn't. Amid all the magnificence—the marble columns, the golden light, the seamless technology—there was an emptiness, a sterile disconnection. Like a perfect photograph where everything was captured except the soul of the subject. A beauty without warmth. A civilization without a face. An apartment tucked into a corridor of cement and chrome. But it was dry. Warm. Safe.

That was enough for now.

Halix'Dra said little, but she was not unkind. Not cruel. Just… detached. Her duties seemed more logistical than maternal. She pointed to where things were. Demonstrated the water system. Taught Jessica how to access rations from the chute. But she didn't linger. Didn't ask questions. Never smiled.

Some rules were obvious. Others were complicated but could be pieced together through tone, repetition, or a series of careful gestures. But there was one rule that stood above all the rest— unspoken in its importance, unmistakable in its enforcement.

The pin.

A small, metallic "X" affixed to every white uniform Jessica wore. It was given to her without explanation, fastened without ceremony—but it became the anchor of her existence. No one else in the city wore one. Not a single person. Just her.

She didn't ask why. Not at first. Something in the silence that followed its placement told her she shouldn't. Because this wasn't a question. It was a warning. It wasn't until much later that she discovered its meaning. The mark of the Aberration. A title that, in a city of over ten million, belonged to her alone.

Even with the strange stares and the colder corners of the city, her life had undeniably improved. She ate more in a single day than she once did in three. She had warm water—real water—with actual temperature controls. Her clothes were whole. Her skin had stopped cracking and bleeding.

But still, a pit formed in her chest, growing deeper with each passing day. She fought the loneliness. Fought the isolation. She even began to mistake Halix'Dra's silence for comfort. For a time, it was enough.

Three months later, everything changed.

One morning, Halix'Dra greeted her with a nod and a half-smile. The next, she didn't leave her bed. No words. No acknowledgment. The woman who had once seemed carved from iron now looked hollow.

Grief clung to her like armor too heavy to bear.

Jessica first noticed it in Halix'Dra's eyes—dull and distant, like someone who had already made peace with the end. Her movements grew sluggish. Her voice vanished. She moved like a ghost, waiting to be forgotten.

*"What have I done?"* Jessica thought, a piercing critical voice rang in her head. *"What changed?"*

Then she noticed the Placard.

It was a small, rectangular screen mounted above Halix'Dra's heart. Every Acadian over the age of sixteen wore one, embedded into their armor like a window into their soul. The number it displayed changed daily. Jessica didn't understand what it meant. Not fully. But she knew it mattered.

She watched how often Halix'Dra scratched at it—like it itched. Like it burned. Like it condemned her. And every day, the number dropped. Not by much. A few digits here and there. But enough. Enough to matter. Enough, perhaps, to mean death.

Halix'Dra's brief, friendly conversations disappeared. Her quiet efficiency turned into absolute neglect. She stopped polishing her armor. Stopped bathing. Stopped cleaning. Stopped eating.

Jessica tried to ignore it, to carry on as before. She kept up with her chores. She tidied the kitchen and scrubbed the bathroom, even if they were barely used. But as Halix'Dra deteriorated, Jessica took on more—dusting the lights, wiping the shelves, bringing food to her guardian's door.

Each day, two bowls arrived through a chute. The food was bland but filling, and usually came with a flatbread or two. The larger was clearly for Halix'Dra, but after a few days, the portions changed. Jessica tried to give Halix'Dra the bowl with more food, but her guardian always chose the smaller one.

Then one morning, Jessica found her guardian sitting on the floor. Breathing. Blinking. But still as a statue. Her gaze locked onto a blank wall.

Jessica's heart fractured.

They barely spoke. They barely interacted. But Jessica felt a quiet bond—a sense of debt. Halix'Dra had taken her in when no one else would. Given her food. Shelter. A place to exist.

Jessica whispered the only word she knew for "eat." No response. She left the bowl and returned with another at lunch. Still no change. By dinner, all three bowls were untouched. Halix'Dra hadn't moved.

Panic clawed at Jessica.

She approached cautiously, trying every word she knew. "I… find… friend… you… eat." She waited for a response, but none came. "You eat… I find friend… you eat… I friend… you friend."

Nothing.

Frustration boiled over. She shoved Halix'Dra's chest. The woman toppled backwards, her body collapsing into a heap—but still, no movement.

Jessica cried—hot, silent tears soaking her cheeks. Then she ran. She sprinted into the corridor and grabbed the first passerby—a burned-faced man with broad shoulders. He shoved her aside. She tried again with a woman, but the woman gave her only a glance and kept walking.

Jessica ran home and collapsed onto her bed, her eyes watering her blanket until sleep took her. When she awoke, Halix'Dra was gone. Her clothes still hung in the closet. Her armor hung from the wall. The CityScreen still in the living room. The bowls were untouched. Nothing else had changed. It was as if she'd never existed.

An hour later, two towering warriors opened Jessica's bedroom door. Silent and expressionless, they motioned for her to follow. Her cheeks still red and puffy, she obeyed.

They led her to a gray door with fresh paint. It opened to reveal a woman in brilliant, polished bronze-colored armor with angular features and eyes as sharp as daggers.

"Adrestas," the woman said, pointing to herself.

Jessica blinked. No one in the Light City had ever introduced themselves to her. Certainly not someone who looked like Adrestas.

The woman repeated the name, this time slower. Jessica tried it. It came out wrong. She tried again. Adrestas gave a shrugging nod of approval.

Then she pointed at Jessica.

"Jessica," the girl said.

It sounded strange to her ears. Like it didn't belong to her anymore. But Adrestas said it back perfectly. Jessica smiled.

Adrestas didn't smile in return. That day, Jessica began

learning. And by nightfall, Halix'Dra's memory had been buried beneath a pile of new words.

Adrestas was nothing like her predecessor. Fierce. Precise. Demanding. For the first time, Jessica became the center of someone's attention. Language was the first priority. For hours a day, she practiced. Mispronunciations earned bruises. Adrestas wasn't cruel—just clinical. Her punishments were methodical. Predictable. It wasn't anger. It was education.

Jessica learned the cost of a mistake.

She began to stutter. Slight at first. Then worsening by week's end. Some evenings, her eyes swelled shut from the beatings. But there was a strange comfort in the pattern—a brutal rhythm that made sense. After every severe beating came a reprieve. A day. Sometimes two. A strange reward for pain.

After three months, Jessica understood a fair portion of the language. Speaking was harder, slowed by her stutter, but she could follow conversations. Adrestas didn't seem impressed.

Lessons expanded. History. Math. Biology. Psychology. Cleaning. Every surface in the apartment had to gleam. Clothes were pressed. Rooms spotless. There were no idle moments. Jessica welcomed it. The busier her hands, the quieter her mind. The harder the work, the further her memories receded. Pain kept her grounded in the now.

Then came the CityScreens. And with them, nightmares turned into reality. The battles were all streamed live, and it was mandatory for every child over the age of ten to watch. Each warrior's armor deployed HoverCams from their upper backs—one to track their movements, capture their technique, and tally their kills or accomplishments. The other focused on how their Phalanx fared.

There were no edits. No soothing narration. Just truth, vicious and brilliant, carved into high definition. The city didn't just show the battles—it worshiped them.

Jessica mostly watched the BloodBorne warriors—the faction she had been assigned to—but the City had the final say. When the fighting reached a fever pitch elsewhere, the feed would shift. Unannounced. Unfeeling.

She saw legends fall. Phalanxes shatter. Blood blur the HoverCam lenses like rain on glass. And in those images, she learned the truth: Acadia was not a sanctuary, it was a beacon of death.

The first time Adrestas forced her to watch, Jessica vomited on the floor. She was beaten for it. The second time, she kept her food down, but silent tears betrayed her. She was beaten again, though not as harshly. The third time, Adrestas didn't need to push her in front of the screen.

She was on it.

Adrestas held the front line with brutal precision. In the shieldwall, she was untouchable—an unyielding pillar against the Roach tide. For a time, Jessica allowed herself to believe she might be invincible.

Then the formation broke.

A spearhead of Roaches surged through a weak point in the line, and Adrestas—separated and alone—began to falter. Her movements grew sluggish, her strikes imprecise. She fought on, but without the Phalanx around her, the difference was stark. She was no longer a warrior—just a woman, standing alone.

Jessica leaned closer to the screen, heart pounding.

That's when it happened.

A Reever, massive and chittering, emerged from the periphery of the broadcast—so sudden it might as well have always been there. Adrestas tried to fight back, but her armor no longer glowed with power; it had lost its charge. Her limbs moved like they were underwater.

The Reever lunged.

Its mandibles closed.

Her leg came off clean.

Jessica screamed. The camera panned away.

Other BloodBorne rushed in, too late to stop the damage. When they lifted Adrestas from the battlefield, the blood beneath her shimmered like oil. The cameras panned away. Jessica watched, unmoving, a knot hardening in her chest. She wanted to ask what had happened—wanted to cry, to run, to fight—but there was no one to ask. So she waited faithfully by the door.

Five hours later, the door opened.

Adrestas rolled inside, her body supported by a metal frame set with four wheels—two large, the other two small. She was pale, her eyes hollow. Unable to help herself, Jessica rushed forward and wrapped her arms around the woman's broken frame. This was strictly against Adrestas' rules, but this one time, she did not resist.

They held each other in silence. When the hug ended, Jessica noticed a single tear tracking down Adrestas' cheek. Jessica turned away, pretending to study the tile floor. She would not dishonor this brave woman.

The next day, everything returned to routine—almost.

Jessica cooked, cleaned, studied, and drilled in language practice with Adrestas. But something was different. Her guardian, though still scarred and iron-backed in posture, softened. She no longer barked orders or struck Jessica when her speech faltered. The beatings were gone. The rebukes too.

And slowly, Jessica began to change. Her stutter faded. Her grasp of the Acadian tongue sharpened. She began to speak—not in fear, but in thought.

That's when the number on Adrestas' Placard began to fall.

## FIVE

Jessica was quick to notice a change on Adrestas' Placard. Large Acadian numbers were still foreign to her, but the smaller ones she had already learned and mastered. And the last two numbers continued to fall. First thirty points in one day, and then forty the next. Her *Score* was falling.

Adrestas was *Weighted*—a term she had only heard in whispers and echoes. A term that felt more like a curse word too foul to be said out loud.

*"What happens when her Score disappears completely?"* Jessica thought. She wanted to give voice to the question, but each time she began to, she choked on her own words, afraid to hear the answer. *"Perhaps retirement. Perhaps she will be moved to a place where war veterans are taken care of and honored for their service."*

The city had abundance—that much was clear. They had enough food, energy, and shelter for millions. *"They must have room for her too—for a war hero."*

She knew Adrestas would soon be taken away, moved to a different part of the city, set up to live her days in modest comfort. In the following weeks, she would sometimes daydream about visiting Adrestas when she was older, when Jessica wore the armor of the Validated and had Roach wax on her blade.

Three months later, that day arrived—the number on the Placard disappearing completely.

Adrestas summoned Jessica to the main room.

Her guardian wasn't wearing her armor. Jessica had almost never seen her without it. Stripped of the metallic bulk, she looked smaller somehow. Fragile. Like a drenched alley cat trying to keep its dignity.

She powered on the CityScreen with a voice command. Its screen lit the room in a cold, sterile glow.

Then, Adrestas turned to Jessica and pulled her close.

The embrace was tight and sudden. Jessica returned it without hesitation, burying her face into the older woman's shoulder. She didn't ask why—didn't need to.

"Where…w-where are they t-taking you?" she finally whispered.

Adrestas pulled away, her voice calm. "No one escapes their fate, Jessica. We can only choose how to meet it. I've earned what's coming. I was once of the First Tier. That grants me an Honorable Release."

Jessica narrowed her eyes at the words. She had never heard the term before. "R-release? You… what d-does that mean?"

A soft smile broke across Adrestas' face. "These last few months have been my best. And that's because of you. But the moment has come." She raised her hand to her chest in salute, bowing low—a gesture normally reserved for the Numberless.

Then she wheeled toward the door.

"W-wait," Jessica said, reaching out.

But her guardian continued on until she was gone, the door shutting with finality behind her.

Thirty minutes later, the screen flickered to life.

Jessica stared at it, heart pounding. She knew. Deep in her gut, she *knew*.

It was happening now.

Adrestas was being sent out to the Killing Field.

*"But that couldn't be right."*

She had witnessed events like this before—dozens, maybe even hundreds of times. Every month, the city made room for the next generation, sending a group of people into the Killing Fields, often unarmed.

"But those were criminals," Jessica told herself. That's what she had always believed. *"What else could they have been?"*

She scoured her memories for something—anything—that Adrestas had said. Some condemnation. A warning. A label. But there was nothing. Not once had Adrestas called them traitors, criminals, or thieves. Jessica had never thought to ask. She hadn't needed to. The assumption was easier to hold onto.

Believing they were wicked made it bearable to watch.

Because the alternative—that Acadia discarded its heroes as

easily as it did its failures—was too monstrous to accept.

Adrestas couldn't be one of them. She had fought for Acadia. Suffered for it. Bled for it.

Jessica had loved her.

And now the city was sending her to die.

On the screen, Jessica watched as the Released gathered at the North Gate, standing shoulder to shoulder in a tight formation. Their faces were void of emotion. Their clothing varied—reflections of the diverse Factions they once belonged to. This month's group was smaller than usual—barely twenty. They ranged in age, though most looked to be in their late thirties or early forties. At the front stood two older men, both near fifty, their faces carved with the grit of war. And yet, despite their age, their bodies showed no sign of weakness. Jessica recognized them instantly—Validated warriors, famous for their mastery of the Arc Blade.

They were the only ones holding swords.

"Wait—no." Jessica leaned closer. "Adrestas has a sword too!"

A third figure stood near the edge of the formation, supported by a white crutch. There she was, clad in a white uniform, her eyes fixed forward with burning focus. She looked larger than life on the screen—so fierce, so commanding that Jessica barely recognized her.

"She's been granted... a sword," Jessica whispered, her voice catching. "She's been granted a sword!" This sudden revelation changed everything—she was going to be alright.

To be granted a sword was an honor—reserved for only the most respected of the Released. All of them had lived with dignity; otherwise, they would have been Rifted, not Released. The Rifted simply disappeared, but the Released had one last chance for glory as they charged into the Killing Fields, their bravery put on display for the entire city to see.

The North Gate opened.

Light spilled across Adrestas' face, and a new camera feed took over—a HoverCam from high above. From that height, the Released looked small and fragile compared to the immense crowd lining the perimeter. Then, from somewhere deep within the city, the Horn of Acadia let out a deep, resonant cry. The ground seemed to tremble beneath its call.

The Released marched forward into the Killing Field as they had done a thousand times before. Except this time, Jessica knew one of them. This time, they wouldn't be coming back.

Another HoverCam shifted across the battlefield, zooming in on the Roach Dens beyond the shimmering energy wall. Movement stirred in the distance—shadows rippling like waves. The horn had awakened them. Drawn by scent, by instinct, and by the promise of flesh.

Jessica leaned in, squinting. The creatures looked small on the screen, distant and almost harmless. But she knew better. Many were larger than most humans, some even as big as apartment buildings. The camera could not show the scale. Only the nightmare they brought with them.

"Maybe she can fight through them. Maybe—"

Then more creatures appeared. A tidal wave of stingers and teeth, of carapace and claw. The hope inside Jessica collapsed.

These weren't the commanding Roaches, the Damnattii who led armies. These were the border beasts—feral, fast, and used as walls of living death.

"The Released don't even have armor," Jessica whispered, so faint it barely reached her own ears. Most of them were wounded— missing arms or legs.

*"Why?"*

She had never asked that question before and now it would not go away.

*"Why was she being punished?"*

The screen adjusted again. The Released were advancing— directly toward the thickest horde. A closer HoverCam tracked the line. A few stragglers had fallen behind, already limping, staggering. But not Adrestas. Despite her missing leg, she held the right flank, swinging her crutch forward like a baton to keep pace.

Then came the final camera shift.

One screen. Both forces.

The Acadians screamed.

And the two sides collided.

It was instant and brutal. The creatures surged forward with feral hunger, surrounding the Released in a wall of claws and mandibles. Yet none of the Acadians ran. Not one broke rank. They held the line, even as they were overwhelmed.

Screams. Blood. Blades of grass cut down by a cyclone of death.

Within seconds, only a handful remained.

Adrestas was the last to fall.

Jessica saw her thrust her blade into a Roach's face—deep, likely fatal—but another creature lunged before she could retrieve it. She looked straight into the HoverCam, calm and fearless, like she was standing in a field of grass, not a battlefield of monsters.

Then she vanished—swallowed by the swarm.

Jessica turned away, gasping. Her knees buckled. Her palm anchored on the wall, holding her upright. She couldn't breathe. Her vision blurred. It felt as if the earth beneath her had vanished, as if she were falling into the same abyss that had claimed Adrestas.

The light overhead burned her eyes. She blinked, and it became a dull haze. She let her thoughts drift—back to memories before the Light City. Before the Wall. Before *he* was gone.

She might have stayed like that forever.

Until the front door opened.

The sound was alien—loud, sudden, without context. Jessica barely registered it. Footsteps. A presence. Someone entered and stood before her.

Jessica rose abruptly, wiping her tears with the back of her sleeve. Rage surged through her—pure and unfiltered. She clung to it, let it replace the ache inside her chest.

She glared up, face tight and unflinching.

It was a woman.

Her armor was sleek, traced with thin, elegant bands of light that curled in intricate patterns—the unmistakable signature of the BloodBorne Faction. She was shorter than most Acadian women, but she moved like someone who had never been told "no." Her face was soft, curved—a rarity in this place—and yet there was steel behind her eyes. She strode through the apartment without waiting for permission, scanning everything, then fixing her gaze on Jessica.

"I am Elena," she said. "Nova Second Class. First Tier. You're now in my charge. Come with me, Jessica."

Jessica squared her stance and crossed her arms. "N-no. I... I don't c-c-care if you're a Numberless of the highest Tier. I stay here.

This is my h-h-home."

She had never spoken that way to anyone—not in the Outer Roads, and certainly not in the Light City. A dam of emotion released inside her. First *him*. Then *Halix'Dra*. Now *Adrestas*.

"Go ahead! Hit me." She stepped forward, exposing her cheek. "You can h-hit me, but I'm s-s-taying here."

She shut her eyes, bracing for pain.

But none came.

Seconds passed. Then a full minute.

Silence.

She opened one eye. Elena hadn't moved. She stood in the same spot, watching her with quiet, unreadable patience. Jessica squeezed her eyes shut again, but the tears came anyway—spilling freely down her cheeks.

Then Elena spoke.

"I live on the fourth floor above ground," she said gently. "It's not much bigger than this apartment. But it has a window. You can see the Trinity from it. That could be your room—if you wanted. Of course, if I move down here, someone else will take it. And you'll never know what it's like to wake up to the light of the city."

The words were so unexpected, so warm, that Jessica couldn't process them at first. No one had ever spoken to her that way—in Acadia or before. Not since... *him*.

"Who are you?"

Elena smiled.

"Just another Acadian. But you? You're something else entirely. You're rare. You're special."

Jessica looked away, ashamed. "I-I-I'm sorry, First Tier. I can barely do my ch-chores. I can barely even speak without... stumbling over my w-words."

Elena's voice softened even more.

"Jessica, what makes you so special is this: aside from your eyes, there's nothing remarkable about you. And in this city... that's the rarest thing of all."

# SIX

Jessica had never had a real bed before. She sat gingerly on the smooth surface, and it gave beneath her weight—soft and warm, like an embrace she didn't expect. Tentatively, she bounced up and down, testing it, half-expecting it to collapse. When it didn't, she let herself fall back with arms outstretched, allowing the bed to carry her. For a brief, impossible moment, she felt as if she were floating.

"Never seen a bed before?" Elena's voice called from the doorway.

Jessica bolted upright, her cheeks flushing crimson. "M-my ap-ap-apologies."

Elena stepped inside, smiling faintly. "This is your room, Jessica. You're free to enjoy it. Are you hungry?"

Jessica's voice was barely a whisper. "A little."

"Then follow me to the kitchen."

The apartment was larger than Adrestas'—two extra rooms and a front chamber that opened into a vaulted central space. A tall window cast a pale ribbon of light across the gray-tiled floor. It was weak, filtered light, but Jessica froze when she saw it. She stared, captivated, as if the sun itself had visited.

The kitchen looked familiar—same layout, same utilities as every other Acadian home she had known—but it held subtle luxuries none of her past guardians possessed. Fine silverware gleamed in organized drawers. A full set of eight plates lined the cabinet shelves. Jessica couldn't recall ever seeing that many plates in one place.

"Ma'am?" she asked hesitantly.

"Call me Elena," the woman said without looking back. "In the apartment, at least. In public, I'm First Tier. That's the Code… the Acadian Code that we must all obey. But here… we don't need to be so formal. What's your question?"

"Why did y-y-you… say I was unique?"

Elena paused, her brow furrowing slightly. "That's not quite what I said." She glanced at Jessica. "I want to show you something, but can your hunger wait?"

Jessica hesitated, then nodded.

"You sure?"

She nodded again.

"Alright. Wait here."

Elena left the room and returned moments later with a small yellow sphere no larger than her fist. Its smooth surface shimmered faintly under the kitchen lights.

"Acadia is the light of the world," she said, holding the orb up. "The last light humanity has. But that light doesn't generate itself. We are its fuel. Its source. Its lifeblood."

She turned the orb slowly in her hand, admiring its cryptic and pulsing beauty.

"This is an Absorber. You've seen them before, even if you didn't know it. They're built into the walls, the floors—trimmed red or white, sometimes flickering with energy. They draw electricity directly from us. Every citizen contributes to the city's power simply by existing. The majority of that energy is harvested from the Innocents while they sleep—when their bodies have no immediate need for it. It is precisely because they generate the lion's share of our power that the AC protects those under the Age of Accountability from Riftings."

Jessica blinked. "I thought th-th-they were just... decorations."

Elena smiled. "No. They're essential. They take the bioelectric current produced by the human body and convert it to energy—used to power lights, shield grids, even hovercraft. Every Acadian is different. Some generate more current than others, and the System measures that. What most don't realize is this: the more energy you give, the more points you earn."

Jessica's eyes widened. "S-so... if someone's bad with a sword... but has a strong c-c-current..."

"They can still rise," Elena finished. "Skill matters, but so does output. This one"—she raised the orb—"is different. It doesn't take just a little. It takes everything."

Jessica's stomach tightened. "W-w-why would anyone let it do that?"

"To serve the city. To raise their Score. To be useful." Elena's voice was calm but heavy. "Do you understand?"

Jessica nodded slowly. "I-I think so."

"Good. Now step back. Farther."

Jessica obeyed. Elena nodded again, satisfied, and turned back to the orb. She took a slow breath, a momentary hesitation appearing in her features, and then latched the device onto the center of her breastplate. The smooth surface of the orb suddenly rippled like liquid. Jessica's eyes widened.

Sensors implanted in Elena's body lit up, glowing in alternating pulses—amber, yellow, white—casting ghostly patterns across her armor. The orb glowed in sync, first faint, then faster. With every pulse, its color intensified. Jessica realized the two light patterns were aligning, syncing into a singular rhythm.

Then came the strain.

Elena's face tightened. Her breaths deepened. The orb brightened with each beat, while the implants dimmed, siphoning energy from her body in accelerating waves. She began to tremble.

It only lasted ten seconds—but to Jessica, it felt like forever.

The orb flared one final time.

And then—darkness.

Jessica shielded her eyes, blinking away the afterimage. When she looked again, Elena had collapsed on the floor, face down. Sweat poured from her like melted wax, her body trembling, her breath ragged and shallow, as though she were trying to lift the world with each gasp.

Jessica stepped forward cautiously. "A-a-are you okay?"

No response.

The little girl stepped even closer, this time reaching out with her right hand. Despite the fear that had crawled into her chest and constricted her breath, she took another step forward. She knelt by the powerful woman's side and grabbed her hand. It was icy cold.

Elena was still awake and blinking, but it was several long moments before she could speak. When she could, she ordered Jessica to help her sit up against the wall. This movement too seemed to cost the woman a great deal of effort. When she spoke again, her voice was only a whisper—only a shade of its former power.

"Now," Elena murmured, her voice barely audible, "we can talk."

Jessica's eyes narrowed, her voice trembling. "W-w-what do you mean?"

"Our armor," Elena said, pausing to steady her breath, "records everything we say."

Jessica blinked. "Why?"

Elena looked her in the eyes. "For whispers… of sedition."

"S-s-sedition?"

"They don't catch everything," Elena admitted, "but… you can never be too careful."

Jessica glanced around the room, uneasy. "C-c-can't they hear us now?"

Elena shook her head slowly, her throat working as she swallowed. "No. And that's what you need to remember. No matter what you're up against—no matter how impossible it seems—there's always a way. Always a solution."

She looked at Jessica for a long moment. "And you, Jessica, are mine."

Jessica stiffened. "Solution? To wh-what problem?"

Elena's answer was a single word, heavy with meaning. "Acadia."

Jessica swallowed.

Elena leaned back against the wall, her breathing still labored but slowly recovering. When she spoke again, her voice was steadier.

"Our armor tracks everything—what we do, what we see, what we say. It's our surveillance. Our accountability. No need for cameras in the ceilings or wires in the walls. Every Validated wears their own monitor. It's how the Acadian System adjusts our Scores—every action, every word, every choice, processed through a thousand equations. It's not perfect, I've heard and seen plenty of things go unnoticed, but sometimes… it's brutally efficient and effective… weeding out rebellion with merciless delight." She said these last words with a surreal, bitter intensity.

She paused, letting the weight of it settle in.

"If we litter, the armor knows. If we are lazy, it knows. And it reports us." Her eyes drifted toward the orb. "But despite that flaw, the Static Armor is a powerful tool. It siphons off excess energy and stores it. When we are fatigued, it gives it back. Keeps us sharp. Maintains our body temperature. It's a technological marvel—with that one fatal weakness."

Jessica leaned in. "And if your e-energy runs out…"

"Then the system shuts down," Elena finished. "And it stops listening."

Jessica's brows lifted. "But… I t-t-thought once you earned the right to speak in public, you could t-t-talk about anything."

Elena let out a rough laugh—like gravel caught in metal. "Earning the right to speak doesn't mean you should. Some truths don't earn you points. Some things said… can cost you everything."

She sat up straighter, her energy slowly recovering.

"And the Golden Orb?" Jessica asked. "It… it took your energy?"

"Yes," Elena said, her voice calm again. She raised the orb in her hand. "Some of us are born different. We produce more energy than most—more by a large margin. We're called Novas."

The orb flickered faintly in her hand.

"We can apply for and receive a Golden Orb. It lets us contribute more… or be used more. Some Novas never see battle. They just sit still, letting the orb drain them day after day." She looked at Jessica, her voice flattening. "But I wouldn't recommend it. Every time you use it, it takes a little more."

Jessica nodded slowly. "O-okay."

Elena's tone shifted, her voice firming. "Jessica… there's something I didn't tell you before. Something I couldn't say with the City's ears still listening. I wish I had more time to explain—gently— but we don't have that luxury. So I'll speak plainly. If nothing changes, you won't survive the Mahghetto."

The word hit Jessica like a cold wind. She'd heard it whispered before, but never dared ask what it meant. Her mouth opened instinctively, but courage failed her. She closed it again.

"The Mahghetto," Elena continued, "cannot be discussed openly with Innocents as merit comes before all. *What* I'm telling you is a violation of the Acadian Code. But you must know. And the Mahghetto…" she paused, "…is hell. It's designed to crush the weak, to break the Dependent. If you somehow make it through, you'll be sent to the Crossing and become a Validated—one of the most powerful beings ever to walk this Earth. But you'll lose pieces of yourself along the way."

Jessica's voice was barely audible. "W-why won't I survive?"

Elena looked at her squarely. "Because you and I are not the same. You're from the Old Blood—the line of Adam and Eve. I thought your kind was extinct." Her voice softened briefly. "We, the people of Acadia, are their departure. Two hundred years of genetic refinement separate us from your lineage. We were bred for war. Tailored. Perfected.

"The Roaches adapt. They change. They evolve. And still, they can't break an Acadian shieldwall on the first charge. Even the weakest among us would outrun your strongest athlete. And that's why you, Jessica..." she said quietly, "...won't survive the Mahghetto."

Jessica's eyes dropped to the floor.

"...Unless I help you," Elena finished. "That's why you're here. That's why I volunteered to be your guardian."

Jessica blinked. "W-why?"

"Because you *must* survive."

"B-but how?"

Elena knelt to meet her gaze. "We have four years before your sixteenth birthday. Four years to turn you into something capable of surviving the fire. I can prepare you—but only if you give me everything. Absolute dedication." She paused. "What I *can't* give you... is the one thing you'll need most: the *will* to survive."

Jessica's voice cracked. "Wh-what do you w-want from me?"

"Everything you can give. And then more." Elena's eyes hardened. "But it'll be nothing compared to what the Mahghetto demands. Can you do that?"

Jessica hesitated. "I-I don't know..."

Elena's voice gentled again. "Listen to me, Jessica. Taking you in earns me points, yes. But the time I'll spend on you... it will cost me dearly. My Score will drop. I will suffer for this. And I'm not the only one. Others are sacrificing for you too. Because if you survive the Mahghetto..."

She stood.

"...you can end this."

Jessica blinked. "End what?"

"All of it. The suffering. The system. Acadia." She stepped forward. "But I need more than consent. I need commitment. Will you give me that?"

Jessica swallowed. "S-sure."

"No. Not enough." Elena's voice turned sharp. "Can you swear absolute obedience? Can you promise that your desire to live will burn hotter than your desire to give up?"

Jessica nodded, trembling. "Y-y-yes."

Elena studied her for a long, quiet moment. "Stand up." Jessica did, and the size disparity was so evident, it accentuated their tremendous genetic differences. A battle raged inside Elena's head. Reason told her the road was impossible, the gap between their two species was so wide, it was insurmountable.

*"And the will,"* Elena thought. *"Even after everything… who's to say she won't break when the pain becomes too much?"*

The girl was a fighter—of that, there was no doubt. She had endured a life of pain, starvation, violence. By all rights, she shouldn't be here. And yet, she was, like a flower forcing its way through a slab of concrete—too stubborn, too defiant to realize it wasn't supposed to grow at all.

Elena didn't like it—but she had to know. She needed to see that resilience for herself. And this, uncomfortable as it was, seemed the only way—or at least the fastest. More importantly, Jessica had to understand. Truly understand.

"Follow me," Elena said, her voice falling to a low monotone.

Jessica obeyed.

Elena led her into the small, shared bathroom. Jessica hadn't seen it yet—and for a moment, the strange opulence distracted her. The toilet rose to her knees—oddly tall. The sink was carved with oversized leaf patterns. The shower was expansive with gleaming hooks and polished steel fixtures. A broad mirror hung above the basin. For just a moment, she was transfixed.

And then Elena stepped in behind her.

Close.

Too close.

"What I do now," Elena said, her voice low and grim, "is so you know what you're choosing. I won't let you enter the Mahghetto in ignorance."

Before Jessica could react, arms wrapped around her—strong, unyielding. The air vanished from her lungs in an instant. She struggled, but it was useless. The room spun. Her mind fuzzed. Up became sideways.

She was being lifted—then dropped.

Hard.

Her body hit the shower floor with a thud. The last breath she had escaped on impact. She gasped but found only silence.

Then Elena returned—holding something.

Wire.

Jessica's wrists were jerked to her sides, bound tight.

"W-what are you doing?" she choked, coughing.

No answer.

A towel dropped over her face. The darkness was sudden and absolute. Panic bloomed. She opened her mouth to scream—but then something hissed.

A switch.

Water.

Freezing liquid slammed into her head. At first, the towel shielded her face, but then the cloth turned on her—soaking through, clinging to her skin. Water poured over her chest, down her arms, pooling under her back.

She tried to breathe. Inhaled fabric.

Coughed. Sputtered. Tried again.

Her breath came in shallow, pitiful gasps—just enough to taste the air between the droplets. But it wasn't enough. Her lungs burned. Her head spun.

She tried to scream again.

Nothing came out.

She could barely manage a whisper. Just a small, pathetic cough. Then the darkness deepened.

*"This is it."* Jessica's mind spiraled. *"She's going to kill me."*

But the thought didn't bring terror—it ignited fury. A molten coil of rage unwound in her chest and shot through her limbs. Her fists clenched instinctively, a raw violence she had never felt before flooded her body.

*"Why?"* she screamed silently. She fought like a caged lion. When her arms were pinned, she kicked; when her legs were secured

by wire, she rammed her head into the woman. For a brief second, the drenched cloth slipped from her face. She sucked in half a breath—glorious, sharp—before the towel came down again, sealing her world in darkness.

Time fractured. Seconds stretched into eternities. Days, weeks, years—her lungs didn't care. They just needed air. Each breath was shorter than the last, but just enough to cling to life for one more moment.

She kicked. She twisted. At one point, she was sure her knee connected with Elena's head. It cost her breath, but the bitterness that followed gave her a savage kind of satisfaction.

She thrashed again, pushing her back against the slick wall of the shower, launching her face just clear of the water. For a fleeting moment, she felt open air again. Then strong hands dragged her back under. Water slammed against her face. Her mind began to spin. Blackness crept in from the corners of her vision like a closing curtain.

Her fists slackened. Her legs gave way. Everything faded. Reality became as distant as the horizon. She could hear noises, but they were so distant she couldn't tell what they were.

She vaguely became aware that the water had stopped. That her body was rolled to the side. Vomit surged up her throat and splattered onto the tile. She lost consciousness.

When she stirred again, she was being carried—gently, almost tenderly—into another room. She was placed onto something soft— a bed, maybe. Her eyes fluttered open, catching only the blur of a face above her. She thought she heard a voice.

Then the blur sharpened. The figure came into focus.

Elena.

Jessica jerked back instinctively, her hands lifting to protect herself.

Elena didn't flinch.

Tears slipped down Jessica's cheeks. "W-why didn't you just let me die?"

Elena met her gaze evenly. "You could have," she said. "But that wasn't my choice. It was yours. You didn't surrender. Even when death was within reach—you chose to fight. That matters."

Jessica wiped her face with the back of her trembling hand.

"D-do I even have a choice?"

Elena nodded slowly, then sat on the edge of the bed, the weight of something unseen pressing on her shoulders.

A long silence passed.

"You have four years," she said at last. "Four years to live however you choose. I won't demand much. You'll eat well. Rest. Laugh, if you can. But when your Mahghetto begins…" she looked down, voice darkening, "…you'll die. Quickly."

Jessica's breath caught in her throat.

Elena exhaled slowly, her expression somber. She looked like someone already burdened by too many losses. Her strength was unmistakable, but in that moment, her sorrow was just as palpable.

Then, something changed in her eyes. A spark—cold and resolute—cut through the grief.

"Or," she said, rising, "I can mold your body into something much more."

She stepped to the doorway.

"I can give you all the tools—strength, skill, discipline. I can train your body, sharpen your mind, prepare you for the horrors to come. I will break you. And then I will ask for more. I will push you to the edge of death. You'll bleed. You'll scream. You'll beg me to stop. But even then, it won't be enough. Because what you need most—the thing that matters more than any technique or lesson—is the one thing I can't give you: the will to go on. The will to rise again when you're broken. To stand when your legs fail. To fight when your lungs scream for rest.

"To survive the Mahghetto, you have to want it more than comfort, more than safety—more than life itself. You'll have to want it like you wanted air just now. When you do, that's when you will be ready to face the Mahghetto."

She paused at the threshold, resting her hand on the frame.

"You don't have to decide now," she said, glancing over her shoulder. "But you will. Soon."

Then she was gone.

## SEVEN

"We need to see what you can do," Elena said after breakfast.

Three long days had passed since the shower incident—since Jessica had nearly drowned at the hands of the only person she trusted. And every time she passed the washroom, she felt it: the phantom pressure of water-soaked cloth, the invisible grip tightening around her throat.

Elena said little that morning. She couldn't—not with her armor still active. Instead, she left the answer in the form of a box.

It sat in the center of the front room like a cold, metal sarcophagus—long, narrow, and coffin-shaped. Jessica knew what it meant. Elena had explained it to her when the warrior's armor was not recording.

But that didn't make it any easier.

Jessica's stomach turned. The box meant the sub-levels. And the sub-levels meant darkness. Tight walls. Air that tasted like rust and echoes.

Elena studied her with unreadable eyes before her voice dipped to a low growl. "I'm going to work. You can stay here if you like. Maybe take a shower."

With that, she disappeared into her room, leaving Jessica alone with the box's looming silence.

Jessica stared at it.

Minutes passed. Maybe more.

Finally, with trembling hands, she climbed inside. She closed her eyes before the lid sealed shut, as if that would somehow make it easier. The world narrowed to darkness and metal.

It was not long before the box shifted. She felt movement, a rocking motion that echoed footsteps. Elena wasn't using a Lifter. She was carrying the box herself.

Jessica gritted her teeth as her body tilted left, then right with each stride. Her stomach lurched. Vomit crept up the back of her throat. She clamped her jaw shut and pressed her palms into her thighs. Panic built. Not a scream—but a still, clawing kind. The kind that curled inward and tried to make her disappear.

*"Don't lose it,"* she begged herself. *"Keep it together, Jessica."*

She thought of Elena. Of the strange warmth buried deep in that storm-hardened woman. If she failed—if she broke—maybe Elena would give up on her too.

Jessica bit her tongue and held on.

It felt like several hours.

Then—*hissss*—the box opened.

Air swept across her face like a rescue. She gasped, dragging in lungfuls of oxygen as if surfacing from an ocean trench. Her arms shook as she pulled herself upright, knuckles white as she gripped the box's rim.

Elena stood above her, one brow raised.

"Well," she said with a gentle laugh. "You shot out of there as quick as a sardine in a shark tank."

Jessica dropped her gaze, shame crawling over her like a second skin. She fixated on the checkered tile beneath her, wishing it would swallow her whole.

"Don't beat yourself up," Elena added more gently. "I don't care for enclosed spaces either."

Jessica looked up. The words mattered more than they should have.

The room around them was large, cold, and functional—a medical bay carved from steel and wire. Suspended machines hung from tracks in the ceiling. Diagnostic tools blinked softly on metal tables. There was a sophisticated workstation complete with multiple projection screens, a hovering interface, and a wall of reactive readers.

"My Second Stewardship is a Medicus," Elena said, setting down a tray of devices. "I work in the Mahghetto's Medicus wing. One of the few places in Acadia where I'm not required to wear armor. No recording. You can speak freely here."

Jessica hesitated before blurting out, "W-w-what are we d-d-doing here?" She hoped her words were calm, but she doubted they were. Her heart was still pounding from being trapped in the metal box.

Elena didn't answer at first. She was scanning shelves, her tone detached. "We're going to have to fix that stutter."

Jessica flinched.

"Don't take it personally," Elena said. "There's no room for stuttering in Acadia. That'll be the first thing we change. But not the last. Today, we find out what makes you different—from us."

Jessica's throat tightened.

"W-w-what do you mean?"

Elena turned. For the first time that day, her voice softened. "You're nervous. That's all right. You're safe here, Jessica. I know that might be hard to believe—especially after the shower thing. But this isn't that. You're not in danger. Not today."

She opened a cabinet and retrieved a small mask—sleek, gray, covered in tiny ridges and ports. She slipped it gently over Jessica's face, adjusting it until it sealed around her mouth and nose.

"Okay," Elena said. "This one's simple. Hold your breath. As long as you can."

Jessica nodded, relief flickering through her chest. *Finally*, a test she could handle. She had always been a good swimmer. Back in the village, she and the other children would dive beneath the pond's surface and try to outlast each other in silence and bubbles. It was the only game she ever won consistently.

She closed her eyes and inhaled deeply.

And waited.

Time slowed.

Her lungs ached, but she held.

At sixty seconds, her stomach clenched. At one hundred, her temples began to pulse. By one hundred and twenty, her body demanded release. She exhaled, gasping, and the mask hissed quietly as it analyzed her output.

She opened her eyes, half-expecting praise.

Instead, Elena only nodded, her expression unreadable.

"Good," she said. "That's a start."

Jessica had always been good at reading people—body language, tone, the tiny signs that foretold danger. It had been a matter of survival. A twitch of the brow, a tightened jaw, the weight of a footstep—those told her when to run, when to hide, when to brace. So when she finished holding her breath for a minute and fifty seconds—five full seconds longer than Sam Justine, the best swimmer in her old village—she expected to see some glimmer of pride in Elena's expression.

She saw none.

"Next," Elena said flatly. "Altitude response."

Jessica blinked.

"We'll simulate Mount Everest's elevation. Then go higher," Elena continued, tapping a sequence on the mask's controls. "When I activate the setting, take a full breath and start counting out loud."

Jessica nodded, trying not to look disappointed. She inhaled deeply. "One, two, three, four—"

Black.

When she came to, the mask was gone. Her head felt like it had been packed with insulation foam, her limbs leaden and unresponsive. Her thoughts swam sluggishly. She blinked several times before realizing she'd blacked out.

The tests didn't stop.

Running. Jumping. Lifting. Throwing. Reflex calibration. Vocal resonance. Cognitive mapping. Spatial orientation. Jessica complied, drenched in sweat and urgency. Each action was a prayer. But no matter how fiercely she tried, Elena's expression became more inscrutable—tight-lipped, calculating, grim.

Jessica had always been a champion. In her village, she ruled stickball like a queen—quick, cunning, relentless. She beat boys older and stronger, then practiced in secret to make sure she stayed ahead. But now? She felt like a toy hammer among laser-forged swords.

When the final scan ended, Elena collapsed into a mag-lev chair. She looked drained, as if *she* had run the tests herself. Jessica remained motionless across from her, a statue of quiet tension. Even her eye twitching felt like failure.

"What's wrong?" Elena asked.

"M-my eyes get itchy."

"Allergies?"

She shook her head. "My eyes just itch when it's dusty."

"That's allergies."

Jessica nodded, embarrassed.

Elena sighed. She reached for a stylus and tapped through holographic readouts that floated in the air. Her voice dropped to a mutter. "Figures."

Jessica's heart lifted—was that sympathy? Or frustration?

"You're so..." Elena began, then stopped, trying to pick a less brutal word. "Less..."

Jessica flinched. "W-what?"

Elena exhaled slowly. "I've read the records. Before Acadia, humans could do some relatively impressive things. The hundred-meter dash in 9.58 seconds. Breath-holding for ten full minutes. One man bench-pressed over a thousand pounds. You? Seventeen seconds. A minute forty-five. Seventy pounds—barely. And I think I helped."

"H-h-how good are—?"

"Acadians?" Elena anticipated. She tapped a virtual graph into existence. "No one knows exactly what we are capable of because no one has taken too much time to measure and quantify it. But the average Acadian's one-hundred-meter dash is six seconds, twenty minutes for holding their breath, and lifting—over a ton, and that's before enhancement. But it's more than just muscle. You produce two watts of electricity daily. That wouldn't light a Tech Pad. We generate five hundred per hour. No allergies. No infections. Our bones can take ten times the stress. Our organs regenerate. Our cells are resistant to vacuum, radiation, bio-corruption."

Jessica was speechless.

"We even digest more efficiently. We don't...defecate nearly as often."

Jessica frowned. *"She's been counting?"*

"I know what you're thinking; she's been keeping track of *'that'*".

"N-n-no," Jessica lied.

"And you're a terrible liar—which is not necessarily a bad thing." Elena said dryly. "Yes, I've tracked and reviewed all of your... markers from the day you arrived in Acadia. Even that."

Jessica's face burned. "But does this m-mean—"

Elena cut her off with a rare smile. "It's not a flaw. It's a baseline."

Then she turned away, muttering again—two minds fighting. One proposing strategies, the other dismantling them.

"D-does this mean I'll—I'll fail?" Jessica whispered.

Elena turned, eyes catching the shimmer of a single tear. Her expression softened.

"No. It means we'll have to recalibrate. Redesign. Adjust the enhancement protocols. But we can *do* this."

Jessica nodded. Her voice barely a whisper. "D-do you believe I can?"

Elena crossed the room and knelt before her. "Yes. But the work will be brutal. The injections, the procedures—they'll only work if you give everything. If you don't push beyond your limits, they'll backfire."

Jessica thought of the shower. The freezing water. The coarse towel. The panic. If she'd been strong, truly strong, she could've stopped it. If she'd been strong, she could've saved *him*.

That was the first time since arriving in the city that she allowed herself to name him—*father*. Not by blood, but by bond. He had fed her when her stomach shrank from hunger, clothed her when the others looked away, taken her in when every neighbor claimed they had too little to share. He had chosen her.

And when he needed her most, she ran.

She obeyed.

She left him behind, swallowed in smoke and screams, leaving nothing but blood and ash.

*"If I were strong,"* she thought, *"he would still be alive."*

"I will be stronger," she whispered. Her voice grew in steel. "I h-have to be." It was then, in the sublevels of Acadia, she learned a truth that would never fade. *"One must earn strength if they ever hope to obtain freedom."*

And in that moment, she found the resolve she never knew she had. She would *not* be weak again. She would not be a creature that would leave fate to chance—like Adrestas. She would not give in or surrender like Halix'Dra, losing so much hope she was physically paralyzed, unable to move or eat. She would not curl up into a ball at night, afraid of the Roaches and their distant screams. No, she had experienced enough fear for one lifetime. *She* would become a thing that the creatures feared.

"I have to be stronger," she whispered, more to herself than anyone else. "I will be stronger."

Elena nodded, her incredibly keen ears somehow hearing the

sound. "Yes, but you still have time to make a decision. No point in…"

Jessica wiped her cheeks and lifted her chin. "I'll d-do it."

Elena studied her for a long moment, her expression unreadable. "What do you mean?"

"C-change me. Make me strong. M-make me into something that can kill Roaches as easy…as…."

"As what?"

"As…I dunno," Jessica answered. "Something…good at killing."

"An Acadian," Elena said with a slightly sadistic smile.

Jessica nodded. "Yes, an A-Acadian."

Elena nodded slowly. "Then let me tell you the truth. These treatments will push you beyond the limits of natural evolution. We'll use focused radiation to break down cellular membranes, temporarily destabilizing your mitochondrial matrix. That lets us rewrite protein chains at the molecular level. Once we disrupt your cell walls, we'll rebuild them with bio-synthetic nanogel scaffolds. It's like breaking and recasting your entire body from the inside out."

Jessica's lips parted in awe and dread.

"Then," Elena continued, "we'll reinforce your skeletal structure with polycarbonic Vantarite filaments—one millimeter at a time. You'll be suspended in a medical cruciform while the auto-surgeons open each limb for deposition. You won't be unconscious—you *can't* be. The system needs your stress response to calibrate immune overrides."

Jessica's voice trembled. "Will it hurt?"

"Pain is… inadequate to describe it," Elena said. "You will beg to die. But if you survive, you'll have ten times the bone density, enhanced neural conductivity, oxygen-saturated blood, and metabolic efficiency."

Jessica nodded, silent.

Elena's voice grew heavy. "But it comes at a heavy price. By twenty-two, your bones will micro-fracture spontaneously. By twenty-five, your nervous system will begin degrading—blurred vision, memory loss, limb tremors. At twenty-eight, your heart may rupture from the bacterial overload. By thirty-two, your intestinal lining will collapse. And that's *if* you survive the treatments."

Jessica breathed slowly. She kind of wished Elena would have mentioned the potential negative effects before she agreed to anything. But then she realized it did not matter—she had already made her choice even before she knew there was one.

"I've made my d-decision, Elena. You can't s-scare me."

"You're sure?"

"Yes."

Elena turned to her ArmGuard, interfacing with the small glowing screen. The testing chair Jessica was sitting on transformed, unfolding into a surgical bed dressed with sterilizing nanofiber.

"Relax your body. We begin now."

The table slid into a chamber embedded in the wall. Jessica clenched her jaw, breathing deep, pushing her panic to the edges of her mind.

"Can you hear me?" Elena's voice came through a Comm-Link.

"Y-yes."

"You like music?"

Jessica was so surprised by the question, she did not answer. She was about to have her body radiatified or something and Elena was going on about music. All the music she had heard before was crap—a bunch of village shamans chanting to offbeat drums.

"What's your favorite kind?"

*"Kind?"* Jessica thought. *"There is no kind of music—it's just drums, low voices, varying pitches."* She had no idea what Elena was even talking about. Her favorite *kind* was the music that ended quickly and did not keep her up late by the campfire. She did not say this though and instead responded.

"I dunno."

"Acadia has its flaws, but it does have an impressive library of old music. Focus on the melody. On the words. When you come out again, can you tell me which one was your favorite?"

"S-sure."

Then Jessica's ears exploded—the walls around her vibrating. Jessica flipped out, her eyes opening, her hands hitting the walls. Elena must have hit an emergency ejection button because she was suddenly in the room again, the bright lights above piercing her eyes.

"What happened? Are you alright?"

Jessica blinked rapidly. "Yeah, I'm f-fine. The r-radia-radiatom radia—"

"Radiation?"

"Y-yeah…it s-s-startled me."

Elena looked puzzled for a moment. She glanced over to her equipment, double checking to make sure. Then she let out a soft, pleasant laugh.

Jessica could not help but be affected by the mirth. She returned the smile. "What?"

"That was…just the music," Elena said. "Sorry, my playlist has a lot of bass—I like a good beat when I'm killing Roaches. We'll start with something a little more mild."

"Oh, I…I've never h-heard something like that before."

Elena's laugh grew in strength, and her smile widened. "I think that's enough for one day. How about we head back to the apartment? Once we're on the surface, we can walk the long way and I can take you past the Hall of Statues. That will be the closest you've come to the Trinity so far."

Jessica's smile persisted. It felt good, warm. It was a tempting offer, she had rarely seen the city, and when she did it was with a specific purpose and destination. As simple as it was, going for a walk sounded like the most exciting thing she could hope for that day. But then the weight of her situation returned to her, and her resolve deepened.

"N-no," Jessica said, more terse than she meant. "Send me b-back in."

The two went back and forth for a while before Elena finally relented, and Jessica returned to the tomb of machinery that would become her new home.

The "music" started, soft, pleasant, an actual beat that the singers seemed to adhere to. Her ears had never heard such life, such harmony. And for about forty-five seconds she was in a state of wonder.

Then the radiation began.

## EIGHT

The pain wasn't the worst of it.

It was the stillness. The waiting. The endlessness of becoming. The radiation made her sick beyond words. Acrid saliva pooled in her mouth constantly. Her hair fell out in clumps. Her skin yellowed. She struggled for breath—not just when walking, but while eating, showering, even sitting still. She had to keep reminding her own body to breathe, as if her autonomic system had given up.

By the third week, she was paper thin. Her muscles felt like sacks of wet sand. Her face grew gaunt, her frame fragile, her bones hollowed. She was a whisper of herself.

Her home studies suffered. As an Innocent, she couldn't be Rifted for academic failure—but failure still had a cost. In Acadia, that cost was more homework. Elena handled most of it, carefully submitting just enough to avoid raising suspicion. Until Jessica received her own Placard, Elena's Score rose and fell based on her Dependent's performance.

Elena petitioned the city to allow Jessica to study from home. Her exemption had been approved so quickly, Jessica wasn't sure the digital ink had even dried before it returned authorized. Apparently, the city did not want the Aberration in public, much less at the schools.

Her only friend, her only lifeline, was Elena.

While Jessica lay tucked in the Mahghetto's Medicus wing, hidden in a corner where only machines whispered, they would talk—about her past, her pseudo-father, her tribe, the way her people survived the Roaches. At first, Jessica felt like a bore, no more interesting than a wart on the bottom of a foot. But Elena listened— really listened—her dark eyes absorbing every word like scripture.

She cared for all her Acadian guardians in different ways, but Elena was something else entirely—a lifeline in storm-tossed waters. Steady, unyielding, essential.

Even before applying to be Jessica's guardian, Elena had gone out of her way to understand her. She'd found a digital copy of an old Earth book tucked away in the Archives titled *Brave From the Inside Out*. Curious whether humans from before the Collapse raised their young differently, she read it cover to cover, wondering if those forgotten techniques might work better for a girl like Jessica.

At first, she thought it was a joke—maybe even satire. She laughed harder in the first few chapters than she had in years. Some parts were absurd to an Acadian: chapters on expressing love verbally, giving physical affection, validating a child's emotions. To Elena, it all seemed... unnecessary.

*"If I didn't love the child,"* she had thought, amused, *"why would I let it live in my house?"*

But then she tried it.

And it worked.

Jessica blossomed like a root finding water. Within weeks, her stutter disappeared. Her eyes lit with confidence. She spoke freely, openly—sometimes for hours. It astonished Elena. Words, hugs, praise... for some reason, they really seemed to matter to this kid.

They talked about everything.

But most often, they talked about music.

Real music—country, epic classical, rap, jazz, hip-hop, punk, even Acadian synthwave, which was most similar to techno. Some of it was terrible. Some of it made her cry. All of it opened a world she didn't know existed. It was like discovering a new sense. A sugar-sweetness for the ears.

But Elena couldn't stay forever. She had other duties to fulfill—fighting on the Killing Field, in the medical ward, in her Second Stewardship. When she left, Jessica remained behind, usually in darkness, music drifting through speakers like invisible companions. Sometimes she studied, squinting at ceiling-projected texts. But pain blurred her concentration.

Music became her only relief.

For thirty days, it became her language.

Then one day, the radiation and body-flaying came to an end. Elena looked at the wounds every day, checking for inflammation or infection.

"Let me see," Elena said, peeling off an Adaptive SolarBracer.

It hissed as it detached—a miniature miracle of bioengineering. The bracers had accelerated her healing to only a few days. They were magic: sealing lacerations, mending shattered bones, reversing infections. If even one had existed in her village, it would've saved countless limbs and lives.

That thought led her to another. A darker one. She had rehearsed the question a hundred times, trying to find the right phrasing. But in that moment, it simply fell out.

"How did this happen?"

Elena blinked, unsure which "this" Jessica meant. "The damage to your leg? That's from the Polycarbonic Vantarite infusion. It reinforces your bones, even if they break. The filtering wasn't perfect, but it's close to Acadian standard." She tapped the recovering limb. "It's healing nicely."

Jessica shook her head. "No. I mean… how did *everything* happen? Where did the Roaches come from? I've seen the ruins— skyscrapers that once touched the sky. How did we go from that… to my village?"

Elena paused. "Do you feel this?" she asked, gently massaging the muscle.

Jessica nodded.

"Well," she began, voice quieter now. "No one kept proper records. History collapsed with everything else. But here's what we know: sometime in the decline of the modern era, governments started to fail. Birth rates plummeted. Global trade fell apart. Greed hyperinflated currencies. It was chaos. And then…we made first contact."

Jessica held her breath.

"A ship the size of a city descended from the sky, landing somewhere in the old state of Virginia. It was a global sensation. People thought it was salvation. That aliens had come to fix what we broke." She exhaled slowly. "But the ship didn't open. Not for fifteen days. No signals. No response. It just waited… until the others arrived."

"And then?"

"When it finally opened, Roaches poured out. No diplomacy. No message. Just death. They slaughtered every living thing in their path."

Jessica's voice barely registered. "Who piloted the ships?"

"The Damnattii."

She'd heard that word before. Her people called them the Gifted. Village children nicknamed them *Three Arms*. Sometimes, they flew past the village in strange vessels, and the Damnattii allowed them to clean the splattered animals from their hulls—a grotesque chore, but one that fed entire families.

Jessica hesitated. "Why do they hate Acadia so much?"

"No one knows," Elena said, brushing hair from her face. "Maybe it's conquest. Maybe it's fear. But Acadia is the last human stronghold. If Earth is to fall, we're the final stone to break. We are the final wall of defense for the next generation of humans."

Jessica chewed on the thought. Then a new one surfaced. "Did you... have children?"

Elena froze.

Stillness clung to her like dust.

"Yes," she whispered. "I did my duty...." Then, avoiding eye contact, she crossed the room. "But enough about that. I have something for you."

She returned with something hidden behind her back, a smile breaking through the silence.

"What is it?" Jessica asked.

"I even wrapped it, like your people used to." Elena held out the object—wrapped in gauze, tied with medical tape.

Jessica raised a brow. "*Our* people—and we still do."

When she unwrapped it, her breath caught.

It was an ArmGuard. Sleek. New. Fully adaptive. Its screen wrapped across her wrist like liquid metal. A flick of her finger triggered a cascading bloom of holograms—navigation, messaging, diagnostics, maps.

"It dipped my Score a bit," Elena admitted. "But the refurbished ones never work right."

Jessica glanced at her guardian's Placard. Elena's Score had dropped—badly. But that could've been from everything over the past few weeks.

Elena hesitated. "Do you... like it?"

Jessica looked up, misty-eyed. "I've never had anything so beautiful before."

Elena pulled her into a hug. "Good. Because it suits you."

Jessica blinked. "But I can't walk yet."

"That will give you time to input your workout routine into your ArmGuard," Elena said with a wink. "By the time that's finished, you'll be walking just fine. After I inject a few billion bacteria into your stomach, heart, and muscles. It won't be pleasant. But it'll fill you with power."

Jessica winced.

"First, you'll learn to walk. Then jog. Then run… then kill."

***

Time passed. Days, weeks, years. It all blurred together. Jessica became something else—something forged. Each morning, she woke in pain. Each night, she collapsed in exhaustion. She followed Elena's schedule to the letter: running, climbing, competing in city-wide tests, studying tactical theory, dueling with blades inside the Mahghetto's training pits.

Her body thickened. Her mind sharpened. Her voice steadied. She was no longer an Innocent from the fringes of civilization. But she wasn't fully Acadian either. She was something else. Something new.

She just hoped it would be enough.

## NINE

Cojax stirred beneath his synthetic fiber sheets, eyelids too heavy to lift. It was early—too early. But not early enough. Sleep still clung to his bones like lead, and yet his body ached to move, like a sun-deprived serpent seeking warmth. He kicked one leg free and used it to anchor the rest of his body out of bed. Both feet found the floor—cold, sterile, tiled in polished chromium.

He raked his fingers through his wavy obsidian hair, then pressed them to the back of his neck. His face was sharp—high-cheekedboned and hawk-eyed, the kind of eyes that could project hatred from across a courtyard. But he rarely let them. Rarely needed to.

He slapped his face lightly and rubbed his brow.

*"You're sixteen now, Cojax. You don't get to sleep in. You think you can drag yourself like this through the Mahghetto?"*

These thoughts were his own, but they had the tone of his father. It was the sharpness of this tone that awoke him completely.

He stood, grabbed a fresh set of pressed whites, and headed for the shower. The moment he stepped in, the water stung like needles—ice-cold and alive. He tensed, grit his teeth, counted to three. On cue, the temperature shifted, enveloping his skin in a programmed embrace.

He could've stayed longer. His Score wasn't being tracked yet—Innocents were still beneath the metrics—but that didn't mean he was free.

Not with a father like his.

*"Dimmed rules."* He exhaled sharply. *"Wish I were a Hellion."*

The Hellion Faction—unrestrained, wild, born to rebel before ever setting foot in the Mahghetto. He knew a few. They didn't press their uniforms or count their seconds in the shower. They lived like fire. Cojax, on the other hand, had been under surveillance since his tenth year.

"Blood and bile," he muttered, eyes darting to the wall-mounted timer.

1:02.78—two seconds too long.

He slapped the valve off and stepped out, dragging a towel across his head. The race was on now. Those two seconds would cost him. He could already feel them hanging over him like an indictment.

He dressed with mechanical precision. The white jacket was stiff, too crisp, resistant to movement. The matching slacks creased like paper, unforgiving to the slightest bend. He hated the uniform. Hated how it made him look like a hollowed-out version of himself. But he buttoned it anyway.

He could not stop his thoughts from adding commentary. *"Brutus' jacket looks like it came out of a trash chute, and no one says a word. Finn oversleeps every day and his father couldn't care less."*

Each button clicked into place like a prison lock.

When he stepped into his boots, they hissed softly, auto-tightening around his calves with biometric feedback. His anger rose. Not fury. Not rage. Just a quiet injustice, coiling inside his chest like steam trapped in a sealed pipe.

*"Breathe,"* he told himself. *"He'll detect it. Even the smallest crack, and he'll exploit it."*

Eyes shut. Inhale. Exhale. Smooth.

Once composed, he exited the hallway. The door slid open on motion-sense, revealing the pristine white main room. Their apartment, positioned at the top of the Praetorium Residences, overlooked the clean geometry of Acadia's skyline—columns of white, red tiled roofs, CargoLifters weaving between hovering transit cones.

It was an exceptionally large dwelling by city standards, but it was still austere. White walls broken only by algorithmic lighting and the occasional structural pillar. He stepped to the far wall, drew his right fist to his chest, and bowed his head. Three full minutes passed.

Then the main door hissed open.

Cojax didn't need to look to know.

The temperature in the room had already dropped.

"Attention," he called out, loud and clear. "Numberless present."

He snapped to full posture, arm across chest, spine locked in place. Adrenaline surged through him. Sweat prickled his collar despite the chill. A part of him still scanned his own uniform with peripheral glances. Near his shoe—was that a fold? A wrinkle?

He was larger than most Numberless, his frame encased in dark alloy plating beneath a blood-red cloak that marked his status. As he moved through the doorway, he passed an Arc Blade mounted beside it—massive, ancient, and powerful.

It wasn't a battlefield weapon.

Not one used against the Roaches.

No, this blade was something else entirely—something ritualistic. It had weight, both literal and symbolic. In the wrong hands, it could be repurposed with terrifying efficiency. Cojax knew that if Titan ever deemed him unworthy, that blade could fall from its place and end him—cleanly, definitively, without a word spoken.

Titan's presence stole the air from the room.

"Report, Innocent," Titan said. His voice was smooth now—deceptively calm. Cojax knew better than to trust it.

Cojax raised his head and dropped his arm. "Sir. Ready for inspection."

Titan circled slowly, glancing at his ArmGuard. Its embedded screen cast a harsh glow across his angular features—jaw like cut obsidian, eyes like polarized glass. Every step he took felt like pressure against Cojax's ribcage. He didn't just assess uniforms. He scanned for weakness.

"Innocent," Titan said at last, stopping mere inches from his son. "You pass visual inspection."

"Yes, sir."

Titan's eyes narrowed. "But explain to me why your shower exceeded its time limit by 2.78 seconds."

Cojax's mouth went dry.

"Sir," he said carefully, "I lost track of time."

Titan didn't blink. "Unacceptable."

"Yes, sir."

"Do you think the Roaches will wait while you finish a shower? That they might be too intimidated by your naked frame to break down your door and slice you in two."

"No, sir."

"Do you think that in the Mahghetto, you will get away with

such luxuries?"

"No, sir."

"An Acadian does not lose track of time—ever. You can't afford to. You've been over your allotted shower time every day this week. I've also noticed that when you are at the Games, you're spending too much time on Dependent activities—such as the CargoLifter Simulator, the Gouger arcade, the Arc Lancer circuits. I've specifically told you that these things are a waste of time, that you should be in the Vortex, or the fighting simulators, or at the track running circuits."

"Sorry, Father. My friends just wanted to try—"

Titan let out a low, violent breath—one that instantly silenced his son. It was obvious he was restraining a temper hot enough to forge steel. "You have to choose strength over weakness, boldness over fear. You are stronger than you know, son. Don't pick the path of the Dependent—you can't afford it."

Cojax swallowed the words building in his throat. He wanted to yell, to point out that the Mahghetto hadn't accepted him yet—that he was still an Innocent. Innocents could take minute-long showers—longer, even. The whole point of the Games was to have a final break between school and the initiation into the Mahghetto.
But Titan didn't care about qualifiers. He only cared about upholding the AC, maintaining his perfect Numberless image.

Titan leaned closer. "You will not be like the others, Cojax. You cannot fall upward, clawing your way forward with mediocrity. You have to be sharper than this, my boy. You have to. This is the year of your Mahghetto." There was an intensity in Titan's eyes that was so visceral, so pleading that it was hard to explain.

Cojax locked eyes with him, unable to force all of the bitterness from his voice. "Understood, sir."

Titan stared a moment longer, then turned away. "Not yet you don't, but you will. They all do eventually. Now, grab your breakfast and head to the Games. You're already three minutes behind. Dismissed."

Cojax thudded his fist to his chest in salute and turned on his heel, retreating to the adjoining kitchen. Titan didn't follow.

As he stepped through the sliding doorway, a body scanner flickered, silently reading the embedded micro-tag in his palm. A soft chime responded, and a narrow hatch slid open atop the brushed steel counter. From it rose a thermosteam tray bearing oatmeal—pale, gluey, and quivering—alongside a recycled-plastic cup of nutrient milk and two slices of processed toast curled at the edges. A faint puff of ionized mist escaped the tray, sterilizing it before delivery.

He took his food and sat at a rectangular metal table, cold and just wide enough to crowd three occupants. Every surface in the room gleamed sterile chrome, designed for hygiene and longevity, not comfort. Beside the food chute, a reheating pod with a thermal resonance coil sat idle, capable of flash-cooking meals in under a second. A shallow gray sink blinked blue when approached, automatically measuring water flow to the nearest milliliter. A tall, humming cryo-fridge stood in the corner, its contents logged, rationed, and encrypted.

Technically, there were only two residents now. His brother Marcus had moved out years ago. But since their father was a Numberless—and Marcus still visited regularly—the third chair remained.

Cojax scowled at his tray. It had been months since he had eaten cheesy eggs, pancakes, or even citrus-synth juice. The moment he was in his sixteenth year—it all went away per his father's orders. No explanation. Just gone. No other Innocent he knew had their food selection reduced. It stung all the worse because he'd only just earned a broader menu two years before. This was meant to be the best two years of his life, yet his meals had the texture and taste of something better suited to lubricating a HoverBucket's engine.

He forced down a spoonful, the texture more like thermoset paste than food. As he grimaced through his third bite, the apartment's front door whooshed open.

Marcus entered with the quiet confidence of a man who commanded thousands. In moments, he crossed the main room and entered the kitchen. The system registered him instantly, scanning his Score through his chest Placard.

"Would you like to dine here, Gamma Marcus?" the house AI asked in its neutral tone.

"Yes."

"Marcus!" Cojax said, his spirits instantly lifted. "If it isn't the

First in the Gap at the Battle of Menoch."

"Hah!" Marcus answered, heading to the food chute. "Rumors, nothing more." Marcus was a boulder of a man—larger even than Titan. His arms were thick as forged steel, his legs built like Corinthian-style pillars. Cojax was no small figure himself, but seated beside his brother, he felt like a shadow cast by a mountain.

"No," Cojax said, his smile persisting. "I was in the Great Forum and saw it for myself on the CityScreens. You ranked number one in that battle. There you were, three stories tall, waving your Arc Lance like the turbine on a HoverBucket."

"Well," Marcus said with a quick wink. "That might have been me. It won't be long before you're out there with me, holding the shieldwall together. Your Mahghetto is not too far off."

A second hatch opened with mechanical grace, revealing a tray that contrasted sharply with Cojax's. It overflowed with golden pancakes, sizzling bacon, a warm blueberry muffin, eggs laced with synthetic cheddar, and a chilled glass of authentic orange juice—the real kind, not the enzyme-reconstructed variety. Marcus sat across from him, placing his tray down with military precision.

"And not too soon," Cojax said, eyeing Marcus' splendid selection of breakfast delights. He grunted, all good humor leaving him in an instant.

Marcus wore the polished bronze armor of a First Tier Gamma Commander—a leader of ten thousand. He had spent a good chunk of his Score on armor upgrades—reinforced breastplates, reactive flares, enhanced sensory embedding in his helmet. Arc veins pulsed faintly beneath the plating, feeding nanocurrent to his embedded systems. The bio-circuitry in his arms flared dimly with each movement. His Placard blazed across his chest with a Score so high it bordered on myth for someone so young.

Despite himself, Cojax was jealous. He knew his brother deserved all the accolades and more, but he was only four years passed his Crossing and already was a Gamma—a Gamma, of all things. Before long, there would be two Numberless at the table—doubling his chance of getting lectured at any given moment.

Marcus caught his gaze. Cojax looked away quickly, flushing red, stabbing another bite of oatmeal with theatrical disgust.

"How are you holding up, brother?" Marcus asked.

There had been a time, before Marcus' Crossing, when the two had been inseparable. They'd sparred, studied, and laughed together, each filling the other's gaps. Cojax was competition and movement; Marcus was ponderous and thoughtful. Marcus had been the only one of the quadruplets who treated Cojax like more than a tagalong.

The others were gone now—four of them went into the Mahghetto, but only one returned. Marcus had changed. Become remote. It took another rotation but he finally came around, rekindling their friendship. But things were never the same. Marcus was now exceptionally busy—weekly battles, work at the Archives, his responsibilities as a Gamma, his role on the First Tier High Order. This little banter was the most they had spoken in days.

Cojax stirred his oatmeal idly. "I'm so tired of this slop. Every morning, same molecular composition, same texture. I think they repurpose industrial sealant and then send it my way."

Marcus chuckled softly, a rare sound. "Yeah. Looks rough."

"It's not just the food," Cojax muttered, dropping his spoon into his bowl. "They said the year before the Mahghetto was supposed to be the best. No classes, no formal drills. But I'm still up before sunrise, rationed warm water that cuts off before I can even lather with soap, and meals that double as armor lubricant. Blazing rot—if this is freedom, I want my old schedule back."

"You can always use the VaporSweep if you prefer—some residences don't even have a shower in the Subterra Residences and that's all they use."

"Ugh," Cojax answered. "It might kill the bacteria but it does nothing to wash away the dead skin. It's quick though, I'll give you that."

Marcus raised a brow. "What exactly were you expecting?"

Cojax gestured bitterly toward his brother's tray. "That, for one. I haven't tasted bacon in six months. And music—don't even get me started." He leaned forward, his voice falling to a whisper. "Father won't budge on anything. He's purged my ArmGuard and gave my Tech Pad away. I'm stuck with static-churned synths on my ArmGuard—that stuff is for infants. And look at those micro-tags running through your skin—do they boost reaction time? Sensory processing? I don't even know. But they look... *alive*. You get to choose your meals. You can visit the Red District—"

"You don't want that," Marcus cut in sharply. "The Red's for those burning out. Dependents. Tier-drained gamblers. You walk those halls long enough, your Score starts bleeding."

"I wouldn't live there," Cojax said quickly, "but I wouldn't mind a visit. They've got stock taps, real music, and you can meet girls. If half the rumors I've heard are true, it's a place I've got to see."

Marcus gave him a knowing look, amusement flickering at the edge of a tired smile. "Don't believe rumors. You won't find a First Tier there. Maybe a few desperate Fourths or Fifths. Besides, you *can* meet girls now."

"Not ones that matter," Cojax muttered. "Without a Score, you're invisible. No female worth her Tier will even acknowledge you. I just—" He exhaled, voice lowering. "I want to get to the Crossing already. I want to be seen. Be *Validated*. I want bacon for crying out loud."

Marcus looked at him long and hard, expression unreadable. "Here, take mine." He slid a piece of bacon over to Cojax.

"I don't want your bacon; I want my own bacon."

Marcus moved to take the bacon back but Cojax popped it in his mouth. "I'm just ready for my chance, you know."

"You'll get your chance," he said finally. "But the Mahghetto doesn't make you visible. It just burns off the parts of you that aren't needed."

"I can't wait for the Mahghetto," Cojax said with relish.

Marcus hit the metal table, his face suddenly turning taut. A rage Cojax had rarely seen his brother display was behind his eyes. "Yes, you can."

He had growled the words more than he had spoken them. Marcus suddenly realized he was standing and sat back down, his hands reaching for his toast. He was about to take a bite but he stopped. His mouth opened as if to speak, no doubt to apologize for his outburst, but no words left him. A higher Tier never apologized to a lower Tier. He took a bite instead.

Cojax shook his head. "I'm sorry. I spoke too brashly."

Marcus nodded. "It's easier to find men who will volunteer to die than to find those who are willing to endure pain with patience."

"Why do you quote those old philosophers? They're outdated, Marcus. Just because they're dead doesn't mean they made any sense."

Marcus only shook his head. "Cojax, look at me. No matter when something is said, no matter who said it, it's worth repeating if it rings true. If you learn from their past, you can avoid many mistakes in your future."

"Who said that last quote?"

"Julius Caesar."

"Didn't he get killed?"

Marcus grunted.

"Now that I think about it," Cojax responded, anxious to keep the conversation light. "I believe he was stabbed a whole bunch of times. Maybe he should have spent more time making friends than crafting lofty quotes that only you and a handful of others would ever remember."

Marcus laughed. "Point made, little brother."

"So, what else is new in your life?"

"Nothing."

Cojax shifted in his chair. "Isn't your…Civil Union in a few weeks? If that's nothing, you're living a life I'm truly jealous of. That's some pretty big news."

Marcus frowned, as if trying to force his mind through a fog.

"What's her name?" Cojax teased.

"They haven't told me yet."

"When do you meet her?" Cojax replied.

"Don't know that either."

"Come on," Cojax persisted. "You've got nothing to share? All this time you've been studying for the Civil Union exam, preparing to be a parent and live with your spouse, and now that day has arrived, you've got nothing more to add?"

"My Score is subsidized after the union."

"My goodness, you're boring," Cojax replied. "You should take lessons from Finn on how to tell a story."

"Is Finn one of your sparks that lives in the Subterra Residences?"

"Yes," Cojax replied, taking a bite of toast, "but don't let him hear you say that. They prefer the term Burrows, not Subterra

Residences."

"That's the official name," Marcus said, his tone flat.

"So? You excited? Nervous? Come on, give me something. What's going on in that mind of yours?"

"Feels like I'm marching into battle—so yeah, a bit of both," Marcus replied. "But I don't even know who my spouse is going to be. I figured they'd at least tell me a name by now, or send a picture or something. But—"

"—But what?" Titan's voice cut in. He had appeared without a sound, causing both boys to stiffen. The air shifted as if it had lost oxygen, the ease between them evaporating instantly.

Titan retrieved his thermosteamed tray from the wall chute while Marcus stumbled over his thoughts, not prepared for the forceful question.

"But now...," Marcus said carefully. "I'm starting to question this whole Civil Union thing. I mean...I'm only twenty-two. I just thought they'd give me more information—where I'm going to live, who I'm going to live with...."

Titan nodded slowly, a gesture that might have passed for sympathy, if such a thing still existed in his vocabulary.

"Civil Unions are the backbone of this city. We need children—citizens—to carry the burden forward. Be grateful. It's an honor few are given. I will not have my son talking like a Dependent."

"Yes, sir," Marcus said, lowering his voice. "I apologize. I'll remember my place."

Cojax, who had momentarily forgotten himself, shot to his feet in attention. "Attention! Number—"

Titan waved him down with a single firm hand. "Too late for that now, boy. Just finish your food."

"Yes, sir," Cojax murmured.

The rest of the meal passed in silence, just like most of them did when Titan was in the room. Cojax focused on his bland oatmeal, avoiding his father's gaze. Marcus, now as distant as ever, dutifully picked at his food, eating it without relish. Whatever part of him existed before the Mahghetto seemed to vanish the moment Titan entered a room. Despite arriving later, Marcus and Titan ate with efficiency, and they left not long after, dropping their empty trays in the hydro-wash and then down the chute.

When he was done, Cojax checked his ArmGuard. A small holographic clock glowed for a moment, reminding him of the time. He dumped his plate into the chute, forgoing the hydro-wash, and moved to the front door. A micro-tag in his palm blinked once, and the door slid open with a soft hiss. Outside, a narrow gray hallway stretched along the building's edge, lined with identical pressure-sealed doors. He ascended one flight of stairs until he reached the landing zone on the roof.

A CargoLifter hovered, just about ready to take off, but it was nearly full. Cojax let it pass. Instead, he walked to the railing and stared out over Acadia.

The city smelled sterile. Purified. Exact. It always did.

He spent more and more time up here lately. From this height, the city looked like a machine—streets lit with low-burning lights that stretched like circuit lines, dividing the city into glowing sectors. Each Faction had its own signature, its own flair of design and custom. Just like its people.

His eyes settled on the city's heart: the Trinity.
Three towering spires, each divided by a beam of pure light, soared skyward in a perfect concert. It wasn't three buildings, not really. Just one colossal tower split by refracted beams, giving the illusion of separation. It dwarfed everything—an iron monolith surrounded by marble and concrete ants. The Trinity projected the city's protective shields, guarding them from long-range enemy fire or orbital bombardment.

Around it stood buildings that looked more ancient than futuristic—white walls, red-tiled roofs, concrete and marble columns. It was like someone had resurrected Athens and given it a power grid. Statues and fountains of the Numberless dotted the forums, while weapons and fallen Roach heads adorned certain Faction buildings and walls. The closer a building was to the Trinity, the taller it stood—fifteen stories at the core, tapering down to two or three near the Wall.

No one built out anymore. When space was needed, they built up. But Cojax hadn't seen new construction in his lifetime. Population caps kept the city locked at ten million Validated—not counting the Innocents or Dependents in the city.

Cojax checked his ArmGuard again and cursed. He was meeting the triplets, not that they cared about punctuality. They were always late.

Another CargoLifter descended. He scanned his micro-tag embedded in his palm across the access panel and stepped aboard. The vehicle surged upward, then coasted toward a platform near the Trinity—fifteen stories high, the closest any non-Numberless could legally get in a flying craft.

Once landed, Cojax disembarked and headed for an elevator, but four Validated from the Saken Faction barged past. One of them slammed his shoulder into Cojax. He straightened, locking eyes with the offender.

Cojax held the stare a second too long.

"Watch it, Innocent," the smallest of them sneered.

Cojax clenched his jaw. Hard.

"My apologies. I'll be more careful next time," he said with a practiced salute.

He took another step toward the elevator—then a fist hit him square in the face. His head cracked against the concrete. The pain was immediate. Stars burst behind his eyes.

He was on his feet in a breath. His muscles coiled. Fists clenched. Training from the Games had kicked in.

"Who the blaze do you think you are, little Rifter?" another Saken said. "Innocents don't use elevators. You take the stairs like every other Point-parasite."

Rage burned through him like fire in his veins. His fists shook, nails biting into palms.

They laughed.

Others passed without noticing. Or pretending not to.

One by one, they entered the elevator. The doors slid shut, leaving Cojax behind. Alone. Seething.

As an Innocent, just walking the crowded streets could be a battle. He was expected to make way, to hold doors, to bow with deference. In his ninth year, he had earned the right to walk freely throughout the city, but that right could easily be taken away if he ever got in the way of someone in the Tiers. What took a Validated five minutes could take Cojax twenty. By the time he reached the base of the Trinity, he was over twenty minutes late—a crime in the eyes of his father.

"Look who it is," came a familiar voice. "I thought being late was our job."

Cojax turned to find his three closest friends—Finn, Hadrian, and Brutus—lounging behind a Corinthian-style pillar. They were triplets, though no one would ever guess it.

Brutus was the largest by far, with a scar slicing from his left ear to the base of his throat. He used his size to his advantage—and had grown very comfortable doing so. His humor had sharp edges, usually aimed at others.

Hadrian, shorter and squarer, had a barrel chest and thin arms, giving him a look of constant imbalance. He rarely joked, which made his dry comments land awkwardly in mixed company. His face changed with his weight, so much so that it seemed to morph week by week depending on how much physical exertion he'd endured.

Finn was tall, lean, effortlessly charming. His wit never felt forced, and people tended to trust him within hours of knowing him. It was a gift he rarely abused.

"I'm just giving you a taste of your own medicine," Cojax said, grinning.

"You can't be running late, Cojax," Hadrian said. "That doesn't light in the Mahghetto."

"The Placard-polisher speaks," Brutus added, squaring up to his brother. "We're not in the Mahghetto yet."

"Easy," Finn said, waving off the tension. Then, to Cojax, "What happened to your face?"

"He's always been ugly," Brutus muttered with a snort.

"Someone hit you," Hadrian said, more serious.

Cojax wiped a small streak of blood from his chin. He examined his fingers and swore under his breath. "Blood and bile, Rift those Eighth Tiers. Probably still have a sheen from their first major battle."

"What'd you do to deserve that?" Hadrian asked.

"Apparently, Innocents from the Saken Faction can't use the elevators. And they decided their rules apply to the BloodBorne now."

"You should've known that," Hadrian scolded, eyes

narrowing. "Your father's a Numberless—he should've taught you other Faction protocols."

"Maybe he and the big guy don't talk much," Brutus teased.

"This is serious," Hadrian continued. "If Titan finds out, and thinks you were insubordinate—forget it. You might as well leap into the Killing Field yourself."

"Whose side are you on?" Finn asked, arms folding.

"Eighth Tiers, huh?" Brutus said with a sneer. "You just let them smack you around?"

"There were four of them," Cojax answered. "They were in Static Armor. They were Validated."

Brutus chuckled softly.

"Don't act shiny," Hadrian snapped at Brutus. "You'd have done the same. Cojax is an Innocent—you don't pick fights with someone above your Tier. That's statute seventeen, article four of the Acadian Code."

"Why don't we head to the fight simulator and scare Hadrian into silence?" Brutus offered with mock sweetness.

Cojax and Finn chuckled despite themselves. Hadrian made for an easy target.

Unbothered, Hadrian flashed a grin. "Why don't you make that same offer to Cojax?"

Brutus stiffened but said nothing.

"Oh?" Hadrian said. "So you only challenge the ones you know you can beat? I think Cojax did more than beat you last time— it was a massacre. You nearly kissed the crest. Face it, Brutus, you're always Beta when he's around."

Brutus stepped forward, but Finn pushed him back with a hand to the chest.

"We just got our Right of Speech in Public restored," Finn warned. "We're standing in front of the training grounds and you two want to start hurling insults again?"

"Keep poking me and I'll break your jaw," Brutus growled at Hadrian.

"Which will get our Right of Movement revoked," Hadrian shot back. "Remember being locked in the apartment for three full months? That was a joy."

"Enough," Finn barked, separating them. "Hadrian, stop

provoking. Brutus, stop taking the bait."

Cojax shook his head. "I wish we could just do it already."

"Do what?" Brutus asked.

"The Mahghetto. Forget all this rot. We've earned every right we can, every freedom that is afforded to us. Right of Movement, Speech, even the Cert to pilot a HoverBucket...." His eyes drifted to Hadrian.

Brutus grinned. Finn pretended not to hear. All but Hadrian had earned the Cert to pilot a HoverBucket. During Hadrian's practical portion of the test, he had accidentally knocked off a chunk of concrete from the eighth floor of the Vixor Faction building. Last time they checked, it was still missing.

"My point is," Cojax continued, "if we start now, we could be done in nine months. Right now, Top Tier girls don't even look at us. But once we're Validated..."

"Top Tier girls won't remember your name if all you've got is Mahghetto dirt on your boots," Brutus said.

"He's got a point," Finn added.

Cojax blinked. "Wait—his point or mine?"

"His." Finn shrugged. "You need Roach wax on your hands. Need to be Sixth Tier or better—and climbing."

"You need to follow the rules," Hadrian added, voice steady.

"I know all that," Cojax snapped.

"Then why rush?"

"Because I'm sick of being treated like a Dependent. The sooner we start, the sooner it's done, the sooner we can get on with our lives. Win glory. Win fame."

Hadrian's tone darkened. "We're not ready. None of us are."

"We'll have to be," Cojax said.

Hadrian hesitated. "There are a lot who don't make it. I've had four—maybe five—friends who started but never reached their Crossing."

"Friends?" Brutus scoffed. "Just because you know their name doesn't mean you can call them a friend."

"Tiber. Alexander. Jacobo—remember him? Always followed us around during The Games."

"Maybe they just failed a section, and it took more time because they had to repeat it," Cojax said, trying to convince himself more than the others. "We don't know what goes on in the Mahghetto. It can't be as bad as the rumors. We're strong. Smart. We'll make it." These words were made hollow by the memory of his four older brothers. Four had entered the Mahghetto, but only one made it back.

"No one lasts more than nine months," Hadrian said. "They either make it—or disappear."

"You're being dramatic."

"No, he's not," Brutus growled. "And I hate saying this—but Hadrian's right. We live down in the Burrows, remember? Not in a top-floor penthouse. Most of the Innocents live down there with us—and we see who comes back and who doesn't."

Cojax flushed.

Finn placed a calming hand on his shoulder. "No offense, Cojax. Your dad's a Numberless. Makes sense you live higher up. But the rest of us? We're down in the deeps. Parents are usually Tiers Three to Six."

"A lot enter," Hadrian said, "far fewer come back."
"You don't know that," Cojax said. "People move around. They get reassigned. You're not even supposed to keep in contact with people from before."

"Some do, sure," Hadrian admitted. "But not most."

"So where do they go?"

Silence.

Then Finn smirked. "Wow. You guys really know how to keep it light." He rolled his shoulders. "Look, we'll all go through the Mahghetto eventually—and we'll get through it. Together. Until then, why even think about it?"

Cojax exhaled. "Because it's hard not to. Everyone treats us like nothing until we pass through it. I just want to be seen for what I can already do."

"What do you think it'll be like?" Hadrian asked. "You think it's just our Faction down there—or all of them? There's probably a hundred thousand trainees in the Mahghetto at any given time. You think we'll train together—"

A horn split the air.

Low. Deep. Trembling.

It sounded again.

Cojax was already on his feet, fists clenched, head raised. He was always the first to move. His chest tightened, an old memory returning. "They're attacking."

## TEN

Hadrian laughed, a quick, nervous sound. "Midday?"

Brutus cocked a brow. "What? You going to get on the Roaches now for not following protocol? Maybe hop the Wall and lecture them on punctuality?"

Laughter rippled through the group.

Hadrian bristled. "They haven't attacked at midday in six months, two weeks, and seven hours. Trust me—I remember every engagement. Down to the hour."

Brutus grinned. "Really? You've been my brother our entire lives and never mentioned your photographic memory. You'd think that would've come up."

"Once," Cojax said.

"Or twice," Brutus added, "or every glitching day since your mouth could form words."

Finn held up a hand. "Let's go find a CityScreen."

Hadrian nodded. "It's a mandatory viewing today."

Brutus opened his mouth, another insult already locked and loaded, but Finn cut him off. "A Major Forum's closest. We can still get a good spot if we move."

"It's been four months, two days, and six hours since we were last there," Hadrian offered.

Brutus rolled his eyes. "And it's been exactly three-point-two milliseconds since your last irritating comment. Pace yourself, Tier Scraper. It's going to be a long day."

They reached the Major Forum quickly—Brutus leading with the kind of hunger he only showed for food and warfare. Despite the dozens of battles they'd all watched, Brutus never tired of the carnage. The blood. The violence.

Thousands of Validated had already assembled outside the Wall, lined up in shieldwalls. CargoLifters and HoverBuckets were still ferrying troops to the Killing Field. A few warriors leapt directly from the Wall, their armor igniting upon impact. What should've been chaos—an impossible choreography of bodies and machines—was instead seamless. Precision-timed landings, synchronized formations. Like a clockwork war machine.

Within moments, the soldiers locked into flawless box formations—phalanxes of two hundred warriors led by Alphas. Ten phalanxes formed a Quorum beneath a Kappa, and five Quorums advanced as one under the command of a Gamma. Over all of them presided the Omega, master of the battlefield.

Cojax knew every structure. Every rank. Every function. But watching from the Major Forum was something else entirely. He stood among the crowd, eyes locked on the towering CityScreen as the battle unfolded in high definition. He knew the tactics. The grid patterns. The standard opening salvos. But beneath all that...

His stomach tightened.

He hated watching.

Even now, years later, the memories clawed at him. The day the Roaches breached. The screaming. The helplessness. He had frozen while others bled. He wasn't proud of it, but he hadn't forgotten it either.

He forced himself to study the formations, the angles, the counter-movements—anything to make it feel like a simulation instead of slaughter. To reframe the battlefield as a chessboard instead of a grave.

He'd lied to his brother. Worse—he'd lied to himself. It was never about girls, or status, or even the city-rationed bacon—though, if he was being honest, he really did miss bacon. No, what he wanted—what he *needed*—was something deeper. A blade meant control. Armor meant resolve. He craved the chance to prove he wasn't just the frightened boy who'd once cowered on the blood-slick ground while Validated warriors fought and fell around him. He had to prove—if only to himself—that he wasn't a coward. That he could stand, bleed, and fall alongside the best of them.

To never feel that kind of fear again.

Down below, the first wave of Validated stepped into the Killing Field. The Roaches met them in kind—dark, spiny beasts swarming forward in a sea of carapace and shrieks. It seemed mostly to be comprised of Class IV Reever Subjugators and Skitterfangs—

an impressive gathering but not nearly as deadly.

Then came the light.

At two hundred yards, the Acadians raised their Blazers and opened fire—surgical beams slicing through the advancing swarm. Behind the lines, the Gougers opened up—squat, ball-shaped vehicles with four cannons. Though they could fly, they were far more effective on land, scaling terrain and launching punishing blasts from fixed positions or on the Wall itself.

For several minutes, it was an exchange of light and blood. Then, as if on cue, the Roaches turned feral.

They charged.

The CityScreens shifted frantically, swapping HoverCam angles every few seconds. A sidebar tracked the warriors in real-time—face, rank, kills per battle, blade-to-blade efficiency, sniper accuracy. The top ten rotated constantly, their battle titles highlighted like trophies.

"Looks like your boy Cineas is on the field," Finn said, squinting at the readout.

"I thought he was still recovering from his rib puncture," Cojax replied.

"Guess not."

Cojax tapped his ArmGuard, fingers gliding across the interface until he isolated Cineas' unit—front line command of a leading Quorum.

Then came the SataniKahns—mostly White Maws but a few Primes sprinkled in as well. Massive. Grotesque. Crowned with spiraled mandibles and bleached, lethal appendages. They moved with the grace of nightmares, their bodies a fusion of bladed chitin and thunderous limbs. Each step tore the ground. Their mouths were serrated maws; their limbs, living weapons.

The first SataniKahn hit the Acadian line—and the screen exploded with light.

"Have no fear," Brutus smirked. "Onar's on the field. He'll keep your boy Cineas from becoming bug paste."

Onar the Slayer—massive, scarred, legendary. The crowd roared when he appeared, his Arc Blade spinning through Roach limbs like a harvesting scythe. He should have been a Gamma by now—or at the very least a Kappa—but he seemed to prefer the front line over taking a command.

Now that the two sides had engaged, the real point-gathering began. Warriors were scored on every detail—technique, kills, efficiency. Bonus titles were awarded: Sharpest Shot, Longest Lunge Kill, Most Decapitations, Best-Synchronized Formation. The crowd cheered each flash of a new ranking.

"Cineas isn't even on the board yet," Brutus taunted. "Meanwhile, my man Onar is Top Three. Again."

Cojax ignored him. His eyes tracked Cineas' unit. Roaches had encircled them, but hadn't yet closed in. Cineas broke protocol—ordered a forward surge instead of waiting.

"Now he's on the board," Cojax muttered. More ArmGuard screens activated around him as others keyed into the same action.

"Took him long enough," Brutus snorted. "I was starting to think he was using a rubber sword."

But Cojax admired Cineas. Not just because he was good—but because he thought differently. While most Acadians stuck to protocol, Cineas tweaked it—subtle shifts, like having only the outer shieldwall use Arc Blades, while the inner ring fired Blazers. It wasn't revolutionary, but it was different. Smart.

Cojax didn't want to follow instructions. He wanted to outthink the battlefield.

Soon, the conflict turned.

The Roaches broke. ArcSpeeders were deployed—sleek, torpedo-shaped vehicles with forward blades, ideal for slicing retreating targets. Too fragile for the initial charge, but devastating in the cleanup.

The CityScreen replayed the top kills, each dramatic strike highlighted in a split-panel montage. Points tallied. Battle titles assigned. The engagement was dubbed the Battle at the Eastern Nook at Midday—a name chosen not for glory, but because no Acadian had fallen. Had one died, the battle would've likely borne their name instead.

Cineas didn't place Top Ten—but he earned the Best Kill award, pinning two Roaches under his shield and torching them at point-blank range.

"Not bad," Cojax murmured.

"Not Top Ten," Brutus countered, giving him a playful

punch. "Onar ranked second."

Cojax rubbed his arm but didn't answer.

The screen began to fade, returning to standby. But just before it blinked out, Cojax caught something—just a flicker. A group entering the field. Not armored. Not Roaches. Not Acadian.

They looked... wrong.

Tattered. Filthy. Their clothes were more grime than fabric.

"Did you see that?" he said suddenly.

"See what?" Finn asked.

Cojax opened his mouth, replayed the image in his mind—and closed it again.

"Never mind."

Finn eyed him. "What?"

"Forget it." Cojax shook his head.

Finn shrugged, then grinned. "Alright. Let's move before this mob turns into a stampede. Best games are filling fast."

But Cojax didn't follow right away.

He glanced once more at the CityScreen, now dark.

And for the first time all morning, he felt cold.

ELEVEN

Cojax found himself smiling as his friends selected the Vortex as their first game. He was, by far, the best at it. Though Finn's lighter frame made him a fierce competitor, Cojax usually dominated. The Vortex was popular and always drew a crowd, but today it seemed especially packed. They were in the Forum of Innocents—the place of the Games—frequented almost exclusively by those who had yet to enter the Mahghetto.

Brutus clapped Cojax on the back. "Looks like your fan club showed up early."

"What's going on?" Hadrian asked, scanning the crowd. "Looks busier than usual."

"Let's find out," Finn said, leading the way to the Vortex observation windows.

The Vortex was a massive, cylindrical chamber that spun relentlessly, forcing players to run along the outer curve just to stay upright. Without the spinning and the barriers, it would take only seconds to cross. But the real challenge lay in the endless, randomized obstacles—barriers to scale, bars to duck, gaps to vault, panels to dodge. They were foam-padded and non-lethal—but the game didn't stop for anyone. Cojax had known two kids who died in there. It hadn't been the obstacles themselves that had killed them, but the relentless, unyielding pace of the machine that tossed them like broken toys.

Cojax stepped up to the glass.

At first, the chamber looked empty. Then she appeared.

A girl.

Small. Red hair. Moving fast. Her face was slick with sweat, her hair tied back but unbraided—a rarity. She wasn't just moving. She was navigating. Every movement was a decision, each obstacle approached like a puzzle. She didn't follow the obvious path, didn't repeat anything. It was unpredictable—and mesmerizing.

"It's the Aberration," Hadrian hissed. "What's she doing here? Has she even earned her Right of Movement? Can she even participate in the Games?"

"She's here," Cojax said. "So she has the right."

"Look at that," Finn pointed. "She just jumped the separating wall into the next lane."

"That's reckless," Cojax muttered. "She doesn't know what's on the other side."

But she kept going. And the more Cojax watched, the more enthralled he became. No one had ever thought to bypass the barriers that way. It was dangerous. Creative. Unique. And as much as he hated to admit it, he felt something else, too.

Not hate.

Maybe jealousy.

"Check her times," Finn said, pointing to the scoring display.

The name "Jessica" appeared next to her scores: 3:06. 3:03. 3:04.

"Jessica," Cojax whispered.

"No," Finn grinned. "I'm Finn."

"No, *her* name's Jessica," Cojax repeated. "No one ever told me her name before."

"Weird name," Brutus muttered.

"She's close to your times," Finn said. "Really close."

"I did 3:02."

"Once," Finn replied. "And she's running consistently."

"Whose side are you on?" Cojax snapped.

Brutus elbowed his way to the glass. "She's the Aberration. She can't be impressive."

"She's cheating," Hadrian said. "You can't jump lanes. That's not how the game works."

"They're still scoring her," Finn said. "She's just figured something out. Honestly? I think she can beat you, Cojax."

"What kind of shell-cracked idea is that?" Cojax growled. "I'm faster. Period."

Finn leaned closer. "She gains time by switching lanes, but she doesn't use it. She slows down afterward. It's like... she's practicing. Not racing."

Brutus chuckled. "Cojax, are you getting beat by the

Aberration?"

"She's kinda cute," Finn added.

Cojax's face burned. "Get Rifted. All of you."

"I think she can beat you," Hadrian said. "Unless she's cheating."

"She's not cheating," Finn said. "And sorry, Cojax, but I'm not so sure you can beat her."

Silence.

Finally, Finn added, "Doesn't mean you're a bad person."

Cojax turned away, fists clenched.

"Where are you going?" Hadrian asked.

Cojax didn't answer. He walked to the end of the Vortex just as Jessica exited. Her face was red, but her breathing steady.

He nodded to her. "Good work. You're really pushing yourself in there."

She didn't answer. She stared past him, toward something unseen. The others arrived. Finn smiled. Brutus scowled. Hadrian looked disapproving.

Jessica gave a polite nod and stepped forward, but Cojax blocked her path.

"You're running pretty fast," he said. "You came close to my top score."

"Close," she admitted. "But not quite."

"Some say you could beat me," Cojax said, his tone teasing.

"Maybe," she said.

"I doubt it."

"You're right."

"Let's find out," he challenged.

"She just ran it a dozen times," Finn said. "Where's the sport in that?"

"She can rest while I warm up," Cojax replied.

"I'm finished for the day," Jessica said. "I've used it enough."

Cojax stepped closer. "What's wrong with a little friendly competition?"

"I admit defeat," Jessica said. "You've won. No competition."

"She's tired," Finn said.

"She's the Aberration. Of course she's tired," Hadrian muttered.

Jessica's jaw tightened. "Maybe I can run it one more time."

Cojax grinned. "Great, let's make it happen."

Five minutes later, Cojax was in his running gear. Jessica was already waiting at the start. She didn't look at him.

He misread it as fear—until he saw the stillness in her eyes. She wasn't nervous. She was focused. Even the jeers from the crowd didn't touch her.

"Blind me, girl," Cojax said. "It's just a game."

Jessica ignored him.

"Get in there," Finn called. "Two laps, then the race."

Cojax grinned and charged into the Vortex. The moment his foot hit the floor, the timer began. He ran his first lap in 3:03.

Finn met him at the exit. "Pace yourself."

"I'm not even winded. Where's the girl?"

"Still at the entrance," Finn said.

Brutus sneered. "Guess she doesn't see you as a threat."

Cojax laughed. "She's wound up tighter than Hadrian."

"Hey," Hadrian said, "I'm right here."

Cojax winked. "You two have something in common."

"I hope she beats you," Hadrian muttered.

"There might not be enough room in the Vortex for Cojax, Jessica, and Cojax's ego," Brutus added.

"If you think it's big now," Cojax said, "wait 'til I set a new record."

He ran his second lap in 3:02.

The crowd doubled. Jessica still hadn't moved.

"You sure you're up for this?" Cojax asked.

Jessica's face was stone. "I'm ready."

They entered together. Dual timers appeared on the screens: Jessica and Cojax. First obstacle: circular holes in a wall. Cojax went high. Jessica went low.

"Did you attend school?" Cojax asked.

"Didn't suit me," she replied. "I'm the Aberration."

Second obstacle: swinging panels.

"You can attend no matter your Tier," Cojax said.

Third obstacle, and then fourth.

"Guardian," Jessica corrected. "I have a guardian."

"Why not attend?"

Jessica exhaled. "You're seriously asking questions right now?"

Cojax shrugged.

Jessica shook her head and accelerated.

She reached a wall with slits, kicked off the side, ran vertically, and vaulted the separating wall.

"Blood and bile," Cojax whispered. It was one thing to see her vault over the wall from the observation glass; it was a different thing entirely to see it right in front of him. He sprinted. Obstacles blurred. He vaulted, ducked, dove—then remembered: the Vortex matched his speed. Jessica was now running at *his* pace.

He had to cross lanes.

He tried to climb. His foot slipped. His chest slammed into the wall. Air fled his lungs. He scrambled, wild-legged, and hauled himself over. His landing was brutal. Groaning, he stood. The Vortex slowed to Jessica's pace. He sprinted. Closed the gap.

She saw him. Her eyes flicked back, calm and unreadable.

She vaulted another wall.

*"Blood and bile!"* He followed. Too hard. He slammed the far wall. Dizzy. Bleeding. He pushed forward.

They exited side by side.

His friends were waiting. Brutus burst into laughter.

Jessica passed him. "Good run," she said softly.

"We tied," Cojax said.

"You were half a second faster."

"We do it again."

"You set a new record."

"Again."

No answer.

His anger flared. He stepped closer. "Think you're special, Aberration? Think you're above my Tier? That you can ignore a challenge?"

Jessica met his gaze. Calm. Intense. "No, I'm tired. Thank you for the race." She bowed low, as if saluting a Numberless, and vanished into the crowd.

Cojax stood frozen, mouth half open.

Finn clapped him on the back. "Let her go. You got the record. And hey, Brutus and Hadrian finally agree on something—

even if it's laughing at your expense."

Cojax didn't laugh. He was still staring in the direction she had gone.

# TWELVE

"And did you stutter while talking to him?" Elena asked, breath ragged. Her armor had just flickered out, its charge depleted, granting them a rare moment without surveillance in their Praetorium Residence.

"None," Jessica replied. "But I feel awful. I walked off like I didn't even hear him."

As instructed, she had recounted everything—every word, glance, hesitation. Elena didn't take her at her word. She never did. The Medicus had already pulled the memory chip from the collar of Jessica's shirt and was scrubbing through the footage. Most Innocents weren't tracked like this, but Elena insisted. Jessica had learned long ago: lying delayed embarrassment but never avoided it.

"I need a drink. Bring me some stock."

Jessica nodded. She padded into the front room, opened a concealed panel on the wall, and retrieved a flask of pale blue liquid. When she returned, Elena popped the cork and took a long pull without a word. Jessica didn't know what was in the bottle—didn't want to. It reminded her of the men back in her village who drank moonshine that dulled their senses and twisted their tempers. All she knew was this: Elena only drank it when her armor was dead and her secrets could be kept. Whatever was in it, made her relaxed, warmer. Human.

"You handled yourself well," Elena said, wiping her mouth. "Don't let guilt twist that."

"I was rude."

"You were Acadian."

"But I don't treat people like that."

"Some will hate you. Others will plot to ruin you. You'll never win them all—not in this city."

"They'll all hate me."

"Yes."

Jessica blinked. "That's bad, Elena. If they hate me, they'll try to get me Rifted."

"Let them hate you—as long as they fear you."

"They won't fear me."

"Then make them."

Jessica shook her head. "You've seen the data. I might be better now, but who knows how long that will last when all of us are training together."

"In some ways, you will never be able to compete. In others, you will far surpass them."

Elena gestured to the monitor replaying Jessica's Vortex match. "Do you know who that boy is?"

"No."

"Then tell me what you saw."

"He's about my age."

Elena narrowed her eyes. "No. See more. You're not some drone. You've been trained to read past the surface. What else?"

Jessica folded her arms, thinking. "He's good. Talented in the Vortex. I probably could've beaten him."

"But?"

"He's not from the sub-levels. I could tell. His suit was perfect. Pressed like a Disciple in the Mahghetto. His friends looked more like real people. One even had wrinkles down his back—like he stored his uniform on the floor."

"Who else keeps their suit perfect and isn't a Disciple?"

"Besides me? No one."

"Exactly. What does that tell you?"

"He has a parent high up. Probably one who demands perfection."

Elena smiled. "Now you're getting it."

Jessica's voice dropped. "He knew me. It was personal. Like he'd seen me before and didn't like what he saw."

Elena nodded. "His name is Cojax. He's the son of Titan, Slayer of the Nartic, a Numberless on the Infinite Council. When you first arrived, Titan was the one who cuffed you and brought you to the Trinity. He spared you from Atlas, who would've cracked your skull open on sight."

"I remember," Jessica whispered.

"Titan didn't want you here either. He just follows rules more than Atlas. But something else is going on. I haven't figured it out yet."

"What are they hiding?"

Elena took another swig. "That's what I aim to expose. If you succeed, you'll fracture the illusion of perfection. And once that crack forms, others will follow. We can change the city."

Jessica fell silent, her mind drifting to Cojax. The brief exchange had been the longest she'd had with someone her age since arriving.

"Cojax will be in the Mahghetto with you," Elena said. "He isn't his father—not yet. But he'll be expected to live up to Titan's reputation. And you, Jessica, are the opposite of everything Acadia celebrates."

"So he'll try to kill me?"

"Probably not outright. But he'll do what the city wants— prove you're worthless, then let Acadia take care of the rest."

"I only did what you taught me. I didn't back down, but I wasn't reckless—"

"—You let yourself get baited."

"I let him win. Or at least made it look close."

"Now he's got a grudge. And we haven't even started."

Jessica lowered her head. "Blood and bile, of all the kids I had to race, I happened to run into one that would be in the Mahghetto with me. I'm sorry."

"Never apologize to me. Learn from it. That's enough."

Elena paused. Her expression softened. "Now tell me the truth. Did it feel good knowing how easily you could have beaten him?"

Jessica smiled. "Like nothing I've ever felt."

Elena laughed—a real, full-bodied laugh. The kind she only let out when her armor was offline. "Don't get too much of a sheen. You beat him because you've trained nonstop for four years. In the Mahghetto, you'll have the early advantage. But they'll catch up fast. Some will surpass you."

"I'm ready."

"Yes, you are. But remember this: Cojax cannot be trusted. No one in the Mahghetto can. They're your competition, not your allies. I've studied them all—Brutus, Finn, Cojax. They aren't evil. But inside that pit, they'll become monsters."

"What happens to someone who gets Rifted in the Mahghetto?"

Elena shrugged. "No idea. Maybe they're dumped in the Killing Field. Maybe chopped up for food. Don't think about it. Especially not the latter. That'd just ruin your appetite."

Jessica gave a faint smile.

"The first test is coming," Elena continued. "They call it the Descension. I call it Rebirth into Hell."

"How bad is it?"

"Bad. But I've prepped for this."

She reached behind her back and pulled out a small red injector.

"What's that?"

"Custom blend. Adrenaline. Painkillers. Nanobots to seal off major cuts. You won't need it unless things go wrong—but if they do, jab it in your arm. You'll survive whatever comes."

"Where did you get it?"

"I engineered it. I'm a Medicus, remember."

Jessica nodded.

Elena continued, more serious now. "I'll stitch a pocket into your uniform where it won't be noticed. Use it with caution. If they catch you, it's over. Also, I'll include a Vision Balancer as well. They can't see you wearing it, so hit the red button on the side three times and it will destroy itself."

"Once I'm in the Mahghetto, will there be cameras?"

"Just in the armor. There's a supply room near your dorm where you can go to get away from everyone if needed."

"And the first challenge?"

"There are cameras in the tunnels, but I'll cover that. It won't be easy, but I know a TechOps whiz who supports our cause."

Elena looked at her, eyes glassy but warm. "You're kind, Jessica. Too kind for this place. But you'll need to bury that part of you. Compassion in the Mahghetto is suicide. Wear a mask. Hide the girl beneath it. Just don't lose her."

Jessica hesitated. "Can I tell you something?"

"While the armor's off? Anything."

"I'm scared."

Elena wrapped her in an embrace. "Good. Not even I could tell. That means you can hide it. That means you're ready. This is the beginning of rebellion, and you, Jessica, are at the heart of it. Together, we will shake off the invisible shackles of our slavery. Know this—Acadia won't see *you*. Only your Score. It will decide everything: what you eat, where you sleep, how long you live. Earn your Score—and they can't deny you the Crossing."

## THIRTEEN

"Report, Innocent," Titan said flatly.

Cojax saluted, heels clicking with crisp precision, then bowed low, the practiced motion instinctive. He had only just arrived home to find his father seated in the center of the room, posture rigid. The glow of a black tablet lit up his chiseled face, eyes locked in scrutiny.

It was rare—jarring, even—to see Titan outside his armor, lounging in the living room as if he were any other man. Cojax hesitated, unsettled by the image. His report, which had seemed so urgent only moments before, now drifted from his thoughts like vapor.

Titan's eyes flicked up. A single glance, hard as forged steel, pulled Cojax back into form.

He launched into his report, detailing the day's activities with mechanical precision. He spoke of his training, his performance in the Vortex, and a brief mention of racing another Innocent. But he said nothing of who she was.

Titan let the silence hang for a moment after he finished. Then, his voice dropped to a low rasp. "You've given me plenty of details I don't care about. Now tell me the ones you left out."

Cojax swallowed. He knew what his father was asking. Titan didn't need to ask—he already knew.

"The girl I raced was the Aberration," Cojax admitted.

"Did you speak to her?"

"A little."

Titan's mouth tightened, his expression hardening. "Spare me your excuses, Innocent."

He set the tablet aside with deliberate calm, then stood. Each step he took toward Cojax was silent but heavy, his towering form casting a long shadow across the floor.

"I already knew who she was. I know more about that girl's situation than you could comprehend. And still, you withheld information. I tell you this because I want you to survive, Cojax. I want you to *rise*. But you need to believe me when I say: she is destruction. She represents the end."

Titan's voice was grave, each word deliberate.

"She's been spared by the Acadian Code. But nature corrects what the Code cannot. She will not survive the Mahghetto."

"Yes, sir," Cojax replied, his voice small.

"Do you remember when she arrived?"

Cojax blinked. The question was simple, but something in Titan's tone made it feel…unordinary. There was something contemplative behind the question.

"I was young," Cojax said slowly, "but I remember. It was my first time at the Wall." It was also his last time—he had never been back since.

"You were the one who spotted her—or so I was told. She looked like she'd collapse at any moment. I thought death would claim her before we could. But she lived. Like some stubborn weed growing in stone. I spared her. I stand by that decision. The Infinite Council did too. But sometimes, I wonder if letting Atlas finish it would've been more merciful."

Titan paused, jaw clenched. "She has no idea what's coming. And when she fails—and she will—she'll poison everything and everyone near her. I don't want you speaking to her again. That's not advice. It's an order."

Cojax hesitated. "Sir… may I ask a direct question?"

"You may," Titan said, voice low. "But remember your place." "At ease," he added, nodding.

Cojax shifted to parade rest, the motion fluid.

"Why is she so dangerous?" he asked. "She seems…small. And why call her the Aberration?"

Titan's gaze narrowed. "You studied the wars, the politics. But did they teach you about viruses?"

"Like… illnesses?"

"Yes. Primitive threats, mostly gone now. But once, viruses nearly ended humanity. They begin unnoticed—microscopic. One becomes two, two become four. And before long, the whole body collapses."

He took a step forward. "She is a virus. A deviation. And like all viruses… she spreads. Slowly. Quietly. Until it's too late. The body becomes sick and is destroyed from the inside."

"I…I don't fully understand."

Titan looked down, brows furrowed. His mouth opened slightly, as if about to say something. Then he paused, reconsidering. When he finally spoke, his voice was softer. "Just keep your distance from her, Cojax. That's all you need to understand."

# FOURTEEN

Cojax smiled. He was glad to have his friends close at hand, despite Brutus making them late. They had only just arrived when the Validated in front had started to talk, and Cojax could not help but feel a tinge of anger toward Brutus. The large boy attempted to defuse the tension by appealing to Cojax's humor. He began to show pictures of Hadrian sleeping. The pictures in themselves were not funny, but he had doctored each one with compromising elements. Cojax ignored them at first, intent on paying attention, but then one picture forced a laugh out of him.

He shoved it down and turned to Brutus. "What do you think would've happened if we didn't show up on time today?"

"Probably given us the day off," Brutus answered.

Finn shook his head, "I was hoping that they'd reset Brutus' ArmGuard so it runs half an hour earlier."

"Actually," Cojax said, "that's still a good idea. Why didn't we think of that before?"

"I'm just efficient with my time," Brutus answered. "What's the point of arriving early if we just have to wait around when we get there? Do you guys know how much more productive your time is when you're with me? Think of all the times you would've shown up early just to wait around until things got started."

"No," Finn answered, "it's not more productive because instead of waiting for things to begin, we're waiting for you to get ready. So you see, we're still waiting."

"And that's how it should be," Brutus answered.

Cojax shook his head. "You shiny little Dependent."

Hadrian pushed into them. "Hold your tongues. He's giving us instructions."

Cojax nodded and straightened. He forced his mind to settle, his breath to level. *"I need to focus. I need to rise."* But beneath his stoic exterior, a storm swirled. His father hadn't said a word before he left.

Neither had his brother. No farewell. No good luck.

"Did your parents say anything when you left?" he whispered to Finn.

Finn's expression tightened. "No. Mother stayed in her room. Father barely looked at us."

Brutus leaned in. "No hugs from the big guy today, eh?"

Cojax exhaled through his nose. "I dare you to call Titan 'big guy' to his face."

Brutus shrugged. "Alright. Next time I see him."

"There's no way," Finn muttered. "You'd be Rifted mid-sentence."

"Please," Cojax said. "You're only saying that because you know we won't see him for nine months."

Hadrian turned on them. "You're all insufferable. We're Disciples of the Mahghetto now."

Cojax gave a sheepish nod. "Sorry."

"Not sorry," Brutus added. "And technically, we're not Disciples until the first trial starts."

The banter died off. Silence closed in again. Cojax stood still, fists clenched so tightly the blood drained from his knuckles. His throat was dry, but his mouth flooded with saliva. His body buzzed with energy he couldn't control. He bounced on his toes and stretched his neck, trying to push the anxiety down.

He gave up on listening to the speech—it was rhetoric, not instruction. Instead, his eyes scanned the crowd, landing on her.

Jessica.

The Aberration.

He hadn't noticed her earlier. She was easy to miss—small, slight, dwarfed by the others. And yet, somehow... radiant. The name alone should have buried any sympathy, but seeing her now, standing with quiet resolve, stirred something in him. "*She'll be Rifted,*" he thought. "*She's too small. Too soft. Too... breakable.*" And yet, he couldn't look away.

They were near the South Wall now—a part of the city they'd never seen up close. The buildings were familiar in design: marbled, angular, flawless. But the air felt heavier, like gravity had thickened.

The speaker stood on a concrete platform, barely visible beyond the crowd. Behind him gaped a massive, rectangular cave.

Man-made. Precise. Its symmetry was unnatural—its darkness even more so. It wasn't the absence of light. It was something worse. Like night had congealed inside.

"You think we're going in there?" Cojax whispered.

"Looks like a Roach tunnel," Finn muttered.

"There's no Roach tunnels in the city," Brutus mocked.

Hadrian nodded. "They call them the Mouths of Hell. Usually sealed. See the blast doors?"

Cojax followed his gaze. Massive steel slabs—ancient and mechanical. Above them was something even more interesting.

A statue. Not white marble, but black.

Obsidian.

Twice the height of any man. Broad-shouldered, horned helmet, axe in hand. In its left grip—a bloody head, severed at the neck. Carved veins dripped liquid that vanished into the ground. The face wore a smile that seemed to *know* something. Something no one wanted to hear.

"Who's that?" Finn asked.

"Pluto," Hadrian answered. "An ancient Roman god of the underworld."

"Shh," Brutus said. "I'm trying to listen."

Finn and Cojax choked on silent laughter.

"Fare thee well, friends," the speaker intoned, his voice rising. "You enter the underworld—not as warriors, but as Disciples of the Mahghetto, to be forged by the Bloodborne Magisters in the ways of war. I send you now into Hell."

Suddenly—drums. Thunderous, deep, and all around them.

The crowd compressed instinctively, drawing close. From the alleys, from rooftops, from behind corners—Validated emerged in full bronze-colored battle armor. Their movements were calm, but their presence was suffocating. Shields gleamed with the BloodBorne symbol. Helms masked their faces. They closed in slowly, encircling the Disciples like predators around prey.

Cojax's lungs clenched. He hadn't even seen them arrive.

"What do we do?" he asked.

"I don't think anyone knows," Finn answered.

Confusion swept through the crowd like static. Some whispered. Some just stood, stiff and uncertain.

"They're testing us," Hadrian said. "Seeing who panics. Who breaks."

"Well," Finn muttered, "I think we're already failing. Maybe we head for the tunnel?"

"That's not a tunnel," Brutus said. "It's a trap. There's no light. That's a tomb. We go in there, we don't come out."

"You sound like a Dependent," Finn teased. "It's just ceremony."

Cojax looked again—and froze.

Jessica was moving.

Calm. Deliberate. She slipped past the others and toward the cave. No hesitation. No glance back. Her eyes fixed ahead like she'd already lived this moment before.

"What is she doing?" Cojax whispered. "She knows something…"

"Well, no one in the front is moving until they receive orders," Finn said. "So, I guess we stand here like fools until someone tells us to do something."

"We stand our ground," Hadrian said. "Rule one of the Mahghetto: never retreat. Especially not down a tunnel that looks like the home of Roaches."

"There's no Roaches in the city," Brutus repeated, his voice a mocking tone.

The Validated stopped. Twenty yards away. The drums ceased. Silence descended, heavy as a hammer strike.

Then one of the warriors broke from formation.

He approached.

Shield in hand. Blade at his side.

He stopped before Hadrian—who trembled slightly, but masked it by clasping his hands behind his back. Then, with effort, he mounted all his courage and saluted, bowing low.

It was stiff. Awkward. But the gesture held.

Other Disciples followed suit—ripples of salutes spreading outward.

The Validated drew his Arc Blade. The weapon hummed with raw, white energy.

Then, without warning—

The blade split Hadrian in two.

# FIFTHTEEN

Time fractured as Hadrian's body collapsed, folding to the ground like discarded meat. Blood sprayed across the concrete, misting the Validated's armor in a fine red fog. The Arc Blade pulsed once more—white-hot light slicing the air—leaving behind the stench of scorched flesh and silence.

"Go!" Cojax roared, yanking his friends by the arms.

Finn ran. Brutus didn't move—eyes locked on the twitching halves of Hadrian's corpse, mouth agape. Cojax shoved him hard.

"Move!"

The drums thundered again, faster, urgent—battle drums meant to chase prey into the pit. The Validated surged forward, Arc Blades igniting in synchronized hums, shields locking into an impenetrable wall. The crowd broke like dry timber under pressure. Panic surged. Screams erupted. They trampled each other toward the tunnel mouth—a writhing, frantic tide of bodies desperate to escape. Blades flashed. Limbs fell. Blood spilled in ribbons.

A Disciple in front of Cojax collapsed. For a breath, Cojax considered helping him—then saw a sword catch the fallen boy across the back, the blade erupting from his chest.

"Faster!"

"There's people in the way!" Brutus yelled.

"If you don't move, my blood's next!" Cojax growled.

With brute resolve, Brutus bulldozed into the crowd, shoving bodies aside with his sheer size. A Disciple hit the pavement hard— cracked skull, limp arms—cut down seconds later.

Cojax caught movement from the corner of his eye—too fast. He ducked. An Arc Blade hissed overhead, its heat grazing his scalp. Another strike came—lower, stabbing for his thigh.

Steel bit flesh.

Pain exploded through Cojax's leg. He gasped, staggered. The blade rose again—aimed at his neck.

But Cojax lunged forward—into the grasp of Finn and Brutus. They dragged him, half-limping, across the threshold into the tunnel. Behind them, the Validated stopped. Blades still drawn, formation rigid. Then—one by one—they began to vanish.

No... not the warriors. They weren't vanishing; the tunnel entrance was closing. The steel doors groaned as they slid shut, severing the last rays of light. Darkness collapsed—whole and suffocating.

Black. Absolute.

Cojax waved a trembling hand in front of his face.

Nothing.

He leaned on Brutus. Finn took his other arm. They pressed forward, blindly, until they stumbled over a body.

"Watch it!" hissed a voice in the dark.

Others were here. Dozens. Maybe hundreds. Whispers and weeping swirled in the pitch. Most had collapsed, scattered along the walls, too stunned to move.

Brutus pulled Cojax to the side. "Sit. They're not chasing us."

"Where's the wound?" Finn asked.

"My leg. Bad gash. Still bleeding."

"Should be cauterized if it's from an Arc Blade."

"It's not."

Finn tore cloth in the dark. "Here—press this on it."

Cojax grimaced, gritting his teeth. "We can't stop here. We have to move."

"There's nowhere to go," Brutus said. "We're sealed in."

"No," Cojax murmured. "There's always a way forward."

He wrapped the cloth tight. As silence fell again, he heard it—an ominous sound in the distance.

Click. Click-click. Like scissors snapping shut—quick and dry.

"You hear that?" he whispered.

The tunnel hushed. No one answered.

Cojax struggled upright. "Help me. The Mahghetto's begun."

"You're not fit to walk," Finn warned.

"I am—I have to be. And we have to find the Aberration. She knew this would happen."

They moved, shuffling past huddled bodies, past the moaning and broken Innocents. Finn kept a hand on the wall, guiding them through the curved tunnel.

It smelled of mold and earth. Damp, suffocating.

"There's a break in the wall," Finn said. "Slime everywhere."

"Should we try heading that direction?" Cojax asked.

"No chance," Brutus muttered. "I'm not crawling into a slime hole."

They kept moving. More openings. More silence.

"We're descending," Finn said.

Cojax wasn't sure. His mind swam from blood loss. His steps blurred. Was he going down—or simply losing himself? Time lost all meaning. It felt like hours had passed. Or maybe just minutes. Pain had made time meaningless.

"Rest," Finn said.

"No. Keep—"

Suddenly, Brutus cried out and fell. Cojax hit the floor, clawing toward him.

"What is it?" he asked.

"I tripped over something," Brutus grunted. "It's huge."

Cojax's fingers found it—a carapace. Spiked, shelled. Cold. Then the head—two pincers, curled and rigid.

"A Roach—but this one's dead," he whispered.

"In the city?" Brutus gasped. "That's impossible."

"It's a Reever, Class II," Cojax said. "But its back should be poisonous."

"How do you know it's not?"

"Because I'm still alive."

Before Finn could respond—clicking. Loud now. Close. And screams.

"This is a den," Cojax said. "A Reever nest. Those gates weren't to keep us out—they were to keep them in."

"Run," Finn barked.

The noise surged behind them—chittering, like metal scraping bone. Disciples screamed. The stampede returned, bodies slamming into them. The three of them pushed on, Finn using the wall to guide them forward, but at their pace, they could not stay ahead of the crowd.

"BLOOD AND BILE!" Cojax yelled as they were knocked aside by someone or something. The mob pushed past, leaving them in the dirt and choking dust.

His bandage slipped. Blood ran freely again.

"I've got it," Finn replied. "Where's the cloth?"

"My shin—ah!"

"Sorry!" Finn yanked it tight.

"We're out of time!" Brutus cried. "Reevers are coming out of the walls. Finn, we can't help him."

"We can do this together," Finn said. "Lift him up."

Cojax grunted against the pain as he was pulled to his feet, a wave of nausea and battle shock passing over him. Blood soaked his pants, heightening his sense of danger.

"We tried," Brutus muttered, then let go of Cojax's arm. For a moment, he paused—something flickered in his eyes. Regret? Shame? Resolve? "I'm not getting torn to pieces in here."

He turned and ran, not even bothering to find out if the others had heard. Brutus didn't even waste a second looking back.

"Blazing Rifter!" Finn cursed.

"Go," Cojax said, his jaw clenched against the fire in his leg. He sat back down, allowing his body to rest. "Get out of here. I just need to sit for a bit, adjust to the pain. I'll be right behind you."

"No."

"Go!"

"I'm not leaving—"

"I need to rest a minute."

A pause.

"Okay…okay," Finn whispered more to himself than his friend. "I'll find help and come back. But you better keep moving when you can, you blazed fool."

Then he was gone.

Cojax lay in silence, pain pulsing through him like a second heartbeat. He forced the bandage tight, groaning from pain. He lay down for a few minutes, resting in the dark, waiting for the nausea to fade. Then by sheer force of will he stood. Trembled. Staggered. Moved.

He heard it then.

Something ahead.

Not behind.

He veered, tried to dodge—but it struck his chest, knocked

him down.

He punched wildly—striking nothing but air.

"Stop," a voice said. Calm. Female.

Cojax froze. Something bit his leg. He cried out.

"You'll feel it soon," she said.

And he did. Power. Clarity. Strength.

"How did you—?"

"Let me fix your bandage."

Her hands were deft, invisible in the black. He reached for her face—she slapped his hands away.

*"She can see."*

"Up. Now. Or stay here and feed the Reevers."

Cojax felt much better—clarity and strength returning, pain completely fading. "I'm with you. Lead the way."

They ran. She knew the path. Her steps never faltered. He followed, half-limping, half-flying. The Roaches stayed close to the walls. He could hear them—clicking, feasting on innocent flesh.

He didn't look. He didn't want to.

And then she let go—vanished into the dark.

"Wait!" he called, his voice breaking.

Silence answered him.

A pinprick of light appeared ahead, faint at first—then it grew, sharpening into a beam that drew steadily closer. Cojax ran toward it. Bodies of Innocents appeared—torn. Dismembered, partially eaten. Roaches closed in. He ducked under the mandibles of one. Vaulted another. Rolled beneath a third. Then—an unbroken wall of them.

He stopped, breath ragged.

*"Think. Vortex. Move like in the Vortex."* He sprinted—up the wall—angled left—leapt—

Mandibles grazed his feet.

Then—he was through and back into the light. He hit the floor, rolled, and rose, breathing hard. Still alive.

## SIXTEEN

Jessica drifted from the knot of Disciples clustered around the massive, circular steel door. Her expression remained composed, almost cold—but her heartbeat thundered in her ears. She felt it in her temples, her teeth. Her breath was shallow, despite all her training.

*"What was that, Jessica? Did Elena teach you nothing? Why did you help him? He's your competition, not your ally."*

She clenched her jaw, pushing back against the voice in her mind. The argument sounded hollow. Weak. She shook her head.

*"Concentrate on the moment. What's done is done. Focus. Breathe. Concentrate."*

She shifted her focus outward. The room they stood in was a vast, circular dome—the ceiling swallowed by shadow, too high for the dim light to reach. The concrete underfoot gleamed in places, sterile and unwelcoming. It felt like a parade ground built inside a bunker: clean, massive, and indifferent to life.

Jessica glanced back at the jagged hole they had crawled through. They had started with just over four hundred. Now, at least three dozen were gone—consumed by Roaches or slaughtered by the Acadians. Most of the survivors huddled in silence or clutched minor wounds, too distracted to notice the threat that emerged.

Black and bronze armor flickered into view like ghosts. The Validated had arrived.

At first, only a handful—silent, towering. Then more followed, some carrying weapons, others simply marching. They fanned out, slow and deliberate, approaching from one side of the chamber.

Jessica turned and bolted.

Behind her, others saw the incoming threat. Panic erupted. Limbs tangled. Bodies surged. What had been a dazed gathering exploded into chaos. Jessica darted between flailing arms and scrambled feet. A tall, wide-eyed youth barreled past her, legs pumping in desperation. She let him pass and fell in behind.

The tunnel they entered narrowed, then opened into another chamber—smaller, but still immense.

A dead end.

The group faltered. They clustered against the far wall like trapped animals. The heavy steps of the Validated echoed behind them.

Jessica ended up in the center of the crowd, jostled and shoved. From her vantage point, she spotted Cojax. He wasn't pressed against the wall like the others. He stood out—a few paces forward, tall and still. There was something in his posture, in his eyes. Not panic. Not even defiance. Acceptance, maybe. Or insanity.

Either the mixture she'd given him had made him fearless— or he had a death wish.

The Validated closed in, weapons swaying at their sides. The leader raised his blade in a sudden flash—steel glinting in the low light.

Cojax didn't move. He didn't even blink.

Gasps filled the room. One girl screamed. The Disciples recoiled in terror—but nothing happened.

Laughter.

Rough, cruel.

The lead warrior lowered his weapon and clapped a gauntleted hand on Cojax's shoulder.

"There might be a few of you worth training," he said.

He turned to his squad. "Strip them. Separate the men from the women. If any of them speaks, silence them. Permanently."

The order was carried out with brutal efficiency. Disciples were yanked from the walls, clothing torn from their bodies. Men to one side. Women to the other.

Bundles of black shirts and pants were tossed at them.

One girl fumbled too long. A Validated struck her hard across the back.

Jessica instinctively moved toward her to help—then stopped. Elena's voice echoed in her memory. *"Charity is not a virtue in Acadia."*

A door hissed open. The female Disciples were herded into a modern, sterile corridor bathed in harsh white light.

"Two lines!" bellowed a voice like iron.

The mob reshuffled instantly, scrambling to obey. Jessica had already positioned herself, anticipating the command—but a thick-fisted Disciple slammed into her back, knocking her to the floor.

She rose quickly—but not quick enough.

A Validated met her with a vicious backhand. Stars exploded in her vision. She stumbled again, arms flailing, but caught herself.

No one helped.

She pushed forward, aiming for a spot in line. No one made room.

"To the back!" a female Validated barked.

Jessica obeyed.

The woman stalked the lines, eyes like cold flame.

"This is the Mahghetto. For most of you, it will mean death—or worse."

Her gaze locked on Jessica.

"You will be tested in all capacities. You will break, then crawl, then break again. Your pursuit is perfection. For now, you have not earned the right to speak. Silence your tongue, or we will silence it for you. Your micro-tags embedded in your palms will keep track of your effort, and your worth. They will be used to figure out who among you will survive and who deserves the Rift. Now move!"

The lines marched.

And the nightmare truly began.

The two lines were split without ceremony—one sent left, the other right. Jessica's group was herded into a corridor, then funneled into a wide room filled with dozens of stark, seamless cubicles. No windows. No sound. Just sterile silence and a faint antiseptic sting in the air.

One by one, they were forced inside.

Jessica stepped into her assigned cell. The door sealed behind her with a hiss. For a moment, she stood still, swallowing the panic that had climbed into her throat. The space was barely large enough to turn around. White walls. No chair. No mirror. Just herself and a blank void.

Her breathing quickened.

Since escaping the Roach tunnel, she'd already made two critical errors—trying to help the fallen girl and allowing herself to be shoved from formation. *"No more mistakes. Focus. Breathe. Concentrate."*

Without warning, the walls illuminated, transforming the space into what looked like an endless white room. Then came the projections—three-dimensional patterns of intricate geometries spun slowly in the air before her. A synthetic voice followed, soft but commanding:

"Identify rotation sequence. Select correct visual orientation."

Six potential outcomes appeared around each shape. Jessica hesitated. Her breath hitched. A second of paralysis, maybe two. Then Elena's training kicked in. Her hand shot out, slicing through the correct shape.

More shapes followed. Faster. More complex.

In the beginning, she kept pace. Minor rotations. Simple alterations. But soon the shapes twisted in on themselves—multi-axis shifts, illusions of depth and distortion. Her mind narrowed into a tunnel of pure logic. The outside world fell away.

She didn't notice the approach.

A hand grabbed her shoulder. She was yanked backward and thrown across the ground like scrap.

She rolled. Hit her knees. Rose.

For a breathless moment, she feared she had failed. Then she realized: all the Disciples were being removed from their cubicles. Only Jessica had been pulled out. The others walked on their own.

No one explained. No one offered answers.

They were herded into formation and marched into another chamber—this one dim, metallic, and hostile. A massive obstacle course snaked around the perimeter. Weight stacks. Vertical climbs. Balance beams worn with use. Swinging cables and crawling shafts. The room looked like it had been built to break bones.

A horn sounded.

The Disciples charged.

In the beginning, they all moved with blind determination—every girl desperate to prove her worth, to bury her weakness. Bodies vaulted, dove, sprinted. Grunts of effort filled the air.

But time became an enemy.

As minutes turned to hours, cracks formed. Gasps replaced grunts. Limbs slowed. Some hesitated before a climb, others stumbled over hurdles. Two groups began to emerge—those who could still move and those who were falling behind.

Jessica held back. Deliberately. She could've led the pack, but she stayed one step behind the strongest competitors. It wasn't humility. It was calculation. Survival. The air thickened with the stench of blood and sweat. No water. No rest. No mercy.

When the first girl collapsed, the Validated didn't pause. They barked commands and hurled insults that stabbed like knives. Jessica didn't flinch. She welcomed the chaos—it kept her sharp.

Then the horn sounded again.

They were pulled from the room, drenched and shaking, and forced back into the white-lit cubicles.

More questions. Mathematics. Memorization. Cognitive sequencing. Some of the queries were familiar—Elena had drilled her for years. But others were alien, the kind of knowledge that only the elite would recognize. At some point, two timers appeared on her screen, both counting down at different intervals, neither aligned to the question set. It was meant to disorient her.

She ignored the timers.

Just keep going.

The cycle repeated. Trial by sweat. Trial by thought. Trial by silence.

Then came the marching.

They were assembled into formation. Taught basic unison movement. Left. Right. Turn. Step.

One girl in the lead made the mistake of asking a question.

She was cut down mid-sentence. Her body didn't twitch. Her blood pooled and soaked into the floor. Jessica recognized the girl; she was one of the first through the Roach tunnel. She had been strong. Powerful. A leader. But now she was dead.

No one spoke again.

Jessica didn't count how many times they were shuffled between rooms. Her body ached. Her mind frayed. In the cubicle, her answers slowed. Shapes blurred. Equations looked like glyphs. Her mind had turned thick and hazy, like trying to solve math through fogged glass.

But she pressed on. Blinked. Re-centered.

*"Focus. Breathe. Concentrate."*

Time dissolved. Hours. Days. Maybe more.

Then—nothing.

The Magisters vanished. The Disciples were left alone in the dark obstacle room. Some leaned against walls. Others wept. A few clustered together, whispering with cracked voices.

Jessica found no one. No arms opened for her. No voices called her name. She curled into a corner and closed her eyes.

The explosion hit like a thunderclap.

She snapped awake, heart punching her ribs. The lights stuttered on. Validated stormed into the room, black visors gleaming.

"ASSEMBLE!"

Chaos surged again. Girls scrambled to obey. Whips cracked. Screams followed. But eventually, formation took hold.

Then—marching. Hours of it. Circles. Turns. Correction. Punishment.

Then—silence. The Magisters left as suddenly as they'd arrived. This time, the room felt... emptier.

Jessica blinked, scanning the chamber. Two girls had been curled against the far wall before she slept. Now they were gone. She wasn't the only one who noticed.

A few Disciples clutched each other, their eyes darting to every corner. Whispers of names. No answers.

Jessica turned away from the fear. She welcomed the dark. Sleep swallowed her.

Another explosion.

Another scream.

"ASSEMBLE!"

Again they marched. Again the whips. Again the fire in her muscles and the stone in her lungs.

Jessica's eyes stung. She caught herself blinking longer than she should. Long, indulgent moments of darkness. Her body begged for collapse. Her legs burned with fire. Her spine screamed.

Still—she marched.

She remembered every nap she'd ever skipped. Every soft bed she'd once ignored. Now she was tempted to trade her future for a pillow and an hour.

She called on Elena's mantras again.

*"Focus. Breathe. Concentrate."*

It was the only thing holding her together.

Finally, the door opened again—and a new set of Validated entered. Familiar. The same ones as the day before. They moved into the center of the room, standing tall. One of them stepped forward, removed her helmet, and scanned the room with calm indifference.

"Yesterday was Day Zero," she said. "It was orientation. Today is your first true day in the Mahghetto."

She paused.

"For some of you—it will be your last."

## SEVENTEEN

Changing into his assigned black uniform was a battle in itself. The dried blood crusted on Cojax's leg fused to his skin like cement, making each tug at the fabric a silent scream. A Validated stepped forward, wordless, and extended an Adaptive SolarBracer—blackened metal reinforced with flexible synth ligature. Cojax had seen such braces before, usually on the warriors who returned half-broken from the Killing Fields. He had never worn one himself.

It was both insult and honor: a crutch meant for the weak, bestowed by those who deemed him just strong enough to be worth salvaging.

He strapped it on.

The brace chafed instantly, biting into the raw edges of his skin. But within an hour, the throbbing in his leg eased. By the time the Disciples were herded into a dust-choked exercise chamber and dropped into uneasy sleep, the pain was nearly gone. Still, the itching gnawed at him. Cojax relented and unlatched the brace. He expected the worst—pus, rot, fevered flesh.

What he found stunned him.

The wound looked weeks old. Scarred over. Healing.

Hope kindled in his chest like a spark in dry wood. Maybe he wouldn't be discarded. Not yet.

The hours—if they could still be called that—melted into a relentless cycle of agony. No sunlight marked time. No schedule softened the unknown. They were stripped of comfort, conversation, even the right to question. Food was tossed like slop to animals. Sleep came in scattered fragments, interrupted by screams, drills, or the sudden bark of a Magister.

After the first week of relentless exercise regimens, they transitioned into hand-to-hand fighting. Techniques were shown once—twice if they were feeling generous—and then drilled under threat of violence. If you failed to master the move, you became the dummy for the next.

Sometimes, they were ordered to beat each other until the floor ran red. But never to the death. That line, for some reason, remained sacred. Perhaps death was considered too merciful. Cojax dominated the fighting, his technique and speed unmatched. He had trained well for this moment without even realizing it. Titan had forced him to use the fighting simulator before all else—and this was paying dividends he never imagined he would collect.

Brutus and Cojax became predators in the Fighting Pit, forged into rivals by pain and steel. One had bulk, the other speed—opposite sides of the same coin, and neither could exist without the other. They were matched often, not just because of their skill, but because they made each other sharper, harder. Deadlier. But Cojax, just barely, was better.

They all broke at one time or another. Fingers snapped like dry twigs. Ribs cracked. Humerus, radius—names of bones they barely remembered, and others they never learned—shattered beneath fists and feet. Muscles tore, bruises bloomed in shades of black and yellow, and skin split like overripe fruit. It didn't take long for the Disciples to learn a bitter truth: a broken bone was a mercy. A fracture earned rest. A SolarBracer, strapped over the injury, accelerated healing so cruelly efficient it became its own punishment—no one was gone long enough to be forgotten. The churn never stopped. Injury didn't hurt your standing. Weakness did. Hesitation. Mercy. Those were sins.

Every day began with the Acadian creed, repeated until it branded the soul:

*"By deeds we rise. By entitlement we fall. Merit before all."*

Each time they awoke, they knew they'd earned another chance at life. Another breath. Another fight. It wasn't given. It was paid for—with shattered knuckles, dislocated joints, and the taste of blood that never quite left their teeth. The number of Disciples shrank, but no one mourned. Not anymore. Death wasn't as cruel as another day of life.

It was brutal.

Efficient.

Even.

When they were fed it was tossed into the center of the

room—sometimes cooked, sometimes raw. They all ate it eagerly, often fighting to guarantee a fair share, their voices used only to create feral growls, warding away the weak. Several times, a gelatinous slop of protein and oatmeal was poured onto the ground—the scraps from the plates of the Innocents above. It was gone within minutes, the Disciples polishing the floor with their tongues. Nothing could be wasted. They needed every calorie and gram of protein they were given.

Days passed. Weeks drifted by, uncelebrated and unwatched. Disciples disappeared like dust caught in a vent. Some broke in body. Others cracked in silence. Cojax watched them vanish one by one, his chest tightening with every absence. Brutus, once loud and confident, rarely looked him in the eye. The fire was gone. Hadrian's death had hollowed him out. Even Finn—who once found jokes in everything—had changed. His smile now came slow, strained, if at all.

And still, the fighting continued.

At night, when even the cold couldn't keep Cojax's eyes open, his mind returned to her.

The girl.

The Aberration.

She had helped him. *"Why?"*

He'd challenged her at the Vortex, even mocked her. And yet—she had intervened in the Mouth of Hell, risking her own life in the process.

It made no sense.

The next morning, their routine shattered.

Without warning, the Disciples were roused and ordered into a dark corridor. Their feet were bare. Sharp pebbles and jagged fragments littered the ground, slicing into flesh with every step. No one dared complain. Early on, two had tried—one claiming to be the son of an important Second Tier. Neither had been seen again.

Eventually, they emerged into a chamber crowned with a natural dome. In the center sat a shimmering pool—clear, cold, impossibly inviting. It looked like salvation. It was not.

Magisters barked new orders.

"Strip down and grab a belt from the wall."

They obeyed instantly, without question. Their bodies were a lattice of corded muscle and hardened flesh, marred here and there by whip scars or the jagged seams of old compound fractures. Any trace of fat had long since been sweated out onto the Pit floor—along with their pride, their hesitation, and whatever mercy once lived in them.

"Swim."

And so they did—lap after lap. With each pass, they clipped another leaden weight to their belts. The weights grew heavy. Breath came shorter. Arms and legs burned. The water turned to tar, each movement a fight against drowning.

Cojax dipped beneath the surface more and more, letting the water bear the weight of his skull. His limbs cramped. His chest spasmed. Even the strong swimmers began to falter.

Then came the order.

"Drop your weights."

Relief was instant. Cojax felt himself float again, weightless and free. He started toward the shore.

Then stopped. Everyone else was waiting.

He corrected himself just in time. One Magister, a brute carved from stone, was watching. Cojax didn't move again.

"Retrieve your weights," the man barked. "If you fail, don't bother coming back up."

The words struck like ice down his spine.

Cojax's mouth dried. He turned, inhaled, and dove.

He plunged into the depths of water, his ears ached. His chest clenched. He swam blind, the bottom always further than it appeared. He held his nose to clear pressure, but it barely helped. He felt like a brick dragging downward.

His fingers clawed the muck at the bottom, searching. Nothing. His movement at the surface had thrown off his sense of direction. He tried to reorient himself with where he was on the surface when he dropped the weights. Still nothing. Minutes passed. The pressure in his lungs built into a scream. He couldn't find it. Couldn't find anything.

*"You're going to fail."*

This thought, unbidden and unwelcome, came from the corners of his mind. His father. His brother. The city. His Score. All of it.

His lungs yearned for air. He briefly contemplated putting his feet against the ground and shooting back to the surface, but then he would be done—most likely killed on the spot.

*"You're going to drown."*

He felt anxiety creeping in, settling around the edges of his lungs. He was going to fail. Was failing. For a moment, it overcame him, the realization more crushing than the pressure around him.

He closed his eyes for a second, forcing in a new calm, pushing back the fear. He was once weak, helpless, hopeless, but he would not be now. He would not be that crumpled boy on the Wall of Acadia who was just waiting to die.

Instead of looking to the mud, he looked up. Most swimmers had already resurfaced. Judging by where they tread water, he pieced together where he had been swimming and where the weights should have landed.

And there they were, half buried but still visible through the refracted light. His mind began to spin as he swam for the belt, his hand clutching it, his feet mechanically pushing off the floor. He kicked upward. His vision pulsed at the edges. His body barely obeyed. He broke the surface in a coughing, sputtering explosion of water and noise.

"Again."

The word hit harder than a fist.

Still choking, Cojax turned away, ashamed. His body trembled. Panic chewed at the edges of his resolve. He didn't want to return to the water below.

The others were diving. Time was gone.

Then Titan's words came back to him as if he were standing on the shore, urging him on. "You are stronger than you know, son."

The words steadied him. His breath slowed. His hands stopped shaking.

*"This will not be my end."*

With new resolve, he dove again.

## EIGHTEEN

Marcus' armor was polished to a bronze sheen, a mirror of both his meticulous discipline and his towering rank. Few had achieved what he had: a rise to the First Tier in just a few short years—a feat even his father hadn't matched. At twenty-two, he was a boy by Civil Union standards, where most candidates were well into their thirties. Yet here he stood, elite among elites. Still, beneath all the polish and posture, his stomach bubbled with unrest; something from breakfast didn't sit well with him.

He wore his composure like a second skin—his breathing steady, his gaze casual, even lazy. He looked far too young to belong, and most in the crowd likely assumed he was staff, another cog helping run the ceremony. But when their eyes drifted down to the Placard on his chest, realization hit like a dropped weight. Deference shifted to reverence in an instant. They knew his name: Marcus, First into the Gap at the Battle of Menoch. The one who vaulted from Second to First Tier overnight on sheer merit.

He had no desire to flaunt his Sacred Score, but in Acadia, it was the currency of worth—the beginning and end of every opportunity, including this one.

Fifty candidates, all from the BloodBorne Faction, all deemed worthy to raise the next generation. They were scarred warriors, hardened and Validated, each bearing the proof of their survival. Only three were First Tiers—a detail no one overlooked. The line formed wordlessly: First Tiers in front, then Second, Third, and so on. Marcus didn't know how Civil Union candidates were selected, but it was clear the system favored the young and high-ranked. The few Fifth and Sixth Tiers present were older—a few pushing their late thirties. A few bore red borders on their Placards, suggesting they were Weighted—their Score was on a negative trajectory.

*"Perhaps,"* Marcus thought, *"they were offered this as a lifeline—a last shot at relevance before being Released... or Rifted."*

They stood within the Trinity—Acadia's most imposing structure. Less a building, more a monolith. It towered over the rest of the city, forged from the same alien alloy used in Arc Blades and Static Armor. Most buildings in Acadia didn't rise ten stories above ground, with twice that number buried below. But the Trinity was triple that height and mostly above ground. It powered the city's defensive shields, purified its water, forged its weapons, and even grew its food. Marcus had never seen most of those sections.

It lacked the grandeur of the rest of Acadia. No statues. No pillars. No elevated arches. Just function. Brutal, unadorned function. To Marcus, it always felt foreign—not built by Acadians, but inherited. As if the real owners might return someday.

Marcus was the third name called. No surprise, given his Sacred Score. He stepped into a modest chamber, well-lit and sterile. His fingers tensed slightly. The room bore carpet, metallic trim, pearl white walls, and a gray vaulted ceiling framed in crown molding. A chandelier hung overhead. It was more refined than the rest of the Trinity, but still sterile. There were four people in the room, most working on Tech Pads. A Third Tier bowed to him and gestured toward a Tech Pad at the center of the table.

"Please place your mark here," the man said.

"Mark?" Marcus asked.

"Your right thumb will do. Place it on the pad."

Marcus leaned forward, his voice low. "I'm... here for the Civil Union."

The Third Tier blinked. "Yes, sir. We know. Place your mark."

"And then what?"

The man's lips twitched. Irritation, quickly buried. Had Marcus been a lesser Tier, the man might have erupted. But he had to be patient with a First Tier. "Sir, have you read the Civil Union Treaties—the document you're now signing?"

"Yes... I have. It outlined expectations."

"And now you sign your agreement."

"But... who am I paired with? Where will we live? Will I still serve in the battle rotation? I haven't even met her... I don't even know her name."

The Third Tier took a breath, speaking now as if to a child. "If you don't know, it means you weren't meant to. As for your pair—it's her."

He nodded to the warrior beside him.

She was tall, with round features and dark eyes. Marcus offered a tight, uncertain smile. He had expected a formal introduction. Maybe even a name. But nothing came. So he simply did as he was told.

He placed his thumb on the Tech Pad. It blinked, shifted colors, and a message appeared on his ArmGuard.

CIVIL UNION AFFIRMED.

He opened it. In seven days, he was to relocate to Room 1003, Weniac Building, First Floor—within BloodBorne territory. A one-bedroom unit. Luxurious by Acadian standards, but much smaller than his father's Praetorium Residence. It came with the caveat that a residence upgrade was possible once children were delivered by Vat.

He clicked on her profile—Aleniana. Fourth Tier. Rising trajectory.

*"At least my future wife is not Weighted,"* Marcus thought—then paused. She wasn't his *future* wife. She was his *now* wife. And they hadn't exchanged a single word. He didn't even know what she sounded like.

He looked up.

Everyone was staring.

"Will that be all?" the Third Tier asked, clearly uneasy.

Marcus blinked. "Oh. I didn't realize…" He stopped, unsure how to finish. Suggestions on how to complete the ill-formed sentence populated in his mind: *"…that there was no ceremony. That it all seemed so functional. That it all felt less sacred than being issued a new Arc Blade."*

He finally settled on, "…how quick the process would be."

He turned to Aleniana and nodded—a gesture meant to convey something. Affection? Solidarity? She returned the nod, stiffly.

The Third Tier waited, then frowned. "Is there anything else, sir?"

Marcus shook his head. "No."

"Then… may I ask you to exit, sir? I've got dozens more pairings to process within the hour."

"Yes, of course. More pairings. For the good of Acadia and

all."

Marcus turned and left, hand instinctively resting on the hilt of his Arc Blade. A habit branded into him from the Mahghetto. Aleniana followed. He slowed, expecting her to walk beside him. Instead, she veered off in another direction.

He paused. Turned away. Then back. On the third time, he jogged after her. He caught up just as she reached the Great Eastern Doors of the Trinity. Most Acadians never saw the inside of the Trinity. For Aleniana, this might have been her first time. Yet she took it in stride, eyes clear, posture straight.

Marcus blurted the only thing he knew. "So you're a Fourth Tier." He regretted his words immediately.

"And you're a First Tier," she replied flatly.

"Yes. Well... looks like we'll be living in the Weniac Building. I know it well. I have a friend who lives there."

"Do you now?"

"Yes, kind of. I mean... well... he was Rifted a few months back, so not anymore."

"You're quite the conversationalist."

Marcus bristled. He was no common Validated. He was a Gamma. Commander of ten thousand. Sacred Score rising. And here she was, mocking him like a Disciple in the Mahghetto. "Is that all you have to say?"

Aleniana stopped. Turned. Saluted. "My superior. I will fulfill my duty. I will honor my oath. I will raise our genetic children to defend the Last City. The Last Ember. That is what the Civil Union requires. Nothing more."

Marcus stared. Then nodded, returning the salute. He realized that more words would not make this strange interaction a conversation. So, like any commander worth their Tier, he acknowledged that in this case, a tactical withdrawal was the better option than a full-on charge. His tone changed, the pride of his Tier falling to one side. "As will I, Aleniana of the Fourth Tier. We will meet again in seven days. Merit before all."

She dipped her head and vanished into the crowd.

He watched her go.

He didn't know why, but he did.

He knew Acadia prioritized function over form. But still, he had expected something more. He had studied for days. Trained for this. He could recite Barian's Nine Assertions of Personality. Knew how to mold a child into a proper citizen. All of that, reduced to a thumbprint on a screen.

It left a hollow space in his chest. Not sadness. Not rage. Just absence. He checked his ArmGuard. No battle calls. No drills. No training. He'd been given the day off, a reward for entering into his Civil Union. His Sacred Score was even frozen for the day.

He considered visiting the Archives—his Secondary Stewardship. It would distract him. Usually, he reviewed historical data. Most of it was about battles and the warriors who had performed heroic deeds, but occasionally there were other things of significance discussed, such as a new discovery by a Scolastica, or an improvement in the waterlines completed by one of the Aquadorians, or an increase in production in electrical output made possible by an ElectraTech. His job consisted mostly of rewriting system-generated summaries to match Acadian standards. But he decided it was best not to. He'd do more harm than good in this state. Mistakes meant lost points.

He stopped in the middle of a crowded causeway. Acadians rushed around him, each with purpose. He stood still. Like the Blinded. Like the soon-to-be Rifted. He had chosen this. The Civil Union. To further his Score. To build something like a family— something his father once took pride in.

Now, it felt like a trap.

His ArmGuard vibrated. It was a message from Sejanus. A First Tier from the Vixor Faction.

"Red District in 30."

Marcus hovered over a canned refusal.

The Red District. Home of the Weighted. The Dependent. The forgotten.

But… he had the day off. And maybe… he needed to see what rock-bottom looked like.

He dictated a reply. "I'll be there in twenty."

# NINETEEN

Marcus felt naked without his armor, like a newborn under the stabilizing glass of a med-pod. Here, there were no ranks, no Placards, no Score. Armor was surrendered at the gates of the Red District and stashed in rows of rotating digital lockers—each spinning like a cog to accommodate the endless demand. When Marcus handed over his gear, the young attendant paused, eyes catching his Placard. A First Tier. Rare. He glanced at a nearby Validated, silently asking if that kind of status belonged here. The response came swift—a cuff to the back of the head. No one was denied the Red District. Not even the elite.

The Saken Faction operated this den of indulgence—loathed by many, used by more. Even the most disciplined warriors occasionally wandered its depths, seeking release. Marcus glanced at his ArmGuard—the only item allowed past the checkpoint. Despite its dark reputation, the district occupied a surprisingly compact space: four city blocks, walled off by high barriers that blocked sight, sound, and shame.

His first impression was... revulsion. The streets reeked of rot and overindulgence. Crushed refuse, broken glass, half-dried vomit— all pressed into a mosaic beneath his feet. It was Acadia inverted: chaos instead of order, stench instead of sterilization. Bodies littered the walkway, slumped in piles, victims of excess. The air mixed sizzling spice with the stench of sweat and decay, clashing like opposing frequencies in his nose.

Yet even here, tradition clung to the bones of the city. White-stone facades, cracked but proud, rose above the filth. Corinthian columns. Arched windows. A ghost of imperial grandeur still clinging to its corpse. But beneath those columns? Madness. Flickering neon signs. Pulsing offers of pleasure, power, oblivion. The city turned inside out—dignity above, depravity below.

Marcus moved carefully, uncomfortable in the crowded

stillness. Unlike the outer city, these people weren't going anywhere. They had already arrived, rooted in indulgence. The collective inertia sickened him—a mockery of merit.

"How can this place even exist?" he muttered, and not for the first time.

A hand clapped his back. Reflex took over—he spun, snatching the wrist of the attacker.

"Easy," said a familiar voice. "You'll dent my pride."

Marcus relaxed only slightly. It was Sejanus—First Tier, Vixor Faction, and frenemy of the highest order.

"Ah, if it isn't Marcus—First into the Gap at the Battle of Menoch," Sejanus said, his voice full of performative admiration. "They say even when the glitching Roaches tore a hole in the Southern Wall, *you* stood like a gate that would not open." The words flattered, but the tone measured. This wasn't reverence. It was assessment.

Sejanus was no ordinary soldier. Once, he had been the better fighter—brilliant, fluid, ruthless. They had met just over eight months ago, when Marcus was still a Second Tier and Sejanus had already earned the coveted First. In those early days, Marcus had taken loss after loss in the arena. Each duel was a lesson. Each defeat shaved points from his Sacred Score and fed them to Sejanus—but Marcus paid the price willingly. Sejanus taught with every strike—philosophy in one hand, the blade in the other.

But then something changed.

Two months later, Marcus began to win. Not with flair, not all at once, but with quiet, relentless precision. An unexpected strike here, a feint there. The victories came small at first, almost imperceptible. But they stacked, and soon they stood as equals. Then Marcus ascended to the First Tier—and the balance tilted.

Sejanus hadn't grown weaker. His form, his mind, his fire remained sharp. Marcus had simply become something more.

And Sejanus knew it.

"If I hear about the Battle of Menoch one more time…" Marcus said with a playful smile.

"And look who else I brought—Ion."

Short and sturdy, he did not look the part of a warrior, but he could hold his shield in the Phalanx line. His strength was in systems and code—an oddity among warriors, but one that earned him a steady rise to Second Tier. His Stewardship in TechOps provided a steady influx of points.

"Ion, you look like a butterfly in a frog tank," Marcus said, trying to lighten the air.

Ion managed a tight smile. He'd fought beside Marcus in the Mahghetto—the kind of bond forged under flickering lights and blood-stained metal. No swagger. No polish. But unbreakable. Most had assumed Ion wouldn't last a full lunar phase as a Disciple in the city's depths. But they sorely underestimated his resolve. He didn't survive through brilliance or strength alone—he simply refused to fall. It reminded Marcus of Laconius.

His breath caught.

The Mahghetto returned to him unbidden—echoes of darkness, of screaming corridors and flickering lights. Cojax is now walking those same buried halls. A chill pressed into his chest.

*"Laconius… Quintus… Haritess."*

Their names whispered through his mind like ghosts.

They had descended together. Four brothers. Only Marcus emerged to see the sun again.

*"And now Cojax is down there, fighting for his life."* Guilt rippled through him, involuntarily tightening his hands into fists. He had not wished his brother farewell, could not. The Acadian Code strictly forbade departing words for an Innocent before the Mahghetto, lest they become temptations to offer advice. But he regretted his decision to uphold the code—not for the first time. His brother could be dead already, lost among the Rifted, and he wouldn't know for months. But what would he have said to his brother anyway— what do you say to someone who has no idea of the terror they are about to experience? Find a bridge and jump? Take a warm jacket? Don't go?

He exhaled, sharp and controlled, shaking his head—once to silence the memory, again to clear his vision. He focused on Ion, then Sejanus, standing nearby. His friends. Alive. Here.

"So, you brought us here, Sejanus, down into the filth and trash," Marcus said. "What's so special about the Red District?"

"We're not being recorded, for one thing," Sejanus answered simply. "No armor means no recording. Our words are our own. We can finally have a real conversation."

Ion and Marcus were shocked at these blunt, overt words. Every Validated eventually realized how much privacy they truly lacked, if not in the Mahghetto, shortly thereafter. But few dared speak about it, much less so bluntly.

Marcus shifted into a defensive posture, his eyes looking around in earnest to see if anyone had overheard. Ion reacted similarly, although he seemed to be looking at the surrounding buildings instead.

"Easy…don't overload your bio-circuitry," Sejanus answered. "I would not speak so flippantly had I not been so confident in the privacy. Come on. Since this is your first visit here, I'll take you to a place a little more relaxed." Marcus and Ion both followed.

The three warriors found a quiet corner in one of the larger taverns—a place called Ankle Biters. The place reeked of sweat and citrus stock, lit by flickering, blue, pulsing lights and lined with patrons in various stages of euphoria or collapse. The furniture was mismatched but heavy—designed less for comfort and more for the likelihood of being used in a fight.

Sejanus ordered three glasses of amber stock, paying for it with a few metal chips neither Ion nor Marcus had seen before. The drink was poured from a squat-necked decanter by a server with pock-marked cheeks and circuit-braided hair. The drink hissed as it touched the metal cups, reacting to something within. Marcus raised an eyebrow.

"Scathian brew," Sejanus said. "Unregulated. Might peel the paint off your stomach, but it'll clear your mind."

They drank.

The first gulp was fire. Marcus felt it coat his throat like molten steel, then flood into his chest, spreading heat like a reactor core. Ion coughed and wiped his mouth, blinking fast. Sejanus just grinned and leaned back.

"Feels good not to wear the Score for a span," Sejanus said, flexing his shoulders. "Out there in the city, you walk into a room and people already know who you are. What you're worth. You forget what it's like to just… be."

Ion, recovering from his drink, leaned forward. "What is this?"

"It's top shelf," Sejanus answered.

Marcus looked around. "Is this what freedom feels like?"

Sejanus scoffed. "No. This is what the *illusion* of freedom feels like."

Marcus, still recovering from the sear of the drink, leaned in. "Then tell me—have humans ever been truly free?"

The question lingered. Not rhetorical. Not dismissive. Real.

Sejanus smirked, but his eyes darkened. "Once, maybe. Or perhaps never. Depends on who you ask. Thomas Hobbes would say no—freedom is a myth, a dangerous one. In the state of nature, man was free to do anything... which meant constant war. 'Solitary, poor, nasty, brutish, and short.' That was the price of absolute liberty."

Ion snorted. "So freedom is chaos?"

"To Hobbes, yes. Freedom meant living without someone to tell you no—and without that, men devoured each other. So they built Leviathans. States. Governments. Armored themselves in authority and called it safety."

Marcus tapped his fingers on the cup. "What about Locke—didn't he disagree with that notion?"

"Locke was gentler. He believed people had *natural rights*—life, liberty, property. But even he said those rights had to be secured by a social contract. Freedom with a leash, basically."

Sejanus leaned forward, the light casting lines across his face.

"Locke thought we were born with freedom. Hobbes thought we had to give it up. But neither believed you could *keep* it without structure. That's the irony. Freedom always demands a cage."

Marcus studied the swirling drink in his hand, his voice low. "Then it's not freedom. Not really. It's just choosing your master."

Sejanus gave a small nod and leaned forward, dropping his voice so low it was barely audible. "And in Acadia, the master is the Score." He leaned back, his dark secret shared, and his voice returned to normal. "Transparent. Brutal. Honest. It doesn't promise you liberty. It promises merit. Bleed for us, and rise. Fail, and fall. No illusions."

"But is that better?" Marcus asked, a marked hesitation in his voice. He knew this was a conversation best avoided, but something seemed to push him on—whether it was the stock talking or some other force, perhaps a subconscious reaction to his newly finalized

Civil Union. "Madison warned that liberty without virtue is meaningless. That the people must govern themselves before they govern a nation. Acadia doesn't want virtue—it wants performance."

"Virtue," Sejanus said, the word thick with distaste, "is subjective. Madison was a dreamer trying to chain the mob with parchment. But Mill... now *he* understood the danger. He said the only freedom worth anything was the freedom to become yourself. As long as you didn't harm others. But even he assumed people *knew* who they were."

Ion exhaled, brow furrowed, struggling to follow the conversation. "But what if you don't? What if every version of you is just who the system shaped you to be?"

"Then freedom," Marcus said slowly, "is a lie we tell ourselves. A myth we dress in different names—Republic, Empire, Acadia."

There was a silence.

Sejanus, for once, didn't answer. He let it breathe. Then he spoke, voice quiet.

"You know what I think?" he said. "I think freedom isn't about choice. It's about *weight*. The weight of your decisions. If they don't cost you something, they were never free to begin with."

Marcus looked at him. "That sounds like something a man says when he's trying to justify chains."

"Maybe," Sejanus said. "Or maybe it's what a man says when he's trying to forgive himself for wearing them."

Ion's fingers curled around his cup. "So what do we do, then? Just... wear the Score and smile?"

"No," Marcus said. "You bleed for it. But you don't forget what it's doing to you."

Sejanus raised his glass again, slower this time. "To memory, then. To ghosts and chains and choices."

Marcus tapped his cup to Sejanus'. "To weight."

Ion hesitated, then followed. "To whatever's left."

The stock hissed again as it touched their lips. The fire returned. But this time, it felt different—less like a purge, more like clarity.

And just as Sejanus opened his mouth to speak again, the tavern's mood shifted.

Five figures entered through the arched doorway—tall, broad, and walking with that unmistakable predator's confidence. Their tunics were coarse, dyed with patterns associated with the Havok Faction—chaotic, asymmetric, edged with deep crimsons and blacks. Tattoos ran along their necks and down their arms, symbols of battle and burn scars barely hidden beneath. Two were women, three men.

They scanned the room and locked onto Marcus and the others, approaching with a confident gait. Patrons began to shuffle away, either out of instinct or a sense of prophecy, parting before the five like a wave before a ship.

Marcus felt his teeth tighten, an involuntary action that happened just before he entered a battle. Sejanus and Ion seemed to sense it as well, as they adjusted how they were sitting, giving them more leverage to act if needed.

"Move," the largest one growled as they approached. "You're in our seats."

He was a brute—an ugliness rarely seen in Acadia, where symmetry and stature were usually curated like sculpture. This man was carved from violence. His nose had been broken so many times it looked like it had been folded in on itself, a crooked ridge between eyes set too deep. Scars crisscrossed his face in angry slashes—not the clean kind left by Roach mandibles, but the jagged, personal kind. Knife work. Human work.

He moved like a conqueror, chin high, shoulders broad and easy, with the swagger of someone who'd beaten men better than himself and grown stronger with each victory. There was something about the way he took up space—like he'd never once considered the possibility of losing it.

Marcus remained still. "We got here first. Plus, there are plenty of seats."

The lead Havok leaned closer. His breath reeked of fermented spice. "Didn't ask for history. I asked for your table."

Sejanus stood, stretching. "I didn't realize Havok Faction needed to steal stools to feel powerful."

The tension spiked. No names. No Scores. No rank.

Just men and women.

The first punch came from the Havok brute—aimed straight for Sejanus' jaw.

He ducked, twisted, and drove his elbow into the attacker's ribs. The man grunted and stumbled back.

Marcus was already moving.

He caught the second Havok by the forearm and shoulder, using his momentum to hurl the man across the table. Wood splintered. Ion, despite being shorter, launched upward like a spring and slammed a knee into the third Havok's chest, knocking the wind from his lungs.

The fight became a blur.

Stock spilled. Glass shattered. Patrons shouted and scrambled out of the way. One of the Havok warriors swung a broken table leg at Marcus, but he caught it midair, yanked the weapon free, and slammed it across the man's shoulder, dropping him like a sack of meat.

Ion grappled with his opponent on the floor, slipping past the man's reach and locking his elbow in a brutal hold. A snap echoed.

Sejanus drove a fist into the jaw of the first Havok again—this time with no holding back. Teeth clattered to the floor.

When the dust settled, the five Havok warriors lay groaning in a pile of broken furniture and spilled drink. Around them, the bar slowly began to buzz again, as if nothing had happened. A few patrons clapped. A few scowled. But no one interfered. The five newcomers had made a grave mistake challenging three elite warriors—two of which were from the First Tier. In the city of Acadia, they would not have dared to make that same mistake, their Scores prominently displayed on their chests. But here it was like the old world; the world where no one could be assessed until the fight had already begun. It was bad luck, really. First Tiers rarely visited the Red District, and these Havok Validated happened to pick a fight with the few who could stand their ground against bad odds.

Marcus stood in the wreckage, chest heaving, stock stinging the cuts on his knuckles. He hadn't felt this raw, this *alive*, in days. There was no Score to gain, no titles to earn—just the pure satisfaction of triumph in its oldest form. His stress, the pressure he'd felt from the Civil Union, bled away with every strike.

Ion limped over, rubbing his shoulder. "They won't be happy when they wake up."

Sejanus chuckled, wiping blood from his lip. "Then we better drink fast."

Marcus sat again, breath finally steadying. He looked at the others—his allies, his rivals, his brothers-in-arms. For a fleeting moment, in the lawless filth of the Red District, he felt whole again.

## TWENTY

Cojax saw her for the first time in over a hundred days. The reunion wasn't planned. No orders had been issued, but the Disciples, both male and female, instinctively fell into formation on the parade grounds. It was messy at first—uncertain how the separate ranks should merge—but they adjusted.

Jessica stood in the distance, her eyes tired but still strong. That same fire she'd shown in the Vortex still burned in her eyes.

A grizzled Magister took the head, instantly sharpening the focus and ranks of the Disciples. "For one hundred days you have been down here, living like animals, each day earning your right to wake up in the morning. This is how our ancestors lived, buried beneath the ground, fighting for survival, eating rats, lichen, and in some cases, the flesh of Roaches. They did all that so you could live like fat Innocents on the surface, safe and warm in beds and blankets, protected by the great Wall. But until now, you knew nothing of their sacrifice, nothing of what the city gave you without asking for anything in return.

"Well, now it is your turn to give—to become the walls that shield the next generation. You started out a group of four hundred and seven, and you're down to two hundred and ninety-four. You are not here because we like you, or we think you're special deep down inside. You are here, because you earned the right to be; you are here, because you refused to be taken by the Rift.

"My name is Octavian and I will be one of your Primary Magisters. Everything you are suffering, I suffered; everything you have endured, each Validated on the surface did as well. Now you know what it means to be part of the Tiers. I am the same Validated that stood at the statue of Pluto on the surface, filling your ears with courage. Most of you did not listen to me then—too busy in side conversations—but I hope you hear me now."

Silence.

"Finally, you're beginning to learn, but we aren't done yet. Not even close. Follow me."

They broke down into a column of fours, the movement seamless, practiced, mechanical.

Cojax did not let his mind venture into the possible torture that awaited him. He found this only built the anxiety in his chest, diminishing his performance at the next challenge. Minutes later, they were in a mess hall, complete with sterile chairs and tables.

It looked so foreign to him he could not stop a wave of apprehension. *What new torture is this?"*

Octavian turned to the crowd, eyeing them thoroughly. "New rights have been afforded you based on your merit: the right to eat like a human—at a table, with a bowl and silverware—the Right to Speak, the Right of Movement. But do not make the mistake of thinking these rights are yours forever—as they must be earned every day. Merit before all."

*"Merit before all,"* the room echoed.

Slowly, cautiously, the Disciples formed four lines at various chutes, a machine scanning the micro-syncs in their skin. Bowls of food began to appear, complete with carbon forged silverware. They sat in silence, each reviewing what the Magister had said. The words were first quiet and whispered, a test to see if this was another trick.

Cojax grabbed a bowl and chose a table near the serving wall, well away from the exits—areas of possible attack. Brutus sat on his right, Finn on his left. They ate in silence until Brutus finally broke it with a whisper. Another two boys sat across from them.

"I'm sorry, Cojax."

Finn nodded. "Me too."

Cojax knew what they meant. The memory still burned—those final moments in the tunnel, the split-second decision to fall behind. Anger threatened to rise again, but he pushed it down.

"You didn't do anything wrong," he said. "Neither of you. My injury was ruining both your chances."

"How did you find the strength to make it through the tunnel?" Finn asked.

Cojax did not know how to answer. *The girl… the needle… the boost in strength."* He didn't know how either of them would react, so he decided to share the news later. He pushed the concern aside, focusing on something more positive. "We've made it this far, and we're still alive. That's all that matters now."

Finn exhaled through his nose. "Hopefully, the worst is behind us. We just need to watch each other's backs and we can avoid the Rift altogether."

"She won't be able to," Brutus said, tilting his head toward Jessica. She had just picked up her earthen bowl and was scanning the tables for a seat.

Cojax began to stand and gesture toward her. Brutus grabbed his forearm and yanked him back down.

"What are you doing?"

"I was going to invite her to sit with us."

Brutus shook his head. "Are you blind? That's the Aberration. She doesn't deserve to be here, much less in a chair." His words were feral, intense—lined with a bitterness that surprised even him.

"She's still here," Cojax replied evenly. "Which means she's earned the right to be. Merit before all."

Finn leaned in. "Cojax, come on. We've survived this long because we didn't take any unnecessary risks. There's no upside to getting close to her. No one's going to bump your Score for kindness—and definitely not for defending the Aberration."

"I'm not some fresh Innocent," Cojax muttered, lowering his voice. "I know how things work. But avoiding her out of fear? That's not survival—it's submission."

"What are you talking about?" Brutus hissed. "We're lucky to be alive, and you want to start attracting fire again?"

"Where's the risk?" Cojax snapped.

"She's radioactive," Brutus said. "The closer you get, the more likely you're going to fall into the Rift with her. She's a weight that will sink all those around her."

Cojax set down his fork, not sure how to respond. His father had said just as much. *But why so much distortion over her? She saved me— I owe her my life.*

Brutus rolled his eyes. "Why haven't they Rifted her yet?"

"They can't just Rift her," Cojax answered. "It's against the Code."

Brutus raised an eyebrow. "Wow. You're starting to sound like Hadrian."

"Don't," Finn said coldly. "Don't talk about him like that."

Brutus backed down, but not out of remorse.

Finn turned to Cojax. "Did your father know she'd be here?"

"He did," Cojax said. "Didn't like it either. Made it clear he wanted her Rifted. But…I don't understand why."

Brutus scoffed. "And you almost asked her to join us? Cojax, you heard Octavian—we're not through this yet. You have to start using your head, not whatever it is you're using now."

Finn narrowed his eyes. "She's so much smaller than us."

"She's our age, just different," Cojax said.

Before Finn could answer, a bowl clattered to the ground somewhere across the room. Every head turned. A mixture of food and silverware splayed across the floor. Jessica stood nearby, alone. A group of Disciples loomed in front of her.

"My best friend is dead," said the one at the front—a tall, striking girl with perfect posture and a cruel frown. "He's dead. And your spot could've been his."

"Get up," barked another—a broad-shouldered girl with a thick build. "You don't eat like us. You eat on the floor. Like the creature you are."

Jessica stood. Her face was unreadable, her movements calm. She picked up her bowl, salvaged what she could of the protein-rich liquid, and stepped away from the conflict. She didn't sit on the ground, but she did not sit in a chair either. She leaned against a wall, eating quietly, one bite at a time, her eyes up and focused on the irate girls.

The large girl started toward her again, clearly not satisfied with the result. "I said—"

"—Enough!" Cojax's voice rang out, echoing off the hard walls. He was already on his feet. Finn and Brutus looked up at him in shock.

"You don't get to dictate where she eats," Cojax said. "You don't even have a Score right now, none of us do. We're all the same—just survivors."

The tall girl locked eyes with him. "Then why do you think you can give advice to the rest of us?"

"We're equals," Cojax replied. "There are only two types of Disciples—those who survived and those who didn't. Your friend's in one group. You're in the other. Whatever that was won't bring him back."

She stepped forward, every movement deliberate and poised. "Aren't you noble, standing up for the Aberration. She doesn't belong here. Haven't you figured that out? She's been cheating this whole time, forcing out others who clearly had more merit than her."

Finn leaned forward with a grin, trying to ease the tension. "Careful—pride has a way of tripping people. Maybe we all can take a seat and talk this out."

Cojax cut in. "Leave Jessica alone. Whether she makes it or not—it'll be because of her, not because of you."

The girl smiled. "So the creature has a name." She was beautiful, full lips and curves in all the right places. Her hair, black and braided, had a sheen to it that glowed. She seemed older by a few years, more sophisticated, her words posh and poised.

Cojax cleared his throat, unsure how to respond.

"If you truly believe in merit, let her fight her own battles," she responded.

"Adriana, come on," said a boy from behind her. "We better get back to eating before we run out of time."

Cojax felt his throat tighten.

Adriana tilted her head. "Are you still part of this conversation? Or did your brain stall out on you?" She turned without waiting for a reply, her braids swaying as she walked away.

Cojax sat down, his face burning red.

Brutus gave a low whistle. "She's Top Tier—what a beauty."

"Once the tension dies down," Finn said, "maybe we can reason with her. She's got a way of pulling people to her side, and I'd hate to stand in her way."

Cojax slumped deeper into his chair, his muscles still taut. "Are you kidding? Sorry—her and reason don't belong in the same room."

# TWENTY-ONE

Jessica ate faster than the rest, her eyes locked on the floor, mouth working silently. Conversation wasn't just pointless here—it was dangerous. Making friends meant making attachments, and attachments didn't survive in the belly of the Mahghetto.

She stood alone near the exit, spine straight, waiting for the next command.

Cojax joined her a moment later, his friends trailing behind. He looked like he was about to say something—then a voice cracked through the air like a whip.

"Form up."

A female Magister's words ended the meal instantly. Bowls clattered into the chute, silverware tossed after them in a blur of motion. They assembled four across, marching in perfect synchronization. The corridor stretched ahead in a long, curving arc. As they passed training rooms and classrooms, Jessica caught glimpses of other Disciples from different Factions through glass and open archways. These other units watched them with quiet fascination, like paleontologists eyeing something ancient and half extinct.

After nearly half an hour, they were ushered into a black-tiled changing room. Orders were barked. Uniforms removed. Jessica stripped quickly, but as she glanced around at the muscle-carved forms of the others—bodies honed to the blade—her cheeks flushed crimson. She wasn't ashamed of herself. Not until now. Not until this moment. She pressed her clothes into a numeric container and left the room at a near-sprint, hoping no one had really seen her.

The room she entered next was large and circular. Dozens of chairs reclined in surgical alignment, like teeth in a mechanical jaw. Hanging from the ceiling was a massive machine, its surface smooth and glossy, bristling with retracted arms—scalpel-tipped, hook-bladed, wire-fed. It resembled a robotic leviathan dreaming of dissection.

Jessica froze. She knew this place.

The Red Room.

Elena had only mentioned it once. Odd name, she'd thought back then—there was nothing red about it. Just gray stone, gray steel. But now she understood: the name was a prophecy, not a description. Each Disciple was guided to a chair. Jessica's was cold against her skin, but she didn't react. Couldn't. She forced herself to breathe, slow and steady. No emotion.

*"Don't show weakness."*

She pictured the land beyond the Wall—the sweeping green hills like rolling waves, the giant tree next to her old home with its gnarled limbs, the soft sound of the river. She clung to the image like a lifeline.

But her grip was slipping.

The rest of the Disciples were flooding in, taking their places, moving with urgency to their chairs. When they sat, restraining devices automatically secured them—one for each wrist and ankle. The machines above her clicked to life. Tubes writhed. Blades spun. Her body tensed.

"I am Thea," said a short, stocky female Magister, her grin too wide to be completely sane. "Learn to master your pain, or it will blind you. And we don't keep the blind."

Her laughter was casual. Practiced. The kind of laugh a woman gives before throwing you into fire.

"Remember this," Thea added. "The path to becoming gods is fraught with peril, but if you keep taking the next step, it will lead you to greatness."

Pain exploded.

Electricity slammed through Jessica, bouncing inside her muscles. Her body seized. She bit down hard, jaw clenched, nostrils flaring. She didn't even recognize the first scream—it was hers, but it sounded like an animal being butchered. Her lungs collapsed. When they refilled, a second scream tore free, followed by a chorus of others. The Red Room sang with agony as all the Disciples underwent the same treatment.

*"Focus. Breathe. Concentrate."*

She forced the memory of her father's voice into her mind,

made it echo in the hills outside her old home. But the pain shredded her thoughts like parchment. This wasn't like any shock she had experienced before. This was deeper, more invasive. More complete. Then the machine descended.

A metal arm lunged forward, targeting her chest. Four needles punched into her skin, spraying blood across her face. The wires slithered in behind them, snaking beneath her flesh. Another arm sealed the wounds. The next targeted her throat. Then her legs. Then her spine, weaving a complex mesh of micro-syncs into her body.

It was mechanical. Precise. A printer of pain.

Tears dripped down her cheeks as the machine laced her with wire. Blood streaked down her body, pooling beneath her. Her skin became a canvas of red.

And then—a glow. Faint at first, then pulsing. The bio-circuitry activated, spreading light throughout her body in seemingly random patterns. The pain faded. Not gone—but... compartmentalized. Like she was watching someone else suffer. A switch had been flipped. She didn't feel powerful—not yet—but she felt different. Changed.

The machine retracted.

Silence returned.

Then waiting.

Thea chuckled again. "You've been given the strength of gods—and yet you sit like shackled animals. Are you Rifters? Or warriors?"

Jessica struggled against her restraints. They held firm. She tried again, funneling energy into her arms. Her implants flickered, lighting her veins like molten wire—but the restraints didn't budge. Other Disciples were rising. Metal cracked. Straps snapping.

Not hers.

Panic bloomed. She tried again. Less power. Less focus. *"I can't do it. I'm going to fail. I'm going to—"*

Cojax passed by. He said nothing. Just tore one of her restraints in half as he moved, subtle, smooth.

"I guess we all need help sometimes," he muttered, then disappeared into the crowd.

With one arm free, Jessica broke the rest. She stood, but nearly collapsed. Her blood loss made the room sway. She caught herself on a chair. Looked down.

The floor was no longer gray.

Now she understood.

The Red Room.

***

They dressed in silence, sliding back into their black uniforms. For those who still bled, the fabric drank in the stains like ink on parchment, deepening the already black weave.

Thea led them back the way they'd come—past the Dining Hall, through winding corridors, until they reached a massive dormitory: it was circular and lined with hundreds of bunk beds around the perimeter, each one rigid and precise.

"Your sleeping quarters," Thea said. She looked at her ArmGuard, gauging the time. "Your assigned bunk has your name on it and all the clothing you will need for the rest of your time in the Mahghetto. You have two hours to meet back at the parade grounds. Shower. Change. And be ready to present yourself for inspection."

A non-audible cheer spread through the Disciples, a palpable excitement. With the integration of bio-circuitry into their bodies, Acadia had made a major investment in their futures, their lives. They were no longer things that could be so easily thrown away—cut down for the simplest mistake.

Once Thea left, the cheer became real. Disciples hugged. Rejoiced. Some of them ripped their shirts off and threw them in the air, whooping as if they had just conquered the Persian Empire. As they moved, their bio-circuitry lit up in places, enhancing their speed and strength. None of them were used to it, and it was often disjointed and jarring, like watching two independent minds trying to coordinate the same movement.

Jessica did not lose her razor focus. She figured most would want to spend their time in the showers, scouring the blood from their bodies. To avoid the lines, she headed there first.

Elena had been right about nearly everything—how the others would turn on her, how they'd blame her for the deaths of their friends. Adriana had wasted no time in rallying the Disciples against her, insulting her, singling her out. It could have been chalked up to stress or grief, but Adriana's venom felt deliberate. Cold. Calculated. Like she'd been waiting for the right lunar alignment to strike.

Only one thing Elena hadn't predicted: Cojax—the boy with obsidian hair and a jaw cut from marble. Elena had pegged him as the biggest threat. Jessica wasn't so sure anymore. She chewed the inside of her cheek, trying to make sense of him.

Her bunk was on the upper tier, near the bathrooms. As she approached, she saw that the frames were built from recycled Vantarite, the metal scarred with long gouges and scrapes running the length of each one. Inside her steel dresser were black training uniforms, socks, combat boots, a thin towel, and toiletries. Folded beneath the basics, hidden in a false bottom, was a Golden Orb—just like the one Elena used to siphon her energy. Jessica closed her eyes and whispered a quiet, "Thank you."

She grabbed what she needed and made for the showers.

They were little more than open pipes protruding from the wall, each marked with a sync-reader. Jessica peeled off her clothes and set them aside. Moments later, another girl entered—her face flashing surprise, then disgust, when she spotted Jessica.

Jessica ignored her. She approached a pipe, swiped her hand across the reader, and water erupted from the spout. She stepped into it.

She expected cold. Instead, it was perfect—somehow the exact balance of warmth and chill. Inviting. Restorative.

*"No,"* she thought. *"Not just warm. Perfect."*

On the far side of the room, the other girl activated her own shower. Jessica pulled her hair under the stream, letting it drape like silk across her face. A long sigh escaped her lips.

"Three months without an actual shower is far too long."

She could have stood there for hours, letting the heat melt her thoughts into nothing. Her worries fell from her like the blood and grime, circling the drain and vanishing without a trace. For the first time in forever, she felt warm.

Then a voice screamed in her head.

*"What are you doing?"*

Jessica froze. Panic surged through her chest.

*"Move, you dimmed girl!"*

Her hand flew to the wall. The water stopped. The warmth vanished. She stood still, dripping, her heart pounding.

*"How long was I in there?"*

She couldn't remember. Seconds? A minute?

She scrambled into her clothes. *"If I'm going to die, I'd rather be dressed."*

The other girl cackled behind her. "You dimmed Aberration. You didn't even use soap."

Jessica didn't respond. She yanked on her shirt, just as they arrived. Three Validated burst in, clad in full armor—battle-ready. The leader drew his sword. It glowed with pale white light.

Jessica's throat went dry. *"I will not die cowering."*

The Validated stepped forward, blade raised. Jessica closed her eyes.

A scream.

Blood spattering across Jessica's face. When she opened her eyes, the girl in the other shower was dead—her body crumpled on the tile, blood still spreading.

Jessica blinked through the spray, then grabbed her towel. She didn't look back. As she stepped into the hallway, she let out the breath she hadn't realized she was holding. More Disciples passed her, towels in hand. None spoke.

The tears came fast. Unwelcome. Sharp. She dabbed at her face with the towel, trying to hide her breakdown. She reached the dormitory, but it was still crowded—Disciples talking, stowing gear, laughing.

Jessica kept walking.

*"I just need to be alone."*

But each step felt like a countdown. They'd executed a girl for a shower that went a second too long. She was so lost in thought, she didn't see who she ran into.

Her towel fell. Red streaks stained her face.

Cojax stood before her—tall, calm, his chest bare. A towel in one hand. A bar of soap in the other.

A voice called from down the hall, "Cojax, wait up!"

He glanced over his shoulder, then back to her. His eyes

flicked with decision. Without a word, he grabbed her arm and pulled her down a side corridor.

"Let go of me!" Jessica snapped, wrenching at his grip.

"They shouldn't see you crying," Cojax muttered.

"That's what the towel was for!"

"Well," he said, nodding to the floor, "you dropped the towel. You can't cry in the hallway."

Jessica tried twisting from his grip, but then stopped. She knew exactly where to go. She led him down a dark passage, through two doors, into a storage room half-buried in broken crates. The only light came from the hallway.

Cojax finally let her go.

Jessica rubbed her arm. Her anger was a living thing now—hot and clawing.

He turned his back. "The rest will see your tears as weakness."

Jessica hissed, "I just watched a girl get cut down for taking a shower one second too long."

"Where? When? Just now?"

"Yes."

Cojax sighed. "How long was her shower?"

"What does it matter?"

He was quiet.

"It must have been over a minute," he said.

She nodded. "Yeah, probably. How did you know?"

"I was... guessing."

"That's an oddly specific guess."

Cojax hesitated, eager to change the conversation.

She eventually filled in the silence, her hands still shaking. She had seen people die in brutal fashion, but this seemed sadistic. "Why kill someone for no reason? What's the point?"

"It wasn't about the shower. It was a warning. A message: don't take more than you've earned. I'd bet it happens every Mahghetto—someone dies in the showers. They gave us warmth, clothes, real beds—just enough comfort to tempt someone into forgetting where we are. And the moment someone does..." He paused, voice cold. "They bleed."

Jessica nodded, his words ringing true. "They'll leave her body there for a few days. Just to make the message clear."

Cojax swallowed, eager to talk about anything else. "What is this place?"

"Storage closet."

"How did you know it was here?"

Now it was her turn to be silent.

He turned, flushed. "I'd better go warn the others we are only allowed one-minute showers." He was halfway out the door before he turned back, remembering something.

"You warned me about the showers. Let me return the favor. Make sure your uniform's perfect. I saw steamers in the dorm. I guarantee we're expected to use them."

Jessica hesitated.

"Thank you."

Then he was gone.

## TWENTY-TWO

The Disciples stood in flawless formation, every jaw clenched, every back a rod of iron. Their faces were blank slates, mirroring the hollow corridors that surrounded them. They were gathered on the parade grounds—a vast, domed chamber carved half from volcanic stone and half from reinforced alloy. The architecture felt like a fusion of cave and cathedral, jagged walls of bedrock rising into smooth metallic arches, as if the earth itself had been molded into Acadia's image.

Cojax stood at the front, his uniform razor-sharp, pressed to perfection. The creases were crisp enough to draw blood. He had insisted they arrive early—though Brutus, as usual, had made that difficult. The steamer had been no match for Brutus' inexperience; his first attempt left his uniform looking like it had been chewed. Only with Cojax's last-minute help had they arrived on time.

Jessica was nowhere in sight, but Cojax didn't need to see her to know. She would be near the rear—blending in, as she always did. That girl could disappear into concrete.

A pneumatic hiss. The door opened.

Three figures entered: Octavian, Thea, and a thinner, shorter Magister. More Assisting Magisters followed, surrounding the Disciples like carrion birds circling a fresh kill.

"Attention! Magisters present!" Cojax's voice rang out, sharp and clear.

In perfect synchrony, the Disciples snapped to form—heads bowed, boots struck stone floor, fists hit chests with a thunderous beat that echoed like an execution drum.

Octavian stepped forward. His polished armor reflected the overhead lights, but it was his eyes that drew attention—cold, experienced, alive with grim anticipation. A seasoned Second Tier, Octavian was the kind of man who had seen dozens of Validated die—some in the Mahghetto, others in the Killing Field—and who would live long enough to watch dozens more fall.

"You've made it this far," he said, voice calm but edged with steel. "But you've still more to learn—as one of your fellow Disciples discovered in the showers. Her death was not an accident. It was a lesson. One meant for all of you. Think before you act. Plan before you move."

He turned slightly. "Thea. Orchulli. Begin the inspections."

"Yes, sir," they answered in unison.

A wave of Magisters moved forward, swarming the line. Those with wrinkled uniforms, misaligned creases, or dull boots were yanked out violently and forced to the front. Some stumbled. None dared resist.

Cojax watched as twenty-two were lined up before Octavian.

The man's eyes scanned the group with scorn so sharp that it could flay skin. "Inspections," he said, "are a tradition that existed long before you came here to the Mahghetto. Ignorance is not an excuse. However..." He paused, gesturing to their glowing veins. "Given the new bio-circuitry laced through your systems, I will allow you one opportunity to correct your failure. Dismissed."

The kneeling Disciples bolted like prey released from the jaws of death—running for the dormitories with renewed desperation.

Octavian returned to the line. "Strength brought you here. But strength is not enough. You must prove your mind—your discipline, your loyalty. You will obey without question. You will forsake brother, sister, lover, parent... all for the glory of Acadia."

Cojax stood still, watching the gaps form in their line. That wasn't supposed to happen. When ranks opened, they were always reformed. He hesitated. Then, slowly, he shifted two feet to his left. The rest followed. They reformed. Cojax was just another Disciple— but for one second, they followed him. Not because he gave an order, but because he took charge.

"Ah," Octavian said, a sickening note of relief in his voice. "Finally, my words are starting to sink in. Always reform ranks. In the column we are stronger; without it, we die."

The silence that followed sent Cojax drifting back—back to the stark quarters of his Praetorium Residence. His father had drilled these lessons into him daily. Not as punishment, he now realized, but as preparation. All the yelling about punctuality, inspections, posture… it hadn't been cruelty.

More Disciples trickled in. Uniforms now pressed. Boots gleaming.

The twelfth to return was a girl—her uniform improved, but clearly rushed.

Octavian's eyes narrowed. "What are you doing?"

"Sir… presenting myself for inspection."

Even from twenty paces, Cojax could see the failure. She'd tried—but she had no idea what she was doing. Steam lines crooked. Sleeves uneven. The leather of her boots only half-buffed.

Octavian's body lit with synced energy. His hand shot out, grabbing the girl by the collar. With fluid violence, he twisted and hurled her in a perfect kata guruma—an old battlefield throw once used to dismount riders. Her body flipped, her weight momentarily suspended, before she crashed against the wall. Her head struck hard.

*"How?"* Cojax's thoughts reeled. That kind of power wasn't natural. It wasn't just muscle—it was grace, precision, augmentation. Octavian had performed it with the fluidity of breathing.

"Girl!" he bellowed. "Find your feet or forfeit your head!"

Somehow, she did—blood leaking from her nose, but spine straight.

Octavian approached again.

"I am not fond of repeating myself."

He threw her again—harder. Her limbs flailed as she spun, landing with a heavy thud.

Jessica winced. Cojax's jaw locked.

"Approach me again in that condition," Octavian snarled, "and it will be your last."

The girl's bio-circuitry flickered as she stumbled upright and limped out of the room, leaving a trail of red on the floor.

When six Disciples still hadn't returned, Octavian raised his hand. "Seal the doors. I declare the rest Rifted."

A heavy clang. Metal slammed into place.

Beyond it were panicked words. "Wait—wait!"

But it was too late.

The sound of finality echoed like a tomb sealing shut.

The Magisters waited, letting the silence stretch. Then Thea stepped forward, smiling with controlled malice.

"You have now earned the right to carry a Sacred Score."

She tapped a panel. A CarrierLift groaned, then hissed open. Inside were Score Placards. Gleaming bronze with black interfaces, humming softly like sleeping machines.

A reverent silence spread.

One by one, the Disciples stepped forward to receive their Placards. Each offering was met with a solemn bow from the Magisters and returned in kind by the student, who clutched the device in both hands as though it were a sacred relic.

Cojax counted.

Two hundred eighty.

Exactly.

Not one more. Not one less.

They had planned it from the beginning.

A chill crept into his bones.

Before he could dwell on it, they were moving again—led through winding corridors, natural rock fusing with artificial structures, the path ahead lit by embedded bio-lights that pulsed like veins.

***

As Jessica arrived at their destination, a Magister waved her on, impatiently gesturing to the farthest scanning tube. They were in a large, rectangular room, a massive machine on one side and scanning tubes just beside it.

She stepped inside one of them.

The glass arched around her. Lights ignited, bathing the chamber in sterile green. A scanner whirled from head to toe—stinging her eyes before fading to black.

Then came the next room: a clattering, boxy machine that dominated the space. Its internals groaned with mechanical life. The smell of rubber and ionized metal filled the air. At one end, a conveyor belt occasionally launched out white-wrapped packages.

Jessica slid her Placard into the receiver. The machine roared to life. It took a few minutes, but then a smaller package, lighter than

160

the others, tumbled out with her name across the front.

She took it to a small table. She already knew what was inside, but opening it still stunned her.

Static Armor. Matte bronze with amber highlights, covered in razor-sharp angular etchings and the symbol of the BloodBorne—an inverted V encircled by rings. There was a helmet, armguards, greaves, a chestplate, and a circular Repulse Shield. The helmet resembled something out of ancient myth, but built from a single piece of advanced alloy, its eye slits covered by reactive glass. A strip of bristled black material ran like a crest across the crown.

"Unless you plan to fight in your uniform," Orchulli whispered to her, "I'd try putting it on."

Excitement surged through the room.

Jessica began with the armguards. They snapped on easily—too easily. When she tried to remove them, they wouldn't budge. Seamless. As if they'd fused to her skin.

Panic flared.

She dug her fingers into the gap at her wrist, prying. Nothing. She looked around. Others struggled too.

*"There has to be a release...."*

Then she stopped. Focused. Willed them to open.

They clicked free—like obedient pets.

She set them down and started over.

This time, she began with the breastplate. She slipped her arms through and envisioned it unfolding—and it did. The armor wrapped around her torso and sealed.

Each piece she added—boots, greaves, waistplate—linked with her micro-syncs. The bio-circuitry synchronized. Her body felt lighter, stronger. Infinite.

When she placed the helmet on, her senses expanded. The HUD activated, scanning faces, calculating distances. It was as though she could see everything—more than sight. *A sixth sense.*

The armor didn't restrict her. It flowed with her.

Around her, Placards lit up—names and scores displayed across black holo-panels.

All read 0.

Then she felt it.

A shift in the room. Quiet stares.

One boy glanced at her Placard, his brows furrowed. He nudged another. That boy stiffened, then scowled.

Jessica looked down.

Her Placard read 1,000.

The only one.

*"How? Did Elena do this?"*

The tension thickened. She expected whispers, accusations, maybe worse.

But before the storm broke, a command rang out. "Form up!"

She moved into line.

*"No,"* she thought. *"Elena wouldn't risk something so obvious. Then who? And why?"*

## TWENTY-THREE

They stood at attention for several long minutes before Octavian finally spoke. "Break for dinner and return to your dormitories. Your ArmGuards now carry your full schedule—learn how to use them. You will be at the parade grounds at 0600 tomorrow. Dismissed."

The Disciples saluted in unison. The Magisters exited in coordinated formation. Then all restraint shattered. Movement erupted. Disciples surged toward Jessica, their hostility no longer contained. Elbows grazed her sides. One shoved her with a casual brutality. Most still wore their helmets, their faces hidden behind mirrored visors, dehumanized.

Jessica removed hers deliberately. If they wanted to come for her, she would meet them uncovered.

One voice barked from the crowd. "Look at the little Rifter. A thousand points and suddenly she thinks she's untouchable."

"She'll be Weighted before nightfall," sneered another.

"Must be a glitch," said a third. "That can't be real."

Then a boy stepped forward—too casual, too timed to be chance—and slammed his armored shoulder into Jessica's jaw. The corner of his pauldron scraped across her cheek, splitting the skin.

Jessica staggered sideways. Laughter broke like shrapnel across the corridor.

The blow hadn't been full-force—the boy didn't yet understand how to sync with his armor—but it was enough. Blood trailed down her cheek in a clean, red arc.

"Watch it," he muttered, words muffled. He had not yet learned how to sync his voice with the speakers in his helmet.

Jessica's reply came without heat. "What?"

Her tone—neutral, even dazed—only fed his bravado. He yanked off his helmet with a flourish, expression twisted in triumph. "I said—"

He never finished.

Jessica lunged forward, syncing her movement with her bio-circuitry, and in a flash of light, she headbutted the Disciple. One smooth lunge, no wasted motion. His nose broke, blood blooming across his face. The crack was audible. The boy crumpled backward, squeaking as his body slid across the polished floor, limbs loose, hands still. Unconscious before he hit the ground.

Silence.

Disciples stared—blinking, processing. A ripple of disbelief moved through them like a change in gravity.

Jessica straightened, the corners of her mouth curling into a sharp, merciless grin. She didn't wipe the blood on her cheek—she wore it. Then she slowly lowered her helmet onto her head, her smile disappearing under a sheen of bronze color. She cracked her knuckles and bladed her body, lowering herself into a fighting stance.

The air thickened—charged, volatile. Violence felt inevitable—like a pot left too long on the flame, the lid beginning to rattle, steam screaming through the cracks.

Then a girl stepped forward. She removed her helmet with a soft laugh, as if nothing serious had happened at all.

Adriana.

"Wait," she said as she stepped forward, calm as a storm waiting to happen, her helmet cradled in one arm like a fashion accessory. "Her Score dropped 200 points."

These words brought all eyes to Jessica's Placard. Her Score was now at 800.

"Harrian's Score also went down. It's negative 50," said a female voice.

Adriana frowned. "Looks like fighting with the pig will make us all dirty. Pity. I would have loved to see it squeal."

"What's your problem?" Jessica said. Unlike the boy before, she had synced her helmet with her voice and her words came out crystal clear.

"You are my problem," Adriana replied. "The random Score on your Placard is my problem."

Cojax had just arrived at the edge of the crowd. He hadn't seen the conflict—but he could read the room. "That's enough, Adriana."

Adriana turned her gaze to him. Then to Jessica. Then back

again—drawing a line with her eyes that everyone else now saw.

"Oh, Cojax, here to uphold the Acadian Code," she added. "Adorable, isn't it?"

Cojax stayed silent, his posture unreadable.

Adriana's smile sharpened. "We all know she is the Aberration—short, misshapen, hair the color of a Demon. The girl's a threat. But here you are, ready to fight for her. Noble. Naïve. Maybe both."

"She's proven she has every right to be here," Cojax replied. "No one is above the code."

"Spoken like a proper parrot," she said sweetly. "The kind who can't think for themselves."

Jessica stepped forward. "I don't need him to defend me."

Adriana turned, eyebrow raised, glancing at all the Disciples that seemed ready to attack. "You sure about that?"

"Hah," Jessica answered. "You know I can handle myself. How's your elbow healing?"

Adriana straightened at this. The two girls obviously had a little history in the Fighting Pit.

"I've earned the right to stand on this ground," Jessica said.

"Then why in the Rift does no one else have a single point on their Placard?" Adriana answered, hissing. "Are you better than all of us? Have we not all bled?"

"I don't know why it was granted to me," Jessica answered, anger seething. Her fists were already balled—she didn't need words. There'd been too much talking already. She'd taken on Adriana before. The girl was bigger, sure, but slow—like a Reever missing five legs.

"Exactly," Adriana snapped. "No one knows why either. Which means, you didn't earn them. And *that's* the problem."

Cojax interjected, "You don't know that."

"Don't I?" Adriana asked, tilting her head. "She just said it herself. Why are you in such a rush to defend her? Tell me, Cojax, are you helping her cheat?"

Cojax frowned. "No."

Adriana's expression lit up. "Ah. So she *is* cheating, just without your help. Glad we cleared that up."

"That's not what I said."

"But it's what everyone heard." She turned to the crowd. "Isn't it?"

Murmurs rippled. Eyes sharpened. Alliances forming.

Adriana stepped back into the center. "You all have a choice to make," she announced. "Defy the system of merit that is the foundation of our city, *or* stand with me, and fight against the Aberration's entitlements."

A few Disciples moved behind Adriana. Then a few more.

Adriana faced them again, smiling as if none of this mattered.

"Those who follow the right path will be eating dinner," she said. "The rest can sit in the dark with the Aberration."

And just like that, it was over. The violence that seemed inevitable disappearing completely. The crowd dispersed as if dismissed by a Magister, all of them heading to the Dining Hall.

Cojax turned—but Jessica was already gone. He stood there, stunned. *"What just happened?"*

He looked over his shoulder. Finn and Brutus remained.

Brutus bumped his arm. "You did it again."

"Did what?"

"You didn't introduce us."

Cojax gave a dry look. "Sorry. I was too busy being accused of conspiracy and treason."

Brutus smirked. "You looked like a fool, I won't lie."

"She planned that whole thing," Cojax muttered. "What is her deal? Why is she so focused on attacking Jessica?"

"No idea," Finn said. "But she took your argument and spun it on its head—now it looks like *she's* the one upholding the AC."

"She just soiled all over your credibility," Brutus added bluntly. "And made it look easy."

"Forget it," Finn said. "Let's go grab dinner."

"We can't," Cojax said. "Now it'll look like we're following Adriana."

Finn frowned. "Seriously?"

"She weaponized dinner," Cojax said, incredulous. "Everyone was going there anyway—but now it'll seem like they're obeying her."

"That's how badly we were outmaneuvered," Finn said. "It's taking us this long just to realize it."

"I don't care how it looks," Brutus growled. "I lost half my blood in the Red Room and I still haven't recovered. I'm eating."

They walked to the Dining Hall despite Cojax's protests. He ate in silence, leaving Brutus and Finn to talk to a few of the other Disciples, and then stood to leave. As he dropped his tray down the chute, he glanced across the room. Adriana sat surrounded by sycophants—men and women hanging on her every word. She caught him looking.

She winked.

Cojax turned away, jaw tight. *"How had she become so popular all of a sudden?"* It all confused him. The conflict. Adriana's new crowd of followers. How his words got somehow twisted. He needed clarity.

Somehow, without realizing it, he found himself back in the storage room, his mind still a blender of emotions. He needed to talk to her. Alone. To get some answers.

He stood at the threshold, his eyes adjusting to the dark. Jessica stood in the shadows.

"Congratulations," she said, her tone even but firm. "You made me look weak and you came off as a hypocrite. Are you trying to make this harder for both of us or just me?"

## TWENTY-FOUR

"Jessica?"

He looked deeper into the darkness, his eyes unable to confirm her identity.

"Put your helmet on."

He obeyed and suddenly the room was fully visible, as if someone had turned on all the lights. He removed his helmet and the darkness returned. He put it back on and his visibility returned.

He approached her, his voice urgent. "Let me see that cut."

"I'm fine. The Red Room took far more blood from me than this little cut. Besides, pain is more abstract now, haven't you noticed?"

Cojax chewed on the words. He first took them as a jest, but then realized the deeper meaning.

"Yeah," Jessica acknowledged. "We now only feel pain to a certain level—a tolerable level. The Red Room made sure of that."

He removed his gauntlet slowly, eyes fixed on the bio-circuitry beneath his skin. A faint shimmer pulsed across his palm. She was right. He had sensed something different—something off—but hadn't placed it until now. All those years ago, he remembered the dying Validated who made no sound, no cry, no plea. Like him, they had left their ability to feel greater pain on the floor of the Red Room.

He shifted his stance, forcing the memory aside. "Why do you say I'm making this hard on you? I was trying to help you."

Jessica exhaled, long and weary, like answering a question she'd heard too many times. "I knew they'd target me. It's basic group psychology—when a system thrives on conformity, it finds unity in a common enemy. It's part of Realistic Conflict Theory—externalization of in-group stress through out-group derogation."

"What?"

"Scapegoating."

"Scapegoating?"

"The word 'scapegoat' originates from an ancient Jewish ritual. During the Day of Atonement, the High Priest would symbolically place the sins of the people onto a goat. This 'scapegoat' would then be sent into the wilderness or sacrificed, effectively removing the guilt of the people by *projecting it onto another.*"

"I still have no idea what you're talking about."

"Didn't you study world history?"

"Sure—just not all of it."

Jessica shook her head, cutting to the chase. "Adriana is unifying people around her by creating an external enemy—someone she can project all of her fear and anger at. In this case, me. I'm an easy target—red hair, shorter, the Aberration."

Cojax scoffed. "Adriana's a loudmouth. If she moves against the AC, she'll get Rifted. She's just another Disciple."

"She's not trying to get rid of *me*, actually quite the opposite. The longer I'm here, the more advantage it gives her. She's using that to pull people to her side, to be unified against something they hate. History is full of examples."

He was about to say that there was no way Adriana was that clever, but then he stopped himself, thinking about the Dining Hall and the people surrounding the incredibly beautiful vixen. Jessica did have a point.

Jessica opened her mouth to continue, but then she stopped, thinking better of it. She changed her words, measuring them out carefully. "Can I trust you?"

"As much as anyone can in the Mahghetto."

"I need more than that."

"On my Sacred Score, you can trust me."

Jessica thought it was ironic swearing by a Score Placard that still had a zero on it, but she didn't question it, as Cojax seemed sincere enough. "Wait here. I need to show you something—it'll explain better than words."

Before he could protest, she was gone. For a moment, Cojax bristled. Maybe she wasn't coming back. Maybe she just couldn't handle confrontation. But then he heard her returning—quick footsteps. She had run.

In her hand was a small Golden Orb, no larger than a child's fist.

He furrowed his brow. "What—"

She raised a finger to the side of her jawbone—some kind of warning. The gesture was alien. He tried to speak, but she held her finger in place until silence fell between them.

Then she pressed the orb to his chest.

It was as if the Red Room had returned to him in a burst of light. His body collapsed beneath him, strength siphoned away in seconds. His vision blurred between the pulsing of his armor and the blinding radiance of the orb. Then—darkness. His helmet blinked out. He fell hard to the floor, air gone from his lungs, every fiber of muscle turned to lead.

*"She's trapped me. She betrayed me."*

He clawed weakly at his helmet, but it was already being lifted from his head.

"You... traitor..." was all he could manage.

Jessica knelt beside him. "Are you always this dramatic? Calm down. I just needed to speak without being recorded."

He tried to speak again, but the words died on his tongue.

"You'll feel fine in a few minutes." Her voice was gentle as she placed a hand on his head. "Just rest. I'll explain everything once your strength comes back."

Time crawled. When Cojax finally managed to sit up, his breathing was labored, as if he had just finished sprinting across the parade grounds. His limbs trembled with every movement.

"What did you...do to me?" he rasped.

Jessica stayed seated. "Your Static Armor records everything. That orb—drains your energy. Without energy, the recording stops. We have about thirty minutes before it reboots."

He flexed his fingers. "My armor... it's stiff."

"It's in its default mode," she said. "No assisted movement or adjusting to your body."

Cojax pushed to his feet, wavering but upright.

"You shouldn't push yourself."

He stood stubbornly for a few more seconds, then relented, settling onto a nearby plastic shipping crate.

Jessica placed her fingers gently on his forehead. "You took it worse than most."

"Doesn't your armor record?"

"It would—if it had charge. The armor they gave us had enough power to be worn once. After that it depends on our body's energy to recharge it."

"Except yours?"

"Yes." She gave a bitter laugh. "Because I'm the Aberration. You've been engineered for energy efficiency. I haven't. My biology is... normal."

He rubbed the edge of his gauntlet. "That orb could be a weapon."

"Not really. Disciples don't have BioLocks, but Validated do. You'd need someone's CI code to do real damage, and that is encrypted."

"Where did you get it?"

She didn't answer.

Frustration crept into his voice. "Alright, enough games. Who are you? How do you know so much? You knew about the Mahghetto. You knew they'd push us into that Roach tunnel. Don't lie."

Jessica met his eyes.

"Admit it."

"I don't belong here," she said quietly. "I'm from beyond the Wall, from the world before yours."

Cojax's jaw tightened. "What you're doing is wrong."

Jessica snorted. "Wrong? Look around you. How many have died since this began? How many never even got a chance?"

"The Mahghetto follows the Acadian Code."

"It violates human decency," she snapped. "It crushes the weak to uplift the strong."

He blinked. No one spoke like that—not openly. The AC wasn't just their law. It was their religion. He was so dumbstruck, he did not have an intelligent reply. The best he could do was to repeat what he had already said. He shifted in his seat, playing for time. Finally, he came up with the response he lacked before.

"The AC is what governs our city, allocating resources perfectly. Harsh? Yes, but also necessary. Without it, we'd lose the war—we'd die to starvation and we would not have men and women strong enough to guard our Wall."

"Maybe. But how long has this war been going on?"

"Over two hundred years."

"And in all that time, have you ever heard of the Acadians trying to talk to the Roaches? Do you even know what language they speak?"

"The Roaches are mindless creatures," Cojax said, his voice rising.

"Not the Damnattii who lead them. Tell me why there's never been even an attempt to broker peace? To communicate with them? In all the history of Acadia, there's not a mention of anything like that."

He did not have a good answer to that, so he simply repeated what he knew. "Because they're Roaches."

"I think there's a different reason altogether. We are so scared of the Roaches, we give up all that we love and hold dear to fight back. Think of who you've lost, not just to the Roaches, but to the demands of Acadia. Who have you lost to Acadia?"

"We've all lost people," he said too quickly.

She didn't press, but the air between them thickened.

"You don't understand," he finally said. "It's merit-based. No bias. No favoritism. Just performance. Some are producers. Some are Dependents."

Jessica gave him a tired look. "You sound like a textbook. Easy to say when you don't know the people that are being Rifted. But, I'm willing to bet you've had someone close to you Rifted who you would not consider a Dependent—a drag on society."

These words struck Cojax to the core—a face flashed before his eyes, unsettling him. He scrambled for words, desperate to keep his world grounded. "We are the last bastion of humanity—the Last Ember," Cojax argued. "We *have* to live like this or we'll be wiped out like the rest of the world—"

"—Then how did I survive?"

That silenced him.

Jessica leaned in. "All I'm saying is, there might be a different path. Just because this is the system we find ourselves in doesn't mean it is the only way."

"You can't talk like this."

"Why not?"

"Because—" Cojax's voice cracked. "Because…"

He was on his feet now, trembling with emotion. Was it fear? No. Rage? Maybe. "You *can't* say those things—they'll kill you."

Cojax stared at her, as if seeing her for the first time. Then he turned and stormed toward the exit, his hand crushing the door handle as he left.

***

Even in the hallway, her words spun in his mind. He looked back once—twice—shaking his head. Her voice echoed louder now than when she had spoken.

Back in the massive dormitory, Brutus called out, "Look who's back. Did you have a good cry?"

Cojax didn't respond. His thoughts were still ablaze with Jessica's words.

Finn approached, laying a hand on his shoulder. "Come on, you've got to see this."

"I need to think."

"Not now. You need to see this."

With a sigh, Cojax followed. Brutus joined them, cracking a joke Cojax barely registered. They arrived at a circle of Disciples watching Romulan demonstrate his bio-circuitry.

"You move it with your thoughts?" asked one of the Disciples.

"More like your will," Romulan explained. He was the tallest in their group, lean and well-toned. The first day he was allowed to speak, he had gravitated toward Cojax and Finn.

"Show us again," Finn said.

Romulan's body lit up—lines of white raced across his arms, chest, and spine.

Cojax watched, distracted. "What's the point?"

Finn grinned. "To see in the dark, obviously. Might come in handy if you need to find the toilet and the power's out."

"Maybe we're supposed to use this with the armor," Romulan said. "Maybe it's linked."

Cojax removed his gauntlet, focusing. A faint flicker danced across his thumb before vanishing.

Romulan coached him. "Picture the light—command it."

Cojax tried again. This time his hand briefly pulsed with energy.

"Whoa," Finn said. "Do that again."

Cojax repeated the process, light flickering and fading.

One by one, others tried, comparing effects, joking, pushing boundaries. Then Cojax put his gauntlet back on and punched the concrete wall. Nothing.

Brutus laughed. "That was anticlimactic."

"I missed the timing," Cojax said. "The light didn't sync with the strike."

They kept trying. Some succeeded. Most didn't.

His mind flashed back to Jessica, when she had headbutted that Disciple only a few hours before. The energy had transferred from her lower back to her spine and then neck. The energy reached her head about the same time she struck the kid. He calmed his mind, letting it drift back to the conversation with Jessica.

His fist struck the wall with precision. A crack exploded through the surface.

Gasps followed. Praise. Jokes. Even a few warnings.

But Cojax didn't hear them.

He was somewhere else—lost in the image of his mother's face. Jessica's words had opened a wound that had never completely healed. Now it tore into him with reckless abandon, uprooting doubt and despair. A question arose he had never dared ask.

*"Why was she Released?"*

## TWENTY-FIVE

Jessica arrived at the parade grounds before sunrise. The air was cold, the silence absolute. They stood at attention for nearly half an hour before being abruptly berated for forming out of Score order. She realized, too late, that her high Score placed her in the Alpha position—front left of the column. The others, all with zeroes, followed in random chaos. With reluctant steps, she pushed to the front. Stares pierced her back like heat rays. No one said a word, but resentment thickened the air.

A pneumatic hiss. A door opened.

Thea stood at the center. "I am here to instruct you in the ways of power unfettered." She studied them, carefully walking past the sharp lines of Disciples. "It's my job to turn you, disconnected, barely functional creatures into beings of such precision and brutality that even the Roaches will recoil at your shadow. You will become Validated—Acadia's elite.

"By now, you've probably realized you've been embedded with some Top Tier Tech, the kind that would make Momma proud if she saw you. I'm sure you've seen bio-circuitry before—perhaps even tried using it. Maybe you cracked a wall and thought yourself clever."

Her eyes cut to Cojax. He stiffened. She didn't linger, but the implication landed.

"You weren't given power to impress yourselves. You were given power to destroy—to crush humans and roaches alike." She fiddled with her ArmGuard and activated a holomap of the Static Armor.

"This armor is woven from spider-silk polymers and reinforced with Vantarite, a reactive alloy stronger than anything the Ancients ever wielded. It is not just armor—it's your second skin. As long as it holds a charge, almost nothing can pierce it. But its power depends on you."

Jessica barely heard the words. She was still replaying last night's conversation with Cojax—how reckless she'd been. She'd spoken as if he were a confidant, not a Disciple. Her trust was a vulnerability, one she couldn't afford. He had every reason to turn her in.

Thea's voice cut through her spiral. "You and your armor are a closed system. Your body generates energy; your bio-circuitry distributes it. If you're idle, you recharge. If you're active, you expend. Burn too much too fast, and you hit what we call the Wall. When that happens, your systems shut down. Your armor won't carry you. And neither will we."

Jessica blinked hard, forcing her attention back. She had to distance herself from Cojax. He was dangerous—not for what he might do, but for how easily it was for her to trust him. That was harder to defend against.

"Since SataniKahns can deplete a warrior's charge in a single strike, each of you is issued a Repulse Shield."

Thea raised a circular shield with embedded light bars, rimmed in bronze-colored metal. "A shield is not a sign of weakness. It is a weapon. A properly channeled shield pulse can incapacitate an enemy or clear a swarm. Learn it. Master it. Or die."

Jessica nodded to herself. She would not die. She had paid too much to let herself simply fade away. Cojax was clearly a liability, and his friendship or pity, or whatever it was, had to stop. He was distracting her from her mission.

Thea continued, "When linked in a Phalanx formation, your shields become one. The closer you are, the stronger the link. This is called the Ion-Phalanx—a wall of energy and discipline. Any hit you take is shared across the whole. Alone, you are strong. Together, you are indomitable."

Jessica's hand flexed involuntarily.

"This unity extends beyond your shields. Your helmets contain Comm-Links and HoverCams. These will monitor every strike, every hesitation. They record your bravery—or your cowardice. Your merit will not be judged by rumors. It will be streamed, scored, and celebrated."

Jessica resisted the urge to spit.

"Now," Thea said, "let us begin with control. Your sensory

implants allow you to channel energy: speed to your legs, strength to your arms. Mastering this flow is simple. Timing it with your strikes—that is where the elite are separated from the dead."

They drilled all morning and again after lunch. In the afternoon, Thea introduced the Arc Blade to the group, pulling one from the edge of the arena and sending a pulse through it.

"Deadly beautiful in the hands of a master," Thea said, running her fingers along the spine of the blade. Though merely a training weapon—passed down through the hands of hundreds—it still carried a lethal grace, its edge whisper-thin and well-tempered with age. "Collect your blades and scabbards from the rack. These will be your weapons for now—until you prove worthy of more. Name them. Sleep with them. Let them become an extension of your will. If you treat them like tools, they'll fail you. If you treat them like limbs, they'll never leave you."

The class obeyed quickly and reformed ranks.

She fiddled with her ArmGuard again and from the ground arose detachable pillars of concrete, each one about as wide as a barrel.

"Now spread out before one of you stabs another in the back," Thea instructed. "Power comes from low stance, core rotation, and controlled aggression—not from brute strength. You'll begin with the Iron Spiral—our foundational stance. Feet shoulder-width apart, knees bent, dominant foot slightly behind. This is your anchor. From here, we transition to the Forward Hook: a rising diagonal slash aimed to break guard and open a weak point along the shoulder or neck. Then the Reaper's Descent—vertical, heavy, and designed to cleave through armor seams. Each motion must flow, no breaks, no wasted movement. Think in arcs, not strikes. Your blade should never stop moving. You are not swinging a club—you are shaping space, cutting it with precision. We'll move next to the Wrath Guard, then transition through the Crescent Arc Form, which we use to counter multi-directional attacks. Match your breathing to your motion: exhale on strike, inhale on reset."

She obeyed her own instructions, moving with a fluidity that made her armor seem like she was born with it. Each strike transitioned seamlessly into the next—elbow tucked, wrist aligned, feet shifting with coiled precision. On the final motion, she exhaled sharply and drove her Arc Blade forward in a descending cut, the blade pulsing white-hot as it activated mid-strike. The sound was more vibration than impact, like a wire humming under tension.

The concrete pillar before her didn't explode or shatter—it simply separated. For a moment, it held its shape, cleaved cleanly down the center. Then, with a faint groan, the severed half slid sideways and collapsed to the ground at a sharp angle, sending a plume of dust across the floor.

Thea lowered her blade and spoke without turning. "That is what controlled power looks like. Your turn."

The Disciples hesitated, eyes bouncing between the ruined column and the Arc Blade still glowing faintly in Thea's grip. For a breathless moment, none of them moved.

"I said your turn," Thea repeated, voice like cracking stone. "Pick up your blades. You will perform the Iron Spiral, Forward Hook, and Reaper's Descent. If your technique is sloppy, you'll lose points. If you injure someone, you'll lose blood."

Static Armor shifted as the Disciples reached for their weapons. Jessica grasped her hilt and drew the Arc Blade in a smooth motion, its weight somehow heavier than before. She glanced at the blade's edge, noting the microfilament channel that would glow once charged—dormant now, but waiting.

Across the circle, Cojax moved into position, his stance already more composed than most. Jessica noticed the way his feet found balance instinctively, his eyes already focused ahead. He wasn't just strong—he had instinct. Whether it was learned or bred into him, she couldn't say.

Jessica dropped into the Iron Spiral stance, knees bent, back straight, core tight. Her feet gripped the floor as if preparing for impact. The class moved in uneven synchrony, Arc Blades hissing through the air like slicing winds. Jessica mirrored the sequence— twist, extend, drive—each motion ingrained deeper than she dared admit. The Forward Hook flowed naturally, her hips turning smoothly into the strike. The Reaper's Descent followed, clean and controlled. But she couldn't reveal the full extent of her skill—not yet. She needed a reason to be this capable. So, she broke her rhythm, misstepped deliberately, and stumbled over her footing.

Around her, others struggled. Some flailed with too much

force, others barely committed. Sparks flew where Arc Blades activated prematurely and carved into the floor or collided with armor.

"Reset!" Thea barked. "You're not swinging hammers! These are precision weapons. If you can't respect the form, then the Roaches will feed you your own ribcage! Can anyone tell me what the most dangerous Roach is?"

"A SataniKahn," Adriana said quickly, eager to earn some extra points.

"No."

"A SataniKahn Line Cracker," Brutus tried.

"Nice guess, but no."

"Damnattii," said Jessica.

"Yes," Thea said, her voice slurring the word. "The Damnattii aren't massive like a SataniKahn, but they are incredibly intelligent—perhaps even more than us. The average is only a hand's width smaller than me. They are the ones who lead the armies of the Roaches, directing them when and where to attack. They wear Static Armor like ours and have similar blades. Quick and nimble, they are a worthy opponent. Most have three arms; some of them four. It's rare to run into one on the battlefield, but if you do, you'll have wished you spent more time in the Mahghetto learning the proper forms. For that reason, all of you will learn to duel, to fight each other with the blade—a noble tradition that still continues in Acadia today. Now, reset and try again!"

By the end of class, Jessica had clarity. She would sever whatever fragile tether existed between her and Cojax. If he was a spy, she would starve him of intel. If he was sincere, she would teach herself not to care.

That afternoon they were given a few hours for personal training and the Disciples split off in cliques. Jessica remained alone. She noticed Cojax glance her way, hesitation etched into his posture—but Brutus grabbed his arm and whispered something. Cojax turned away.

She ran laps, her body a metronome of motion. A three-minute mile—meaningless here. Others soon raced past, some using their micro-syncs too early and slamming into the walls.

Jessica remained in the Alpha position, directing and

commanding the group as they marched. But it made her dangerously visible, so she shed points throughout the day, careful to make sure it didn't look intentional. Perhaps that was all Adriana needed to see—the Aberration not in the Alpha position. It was a lie she told herself, one that she could hardly believe.

By nightfall she had fallen to the Beta position—a welcome relief. After dinner, she slipped into the storage room, eager to get away from the crowd of Disciples. Her charge was gone. Her limbs ached.

Cojax arrived moments later. He raised a finger to the side of his jawbone—mimicking her gesture from the night before, a symbol that he wanted to talk.

Jessica studied him. She thought about walking away. Or at least telling him to leave her alone. But he looked so earnest in the low light the words she had practiced all day suddenly failed her. Instead, she walked toward him, the Golden Orb in hand. Their hands met briefly as he took the strange device. Then, without hesitation, he plunged it into his own chest.

He collapsed.

It was a few minutes before he could speak clearly.

"I have to know. Where did you come from?" he asked.

Jessica's eyes narrowed. No one had ever asked. Not Elena. Not the Infinite Council.

"You don't have to be afraid of me."

"I'm not," she replied.

"Then tell me."

Jessica hesitated. "Why do you want to know?"

"Because I need to know if I can trust you."

"I'm from a village outside the Wall—about two hundred people lived there."

"Two hundred people?"

She nodded.

"No tech?"

"Some old stuff. A few handheld radios. A few guns. Tractors. We did most things by hand."

"And why didn't the Roaches attack you?"

"They lived alongside us in peace. We actually traded with them on occasion."

His resolve faltered. "You're serious?"

"Yes."

He believed her. As crazy as it all sounded, he believed her. He had seen her walk through the Killing Fields himself, seen her enter the city with her red hair whipping in the wind. He *knew* she was from outside the Wall, and it was still hard to fathom.

"So your people were at peace with the Roaches?"

"Yes, my grandfather would talk to them regularly. Sometimes they'd give us the scraps of what they didn't need—mechanical parts, broken machines, rusted tools."

"This is incredible," Cojax said. "We have to tell someone— tell everyone. If your people can have peace, why not the Acadians?"

"No," Jessica said firmly. "You can't repeat this to anyone. The moment you utter a word of this, we're both dead. The only reason I'm alive is that I've never told this to anyone—at least not while I was being recorded. Do you understand?"

Cojax stood up, pacing the room. "That doesn't make any sense. Why wouldn't they ask you about that—about any of this? We lose hundreds of thousands of Acadians every year in this war. Are you sure they never questioned you? Maybe you just didn't realize you were being questioned."

"I had to learn the language first. After that, I only talked to a handful of people—almost all of them were my guardians. I only told one of them and that was in secret."

"Why wouldn't the Infinite Council question you?"

Jessica's voice was like ice. "There's only one reason why."

"Because they already knew," Cojax whispered.

That broke something in him. A tumbling cascade of thoughts mixed with emotions, all of them leading to one final conclusion.

"This war… it's a lie."

She didn't answer.

"Why would they want the war to continue?"

Jessica shrugged. "I don't know."

"Blood and bile, why?" he cursed, hardly able to believe his own words. He began pacing again, his mind racing to new possibilities. "My father knew. My father knows."

"How would he know?"

"His name is Titan and he was one of the two Numberless who found you at the Northern Gate. He's part of the Infinite Council."

He clenched his fists. His mind spiraled—his mother, the Killing Field, her Release.

"He knew," Cojax whispered. "He knew… and he let her die."

# TWENTY-SIX

Marcus had borrowed a CarrierLift from the BloodBorne faction building, costing him a few points in return. But the price was of little concern—his Civil Union had greatly subsidized his Score, allowing him the occasional guilty pleasure of studying ancient history: the pride of the Romans, the oration of the Greeks, the mistakes of the Americans, the customs of the Chinese, the collapse of the EU, globalism, and the fractured world that followed. For two hours a day, he could indulge in his reading and suffer no deduction—a luxury he had never experienced before. He felt embarrassed by it, almost ashamed, especially the way Aleniana would look at him as he read from his Tech Pad, poring over the deeds and rhetoric of people long turned to dust. Her gaze cast judgment so intense, he could feel it from ten spans away.

The CarrierLift proved its worth, allowing him to move all his possessions in one trip—offsetting the cost of borrowing it in the first place. It was sleek and wheeled, worn but well-maintained, as were most things in Acadia. Though primarily used for official duties, it served him just as well now. He packed everything in: his uniforms, undergarments, Blazer, Arc Spear, a second suit of armor that had cost his Score dearly, his Tech Pad, and his prized possession—a broadsword better suited for dueling. It was modeled after a Claymore, though not as long. Straight, heavy, and brutal, it could hemorrhage an opponent's shields even with a glancing blow. He still used his Kopis when fighting Roaches—their tight, clawing swarms made the smaller, heavier-ended blade ideal.

He looked over everything with pride. All of it earned. His Score had dipped with each request, each allotment, but it had always recovered. His battlefield skill more than compensated for the treasures he acquired. And now, with his subsidized Score... well, suffice it to say, things were looking up for Marcus, First into the Gap at the Battle of Menoch.

He was halfway unpacked when someone knocked at the door. He looked up, hope rising—then deflating just as quickly, like an exploding Ankle Biter.

They had been married for months, and he still did not know the woman who was now his wife. They spoke, of course, but only functionally.

"Where are you off to?"

"The battlefield."

"Oh. Well. See you later then. Give those Roaches hell."

"Alright."

And that would be considered a long conversation.

The closest they came to something meaningful was when a Reever had torn open her side. It was moderately deep—and bloody. She could've hailed a Medicus via her ArmGuard, but that would've drained her Score, transferring points to whoever treated her. Medici each carried a Solaris—a medical device that harnessed solar radiation filtered through adaptive nanocrystal lenses, accelerating cellular regeneration and sterilizing wounds in seconds. But using it came at a steep cost. So she'd tried to stitch herself up instead—and made a horror show of it. She spread thread at odd angles, sometimes stabbing too deeply, sometimes not enough. Marcus didn't get queasy, but he'd reached his limit when a squirt of blood shot across the room.

She protested. He insisted. It wasn't until he pulled rank that she relented.

As he worked, he noticed the scars—old, messy, patchy. She talked while he stitched. Mostly about nothing. How it happened. How she'd cut herself in mundane ways. And for one strange moment, she wasn't a stranger. She was a person. But the moment passed so quickly, he wasn't sure it had happened at all.

Aleniana entered, arms full—two boxes in hand, her Blazer and Arc Spear strapped to her Static Armor. She hadn't walked far, but burdened as she was, Marcus was surprised she hadn't dropped something along the way.

"You can use the CarrierLift," he said, nodding toward the cart beside him.

"No," she replied, voice thick with contempt, as if he'd just offered to kidnap her siblings.

"It's fine," Marcus said, confused. "Easy to use. The top just slides open."

"No," she repeated, her eyes narrowing.

Marcus nodded slowly, grateful he still wore his armor. She looked just angry enough to strike him. He shrugged, pushed the cart out, and returned it to the ground floor. The Acadian System acknowledged the return and deducted a precise amount from his Score. He barely noticed. Aleniana's icy demeanor occupied his mind completely.

He turned toward the family room and found his favorite chair, Tech Pad resting against it. This new home was larger—three rooms: one primary, two secondary. A bigger bathroom, kitchen, dining area—all prepped and equipped to handle six incoming babies.

Technically, a Scholastica Genetica would bring the babies into the world—growing them in vats. He and Aleniana wouldn't receive the children until four months after inception. They'd arrive three-quarters of the way into the gestation, suspended in purple vat liquid, monitored for two more months until…well…until he was a father.

*"But a father of what?"* Marcus wondered, surprised at the unease in his mind. Acadia had his genetic code. He'd always assumed the offspring would be his, that they'd mix his DNA with Aleniana's. But now, doubt gnawed at him. He remembered his triplet brothers—all born the same day, yet as different as snowflakes in winter.

"Ehh," he muttered, disturbed.

He looked toward the shelf. Six vats. Empty for now, but already ominous. Monitoring them wouldn't be difficult. The instructions on his ArmGuard were clear: check for cracks, maintain stable temperatures, ensure milestones were met. It sounded more like baking than parenting. Unless the oven exploded, it was mostly a waiting game.

He picked up his Tech Pad, eager to escape thoughts of half-formed babies floating in synthetic goo. Aleniana made two more trips to finish moving her belongings. At one point, Marcus had stood to help, but the look she gave him froze him in place. He didn't move again until she was gone.

When she finally sat across from him, she looked exhausted.

Sweat beaded her brow. Dark circles weighed under her eyes. She always woke early and returned late. Where she went, Marcus didn't know. Her Second Stewardship was as a Scholastica Biologica—some sort of plant doctor, or maybe a plant geneticist. He wasn't sure. And asking felt like he'd be putting his head in a bear trap.

"Well, here we are," Marcus said, forcing a smile. He regretted the words instantly. He was smart, always the top among his peers— but since the Civil Union, and especially around his…his wife, he was reduced to stating the obvious.

*"She must think I'm an idiot,"* he thought.

"And here I go," Aleniana replied, standing slowly.

"We just got here," Marcus said, another obvious remark. "Stay. Rest. You look like you need it."

Despite the separation in Tiers, despite his higher Score, she erupted in anger.

"That would be what you want, wouldn't it? For me to rest, to curl into a ball like some monumental Dependent—your Dependent! I'd love to sit here flipping through the ramblings of people so long dead their bones have crumbled into dust. But I have a Score to maintain!"

Marcus stood in shock, mouth agape, like a fish gasping on dry land. She couldn't speak to him like this—not here. Not in Acadia. He rose, anger surging. He was a First Tier. A Gamma. A commander of ten thousand. Son of a Numberless. First into the gap at the Battle of Menoch.

"Listen here," Marcus snapped, jabbing a finger like a blade. But the words wouldn't come. He didn't even know what they were fighting about.

"I'm a First Tier," he finally said. "Not some glitching isotope from the Red District."

"Oh, is that so?" Aleniana shot back. "Funny, I didn't realize you were in the First Tier. I hadn't noticed your fancy meals or extra armor upgrades. I can't even afford to maintain my Static Armor— and you have two Arc Blades. What do you do with the second one—wipe your butt with it?"

Marcus was thoroughly confused now.

"No, I can't rest. I can't wait. I can't sleep in!" Aleniana screamed. "You dimmed Rifter! I hope the Rift swallows you whole! I hope the next Roach rips off your head and pukes wax down your throat!"

That was too far.

He reached for his ArmGuard. Hovered over the report button. He'd only used it once. Didn't know exactly what happened when it was pressed—but it somehow flagged the conversation for the Acadian System to review. If he didn't report it, and somehow the Acadian System found out anyway, he'd lose points as well. In a city of ten million, order came before mercy. Subordinates couldn't be allowed to disrespect superiors—not in Acadia.

He remembered the only time he had used it. A group of Tenth Tiers, cocky from a run on the Killing Fields—probably their first battle after the Crossing in the Mahghetto. They ran into him, knocking something out of his hands—a Tech Pad or stylus of some sort, he could not remember. One of them insulted him as they sprinted off. His first instinct was to run after them, bash their skulls together, maybe see what color their brains were. But fighting outside dueling arenas was prohibited. So he reported them. The next day, he only saw two of the warriors, but they bowed before him like he was a Numberless, apologizing so quickly and frequently it all slurred together.

Now, as his hand hovered again, ready to flag the conversation for the Acadian System, something in Aleniana broke.

"I can't..." she whispered, voice trembling. "I can't keep up. I can't match your Score. I can't keep going like this..."

And suddenly it clicked. Her early mornings. Her exhaustion. Her Tier would never match his. Not now. Not ever.

"But you're Third Tier now," Marcus said gently. "That's better than when we met."

"I haven't slept since," she said, tears streaking her face. "I'm doing everything I can..."

"It's okay," Marcus said. "Third Tier is fine."

Her words came in sobs now. "I just can't... fight like you. I'm not as good. And the children... what will they think of me?"

He pulled her closer, not into a hug, as such things were... well... not forbidden, but certainly not common. One adult hugging another who was not your pair just seemed weird—like a sword with two handles. Of course, she was his pair, but it still seemed weird.

Hugs were for Dependents who had not even earned the Right of Speech. The last person he hugged, or rather that hugged him, was his mother—right before she was ripped apart by Roaches. It's odd that popped into his head at that moment.

Their breath mingled. Their skin nearly touched. Not quite. But almost.

Then her armor flashed—a discreet shift in its luminescence. To the untrained eye, it meant nothing. But in Acadia, everyone saw Scores first.

Aleniana was now Fourth Tier.

Her outburst had cost her dearly.

Marcus' Score had dropped too. He hadn't reported the infraction in time.

He shook his head. "How did it know? How did it know to monitor this conversation? Cameras? Voice tone? Heart rate?"

"I have to go now," Aleniana said, wiping tears from her face. She straightened her back, stepped away, and saluted.

"I forgot my place, First Tier Marcus of the BloodBorne."

"It wasn't me," he whispered.

"I know."

"It's almost night. Please...," but he didn't know how to finish that sentence. She was beautiful in that moment, her cheeks glistening, her body more relaxed than rigid. This was his wife but she was a stranger in so many ways. He knew more about the types of Roaches and how each of them could be killed or how they would try to kill him. He wanted her to stay more than anything. "Please...please stay with me."

Aleniana looked so distant in that moment that in his mind's eye, they were leagues apart, two people on different continents separated by an ocean of differences. She hesitated a little longer, and for a moment Marcus thought she would stay, but then she turned without another word, retrieving her Arc Blade, helmet, Blazer, and Shield and headed for the door, no doubt off to volunteer for a shift at the Wall.

## TWENTY-SEVEN

Cojax retrieved his thermosteam tray, enjoying the sweet smell of his food. It had everything he had ever wanted and more: golden pancakes, sizzling bacon, a warm blueberry muffin, an omelet topped with synthetic cheddar, and a chilled glass of authentic apple juice—the real kind, not the enzyme-reconstructed variety.

He sat down first, Finn joining a second later.

"You know," Finn joked, "I hate to say it, but I really like being in the First Tier." He likewise had a spread of food that was fit for nobility. It was different, as he had selected sausage instead of bacon and waffles instead of pancakes, but it was all made with the same quality. He was the second one to retrieve his food, just after Cojax, as was his right as the Beta.

The rest of the Disciples filed in after, forming into four lines next to the chutes. First Tiers went first, followed by Second Tiers, and finally by Third.

In only two weeks, Cojax had risen to the Alpha position, his rage translating into motivation. Jessica's conversation had not only upset his world, it also fueled it—pushing him to new levels of success. He became a driving force, his momentum carrying from the parade grounds to the lecture halls and into the dormitory. Instead of talking at night with the other Disciples, he preferred to practice with the blade alongside Finn, Romulan, and Jessica. The harder, the better. It gave him clarity.

Finn wasn't far behind. Shortly after Cojax claimed the top spot, he rose to number two.

"It's odd there's only three Tiers in the Mahghetto," Finn said. "Why make it different than Acadia?"

"It makes it simple," Cojax answered.

It was a few minutes before Brutus, Romulan, and Callista sat down, their food selection not nearly as glorious. Brutus had a bran muffin, a meat stick, powdered eggs, and water with a hint of flavoring. He scowled as he looked first at Cojax's food and then at his Placard, a clear resentment of his Score. He was near the top, but he was still Second Tier, unable to close the gap between himself and his friends. More Disciples crowded around, all eager to get seats around the Tier Setters—the rising few. These had become their new core of friends, all displaying a unique loyalty—Romulan, Callista, Sandrix, Ester, Horacio, and Havish. There were more, but the others seemed to float from group to group. These followed Cojax not because he was just the Alpha, but because they respected him as a leader. Romulan was tall and eager, with the boundless energy of someone who hadn't yet learned caution. Callista—short, sharp-eyed, and undeniably beautiful—carried herself with the confidence to match. Sandrix moved at his own pace, slow but steady, the kind of reliability you could set a clock by. Horacio, a genius of design and spatial sense, could judge the distance between two walls to the exact inch without measuring. Havish was quiet and reserved, but lethal with a blade—like most who prefer silence over boasting.

Having a higher Score came with a little popularity. When Adriana finally retrieved her food, Cojax raised a fork of cheesy eggs and winked. She rolled her eyes before finding her normal table, a smaller space in the back. She still had a following but had lost much of her influence.

"What a Dependent," Cojax said.

"Who?" Finn asked.

"Adriana," Cojax answered. "She came down here trying to play a different game, to change the rules to suit her. Now she looks like a fool."

"Yes, a fool," Finn said with a distant look. "A beautiful, slightly taller… possibly kissable…"

"Egh," Cojax answered. "She's a beast."

"I'm with Finn on this one," Brutus answered. "She might have a lower Score, but her looks are Top Tier."

"Yeah, until you get to know her," Cojax answered.

"Maybe we just don't know her well enough," Brutus asserted.

"No," Cojax answered.

"If she were an ally, we'd own this place," Brutus said.

"An ally?" Cojax said. "Is your helmet too small for your

head? Remember how she tried to manipulate the system, how she insulted me? You saw how one of her lackeys attacked Jessica."

"You mean the Aberration," Brutus answered.

Cojax tightened his jaw, clear anger flashing through his features. The two friends would never agree on this point. His eyes floated over to the red-headed girl in the corner. She sat at a table with a few others, but only out of necessity—there were no more available seats. She never wasted time. Even now she was studying the various Roach species on her ArmGuard while she ate.

He had wanted to invite her to sit with them, to share in their conversation, to get to know his friends that much better. Brutus and Finn argued against it, both for very different reasons. Brutus simply asserted that "she's the Aberration" as if this were a well-thought-out assessment. Finn, on the other hand, thought it might undermine their fragile shift in popularity, forcing Disciples to once again make a choice.

Finn noticed the direction of his gaze and leaned forward, speaking so only Cojax could hear. "Give it a few weeks, and then, she can come sit with us. Last thing we need is to give Adriana more fuel for the fire. Wait until everyone is a little more comfortable with…the…I mean, Jessica."

Cojax relented, looking back down at his food. He had spoken with the girl almost every night—a highlight of his rather repetitive day. She was so different than he had first thought, warm instead of cold, thoughtful instead of demanding. But no one else seemed to notice, or care. She knew a truth that could very well change the war—change the entire city. And yet no one knew. Jessica was a Second Tier and most treated her as if she were invisible.

*"Better that than something worse,"* Cojax thought. The dynamics of the class had shifted with him at the top, completely undermining Adriana's ability to do anything but sulk. A few more weeks and any influence she had would be gone completely.

"What did you all think of the Damnattii image Magister Octavian showed us the other day?" Romulan asked.

"I thought they'd be taller," Finn answered.

"I'd cut them down as easily as I pummeled Romulan the other day."

Romulan turned red. "Well, if you used your blade more like

a sword instead of a club, I might stand a better chance."

"You know who would have really loved to learn about the Damnattii?" Finn said with a faint smile.

"Hadrian. He loved collecting those battle cards," Cojax answered, reflecting his friend's smile.

"Sure," Brutus answered. "But even if he...," He started, stumbling on his words. "...if he made it past the first day, he would have never made it this far. It was a mercy."

"He would've done fine," Finn argued.

"He didn't have the will," Brutus replied bluntly. "The Games nearly broke him."

Cojax rested his fork. "Remember when he glued a metal plate to his chest and said it was a Placard?"

Finn chuckled. "He begged for Scores. I kept asking him for water, even when I wasn't thirsty. Promised him a thousand points, and he ran like it was his life."

They laughed, just for a moment.

"He'll be missed," Cojax said quietly.

"He's gone now," Brutus said. Final.

"I hope that doesn't happen to us," Finn whispered.

"We're Top Tier," Cojax said, forcing a smile. "They can't Rift everyone."

Brutus clenched his jaw, nodding to Adriana. "Not if she has something to say about it. She's planning something. And we need to be ready to adapt."

"She's not Alpha," Cojax said.

"She can't touch us," Finn added. "Our Score is what matters. Let her plot. Let her plan. She's nothing but a Mid Tier."

Brutus didn't back down. "Still... influence is influence. We don't have to like her to use her."

"We better get into formation," Cojax said, eager to change the one topic that Brutus just could not let go of. "We've got Blazer training first thing in the morning with Magister Orchulli."

## TWENTY-EIGHT

The following morning, the Disciples were herded into a long, rectangular chamber—low ceiling, endless length. It resembled a forgotten mineshaft, industrial and uninviting. A Magister informed them this had once been a coal tunnel. Now, it was a gun range.

The walls were padded with a strange, spongy material that flexed without yielding. Along one side, an arsenal stretched—Blazers, Reachers, Hedgers. Familiar weapons and fearsome ones. Yet not a single neck twisted to gawk. The Mahghetto had burned out that kind of curiosity.

Jessica's eyes found the Blazer first. Mid-range, standard issue. Its contours were clean but boxy, a two-finger trigger flanked by colored buttons, a blunt energy pad on the stock. Utilitarian. Ugly. Deadly.

Orchulli stepped forward—lean frame, shoulders squared like a born performer. He picked up a Blazer and twirled it with an ease that mocked its weight.

"Once upon a time," he began, letting the weapon drift lazily across the room, barrel grazing several faces, "Disciples flinched when I flagged them. Seems we've bred that out."

Then he fired.

A Disciple in the second row took the hit square in the chest. His shields caught it, but he stumbled back, startled, clumsy. His body language screamed injury, though no damage showed.

"There it is," the Magister said dryly. "Hesitation. Back in line, maggot. You're still breathing. Move."

The youth saluted and stepped back—just in time for a second, heavier blast to crash into him. This time the light hit like a cannonball, knocking him into a roll.

"Blazers," the Magister said, now in a hush, "have options. No magazine, no reload. You are the source of their power. You there, second row."

He pointed the muzzle directly at Jessica's forehead.

She answered without flinching. "Blazers rely on energy. The trigger initiates the release, but the power level determines projectile mass and behavior—like the Arc Blade."

A flicker of approval twitched across his face. "Yes. And that determines not just the number of shots, but also the type of projectile discharged. There are ten types—armor-piercing, Super Nova, cutter, tracker... too many for your tiny minds. You'll learn—eventually, after I've explained it a dozen times.

"In this room, on this range, I am your glorious master, ruler of all that happens. I don't care about your Score. I care if you can shoot. That's why I'm here. Orchulli—Master of the Blazer. Second Tier. I earned it six years after the Mahghetto. But everyone calls me Orch."

He spun toward a Disciple at the end of the line. "That's impressive, right?"

The girl hesitated—half a second too long.

Boom. A head-sized sphere of light launched from his rifle and slammed her into the ground. She wobbled upright, disoriented but breathing.

"Direct hits won't breach your shields," Orch said. "But they'll remind you that you're mortal. So why use Blazers at all?"

His eyes found Jessica again.

"Roaches have carapaces, not shields," she replied. "The right projectile, right place—they'll puncture. Damnattii have shields, and every shot depletes them."

He chuckled darkly. "Good. Some of you actually watched the CityScreens for intel, not just entertainment. I'm glad to see that my good friends weren't dying on the Killing Fields for no reason."
Jessica bit her lip. That knowledge might've saved her from a projectile—but it had marked her.

"Swords are faster," Orch said, beginning to pace. "But these? Blazers are power condensed. They ignore wind. Distance. They cut with light. Ancient humans used metal slugs. That tore flesh. This—" he fired another shot, slicing a nearby target in half. "This tears reality."

Then he stopped. Stared. Raised the rifle.

It pointed straight at Cojax.

Orch opened fire.

Cojax caught the first three rounds—helmet, legs, ribs—and dropped. But he adjusted quickly, using his arms and weight to deflect the next blasts. He ducked, pivoted, absorbed. Then a ball of energy slammed into his head. He flipped backward, armor flaring. More shots followed—relentless. Cojax rolled, absorbed, endured.

Thirty, maybe forty rounds.

The firing speed slowed as the Magister gauged his shots. Then a final projectile hit Cojax square in the chest and his shield broke, his armor slumping.

Finally, Orch grinned. "Impressive energy signature, Mr. Cojax. You'd make a fine battery."

Cojax returned to formation, stiff, armor sagging, but standing.

"Remember," Orch said, addressing the room, "Blazers are economics. Each shot drains more from your enemy than it costs you. They don't win battles—they soften them. You won't see my swordplay on the Screens. But I've brought down enemies by the hundreds. With this."

He raised the Blazer.

"Now. Retrieve your weapons."

Cojax went first, still breathing hard. Jessica followed, resisting the urge to look around.

"Recharge time, Mr. Cojax?" Orch asked. "Thirty minutes?"

"Twenty," Cojax replied.

"Impressive," Orch nodded. "Must be your mother in you."

Cojax stiffened. He didn't speak. He couldn't.

"When you're transporting your weapon, your barrel should be pointed either up at the sky or down at the floor," Orch instructed. "Never at your squadmates. When you hear 'Fix Blazers,' slap it to your back. Like so."

He demonstrated. The rifle locked in place without a sound.

"Now you try."

Weapons swung.

"What are you doing?" Orch barked. "I literally just told you the command and 'now you try' was not it."

Confusion.

"Fix Blazers."

Several dozen rifles clunked to the floor. Only one stayed put. Jessica's.

She winced.

"Ah. Forgot to mention," Orch said, smirking. "It works with your bio-circuitry to lock onto your armor. You have to *will* it into place—like you did to open and release your armor. Try again."

This time, no one fell for it. Orch laughed at his own game. Then he repeated the correct command, "Fix Blazers."

Most still failed. Too hard. Too clumsy. Too slow. Jessica moved like she'd done it a hundred times. Orch noticed.

He stepped in close. "Fix Blades."

A handful moved—Jessica didn't.

"Jessica," he said. "What's the command to sling your Blazer?"

"Fix Blazers, sir."

"And what did I say?"

"Fix Blades, sir."

He smiled faintly. "Attention to detail saves lives. Out there—and here."

He turned away.

"Last row. Step to the red line."

The Disciples obeyed, heading to the front of the class and squaring off with the firing line, the bodies bladed toward the 100-yard range.

The room shimmered as the HoloSynth Array activated, casting high-resolution spectral projections across the range. Dozens of Roach constructs emerged—fast, erratic, semi-transparent phantoms with jittering limbs and razor-thin outlines. Their movements were so fluid they might have been real. The projections even left heat trails in the air, as if daring someone to believe they weren't just light and code. Among the Roaches were pillars of concrete, many of them mimicking the openings of Roach holes or rock outcroppings.

"Radial Motion Optics off for now. Iron sights only. Open fire."

Beams of light streaked wildly. Most missed entirely.

Orch was not surprised, but he certainly wasn't impressed. "I guess I should just be grateful most of you were able to find the trigger. Open fire."

The Disciples obeyed, eager to prove their Tier. They had been studying with the Arc Blade for weeks now, their confidence growing. Most had seen the Blazer as an inferior weapon, something that only Dependents used and one that they would quickly master. They were wrong.

"The Blazer is not a butcher's knife," Orch said. "It's a weapon of finesse and skill. You must first learn to use your iron sights just in case your fancy tech fails you in the field. The rear sight has to line up with the front; the little ball should be seated into the saddle. Most of you are anticipating the recoil from the Blazer and your barrels are dipping before you even pull the trigger. Let's give it one more try. Open fire."

Within moments, Orch called for a ceasefire. "I didn't think it was possible, but you're actually getting worse. The only thing safe down range are the actual targets."

He let out a long breath. "Let's try a different tack. Step back. Jessica. Front and center."

She obeyed, charging her weapon silently. Orch's voice dropped low. "Have you held one before?"

Jessica said nothing.

"Show me."

She fired three shots—wide. Purposefully.

Orch leaned in, voice barely audible.

"You're not fooling anyone, girly. Impress me—or I'll make you pay."

Jessica swallowed hard. *"He knows."*

Panic bloomed in her chest, tight and suffocating. She had fired a Blazer hundreds of times—many of them in this very chamber. Elena had insisted on at least some experience with the weapon because if she failed the qualifications, it would mean her Rifting. That alone had been reason enough. But Jessica had gone beyond the basics. She hadn't just trained—she had fallen in love with the weapon. The weight, the recoil, the heat in her arms when she overcharged a shot. It became her escape, her obsession. Elena had risked everything by smuggling her into the Mahghetto to train after hours. It had been reckless, illegal, unforgettable. And now, Jessica was paying for it—not because she was inept, but because she was too good. Too smooth. Too precise. Better than someone with her Score had any right to be.

"A sniper sees everything," Orch said. "I'm watching."

She opened fire, this time markedly better, but still not great. She hit two out of three targets and the interactive projections reeled in pain, hissing at her with fury and screams.

Orch shook his head. "What am I going to do with you?"

Jessica raised the rifle to fire again. Orch kicked her—hard. A charged boot slammed into her spine. She flipped, hit the ceiling, then crashed through a training projection. She rolled. Came up on one knee. Aimed at Orch.

She was ready to fight.

Orch grinned. He was enjoying this whole spectacle more than he should have. "We have a Disciple downrange. Must've wandered off."

A pause. Then a grin. "Ten of you. One of her. I'm not the best at math, but it seems like even odds. Jessica, your objective is to disable their weapons. The rest of you, shoot her until she yields."

Panic seized her spine. "*No,*" she thought. This wasn't the test she'd expected. It wasn't a spar—it was an execution. Ten rifles shifted toward her.

Then the range erupted.

Beams of light seared through the air, hammering the walls, floor, and ceiling in a wild, erratic barrage. Jessica dove, barely slipping behind a concrete barrier. It absorbed a few hits before sizzling, its surface eroding in ragged chunks as if gnawed apart by invisible teeth.

Her breath caught. "*Will he stop them once my armor loses its charge? Will he even notice when it does?*"

Elena's old lessons surged forward—footage of Blazer wounds, cauterized craters punched through unshielded flesh. She swallowed hard, centering herself. She needed to focus. She needed control.

"*Focus. Breathe. Concentrate.*"

Then she saw it. Her ten opponents were missing. Badly.

Light scattered everywhere—none of it accurate. Despite the numbers, they couldn't shoot. A sharp grin split her lips.

She rolled from cover, Blazer raised. The first shots she fired weren't lethal—just disorienting. Flash Bangs exploded in bursts of white light and thunder, scattering five of the Disciples like startled insects.

She moved.

Four tight blasts from her rifle turned two Blazers into shrapnel. Metal hissed and split, the energy cores rupturing. That was the trick: aim for the weapon, not the wielder. It worked. The panic set in.

A few tried to flee. Big mistake. She dropped two more rifles. Then pain. A bolt slammed into her shoulder, twisting her sideways. She let the momentum carry her into a dive, rolled, came up firing— another Disciple's rifle exploded in their hands.

Half down. And she was only getting started.

The rest regrouped. Five of them, smarter now, using cover.

They moved in formation—alternating fire, communicating by Comm-Link. Left. Right. Left again. Predictable, but punishing. Jessica took four hits, armor flaring with each one.

*"Adapt or die."* One of Elena's old war maxims.

She pressed herself low, letting two blasts scream overhead. Their rhythm was perfect. Too perfect. She saw the flaw.

The firing alternated with such predictability, it was mechanical—one side fired, then the other. In that heartbeat between volleys, she moved.

The left side paused.

She ran. Leaped. Twisted mid-air like a falling feather. She hit the ground behind them, her Blazer snapping up before they even turned.

Three targets.

One tried to call it in. "She's—"

Jessica fired. A LightBomb flared against the girl's back, sending her cartwheeling through a target. The other two hesitated— long enough to lose their weapons.

Two left.

Jessica sprinted, heart pounding, lungs burning. She needed position. Energy. Cover. Her last LightBomb had sapped precious energy from her shields.

She dove behind a concrete barrier near the firing line. The range fell silent, save for the low whine of discharged Blazers and the breathless awe of the onlookers behind the red line. The smell of ozone mixed with metallic soot filled the air.

No one moved. No one gave her away.

She peeked out. A pair of boots shuffled across the far edge of a target.

She switched ammo types. Fired. A thin projectile designed to pierce the hard carapace of a Reever's skull. It hit her target in the helmet with so much force, he flipped back, his weapon breaking from his grip. He panicked and turned, crawling toward his weapon.

Jessica was already running.

She snatched the dropped rifle and aimed both barrels at his chest. According to the rules of this wicked game, he should have been out already, but he lunged for his weapon.

She twisted but he grabbed her Blazer. The struggle began. He was stronger. He used one hand to hold the weapon, the other to pummel her. She took two hard hits to the helmet. Her shield still held, but her head rocked from the impacts. He had synced his strikes perfectly with his bio-circuitry. Without a helmet, each strike would have caved her skull. He spun her, dragging her like a ragdoll. Slammed her into a target.

She held on.

He twisted again—another slam. She gritted her teeth. *"Think."*

He had the front. She had the trigger. She pulsed energy into the grip. The Blazer vibrated.

He noticed—too late.

It exploded.

The LightBomb ripped into his chest, hurling him backward. Jessica stood, barely. Her head rang. Her vision tunneled. She checked her second rifle. Still charged.

Then—nothing.

Her armor failed. The charge dissipated. Her limbs suddenly dragged with dead weight. She lowered the Blazer, pretending calm, but her arms trembled. She took a knee, her breath coming in ragged wheezes. This wasn't strategy. It was survival. Her first Blazer was toast. The second had a shot or two left. But she was slow. Vulnerable.

*"I need to yield."*

But she didn't. Her pride overcame her survival instincts. *"I can do this. I can still win."*

A shadow flanked her. One last enemy. Medium build. Close. Too close to miss. Her hands tensed. Her breath locked in her throat.

A flash.

Jessica was thrown to the ground. But she didn't fall alone. The other boy tumbled backwards, weapon spinning out of reach.

Jessica blinked.

Orch stood where she'd been. Smoke curled off his armor. He looked amused, an oddly genuine smile on his lips. He had taken the hit for her. He had saved her.

"Not bad, little girly," Orch said. "Not bad at all."

## TWENTY-NINE

Cojax and Jessica met again that night—it was becoming their unspoken routine. Her armor had long since drained its charge; his still hummed faintly, pulsing along the edges of his limbs. This time, the Golden Orb only brought him to his knees—not flat on his face like before. A marked improvement.

He rose slowly, lungs drawing in air like he'd earned it.

Jessica grinned. "Congratulations. You've now been Alpha longer than anyone else—and with a healthy lead. Finn is the Beta, right? Is he your friend?"

"Best of friends."

"He seems talented."

"And funny," Cojax added. "Once he gets going with his stories, you'll be laughing so hard you'll forget to breathe."

"And the other one?"

"Brutus?" Cojax chuckled. "He's funny too—but in a different sense. He's the type to snap your photo and edit it in a creative way. It's funny—unless you're the target. We've been close since we were kids. There was another brother, Hadrian... but he didn't make it."

Jessica's posture straightened. Her voice turned serious. "Why are you protecting me?"

Cojax met her gaze. "Why did you save my life?"

She frowned. "What are you talking about?"

"In the tunnel," he said. "You guided me out. I know it was you."

"No, I—"

"Oh, come on," he said with a light laugh. "I'd bet my Placard on it."

She didn't reply.

"Close your eyes," he said, extending his hand. "Now, give me your hand."

"You should've asked in the reverse order," she said, smirking. "Now I can't even see where your hand is."

He reached forward and gently took hers. It was small, smooth—like sculpted marble. He repositioned it slightly.

"There," he said with quiet certainty. "That's exactly how you held it. That's how you led me through the Descension."

She laughed. "Do you use that line on all the girls?"

Color rose to Cojax's cheeks. He released her hand, rubbing his palms together to disguise the sudden tension.

"That proves nothing," she said softly.

"You're still not telling me everything," he said.

"About what?"

"About why you're truly here—what you're hoping to accomplish. I know you've been helped, and don't tell me you haven't. I've never seen someone handle a Blazer as well as you did today. And you're much better with the blade than you're letting on."

Jessica looked down. Something flickered behind her eyes—a storm of conflict, restrained by force of will. "I want to trust you."

"Then do," Cojax said gently. "I already trust you."

"Why?"

"Because no one risks their life for someone else in the Mahghetto. No one. You did."

"That doesn't mean anything."

"It does to me," Cojax said, his voice and eyes lowering. "I'm ashamed to admit, I was terrified in that cave. Pitch black with nothing but the noise of the Reevers in my ears. It... would have been a bad way to go."

He looked so vulnerable in that moment, so small. Without hardly thinking, she pulled him into an embrace. Deep and sudden. Her arms drew him into a warmth he hadn't felt since childhood.

He froze, unsure how to react. Of course, he *knew* what a hug was—technically. But in Acadia, such gestures were reserved for children, not Disciples of the Mahghetto, or even Innocents for that matter. The last hug he had received was from his mother—on the day she was Released. She had held him just like this, in defiance of the Code. That single act might have cost her everything.

And yet, it was all he had left of her.

He hugged Jessica back.

His hand slid to the back of her head. Her hair was soft, silky. He closed his eyes and held her. When she finally pulled away, the absence felt cold.

"Thank you for believing me," she said.

He nodded. "That's my first hug in a long time."

"Why is it," she asked, "that you Acadians insist on showing as little emotion as possible?"

"You lose points if you don't."

"Why?"

He blinked, confused. "...Because hugs are for children."

"Not where I come from. Friends, family—anyone leaving or returning gets one."

He tilted his head. "Odd. What does that accomplish?"

She shot back, "What does *not* hugging accomplish?"

Cojax considered it—but didn't let it show. "It's just a silly tradition. Takes time."

"If it's so silly, why did you hold on for so long?"

He looked away. Her words stirred something deep. His mind drifted again to his mother—to her arms, her scent, her final gaze.

"What are you thinking?" Jessica asked softly.

He blinked and met her eyes. "Nothing."

"Why the sudden silence? You can trust me."

He smiled faintly and sat back down. "Now you're stealing my lines."

"Fine. You don't have to tell me."

After a long pause, he spoke. "My mother was Honorably Released."

Jessica sat beside him, her voice gentle. "Why?"

"I don't know. I was young. But I remember the day like it was yesterday." He stared at the far wall, his voice distant. "She hugged me—really hugged me—after the noon meal. Not the usual side-pat. This one felt... final. Then she walked out the door and that was it. They sent her into the Killing Field. Called it an Honorable Release. I watched her die on the CityScreens."

Jessica's hand closed over his. "I'm so sorry."

He flinched at the contact but didn't pull away. If anything, the touch steadied him.

"She was talented," he said. "Strong. My father always said

she was First Tier once. I can't understand why they Released her."

"She didn't deserve it."

"Everyone here has someone they lost. If not to the Killing Field, then to the Rift. Parents, siblings, mentors—it doesn't matter. They just vanish."

"All those lives… gone before their time."

"That's not fair to say."

"What about your mother?"

He hesitated. "There had to be a reason."

"What reason could there possibly be for taking a mother from her child?" Jessica's voice trembled with fury.

He pulled his hand away, eyes dropping to the glowing lines of his ArmGuard.

"It's not right," he admitted. "But it doesn't matter. Unless your Placard reads 'Numberless,' no one listens. We're too small to change anything. Maybe it's better this way. Maybe this is what our society *needs* to survive."

"I would've died here without help," Jessica said. "Acadia would have crushed me. Like Hadrian. Like your mother. I would've been another casualty."

He felt it then—something shift. He looked at her face, the stubborn strength in her jaw, the fierce defiance in her eyes. It mattered to him. She mattered to him.

Until now, he'd told himself he protected her to repay a debt. That excuse no longer fit. He reached out, brushing his hand through her hair again. That impossible red—so unlike anything else in Acadia.

Then he pulled away.

"I knew you had help," he said. "You were too prepared. You knew about the Roaches. The mental tests. Your body was already conditioned. Who's helping you?"

"The who doesn't matter," she said. "The *why* does."

She leaned in again and took his hands.

"You're right—one person feeling the way you do isn't enough. Even if hundreds feel it, nothing changes if no one speaks. But there *is* a way. I know how."

Something clenched in Cojax's chest. As if invisible wires cinched around each rib. His lungs felt too tight. His thoughts too loud.

He leaned forward, drawing in a long breath, steadying himself for what came next. But just then, his armor flickered—and began to hold a charge.

## THIRTY

"Aletorian and Orium," Romulan said in a whisper. "And two more I didn't know."

Cojax stirred at the slight noise, grabbing his blade at his side. It was halfway out of the scabbard before Finn spoke.

"Easy, Cojax. There's no danger. Why do you sleep with that thing so close? You might cut your own foot off one of these mornings."

"I heard voices," Cojax replied. "Everything all right?"

"Yeah," Romulan answered, "but ten more were Rifted. I got up to use the bathroom and they were already gone—carted off in the night."

"Ten more?" Cojax asked.

"We're down to two hundred and sixty," Finn added. "Orium knew his time was up; he was just telling me the other day. I was hoping we were done with the Riftings."

Cojax stood up, feeling the weight of the news. "Well, best not to dwell on it right now. We'd better get up and moving. Hey Sandrix, time to get up."

Once they started moving, the noise stirred life in all the others. The dormitory was massive but the sound had nowhere to go, so it was also noisy. Cojax glanced over to Jessica's bed. It was empty, as expected. She was usually the last to sleep and the first to wake up, always studying the Roach Infograms, preparing for the next set of exams. The exams were easy enough—spot the weak part of a specific Roach, but she still took it deadly serious.

The morning after a Rifting was always a brutal reminder of how fragile life could be. The Scores added a measure of security, the first Rifted would always come from the bottom, but that didn't make it easier to swallow.

Before breakfast, Cojax led the class on a run in full armor, charging through the caves in a battle formation, their shields raised,

Arc Spears in hand. Cojax pulsed different formations as they moved, adjusting to the terrain. The pulses were an odd thing. Not quite telepathy but not far from it either. When shields were linked, a pulse from the Alpha was like briefly seeing a picture in the mind. Some saw colors, faces, or landscapes—each one different. It was quicker than giving orders, more concise, relaying the correct formation in milliseconds. After the Disciples learned to associate the image they saw with a specific formation, it proved incredibly efficient.

The day progressed like many of the others—blade training, lectures on Roaches and their weaknesses, weight training in the afternoon. It was brutal, but also familiar. And there was a certain comfort in the repetition of it.

That all changed when *he* arrived on the parade grounds just after dinner.

***

Jessica's Score had received a substantial boost from her conflict at the firing range. She was now First Tier—a remarkable feat given everything. At the time, she was unsure if Orch was trying to help her or get her killed. She replayed the events over and over in her mind and still could not make up her mind about it. Either way, it made her feel uneasy. Orch was unpredictable.

*"I just got to stay a First Tier,"* Jessica coached herself as they lined up on the parade grounds. There were only fifty of the coveted First Tier positions, and she could not help but enjoy the benefits it brought. She hated herself for it, as it felt like a betrayal to who she was as a person, but the food selection alone made life much better.

*"I can do this."* It was not the first time she had thought this, but it was the first time she completely believed it. She was already halfway through the Mahghetto and now the path ahead had become much more predictable and clear. Even if they lost ten Disciples every month for the rest of the Mahghetto, there would still be two hundred left and her among them.

A pneumatic hiss. Validated began to enter the parade grounds—not the familiar Magisters they had come to know, but helmets and Placards marked with the symbol of the BloodLetters Faction.

"Attention. Magisters present," Cojax announced.

The Disciples all saluted, bowing their heads, their heels clicking together in concert.

Jessica sensed a new danger. A new test. Whenever they seemed to get their bearings, the Magisters had upended their world—changing the rules of the game. Her hand twitched to go for the blade at her side but she resisted, if only barely.

Then *he* arrived.

"Attention. Numberless present," Cojax announced.

Jessica's body froze. *"A Numberless? In the depths of the Mahghetto."* She did not have to see him to know who it was—the man who wanted her dead the moment she entered the city. Even though it seemed impossible, Jessica could have sworn he was larger and more oppressive than before. She swallowed hard, trying to force her hands not to shake. It didn't work.

"I see a Numberless' duty has no end," Atlas bellowed. "Alpha, step forward and report."

Cojax obeyed quickly, taking one giant step forward. "Two hundred and sixty Disciples, all willing to fight for Acadia."

Atlas placed his hands behind his back and looked at the ceiling, as if carefully considering Cojax's words. "One among you is different than all the rest, a stain on a white cloth, a weed among flowers." He began to walk past the Disciples, inspecting each one. It was at the end of the day, so their armor did not have a sheen like it did in the morning.

Jessica felt her heart stop, each step pronouncing judgment. She tried to force calm in her head. *"Merit before all. I've earned the right to be here. He's only trying to scare me."*

He was in the third row now. His steps sounded like hammers on the polished floor. He was taking his time to find her, enjoying the moments that passed. Despite the fear, she felt a rage bubble up in her chest. She latched onto it, allowing her a temporary bravado. But it was fading as the logic began to seep through it.

*"This is all wrong. Where are the normal Magisters from the BloodBorne Faction? Why are all the others here?"* It felt like the Descension all over again—fear, anticipation, despair.

Atlas stepped into the center of the class. Unsheathing an Arc Dagger from his waist, he sent a surge of light through the blade, illuminating his rough face with perfect clarity. "I am Atlas, a Numberless and member of the Infinite Council. I am he who single-handedly slew three SataniKahns in a single battle." The large man paced as he walked, his voice echoing in the spacious room. "I am he who turned the tide at the Battle of the Collapse and he who saved Erelida, a Numberless of great renown. I have been given the title of Son of Destruction. To face me on the battlefield is to face death. Numberless do not usually descend into the Mahghetto, but I am here because I serve two masters—merit *and* necessity. Today, I do the bidding of the latter."

He turned around sharply. "There are several here who do not belong, but one is chief among you." He stopped in front of Jessica, his eyes boring into her.

He looked up, a sadistic smile on his face. "None of you seem to know of whom I speak, but I don't blame you, as *she* is the one who violated the Code."

Then he grabbed Jessica by the back of the armor, creating an audible and persistent crackling noise as their shields competed against each other. He threw her toward the front of the room, her body twisting and turning. She corrected her spin, but still landed wrong. Despite this, she had her blade drawn before she hit the ground, her eyes narrowed at the Numberless before her.

If he was surprised she had drawn her Arc Blade, he did not show it. He continued his slow, methodical walk back up to the front of the room.

The attack did not come from the front but from the sides. Four Validated grabbed her, each taking a limb, their shields cracking as they connected with her armor.

"The Aberration was given one rule to follow—and she failed to even do that," Atlas pronounced. "To wear the mark of the Aberration, but the pin she was instructed to wear, the one she was entrusted with, was left on her clothes after her Descension. Discarded. Ignored. Well, I am here to correct that mistake. Remove your helmet."

Jessica fought against their grips, twisting and straining against the bodies that held her, desperate to build enough momentum to break free. One of them surged energy through their fist and drove it into her gut, unleashing a burst of light that lit up the room. Her armor absorbed the impact, but the force still lifted her off the ground.

Atlas was only a few paces away. "Drop your blade and remove your helmet."

She hated herself for it; she let her anger slip. She knew she was undone. If she failed to obey, they would only beat her until her shields lost their charge. Worse, she would be accused of violating an order from a Numberless—a violation that very much could result in death.

She dropped her blade. Her right arm was released, allowing her to unclip the strap of her helmet. She pulled it off, letting it fall to the floor. Despite her acquiescence, she could not remove the defiance from her eyes.

"Good, girl," Atlas said with a wicked smile, his Arc Dagger blazing with a trail of light. "Freeze up like a rabbit caught in a snare." He then turned to the Validated. "Pin her to the ground, and hold her head."

A hand pulled on her forehead, flattening the back of her skull to the ground. Atlas knelt next to her, bringing the hot glowing dagger to bear. Her eyes widened against the heat, but she stopped herself from struggling. She would not let her fear show.

Then he started cutting. The dagger cauterized as it cut, filling the room with the scent of flesh. It was not the pain that tore at her, as that only came across as a distant thrum; it was imagining what he was doing to her face—what he was carving into it.

She screamed. Her rage uncorked. Atlas had a talent with the blade but he took his time, enjoying the process as the seconds passed. She screamed again—this time shrill and pitched. For half a second, she thought he'd drag the blade through her eye. She kicked so fiercely, one of the Validated fell back.

"Hold her!" Atlas yelled.

One of the Validated plunged a syringe into the side of her neck. The effect was almost immediate, the world around her shrinking. Her vision faded until it disappeared completely.

"I said hold her, not put her under," Atlas hissed. He punched the Validated who had administered the sedative, sending her tumbling backwards from the impact.

"Enough!" said a voice from behind.

Atlas stopped at this, but not out of fear—more out of curiosity. Had someone dared order a Numberless? He turned back to his work, ignoring the voice.

"If you kill her, you will violate the Acadian Code. Not even a Numberless is above the Code!"

Whoever this was had the confidence of a god or a death wish; Atlas could not decide which one. He would finish here and then turn to deal with the errant Magister who would defy a Numberless.

"I exercise my right as an Acadian and challenge you to a duel!"

Atlas was about to complete the design when suddenly he was struck in the side in an explosion of light and force. He tumbled sideways, end over end. He covered his head before hitting the wall, which cracked from the force. His armor had taken the brunt of it, but his head hit hard, opening up a gash just above his eyebrow. He roared as he found his feet, facing this new enemy, an Arc Blade crafted in the Falcata style already in hand.

When his eyes rested on the opponent, he noticed that other Validated had surrounded him, their weapons out. They had not moved in, but they would not hesitate if they were ordered to do so.

That's when Atlas realized who it was—who dared interfere with his justice. It wasn't a Magister at all—it was a Disciple, the Alpha of their class. And then to his even greater astonishment, he knew who this boy was—he had met him before.

*"It's the son of Titan."*

"I accept your challenge, boy," Atlas answered. He walked over to the wall, pulling out a large, two-handed weapon. With two blades in hand, he returned to the parade ground floor.

Cojax also went to the wall, picking up a shield. He was tempted to take two blades, as the Numberless had, but he still had not mastered one blade, let alone two. They had trained with the shield. He was much more familiar with it.

Atlas surged forward, his Arc Blade igniting with a fierce white flare as energy poured through its spine. Cojax braced, but the first blow landed like a meteor. Six inches of crackling light-edge smashed into his shield. It flared golden, absorbing the strike, but the force pushed him back.

Atlas barely acknowledged the effort. "At least you recover faster than your father." His voice boomed across the chamber. Then he shifted from criticism to instruction.

"You're using your blade like an ax—chopping and cutting. The Arc Blade isn't just steel—it's a conduit. A disciplined user can focus that power into the edge, creating a molecular disruption field—what you see as light."

Cojax decided to cut the conversation short and rushed in, his shield raised. They exchanged a wild fury of blows. One came close to clipping his head, but he ducked just in time.

Atlas laughed, speaking with venom in his voice. "But in the end, none of it matters if you don't know how to use it."

Without warning, Atlas struck again. Cojax dodged the first swing, ducking low and thrusting upward—only for Atlas to catch him with the butt of his blade. His helmet rang like a bell as he stumbled, and another blow swept him to the ground.

"Get up!" Atlas barked, stepping back with predatory calm. "Our duel is not finished yet."

Cojax scrambled to his feet. His response came wild, untrained—a wide swing that Atlas dodged without effort. Atlas moved in, raining blows, striking the shield and blade in quick succession. Cojax found himself stepping back, unable to block the attacks as they came for him.

"Do not retreat!" Atlas exploded. "You are Acadian. You hold the line!"

The next strike clipped Cojax's side. His armor shimmered, venting heat. He reeled.

"You're not bleeding yet," Atlas spat. "Be grateful."

The next blows were merciless. One across the knee. Another to the back of the head. It was a brutal display, Cojax the nail, Atlas the hammer. The Repulse Shield gave out first, all energy depleted. The Numberless sliced it in two. Cojax's shields lasted longer, but not by much. He took blow after blow, until he didn't.

Three rapid hits broke through his rhythm, sending him sprawling. He rolled, gasping. His armor—dim now. Out of charge.

"You've learned nothing," Atlas sneered. "Learn to use a

blade before you challenge someone with it."

"You violate the Code if you kill her," Cojax rasped, a newfound anger in his voice. "Merit before all—isn't that how it goes?" He laughed, a pitiful but grating sound. He slowly pushed himself to his feet, his blade raised. He was unsure if Atlas had killed Jessica, unsure how he managed to find his feet, unsure why he just didn't seem to care anymore. His anger was the only thing certain—not just at Atlas, but the whole system. It was a farce, a lie. And the one person who truly saw the system's hollow core now lay on the floor—unmoving, lifeless perhaps, or caught in the slow bleed between dying and dead.

Atlas turned back, tossing one blade against the wall and raising another.

"Sir," one of the Validated said, "his armor has no charge. You've won the duel."

"And yet, he still stands, blade raised."

Cojax roared and attacked—three wild, erratic swings that forced Atlas back. One connected. A direct thrust to the chest. Atlas' armor flared with blinding light, the impact staggering him. Shock passed through his face for a second.

Cojax had somehow pushed energy through his depleted armor—just enough to surge the blade.

But it had cost him everything.

Atlas came back with fury. Cojax couldn't keep up. More strikes landed—opening cuts across his leg, his ribs, his shoulders. Then a fist collided with his jaw. The bone cracked in three places. Cojax hit the floor hard, blood spraying from his lips.

But Atlas was beyond reason—beyond rage. He hurled his sword aside and lunged, abandoning technique for something far more savage. He was more beast than man. Fists slammed into Cojax's helmet, again and again, until blood slicked the floor beneath them. The armor absorbed what it could; the helmet kept his skull from collapsing entirely—but only barely.

Only then did Atlas rise—breathless, bloodstained, his fists still twitching from the fury.

"Remove this creature from my presence," he said coldly. His gaze swept across the stunned Disciples. "Bravery and stupidity often wear the same armor—but only one is rewarded in Acadia."

Two Validated obeyed, dragging Cojax's shattered body across the floor. Each scrape of metal echoed like punctuation to the lesson, until the doors hissed shut behind him.

215

## THIRTY-ONE

Cojax awoke in a panic. His throat was raw—scorched as if he'd swallowed fire. Instinctively, he reached for his jaw, but his hands met thick, rubbery tubes embedded in his mouth. He gagged. For a horrifying moment, he couldn't breathe. His chest tightened. Air rasped in through the obstruction, sharp and metallic-tasting, but it wasn't enough to kill the panic clawing through his ribs.

He thrashed.

He was trapped—sealed in a compartment scarcely wider than his shoulders, with no room to even turn around. Metal pressed in from all sides. The tubes ran from his mouth down the side of the chamber, vanishing into the wall like surgical leeches. Then, without warning, the wall pulsed.

From it, hundreds of black, snake-like filaments slithered out in perfect unison.

They moved together, tracking his flailing limbs, adjusting with the precision of thought. Cojax kicked at them, screamed—but no sound escaped. The tubes stole even his voice.

He struck the walls. Again. Again. Nothing.

Then came the hiss of gas—sweet, cloying, unnaturally warm. It misted around his face like fog.

He blinked.

And the snakes were gone.

He jolted upright, arms grabbing for purchase. His mouth was clear. No tubes. No restraints. Just cold air and a distant antiseptic tang. He touched his lips, then his jaw. Whole. He ran his hands down his chest. His ribs—mended. His blisters—gone. The memory of distant pain lingered, but the evidence had been scrubbed clean.

*"Am I dreaming again? Or waking up for the first time?"*

A sudden flood of white light spilled into the chamber. The ceiling split open, and the drawer-like pod he lay in slid forward into a larger chamber. He squinted against the sterile glare.

Two figures stood waiting. One wore radiant white, the other bronze-colored Static Armor. Both bore the posture of the Validated. Cojax hesitated, unsure of what protocol demanded.

He sat up slowly, knees over the edge of the pod. Memories returned in a flood: Atlas' blade cutting him to ribbons, the fist crashing into his head, the failure, the punishment. He rubbed his jaw again, still disbelieving its wholeness.

The woman in white stepped forward. She was thin, with shoulders too squared to be called elegant, but her voice carried weight. Her tone made gravity seem optional.

"A new set of armor is in the next chamber. You're already late. Each second you waste, you lose points."

Her words weren't a suggestion. They were law.

The armored Validated stiffened. "Elena, our orders were to be silent."

Elena turned her head just slightly, her voice soft but razor-sharp. "You forget your place, *Landria*. I am Third Tier. You're two Tiers beneath me. Don't speak unless instructed."

Landria bristled. "You're Weighted, Elena. And falling fast. You may outrank me now, but not for long."

"Speak again," Elena said coldly, "and I will report your insubordination."

That shut her up.

Landria saluted in silence, lowering her head.

Elena returned her eyes to Cojax—bladed, humorless. "Move, boy. Your class started lunch five minutes ago."

That was all the permission he needed.

Cojax scrambled out of the pod, realized with a start that he was completely naked, then bolted into an adjacent room where a new suit of Static Armor lay beside a fresh uniform.

He dressed fast—armor latching into place like an old friend reuniting. He flexed his fingers and rolled his shoulders.

Then he was moving.

The corridors beyond the Medicus wing were unfamiliar, but he ran anyway. Signs were meaningless—he followed the smell of heat-processed food and the sound of boots on polished tile. By the time he reached the Dining Hall, his lungs were burning, not with exhaustion but with panic. By his count, he had been out the entire morning.

His class was just filing in. Cojax quickened his pace, ready to resume his position as Alpha, as was his right. That was his place—he'd bled for it. But as he rounded the final corner and stepped to the front, his feet slowed.

Adriana stood in the Alpha position.

Finn was nowhere in sight.

She didn't flinch when she saw him. Neither did Brutus, who stood to her right, massive arms crossed, eyes like two dead stars.

Cojax stepped forward anyway, expecting the line to part.

It didn't.

The air stiffened. Eyes turned to him—thirty Disciples watching his every move.

Their gazes followed a grim pattern: first his face, eyes narrowing at the fresh but healing marks that ran down his cheek; then his neck, mottled in lingering bruises; then the Placard.

That was where they hovered.

His Score.

It had dropped.

"What?" Cojax asked, breath still catching.

Brutus shook his head. Not in defiance. Not in scorn. But with something colder. Indifference.

Adriana's lips barely moved. "You were gone too long."

"I didn't die," Cojax said.

"No," she said calmly. "But your points did."

And behind them, the class said nothing. No sounds of recognition or celebration. No voices to welcome him back into the fold. Just the scrape of trays on steel and the low hum of the food synthesizers.

He was still standing. Still breathing. But somehow… he had already been replaced. His mind could not fathom the change—even if he missed a morning, Adriana's Score was nowhere near the Alpha position. It wasn't just improbable for her to rise so quickly in the ranks—it was impossible.

Adriana's eyes dropped to his Placard.

"Well," she said coolly, "the insubordinate son returns. And not a moment too soon."

Laughter rippled from the three leading Disciples flanking her—Brutus among them.

Cojax followed her gaze down to his chest. His Placard glowed dull red.

Tier Three. The number glared at him from the corner. But worse—far worse—was the center reading:

5,000.

A thousand points beneath the lowest Disciple.

His hands trembled at the sight. *"How is that possible?"* Only the evening before, he had stood at the pinnacle—Alpha. Now he was a ghost, irrelevant and forgotten.

"Fall in line, Dependent," Adriana ordered, her voice casual, almost amused. "Unless you want me to put you there myself."

Cojax wanted to fight back. Wanted to scream. But her position as Alpha meant her word carried authority—unless directly contradicted by a Magister, her orders were law. He saluted, the motion stiff with suppressed fury.

Adriana returned the salute half-heartedly, stepping forward and shouldering past him without another word.

He took his place at the rear.

The Dining Hall was quieter than expected. Whispers buzzed at the edges, but no one spoke to him directly. Cojax collected his tray last—a pitiful scoop of pale protein-enriched oatmeal and a strip of dry toast. Around him, other Disciples feasted on roasted meats, noodles, sauces.

He clenched his jaw. His food was an insult.

Passing Adriana's table, he saw her surrounded by loyalists—Brutus among them, his massive frame spreading across two chairs. The sight made bile rise in Cojax's throat. Then he spotted Finn, seated alone at the far end. The moment their eyes met, Finn stood. His smile was forced. But his eyes—his eyes were haunted. Cojax slid into the seat across from him, nodding toward the tray.

"Why do you get meatballs and I get prison slop?"

Finn gestured to his Placard. "The perks of being in Tier Two."

"You're in Tier Two?" Cojax furrowed his brow. "What happened to your face?"

Finn smirked, revealing a dark bruise beneath his eye. "You

should see yours. You've got a mark running down the left side of your face to your jaw—almost surgical in how straight it is."

Cojax ran his fingers down the line of raised skin. It felt alien. Wrong. He stared at his food, his appetite gone.

"How long was I out?"

"A week," Finn said softly. "We thought you were dead. You had internal bleeding, six broken ribs, a shattered collarbone. Coma for two days."

"They told you all that?"

Finn leaned in. "Not officially. Someone else told me."

"Who?"

Finn pressed a finger to the side of his chin. A silent warning. Armor recorded everything.

Cojax nodded.

"I've been out for a week…," he repeated.

"It's been long enough for everything to change," Finn said. "Adriana's Alpha now. Brutus is Beta."

Cojax blinked. "You were Beta."

"I was Alpha for a day," Finn said with a tight grin. "Then Adriana did what she does best—manipulated the system. She staged disruptions, triggered point penalties across the class, and let me take the fall. Within hours, she set in motion a plan that upended everything. Brutus just stood by and watched it happen. Then they came after Jessica and me. Early morning. Showers. No armor."

His voice dropped, filled with quiet rage.

"I fought along with Romulan, Sandrix, and Callista. We held them off as best we could. But they threatened worse unless we broke up our group and tanked my Score."

"You deliberately dropped points?"

"To protect our group. To protect Jessica."

"They can't do that."

"They did." Finn's jaw tightened. "It's been five days. No consequences."

"And Jessica?"

"She's over there," he said, nodding. "She's eating on the floor. Adriana's order. Not official—just implied. They told her that if she obeys, the beatings stop."

Cojax moved to rise, but Finn grabbed his wrist. "Don't.

Helping her makes her more of a target. Things have stabilized now. If Adriana stays in the Alpha position, and we don't group up, I think she'll let things stay how they are now."

Cojax's eyes drifted to Jessica. She looked fragile—wounded. Her eyes stayed fixed on her tray. Cuts lined her face. Fading bruises marred her neck.

"Don't look at her either," Finn warned. "Adriana notices everything."

"And Brutus?"

Finn's expression soured. "He made a deal. He didn't fight with them. But he didn't stop them either. Just stood there. The same day my Score plummeted, his rose."

Cojax clenched his fists. "That little Rifter."

"He always wanted to beat you at something. Now he has. He's the Beta. You're at the bottom."

"How did Adriana climb so fast? She was Mid Tier at best."

"She staged matches. With the new Arc Blade and Spear training, point swings depend on how convincingly someone wins. Some of her fights were clearly staged. Disciples let her dominate them for safety or favor. That's how the rankings shifted."

"But why would anyone throw a match?"

"Because it's better than getting Rifted. And because people are scared. Adriana has built a kingdom of fear. And we're living under it."

Cojax looked down at his tray. His fists trembled. "Have there been any new Riftings?"

Finn shook his head. "No, and there likely won't be for another three weeks. But now that Adriana is in charge, people would rather bend than face a beating in the showers."

The rest of the meal passed in silence. Soon after, their ArmGuards prompted them to fall into formation. Training followed. Cojax expected punishment, humiliation, perhaps another beating. But instead, he was ignored. The Disciples formed by Tier. First Tier closest to the Magisters. Second just behind. Third Tier—his Tier— was scattered at the edges like unwanted debris.

He picked up a training blade. It felt unfamiliar. He tried to mimic the others. Watched. Studied. And for his efforts, his points began to tick down. Observation was penalized. Inactivity was weakness.

Every time he paused, he lost ground.

By the time dueling began, Cojax was seething. *"Finally,"* he thought. *"A chance to climb back up."*

But no Magister paired him with a fight.

He was invisible.

When he tried to challenge someone, he was told only higher-ranked Disciples could issue challenges to lower ones. And since he was the bottom… he couldn't challenge anyone. An hour passed before a Magister tossed him a bone—a bout against a lean girl barely above him. He charged too quickly, overcommitted, and lost within two minutes.

A Second Tier Disciple sneered, "That was the Alpha? Unbelievable."

Humiliation surged in his gut. In the next bout, he swung with blind fury—unfocused and desperate.

He lost again. More points vanished. His mind crumbled. The rest of training passed in a haze. The blade felt heavier. His body slower. His spirit dimmed.

That night, he wandered the edge of the dormitory, eventually stumbling into the darkened storage room where he and Jessica had once found brief solace.

But she wasn't there.

Instead, Finn stood alone, gripping two Arc weapons—one in each hand. His posture was solid. His eyes unreadable. Cojax collapsed onto a crate, shoulders sagging.

Then Finn spoke. "Get up, warrior. Your training isn't over."

Cojax's head lifted slowly. "Yes, it is."

"They haven't Rifted you."

"They might as well have," Cojax snapped. "I was destroyed by the weakest Disciples. I'm a joke, Finn. I'm nothing. I'm a week behind everyone in training. I didn't think that'd mean much, but it's everything. The Magisters don't even acknowledge me."

Finn's voice rose. "I left you in the tunnels. I won't leave you again. Atlas crushed you. Adriana plotted against you. Brutus abandoned you. But I'm still here. I'm still fighting."

He tossed an Arc Spear to the ground at Cojax's feet.

"Pick it up."

Cojax stared at it. He hadn't even trained with the Arc Spear yet. "I've got nothing left in me. I need some time to think. To process all of this. I can't."

"I don't care." Finn's eyes burned. "They can Rift me tomorrow—but you'll fall tonight if we don't fight. Pick. It. Up."

Cojax stood, rage boiling over, drawing his blade. "What do you want from me! I'm finished."

He struck with full force.

Finn blocked, and the collision of blades released a shockwave of light, thunder-cracking through the room. Both stepped back, stunned by the intensity.

Then Finn's voice softened. "You have more in you than the rest of us. I saw it the day you punched the wall. The day you stood against Atlas. The energy you emit… it's not normal. You're a Nova, Cojax."

Cojax shook his head. "Atlas broke me. I'm nothing. I stood up against a Numberless and what do I have to show for it?"

"You have my respect."

"How many points is that worth?"

"None," Finn admitted. "But it's all I've got left to give."

At that moment, Jessica entered the room, Arc Blade in hand. She was followed by Romulan, Sandrix, Ester, and Horacio—all of them had suffered tremendous loss of points. Three had even dropped to the Third Tier.

"You two already start?" she asked.

Finn shrugged. "He's still warming up."

Cojax looked at her—dirty, bruised, tired—and yet, somehow, still unbroken.

"Let's go," she said. "Vacation's over."

"Vacation?" Cojax frowned. "You two think I was enjoying coconuts, lounging on a beach somewhere, like some Dependent from the modern era?"

"Your skin does look a little more tan," Finn admitted.

Cojax growled.

Jessica stepped between them and raised a finger to the side of her chin. A message clear as glass: She had something to tell him and couldn't do it until their Armor had been drained of energy.

Cojax nodded. He knew the bait. She could've grabbed the

Golden Orb and drained his energy, but then the others' armor might record a glimpse of the Golden Orb in the process. They had to train until all of their armor had drained of energy.

He was tempted just to walk away, to ignore whatever message she had to share. *"Haven't conversations with her cost me enough already?"*

But after taking a long, deep breath, he pushed this petulance aside. Eventually it was curiosity that overruled his stubbornness. He lifted the blade.

"Alright, Finn. Show me what I missed… while I was on vacation."

## THIRTY-TWO

Two hours later, the small group of Disciples collapsed onto the cold floor of the storage room, their bodies spent, their armor suits flickering with residual static. Every breath was a battle. Their internal battery indicators blinked empty.

They had pushed themselves harder than ever before—driven by their collective frustration. It was not long before the other Disciples stood to leave, each offering Cojax what they couldn't in public—quiet words of gratitude for his return and relief that he was still alive.

Jessica and Finn had rotated through bouts with Cojax, who had been stiff at first, but sharpened with each round. Somewhere between exhaustion and instinct, he'd found a rhythm again—his footwork clean, his attacks precise, his defense tighter than it had been since the Mahghetto began.

It wasn't enough to win. But it was enough to hope again.

Cojax had always known Finn was skilled, but not like this. Beneath his usual mischief and laughter had been discipline, refinement. His strikes were surgical. His posture never overcommitted. It was clear—Finn had been holding back in public. He'd learned to mask his strength with a smile.

Jessica was another story entirely. Her footwork was light, reactive. Her strikes lacked power but not purpose. She wielded her blade like an extension of herself, each movement composed and clean. It was more obvious now that she too held back, otherwise she would have swept the Mahghetto with ease.

Jessica whispered, "Our charge is gone."

Finn sat up instantly. His eyes locked on Cojax. "Now, we can finally talk."

He rose to his feet and limped over, planting himself in front of Cojax like a wall of judgment. His voice cracked with rage. "Tell me why she's worth it."

He pointed at Jessica, his finger trembling with restraint. "Why is she worth all of this?"

Cojax's chest tightened. "I didn't make you protect her."

"I trusted you," Finn snapped. "I trusted you wouldn't throw yourself to the lions unless it mattered. You nearly died fighting Atlas—for her. Now tell me why. Don't feed me 'I was upholding the AC' garbage. I deserve more than that—all of us in our group do. I had to choose between you… and my brother."

The words struck like a blade in the gut.

Cojax lowered his head.

He hadn't seen it that way before, but now… now it was clear. He had dragged Finn into his personal crusade, and Brutus, selfish as ever, made the choice to abandon Finn so he could save himself. In most lights, especially in the Mahghetto, it seemed like the best choice—the logical one.

"Is this because you like her?" Finn hissed. "Is this some twisted infatuation? Is it worth everything we've lost?"

Cojax raised a hand. "Just… give me a second."

He took a breath. Then another.

"This isn't about my feelings. And it's not about the AC. It goes deeper than that." He looked up. "Jessica is the truth."

Silence followed. Neither Finn nor Jessica responded. The room felt heavier, the darkness pressing in around them.

Cojax pushed on. "Finn, there are people outside the Wall. Villages. Cities. They're not at war with the Roaches. And I think the Infinite Council knows."

Finn's voice dropped. "How?"

Jessica and Cojax took turns telling the story—about how Jessica was never questioned, about how her people were at peace with the Roaches, and how there were other human settlements beyond the Wall. Finn took it in stride, not interrupting nearly as much as Cojax had the first time it was told to him.

By the end of it, Cojax's voice fell low. "I doubted at first—it seemed impossible. But then I recalled one thing from a distant memory. The day Jessica arrived, Atlas had issued a warning to my father. Only I was close enough to hear it. He said, 'Her presence threatens all of Acadia.' How would he know the threat she represented unless they already knew what lay outside the city?"

Jessica hadn't known—at least, not that part. Cojax had never shared it before—not the words from Atlas, not the way his father had intervened. Hearing it now, spoken so plainly in the dark, made the tension in her spine coil like wire.

Cojax took a step forward, his voice now a whisper edged with fire. "At the time, I thought it was fear. Or madness. But now I know—he meant the system. She's a threat to the system because she proves it's a lie. That survival doesn't require absolute obedience. That the war doesn't have to continue. That beyond the Wall, people live without Arc Blades, without Placards, without the culling of the weak. And that makes her dangerous."

"We're slaves," Jessica added. "We're slaves chained to a system of merit, pain, and death."

"Well… what difference does it make?" he said. "Even if it's true, there's no way to tell anyone. Jessica says the armor records everything. You start talking, your Score is docked or worse before you can finish your first sentence. This information means nothing if it lives and dies with the three of us."

Jessica's voice cut through the dark—calm, but resolute. "If it gets out, it could end the war."

Finn looked up. "Even if you could—what then? The war ends. Great. The Tiers stay. The Numberless still rule. Nothing changes."

Cojax moved closer. His voice dropped. "If the war ends, there's no more justification for the culling. No more Mahghetto. No more forced scarcity to justify their order. Hadrian might still be alive. My mother too. The war gives them power, Finn. Without it, the foundation crumbles."

Finn shook his head. "That doesn't track."

Cojax didn't blink. "Let me put it this way. If you owned a house, would you let strangers rifle through your belongings?"

"No."

"But let's say a trusted source told you there was a bomb under your floorboards. And then someone shows up claiming to be an expert. You don't know them. But suddenly, you let them in. The threat makes you compliant."

Finn's brow furrowed, but he said nothing.

"That's what the Roaches are," Cojax said. "A perpetual

bomb under our feet. So long as we believe the danger is real and constant, we'll accept any intrusion—rankings, starvation, death. We'll let our brothers be cut down and blame them for falling. We'll beg to climb a ladder that leads nowhere."

His voice faltered, then steadied.

"They sent my mother to the Killing Fields. And I never even questioned it. Until Jessica."

Finn stared into the shadows for a long time. "So how do you spread that truth? Like I said—talking gets you killed. And even if it doesn't, who would believe it?"

Cojax turned to Jessica. "You never told me your plan. Not really."

Jessica hesitated. Her jaw worked side to side as she calculated what could be safely said. Finally, she nodded and met Finn's eyes.

"You put faith in Cojax while he was unconscious," she said. "Now it's time I placed some faith in you—in both of you."

She exhaled.

"Four years ago, my guardian, Elena, approached me with a way to end the war. She said she was part of a group—small, hidden, dedicated to pulling down the system from the inside. I never met the others. I assume for safety. But she did teach me secret hand signals so I can nonverbally identify them—a way to quickly assess someone's loyalty." She made a sign with her left hand—a small box with three fingers flared. It was discreet, easily missed.

"Elena believed in me. She trained me. Prepared me for the Mahghetto. I saw the mental tests years ago. The physical ones too. I've studied the Arc Blade, Arc Spear, and Blazer for almost four years."

Finn blinked. "Four years?"

"Yes."

"You should be *way* better."

Jessica frowned. "Well, only two years were actually weapons training. And don't mock me—you've been genetically modified for combat. I haven't. Also, I don't generate enough energy to charge my armor."

Finn's smirk vanished. "What?"

"I can't power it on my own," she said plainly. "When it's drained, it stays that way—unless I use the Golden Orb. Every day, it gets recharged. Every morning, I start fresh."

Cojax leaned forward. "Where's the power coming from?"

"I don't know," Jessica admitted. "Elena wouldn't tell me. Just said it would be ready."

Cojax's eyes narrowed. "I met her. In the Medicus wing. Thin. Sharp. She's the one who woke me."

Jessica nodded. "That's her."

"She's slipping in the rankings."

Jessica froze. "What?"

"She's still Top Tier," Cojax said, "but the other Validated— Landria—said her Score's dropping. Fast."

"That can't happen," Jessica muttered. "She's a Nova."

"She looked tired," Cojax said. "Exhausted, even."

Jessica's lips pressed into a tight line. She looked ready to speak, but Finn jumped in.

"So… what's the plan?"

Jessica didn't hesitate. "I reach the Crossing."

"That's it?" Finn scoffed. "That's your grand plan?"

"When the Mahghetto ends," she said evenly, "the Crossing is broadcast to every Praetorium and Subterra Residence in the BloodBorne faction in real-time. The ceremony is public. Several hundred Validated show up in person."

"And?" Finn asked.

Jessica's eyes darkened. "That's when I speak. That's when I tell them the truth."

Silence.

"Once I cross, I become one of them. I gain a voice. A voice that can't be silenced without consequence."

Both Cojax and Finn knew exactly what she meant.

They had never seen the Crossing—not with their own eyes. Innocents weren't allowed to watch it live, lest it reveal something about the future trials in the Mahghetto. But they'd heard the stories. The ceremony marked the end of the Mahghetto, the final validation of those who survived. It was whispered about in awe, spoken of like a legend only the strongest ever got to tell.

Jessica's voice broke the quiet. "During the ceremony, each Disciple receives their commission into Acadian society. Once they're Validated, they recite their lineage—briefly—one minute or less.

Names. Accomplishments. A condensed legacy."

"And that's when you'll share yours," Cojax said, lips curling into a grin.

Jessica nodded. "Along with some highlights. Like the time my great-grandfather brokered peace with the Roaches. Should raise a few eyebrows at the very least."

Finn blinked. "You're going through all of this—for one minute?"

"There's more to Elena's plan," Jessica said. "She made it clear this wasn't just about me. She spoke of hundreds—maybe thousands—working behind the curtain. I don't know what's supposed to happen after my speech. She didn't tell me. Said it was safer that way."

"So you're the spark of rebellion," Finn said. "And something is supposed to happen in the wake of it."

Jessica nodded once. "Exactly."

Finn suddenly sat down on a nearby box, his legs once again losing strength. "Blood and bile, you're talking about a full-blown insurrection. Blood and bile, why couldn't Cojax's actions have been traced back to a simple crush—that would have been so much easier to understand. You're both talking about overthrowing the government of Acadia, do you realize that?"

"Yes," Jessica answered.

"I think I'm going to lose my dinner."

"I hope Elena has something big planned," Cojax muttered. "Because only the BloodBorne will hear what you say—and probably not all of them."

"It'll spread," Jessica said with conviction. "Elena was sure of that. The BloodBorne are huge, and tightly woven. Other Factions will get word and it *will* spread."

Finn exhaled through his nose, eyes flicking between them. "This is insane," he whispered. Then his lips curled slightly. "I'm in."

Cojax smiled. "Just like that?"

Finn shrugged. "Why not—I lost my brother this week, my Score, and now potentially my city. Besides my meal selection, I don't have much left to lose."

"And now you know why I've been protecting her," Cojax said.

"If we can just keep Jessica in the Second Tier," Finn said, "I think we've got a shot."

"Why the Second Tier?" Jessica asked.

"They won't touch the Second Tier as long as there is a Third Tier," Cojax answered.

Jessica nodded slowly. "Good point."

All eyes in the room drifted to Jessica's Placard. She was in the Third Tier. It was the upper half of the tier but still a potential victim of subsequent Riftings.

"With Adriana as the Alpha," Finn said, "I don't know if it's possible."

"There's only one time Adriana was put in check," Jessica answered. "That's when Cojax was the Alpha and you were the Beta. He ensured that merit prevailed and it undermined Adriana's underhanded schemes. The only way I'm going to make it to the Crossing is if Cojax's Score gets restored."

They all turned to look at Cojax's Placard. The number was abysmal. A thousand points behind the next Disciple.

Finally, Cojax spoke. "We only have three weeks before the next Rifting. Is a climb that quickly even possible? Given that everyone's Score will be increasing at the same time? I looked at the schedule and our training is transitioning to Formation drills, Roach studies, physical fitness, and the Blazer. Between now and the Rifting there are only four Arc Blade trainings—and that's the only time we can duel. If I had four duels with the highest Tiers, and beat them soundly, I might have a chance, but none of them are going to risk their Score."

"I think we can use that to our advantage," Jessica answered.

"How? I can slowly climb in the rankings, as I did before, but not at a pace that will make a difference. My Score is so low, I'd be lucky to reach the next lowest Disciple before the Rifting."

"I have a plan," Jessica said with a knowing smile. "It's basic psychology—aversive fixation."

"Aversive fixation?"

"People struggle to ignore what they loathe. The more they despise something, the more they obsess over it."

## THIRTY-THREE

"I challenge Cojax." Brutus' voice boomed across the training room, silencing everything. Lunch had ended only moments ago. Most of the Disciples hadn't even drawn their blades yet for practice.

Cojax froze.

Brutus stood at the center of the parade grounds, Arc Blade drawn, its hum pulsing with quiet menace. His broad shoulders squared with ritual precision, his expression unreadable. The tip of his sword leveled at Cojax with purpose—not rage, not mockery.

Just finality.

Cojax's thoughts raced. *"Why?"*

The room buzzed with murmurs. Disciples turned to watch, forming a wide circle around the two boys. It wasn't every day that the Beta issued a challenge to a Disciple from the Bottom Tier.

*"It doesn't make sense... unless..."* A wild hope bloomed in Cojax's chest. *"He's helping me."* He latched onto the idea like a drowning man grabbing driftwood. *"He's trying to raise my Score. That's it. He knows how the system works. Beating me won't help him much, but if I put up a fight—even win—it would surge my points."*

With new confidence, Cojax flexed his shoulders, stretching them in preparation for the bout. *"He hasn't abandoned me. He's been playing both sides this whole time—waiting, watching, preparing.*

*"Brutus must've figured all of this out the moment I was beaten. Maybe he saw what Adriana was planning and planted himself close to her. A double agent. A friend in enemy armor."*

Thea stepped into the circle, her boots echoing against the floor.

"A challenge has been issued," she said flatly. "Is it accepted?"

Cojax nodded. He had no choice. Decline and his points would suffer. He might as well jump into the Rift himself at that point. He stared at Brutus for several long seconds, searching for any sign of camaraderie. A flicker of recognition. A smirk. A twitch of a finger.

There was nothing.

Still, he couldn't shake the feeling. *"It's all an act."*

Cojax dropped his helmet into place and drew his Arc Blade. The weapon buzzed to life in his hand. Behind him, Finn approached and leaned in, whispering just loud enough to be heard.

"I think he's trying to help you. Remember what we practiced."

Cojax's heart leapt. He whispered back, "Did he tell you about this?"

"Begin!"

The Magister's bark cut the air like a blade.

Cojax barely had time to take a guard position.

Brutus didn't hesitate.

He charged—*fast*. His body moved like a machine, honed and brutal. Cojax's reflexes barely caught the first strike, his blade deflecting the attack with a shriek of energy.

*"He's making it look real. He has to for the sake of the Magisters."*

They circled, blades singing. Brutus kept his distance at first, engaging with formal strikes, controlled movements. He looked like he was treating Cojax as an equal.

But that changed.

Brutus lunged, and this time his movements weren't measured—they were relentless. A flurry of blows rained down. Cojax blocked, parried, fell back.

*"Just stay focused,"* he told himself. *"He's just putting on a good show. Wait for when he opens up his guard."*

Then a strike slipped through—*hard*—hitting Cojax in the side. His armor flared with light. The impact drove him two steps backward.

Brutus pressed in. Another strike. Then another. Cojax barely saw them coming. A hit to the helmet. Another to the thigh. The Magister couldn't even call them fast enough.

Cojax broke away, gasping, his body flaring with exhausted heat. He looked to Brutus, trying to find some signal—some hint that this was all for show.

But Brutus wasn't holding back anymore.

He wasn't helping.

He was dismantling him.

Brutus became the hammer. Cojax, the nail. Every blow cracked the air with light. His Static Armor flared and dimmed with each strike. Cojax couldn't answer. His footwork collapsed. His timing faltered. There was no breathing room, no chance to recover.

In desperation, Cojax lunged—leading with his shoulder, reckless and wild. He took another blow to the head, another to the ribs. He swung upward, a blind strike.

Brutus had already seen it coming. The Beta knocked the blade aside and twisted, disarming Cojax with brutal efficiency. The Arc Blade skittered across the floor.

Cojax stumbled, trying to recover—too late.

Brutus raised his weapon and slammed it upward, striking the base of Cojax's helmet. The blow didn't kill—it couldn't—but it sent an explosion of light through the armor's failsafe system.

The helmet tore free.

Cojax fell to his knees, blinded and humiliated. His face was exposed. His Score plummeting.

The crowd was silent.

He had forgotten to latch the helmet—a novice mistake. The blow hadn't just taken his weapon. It had taken his pride.

"That's match," the Magister declared. "Fifty to zero. Brutus wins."

Brutus removed his helmet, grinning ear to ear. The kind of grin that didn't hide satisfaction—it showcased it. He stood like a god among mortals, basking in the silent applause of dominance. Before Cojax could catch his breath, Adriana and her entourage swarmed Brutus, laughter breaking out around them like wildfire.

Cojax stared at the crowd, barely seeing them. His limbs ached. His face burned. But it was the isolation that hollowed him out.

It wasn't just a loss—it was flawless defeat. He hadn't scored a single point. A white-hot rage surged through his body, flooding his chest with pulses of light. His armor glowed faintly as the internal charge fluctuated with emotional overload. He took a step forward, fists clenched, breath ragged—

Finn grabbed him, locking an arm across his chest before he took two steps.

"Magisters," Finn hissed into his ear. "They're watching. Conduct unbecoming. You throw a punch now and your Score goes into free fall."

"Look at him," Cojax seethed, barely restraining the growl in his voice. "He's laughing at me—at us."

Brutus turned, loud enough for everyone to hear. "He's throwing a tantrum because he couldn't win. Just because your daddy's a Numberless doesn't mean you can swing a blade, Cojax."

The words hit like a boot to the ribs.

Finn pulled Cojax toward the back wall, his voice sharp and low. "What were you doing out there? You forgot everything we drilled last night."

Cojax snapped back, "I thought I was fighting my friend."

Finn shook his head. "He used that against you. You let your emotions guide your blade. He fought like a tactician. You fought like a storm."

"That's your brother."

"He *was*," Finn said, cold and final. "Not anymore."

Cojax's voice cracked. "I was already hanging by a thread… and he set it on fire. A perfect defeat, Finn. *Perfect.* How do I come back from that?"

Finn's expression softened just enough to let compassion in. "First—you breathe. You fought a Numberless and held your own— at least for a bit. You've come back from worse. And you didn't drop as many points as you think. He was the Beta. He was expected to win."

Cojax closed his eyes. The adrenaline drained from his limbs, leaving only the ache.

"But why?" he whispered. "Why destroy me like that? What does he gain?"

Finn didn't hesitate. "He's trying to survive. Aligning with us doesn't do him any favors right now."

The next hour passed in a blur. Cojax was challenged three more times—low-ranked Disciples hoping for easy points while the wound was still fresh. He lost all three, but each match was closer than the last. He took Finn's advice to heart, fought with focus, not fury. And while the sting of Brutus' betrayal still throbbed in his gut, the fire inside had begun to change shape.

Training ended. They were marched to the classrooms—white, sterile cubes where learning was forced and failure penalized. The exam covered Roach species identification—traits, vulnerabilities, attack patterns. Cojax aced the questions he'd studied before his fall. But the rest? A disaster. While others had learned, he'd been lying in a coma and stumbling through recovery. He handed in his Tech Pad, his failing score already projected on the wall.

His Score dipped further.

By the end of the day, he felt hollow. The hope Jessica and Finn had given him the night before had flickered and gone out like a dying flame. He would have gone straight to his bunk, buried himself in sleep and silence—but Finn and Jessica wouldn't allow it.

They were joined by Romulan, Sandrix, Callista, Ester, and Horacio. They dragged him to the storage room, shoving a blade into his hand. He first fought with frustration. Then rage. The longer he swung his blade, the more his mind processed his situation. And then something new—an emotion that poured over him like water. He was going to get Rifted; that was just a fact. Jessica's plan had merit, but it relied on too many variables.

He had three weeks to live—the last three weeks of his life. Whether Rifting ended in exile or death, he knew he would not be coming back. In that moment, as sweat bled into his eyes, he had perfect clarity.

*"If these are to be my last few weeks, I'll spend them doing all I can to protect Jessica. She's the only thing that matters now."*

The blade moved differently in his hands after that. It was no longer about him, his Score, his pride. It was about something greater. Someone greater. It was about a girl from outside the Wall. It was about the freedom of his people.

Jessica froze mid-parry, lowering her Arc Blade. "That's where you need to be."

Cojax blinked. "What do you mean?"

"Whatever you were thinking just now," Jessica said, "that's your state. Your focus was perfect. Clean. Your form was tight—the only thing holding you back now is your knowledge of the remaining forms."

"It's easier to focus here," Cojax replied, his eyes burning into the pitted cement wall. "At least here I'm not the butt of a joke by someone I once trusted."

Jessica stepped in. "What were you thinking about?"

Cojax turned toward her, surprised by the softness in her voice.

Her face caught him off-guard—battle-worn, bruised, but somehow radiant. His breath caught. The fire inside dimmed into something gentler.

"I guess… I was thinking about…" His voice trailed off. His cheeks reddened. "Doesn't matter. If I tell you, it'll lose its power."

Jessica raised an eyebrow but didn't press.

Finn smirked. "You two are insufferable."

Jessica rolled her eyes and changed the subject. "We need to get you on the Spear. Not many are using it yet. It's not as flashy, but it gives you reach—keeps your opponent back. And right now, space is your best friend."

Cojax nodded, a new determination in his eyes. He was done chasing redemption. He was building resolve.

Jessica handed Cojax an Arc Spear.

It looked unimpressive—just over two feet in length—but once extended, it became a weapon worthy of the Mahghetto. Eight feet long, crackling with power.

"How do I open it?" Cojax asked, eyeing the compact cylinder with uncertainty.

"Same as the Arc Blade," Finn replied. "Just grip the palm pad and focus. And uh… don't stand too close to me when you do it."

Cojax raised an eyebrow, then tightened his grip.

The weapon responded in a heartbeat. It extended outward with a low hiss and a mechanical snap, quadrupling in length. The tip surged with pale light as he sent a pulse through the handle. The spear felt alien at first—longer than what he was used to, slower in the hand. But he liked the way it looked.

Jessica stepped beside him. "The nice thing about the spear is energy efficiency. The charge is focused at the tip instead of across the full length like the Blade. Less energy required—but that also means precision is everything. Block with the shaft, strike with the point. Got it?"

"Got it."

"Good. Now get into the primary stance. Let's start from there."

Jessica stepped back, her posture impeccable as she demonstrated. "Feet shoulder-width apart. Dominant foot back, toes angled—spear forward but close to the body. Keep your core tight. This is the Forward Guard."

Cojax mirrored the position—clumsily at first, then with greater intent.

They went straight into drills, shifting grips from mid-shaft to rear, cycling through Thrust-Ready, Mid-Parry, and Overhead Riposte stances in seamless rotation. Jessica barked corrections between movements. "Slide your back foot when you lunge! Don't cross your centerline when recovering!"

Finn joined in the rhythm, calling out sequences. "Cut, cut, thrust. Rotate grip! Now sweep left—centerline block!"

The spear crackled each time Cojax pulsed energy into the tip. It demanded a different mindset than the Arc Blade—more reach, more patience. He struggled to keep his stance grounded during lateral movement. His hips turned too much. He overcommitted on thrusts. But he adapted quickly.

Sweat glistened under their suits, armor plates humming low from depleted energy. Breath came shallow. Even the air in the storage room felt thick with exertion. Slowly, the warriors got their fill. The majority of Disciples eventually retired early, leaving just Finn, Cojax, and Jessica behind.

"I think that's enough for today," Finn panted, dropping to one knee. "Let's sleep before we collapse."

"I need Cojax," Jessica said, too suddenly.

Her face reddened as the words landed. Too sharp. Too urgent. She cleared her throat and tried again with a more level tone. "I mean… I need Cojax to stay. He missed a lot. He needs the physical training, sure—but he failed the written exam. I've got notes. He's got to catch up."

Finn tilted his head. "Notes? On what?"

"On my ArmGuard," Jessica replied, her voice laced with a flicker of annoyance. "You didn't think it was just for checking our schedule, did you?"

"You want me to stay too?" Finn asked, eyebrow raised.

"No," Cojax said quickly—too quickly. He softened, grinning. "You go ahead. I need the review, and you'd be bored to death."

Finn squinted at them, suspicious. "What's going on with you two?"

Cojax looked at Jessica. Jessica looked at Finn. The silence said more than either of them would.

Finn exhaled through his nose, shaking his head as he turned toward the door. "Alright. Just don't stay up too late. Sleep's worth more than a hundred points."

As their footsteps faded, a quiet settled over the storage room—tense, expectant. Cojax exhaled slowly. He turned to Jessica, a faint smile tugging at his lips.

She didn't smile back.

Her face had returned to its usual disciplined neutrality. "We better get studying."

Cojax's heart sank a little. He hadn't expected anything dramatic—no confessions or tearful thank-yous—but after nearly dying to protect her, he'd expected… something. A nod. A kind word. Something personal.

But Jessica was all business.

"Cojax," she repeated, firmer this time. "Let's begin."

"Right," he said quietly. "Sure. You're right."

She paused, studying him. "What?"

"I just thought…" he started, but then stopped, hoping she'd fill in the gap.

She didn't.

The silence stretched.

Cojax looked at her—those wide blue eyes, almost mythical in a city of hard lines and gray walls. In that moment, he realized how foolish his expectations had been. He didn't even know what he wanted from her—maybe kindness, maybe recognition, maybe… something impossible.

"Never mind," he muttered. "Let's get started."

Jessica nodded and sat down, tapping through her ArmGuard until the screen glowed with pulsing blue light.

Her notes were staggering—organized, annotated, cross-referenced. Each species of Roach had its own entry, complete with diagrams, behavioral profiles, anatomical vulnerabilities, and recorded weaknesses.

"You took all of this?" Cojax asked.

She didn't look up. "I knew you'd need to catch up."

"Impressive."

"Thanks."

Again, that word seemed so foreign in the Mahghetto. He watched as she moved quickly through the entries, summarizing the material with surgical efficiency. She barely took a breath. Her voice was clear but strained by the time she reached the end.

"How does your ArmGuard still have power?" Cojax asked. "I thought your armor couldn't hold a charge."

"It can't. But the ArmGuard's different—it has a reserve battery. You just have to enable it manually. Settings tab, fourth menu down."

She tapped the screen again, loading a more detailed breakdown of each creature.

"Okay," she said, "now we'll go over them one by—"

"No need," Cojax said, cutting her off with a grin.

She looked at him sideways. "What do you mean, 'no need'?"

"I remember all of it. Every image, every entry. I have it all right here." He tapped the side of his head. "I don't have a photographic memory—at least not like Hadrian's—but it's decent enough."

Jessica narrowed her eyes. "That's so unfair."

Cojax raised his hands in mock surrender. "Hey—I didn't design me."

Her face twitched—half-annoyed, half-amused.

"You know how many hours I've spent memorizing all this?"

"What? One? Two?"

Jessica shook her head, a frustrated smile playing on her lips. "Unbelievable."

"Just part of the charm," Cojax replied, finally relaxing into his seat.

Jessica could not tell if he was serious or not. "More."

"It can't be more than two hours," Cojax replied.

She wanted to hit him.

"If it's more than three hours…"

Jessica landed a clean strike on Cojax's arm. The hit barely nudged him—but he staggered backward, clutching the spot as if she'd shattered the bone.

"Ow," he said with mock agony. "That was my broken arm."

Jessica rolled her eyes. "Well, that took way less time than I expected. Maybe we'll get more than a few hours of sleep tonight."

Cojax raised a finger to the side of his chin. "Our armor still has no charge. We can stay a little longer."

"Your armor still has no charge," Jessica corrected. "Mine won't recharge—ever."

"That's not necessarily a bad thing."

Her eyes narrowed. "One swing from an Arc Blade could split me in half—and you call that *not* a bad thing?"

"Well, if you say it like that…" Cojax shrugged. "But think of it this way—I only get a few minutes of conversation before my charge comes back. You could talk all night if you wanted."

"And who would I talk to?"

"Well," Cojax said, smirking. "If you were split in two, you could talk to your better half."

Jessica balled her fist again, but this time the blow didn't land. Instead, she laughed—short at first, then longer, more uncontrolled.

Cojax laughed with her. Something about the absurdity of the day, or maybe the unspoken pressure boiling between them, turned the exchange into something far more ridiculous than it should have been. The tension burst like a cracked seal.

During a lull in the laughter, Cojax snorted.

Jessica gasped and then burst out laughing again.

"You would've gotten away with that," she said between breaths, "if you hadn't done it *right* as I was inhaling."

Cojax's cheeks flushed. "I maintain that was completely involuntary."

Jessica was still giggling. "Just when I start to think you Acadians are flawless, you snort like a startled guinea pig."

Cojax blinked. "Guinea… what?"

But she didn't answer. Instead, she stepped forward and wrapped her arms around him.

It was sudden—unexpected—but desperate. Not soft, not flirtatious, not performative. It was the kind of embrace that trembled beneath the surface. A crack in her otherwise disciplined shell. Her usual composure shattered.

Cojax froze for only a moment before wrapping his arms around her in return. Not as tightly. Not as confidently. But with the kind of intensity born from near-death. From drowning.

"I can't lose you again," Jessica whispered, voice thick with restrained emotion. "When I awoke… and you weren't there…"

"Don't worry," Cojax murmured, his tone low, strained. "I didn't feel anything. They can only break you so many times before the nerves go silent."

"Don't talk like that," she said sharply.

He pulled back just enough to meet her eyes. There, in the dim flicker of light, he saw her—not the rebel, not the infiltrator, not the planner—but the girl who had saved him.

And who had changed him.

He brushed a hand through her hair, slowly, deliberately. The softness of it struck him.

"You're more important than you know," he said. "And there's something I want to tell you. It might not matter to anyone else—but it matters to me."

She didn't interrupt. She just waited.

"I believe in you. In everything you're trying to do. That's why I stood against Atlas. Because I couldn't… I couldn't bear the thought of—of losing you. Not like that."

"Cojax, you don't—"

He gently took her hands in his, locking eyes with hers.

"Jessica," he said, voice steady despite the pounding in his chest, "before they take you, they'll have to go through me."

The words rang louder in the quiet than he expected. Final. Unapologetic.

Jessica parted her lips, ready to argue, but her breath caught in her throat. Her chest rose with emotion she could no longer suppress. A single tear slid down her cheek, trailing like a quiet confession.

She scooted closer, slowly, her forehead resting against his chest. She could almost feel his warmth, his heartbeat through his armor—it was all real. He was still here.

"I can't lose you," she whispered. "Please. Don't leave me again."

Cojax tilted his head down, his breath brushing against the top of her hair. A soft smile crept across his lips, crooked and boyish. "Well, that's not plan A."

Jessica pulled back just enough to meet his gaze. Her cheeks were flushed, her voice a whisper. "Plan A?"

"Yeah," he said, brushing a strand of hair from her eyes. "I just mean… if every other option fails—if no one else can take your place—then yeah, I'll step up. I'll take the plunge."

Her laughter came like a breeze—quiet and shaky, but genuine. "Let's make sure that option stays off the table."

Their eyes lingered on each other, the moment stretching out—bare, unsheltered.

Jessica slid even closer, her hand rising to his cheek. She hesitated for only a second, then leaned in and kissed him—soft at first, searching. The kind of kiss born from long-held tension and the fear that time might run out. Cojax froze, stunned, then melted into her embrace, one hand cradling her waist, the other behind her neck.

They stayed like that—armor dimmed, breath shared, weightless for the first time in days. When she pulled away, barely an inch, her voice was barely more than a breath. "You better not make me regret that."

Cojax smiled, his thumb brushing the corner of her mouth. "You won't."

## THIRTY-FOUR

Cojax jerked awake, a rotten smell hitting his nose. Someone was throwing up in the bunk next to his. His mind clawed its way out of sleep, dread thickening in his chest as memory caught up to him— Titan's fury, Brutus' betrayal, Jessica's kiss. All of it. It returned in waves, salt poured on a still-bleeding wound. He'd been lucky enough to fall asleep. With his mind racing as it was, there was little chance he'd fall back asleep.

Next to him, the Disciple was still retching. It was a wet, violent sound.

"Sandrix?" Cojax rasped. "You alright?"

There was no answer.

Cojax sat up, instinct overriding confusion. His hand found the Arc Blade beneath his pillow. He pulsed the blade. A cone of pale white light shot out.

Not a Disciple. Not even close.

A Reever. HoverBucket-sized. Its segmented body slumped over the lower bunk, twelve legs twitching in the dark. Its head was halfway into the mattress, buried in gore, its six serrated pincers pulled back so its mouth could feast. Blood and pulped flesh slopped around the mandibles, now idly chewing, as if savoring a midnight snack.

The light blinked out.

Wet choking resumed.

Cojax's mind faltered. He wasn't dreaming. This was real. Somehow—impossibly—one of the creatures had gotten in. He pulsed again. The light flared, and the Reever twitched, reacting. Pincers pulled outward like twin guillotines.

Cojax screamed and stabbed, driving the Arc Blade between the Reever's eyes. The blade slipped through its armored carapace with a jarring resistance before bursting out the back of its skull in a geyser of green ichor.

The creature convulsed. Its legs scraped wildly against the bunks with that infernal scissor-snap sound. The smell hit like a toxin. Cojax shoved harder, twisting the blade for good measure before withdrawing and sheathing it again into the soft brain box. The Reever's limbs twitched once more, then dropped limp.

Silence.

Then a chorus of soft, methodical clicks filled the dormitory. The sound of scissors, hundreds of them—open, close, open, close. Cojax ducked and reached beneath his bed, fumbling for his helmet. His fingers slipped against blood and bile. Sandrix's. He clenched his jaw and pulled the helmet on, HUD flaring to life.

The room came alive.

Reevers were everywhere—at least two dozen and more still emerging from a gaping breach along the far wall, their legs snapping in mechanical rhythm as they fanned out with intelligent intent. They moved between bunks like panthers, waiting for perfect angles of attack. Cojax's HUD was sparking with color, picking out multiple creatures and their class. Reever Subjugators, Class III.

One turned its armored head toward him. It knew.

"Roaches!" Cojax screamed, voice amplified by the helmet. "We're under attack!"

Disciples snapped awake, groggy and dazed. Then the first screams erupted. All stealth disappeared as the creatures attacked.

One Reever lunged, lifting a Disciple from their bed and biting him clean in half with its mandibles. Blood rained down the bunk posts. The room came alive with movement on both sides, Disciples grabbing weapons, bunk beds shifting, creatures swarming in.

"Fall in! Arm yourself! They're inside!"

Cojax leapt from his bunk, boots hitting slick concrete. He was already armored—Static Armor cinched tight around his chest and legs. A habit born from Jessica's warnings. Never sleep unarmed. Never sleep vulnerable.

A Reever lunged toward a pair of Disciples still frozen in shock. Cojax barreled in, his Arc Blade burning. Instead of attacking the head, as the creature expected, he swept for the legs, severing four in one quick swing. It shrieked and crumpled, skidding across the floor into an overturned bunk.

"Finn! Romulan! Ester!" Cojax yelled.

Two out of the three replied, but he did not see who.

"We need to create a barricade with the bunks. Keep the creatures out and funnel them to a spot we can hold."

"I'm on it," Finn yelled. "I'll start on the far side. Someone cover me."

"I've got your back," Ester yelled.

The scene was sheer chaos. Disciples everywhere, some half armored, some completely naked. The Reevers had no tactical plan, no line of attack. They just swarmed forward, snapping at anyone in their view.

Cojax worked quickly along the wall, flipping bunks with enhanced strength. The first two tipped easily. The third snagged on something. He crouched to investigate—

A Reever shot forward, jaws snapping shut around him in a brutal, bone-cracking strike. His armor exploded on impact, flashing light. His Arc Blade skittered across the floor, out of reach. Weaponless. Pinned.

He struck the creature with both fists, charging each blow. The first cracked its carapace. The second opened it. The third ruptured soft tissue beneath. The Reever shrieked and twisted, trying to shake him off.

Then it went limp.

An Arc Spear punched through its skull—tip to thorax. Jessica wrenched the weapon free and kicked the corpse aside. Cojax shoved the limp mandibles away as she passed him her Arc Blade.

They fought back-to-back. Jessica gripped the spear, Cojax the blade. A Reever surged forward—Cojax ducked beneath its legs and drove the blade up into its belly. Jessica's spear swept through another, the force of the strike nearly splitting it in two.

For a moment, they held the line.

But only for a moment.

"We need a wall with the bunks!" Cojax barked. "Finn's working the far side."

"I'll cover you," Jessica answered, lunging her spear through another Reever's throat.

He tipped the beds into place, slowly forming a barricade. More Disciples caught on and started to join in—ten, then twenty—

dragging, stacking, reinforcing the growing wall. Territory was reclaimed inch by inch, creatures killed or driven out.

The wall held—barely. The Reevers pushed constantly, their weight pressing in like a tide.

"Anchor them with Arc Blades!" Cojax called.

He did it himself first—driving his blade into the concrete, burying it nearly to the hilt. The bunk stopped shifting. Others followed his lead. With time, the makeshift structure became a jagged, defensive rectangle, open only at one point on one side.

At the gap, Finn and a handful of Disciples linked shields, bracing for the next assault. It wasn't elegant, but with the walls erected, they had a little room to breathe.

Cojax grabbed a discarded blade on the floor and climbed atop an upright bunk at the camp's center. From that vantage, the whole battle unfolded.

Across the dormitory, Adriana and Brutus were building a similar fortification—though with far less urgency. Their side hadn't been hit as hard. Over one hundred and fifty Disciples surrounded Adriana, shields up, weapons drawn—most of them clean.

Cojax barely spared her a glance before his eyes locked on a cluster of Disciples—thirty or more—pinned against a far wall. They were holding on—but just barely.

*"They're trapped!"*

Cojax patched Comms in with Adriana, their commanding officer of the battle. "Adriana, we have a few dozen Disciples out in the open. You have the numbers. Push out and cut them free."

No response.

"Adriana!"

She was either purposely ignoring him or had severed Comms entirely. Regardless, the trapped Disciples were doomed if they weren't reinforced soon. He turned his head to the Disciples below in their little defensive camp. There were about fifty in total—many of them only now starting to don what armor they could find. Most had blades, a few spears.

He jumped from the bunk and his legs lit up briefly, absorbing the impact.

"What's wrong?" Jessica asked.

Finn and Romulan joined his side. Their armor was already

covered in Roach wax and gore.

"We're holding at the front," Finn reported. "We have over a dozen with linked shields. As long as they're not flanked, they should hold with ease."

"Good. But we have a group pinned down across the room. Adriana easily has a hundred and fifty Disciples at her back and instead of helping, she's fortifying her position. Without reinforcement, the Disciples over there will fall."

"If we only had a few Blazers," Jessica opined. "We could soften them up without getting too close."

"What do we do?" Romulan asked.

"Adriana's the commanding Alpha," Finn said. "This should be her call."

"She's staying put," Cojax said. "But maybe… there's another way."

It took several minutes of work before Cojax's idea began to take shape. The bunk beds, forged from Vantarite—the same alloy used in their armor—were harder than anything found naturally on Earth. Arc Blades could cut it, but only with effort and patience. Soon, two bunk beds became one and his mobile structure stood finished. Crude. Misshapen. But solid.

"Make some noise at the gate," Cojax said from inside the makeshift structure. "Try to draw them to the front so we can sneak out the back."

There wasn't a true gate—just bodies and shields at the front. But they seemed to understand regardless and started to perform the Death Rattle, an Acadian battle chant that was magnified by the speakers in the Disciple armor.

Then Cojax, Jessica, Finn, and seven others scaled the barricade and slipped into the madness, hefting the tank-like structure along with them.

Like the Trojan Horse thousands of years before, they went undetected at first, their mysterious moving shape not drawing the ire of the creatures. The ten inside were all volunteers, all covered in Roach wax and gore. Most had known one or two of the Disciples that were trapped, the rest followed Cojax because he was once the Alpha.

They rumbled forward, heading to the left side of the room,

the original source of the Roaches. Bunks were shoved aside, corpses stepped over, blood slick beneath their boots. Twice they had to climb over collapsed bunks, exposing themselves briefly. They took down any Roach stragglers quickly—no sound, no hesitation.

"We're almost there," Cojax said. "Keep moving—slow and steady."

Through his slat, he could see them—twenty Disciples still standing. Desperate. Cornered.

Then the Roaches paused. A shift in the air. A scent. A sound. Cojax saw them twitch. Mandibles flared. The clatter of legs grew louder.

"They've spotted us," he said. "Ramming speed!"

Finn blinked. "What happened to slow and steady?"

"Ramming speed!"

This was not a command they had practiced or even discussed. But the nine Disciples followed Cojax's cue, sprinting forward with the bunk beds in hand. Their combined strength and momentum became a battering ram as they knocked several of the creatures to the side, each one thudding as they hit metal.

They all began screaming. Blind, bold, and bloody, they drove on until their bunks reached the line of Disciples.

"Open the front door!" Cojax said.

There wasn't a real door—just a panel, cut three-quarters through.

Two Disciples peeled it open. It was less of a door and more of a hatch, just big enough to squeeze a person through. Once open, no instructions were needed. Disciples began to pour in one-by-one.

Finn was by the entrance, ushering them inside. "Head to the back. Keep the path clear. Keep moving. Go. Go." The space was quickly eaten up as the last warrior crowded inside.

Then came the scrapes.

A low screeching—chitin on metal.

The Reevers attacked the bed frames, their powerful jaws compressing the metal on all sides, testing the structure's strength. One of the metal sheets broke inward, but the press of bodies prevented it from opening completely. Claws scraped against the Vantarite bunk frames. One of the creatures crested the top edge, its spined legs curled around a metal bar as it peered down at the cowering bodies below. Another followed. Then two more.

"They're climbing over!" someone shouted.

Cojax shoved to the center. "Shields—up! Form a ceiling!"

Those few who had shields raised them up. The rest became manic with energy, swinging spears and blades alike. Finn stabbed a creature through the head and its blood gushed out in a black wave.

Another creature snapped its jaws, barely missing a taller Disciple before hooking onto one of the bunk bed supports, trapping itself from escape. Romulan put a blade through the thorax.

Then, without warning, the creatures began to retreat.

The closest Reever hissed low, like a signal. As if summoned, the others peeled away, falling back. One by one, they disappeared into the breach they had emerged from—clicking as they vanished, like fading metronomes counting down something unseen.

Silence fell, heavy and surreal.

Cojax's chest rose and fell with ragged breath. He stepped through the hatch, just in time to watch the last of the Roaches vanish into the dark, their spiked legs dragging behind them like fading shadows. The hole in the wall began to disappear as a latch mechanically lowered over it.

It was over.

For now.

A cry rang out—hoarse, unrestrained. Then another. Then dozens. The Disciples began to cheer. Tired, wounded, armor covered in gore and limbs shaking, they still raised their voices. A surge of relief swept through the bunk-barricade as weapons were lifted high. They had survived.

Jessica did not cheer like the rest. Something felt off—like a raindrop striking skin beneath a cloudless sky. Then it hit her, a realization she would never speak aloud, though others would come to it in time. The floor of the dormitory was empty of the fallen. The bloodstains remained, vivid and wet, but the bodies of the Disciples were gone—carried off by the retreating creatures, who now feasted upon them in tunnels of metal and concrete.

## THIRTY-FIVE

No one slept that night. The Roaches came two more times. Each time, they were beaten back, but not without cost. The Disciples spent the time reinforcing their defenses—cutting better connection points between the bunks, reinforcing the wall, cutting murder holes, shoring up gaps the Reevers had managed to make.

By the morning, there were two fortresses inside the expansive dormitory, complete with access ports, towers, and ramparts. Adriana's fortress was much bigger and housed the majority of the Disciples, but Cojax and Jessica's defenses were much better laid out and reinforced.

Cojax checked the schedule on his ArmGuard. "Looks like we have to be on the parade grounds before breakfast."

"Parade grounds?" Romulan said. "What are you talking about? Roaches breached the city? The Magisters will want us on the Wall defending Acadia, not running through the corridors."

"No," Jessica answered. "The Magisters were the ones that released the Roaches into the dormitory."

"The city isn't under attack," Cojax said, pointing to the large metallic lids on the wall. "That's where the Roaches came from and that's where they returned."

"Right," Romulan said, surprised at his own naïveté. "Of course. But that means we've had Roach tunnels connected to our dormitory this entire time."

Finn joined their small group, his voice light and full of life. "How'd everyone sleep?"

"I wouldn't know," answered Horacio in his low, baritone voice. "I was on the tower all night."

"None of us slept," Cojax said. "But it's nothing we aren't used to already. Who did we lose last night?"

"Sandrix and eighteen others," Finn answered solemnly. "That brings our count down to two hundred and forty or so.

There…were no bodies to count, but I was able to figure it out by referring to the roll on the ArmGuard."

There were no slow starts that morning—no one could afford it. They had to clean their weapons, polish their bronze, and reorganize their clothes. The room was still a mess—stained in blood and Roach bodies.

They arrived at the parade grounds early, as expected. Adriana and Brutus had fallen from the top spots—a reflection of their inaction at the battle, but not by much—they were still in the First Tier. Conversely, Cojax and his friends had surged in points. He began to feel his luck had changed, that the tides of fortune had shifted again. But a few thrown matches and threats later, Adriana and Brutus were back in the Alpha and Beta position. Cojax, on the other hand, despite the boost, was still so far behind.

Octavian took center stage in the parade grounds. "For perhaps the second time in your lives, you know the fear that the Roaches bring—the unrelenting struggle, the pain, the death. I hope you know that while you slept, ate, studied all these years, the Acadian people were dying to protect your freedom. While you watched us on the CityScreens, we gave our blood, our bodies, and our lives so that you may live. With the terror you felt last night, the friends you lost, I hope you never forget the price of your freedom.

"Like demonic gods from the past, your ancestors eventually rose from the depths of the earth, and reclaimed the land above, building walls to protect our people. Eventually, the Wall was built, forever separating us from the numberless horde of creatures. It now falls to you, to take up this gauntlet, to become the shield of Acadia, to sacrifice so that others may live. You're dismissed. Go grab breakfast and report back here for blade training."

At the word breakfast, Jessica's heart froze. This was it—the beginning of her plan, one that would either save the one she had come to admire or abandon him to the Rift.

*"I can't lose him."*

As they marched to the Dining Hall, she replayed the plan in her head. There were always unknown variables, but she accounted for everything she could.

*"It could work… it should work. I just have to be patient."*

She was the first to sit down at the tables—a break in routine as most grabbed their food first. Her seat had been well selected, right next to the table where Adriana always sat. After grabbing her food, the Alpha stopped, noticing Jessica's change in seating. Feigning indifference, she settled into her usual seat—directly back-to-back with the Aberration. Adriana's table filled, Jessica's did not. None of the Alpha's sycophants would dare sit next to the girl that had been singled out by a Numberless, and so they selected another table further away, effectively dividing them.

Once all Disciples had retrieved their trays, Jessica tapped a spoon against the table—a piercing sound but one that was easily missed among the conversations in the room. From all different tables, Disciples stood, moving in, repositioning their seats next to Jessica. Cojax was to her right, Finn to her left. Romulan, Callista, Ester, Horacio, Havish—they were all there in an instant.

This created a stir among Adriana and her followers—one that did not stop their conversation, but it certainly slowed it.

"Alright," Jessica said. "Time to have a little fun with Pavlov's dogs. Finn."

"Me," Finn said. "I don't know what that means."

"Tell us a story," Cojax said. "Make it a good one and I promise the rest of us will laugh."

Then Finn started to tell stories: some were true, most were false, but they were all so compelling that it was difficult to focus on anything else. Conversations around them crawled to a halt. The Disciples were forced to listen, entranced by the way Finn weaved his words, but they were also annoyed by it, as if they were being forced to listen against their will. Conversation in the Mahghetto was usually hushed, demure, diminished. Laughter was seldom outside of the dormitory, although not expressly forbidden.

Now their little group of friends were upending social protocol—forcing all else to listen. It was jarring going from the silence of the day before to this.

"This is going to get us attacked in the showers," Cojax whispered. "Jessica most of all."

"Don't worry," she answered. "We'll have to stick together and shower at odd times—defaulting to using the VaporSweeps as much as possible. They are much quicker."

"Egh," Romulan said. "I hate the VaporSweep. You might be

sterile, but it never makes me feel clean."

"Tell her about the time you tried your father's armor on," Finn said.

Cojax frowned. "There's nothing to tell."

"Tell it anyway."

"One time," Cojax said, "I tried my father's armor on."

The group paused, waiting for more.

Cojax finally shrugged his shoulders. "What? That's it. That's all there is to the story. You pretty much told it."

Finn jabbed a finger into Cojax's chest, "But what did he do when he found out?"

"That's not the story you asked me to share," Cojax said, his concentration shifting to his food. "And that's not one I care to share either."

"Titan made him wear it the rest of the day," Finn said with an explosion of laughter. "The kid was only ten. His entire body could have fit through one of the armholes! Titan made him go to school like that! It looked like he had been swallowed by a HoverBucket."

Laughter followed—genuine, unabated laughter. The kind of sound that existed when they were Innocents in the Games, when the Mahghetto was some abstract and uncertain concept.

Cojax shook his head. "You wore it too."

Finn smiled. "Yeah, and what did he do to me?"

"He told you never to wear it again," Cojax said with feigned bitterness. "That's not fair. I spent the rest of the day drowning in a sea of plated armor, and he lets you off with a weak warning. I'm his son."

Brutus did not know what to do. He kept turning around, a rebuke on the tip of his tongue, but then Adriana would pull him back. Instead, they tried to ignore it. They eventually gave up and finished their meal early, lining up in the hall.

"Pace yourself, Finn," Cojax said. "You've got to keep this up for three weeks—you sure you have enough stories to stretch it out to then?"

"I'm just getting started."

During blade training at the parade grounds, Cojax was punished for the free-flowing conversation—not by the Magisters, but by challenges in the dueling arena by Adriana's Lower Tier sycophants. They saw him as the leader, as the one behind their little band of renegades, and punishing him was the easiest path to silencing the group. Finn, too, was challenged—but his swift victory cooled any further ambition to silence the storyteller.

Before the duels, Jessica leaned over to Cojax with some final advice. "I want you to lose, but make it close."

"Lose? I can't afford that right now."

"We're playing the long game, not chasing short wins. Laugh while you fight—just like in the Dining Hall. But when you lose, let the laughter die, as if the defeat drained everything from you."

"Well, that's easy enough—that's exactly how I'll feel," Cojax said.

"Good, that means this might work."

"Might work?"

"It will work… we just have to stay the course."

"But I'm so far behind everyone right now."

"It will work," Jessica repeated.

## THIRTY-SIX

The final strike exploded against Finn's chestplate, shorting out the last of his armor's charge. He stumbled back, bracing against the sudden weight that crashed down upon his limbs.

"Blood and bile, Cojax," he muttered, catching his breath. "If you're going to start hitting that hard, I'm going to need to start wearing one of those Pulse Beacons."

Their small group had gathered once more in the storage room, steel ringing against the walls as they drilled their swordwork. Only a week had passed since the Roaches' first assault, yet the danger never lifted—each night brought another test. Sometimes it crashed upon them in full assaults; other times it crept in as probing strikes against their defenses.

"I wouldn't let my blade cut you," Cojax replied, lowering his Arc Blade. "Who's next?"

Romulan stepped forward without hesitation. Tall, loyal, fearless—but too rigid. Jessica knew his strengths the moment she saw him move, and more importantly, she saw his flaws. His form was precise in stillness, but each time Cojax shifted angles or leveraged uneven footing, Romulan's timing fractured.

Jessica circled to the side, voice sharp and deliberate. "You're fighting a living opponent, not a statue. Swordplay isn't about holding perfect form—it's about adapting without losing structure."
Romulan lunged, and Cojax countered with a shallow feint, cutting low and to the side.

"Adjust your rear foot! More weight on the ball," Jessica called out. "You're collapsing inward."

Romulan overextended. Cojax twisted, driving a shoulder into his chest, forcing Romulan back with a grunt.

"Center your mass. Lead with the blade, not your body," she instructed. "Now reset. Again."

They clashed once more. This time Romulan held tighter,

improved. But it only bought him seconds. Cojax's relentless blows chewed through the charge in Romulan's shield. Every impact bled light. When the final surge struck, the shield gave a spark and died.

The tall Disciple dropped to one knee, panting.

"That's it," Jessica said. "Good work, both of you. We've really hit our stride these last few days."

Cojax grinned, sweat slicking his brow. The swordplay had cleared his mind in a way no talking ever could. "I've still got charge left. What about you, Jessica?"

She shook her head. "I need to rest."

She didn't elaborate. Both of their armor was still recording. Any comment about her depleted reserves would be logged. She could teach—but stepping into a duel now would be reckless.

She required two charges a day now from the Golden Orb. One at dawn for training. One at night for the battle with the Roaches. It was always waiting for her in the storage room with a fresh charge.

Cojax's face fell, so did his guard. The blade had been his only escape. In motion, he could forget the weight of his Score, the fragility of his standing. But now, with the adrenaline draining from his veins, reality slammed back into place. His chest tightened. Breath came shorter.

He had performed brilliantly in the nightly battles—leading swift, flanking maneuvers against the Roaches, exploiting their chaos with ruthless disorder. More than once, he'd returned drenched in Reever wax, his armor steaming from the heat of combat. He'd commanded. He'd survived. He'd killed.

But none of it mattered.

For all his grit and bloodshed, he hadn't climbed. Not really. Only now, he had barely tied with the lowest-ranking Disciple.

"We'd better check the wall," Horacio said, tone grim. "No telling what the Magisters might have planned for tonight."

The words cut through the room like frost. Since the first breach, the Roaches had returned every night—relentless, evolving. It wasn't just Reevers anymore. Ankle Biters, Twisters, Erupters, Launchlings, and Leapers had begun to appear, slithering through corridors no one thought reachable.

Jessica led the return to the dormitory, shields locked tight—

four across the front, two deep on each flank. Weapons drawn. Traversing through the Mahghetto had become a dangerous endeavor. More than one Disciple had vanished without a sound on the way to the showers or the Medicus wing.

At the dormitory threshold, they broke formation. The danger hadn't disappeared, but the pressure lessened. If Roaches came now, the holding grates would shift first—giving them precious seconds to prepare.

Cojax sheathed his blade and surveyed their stronghold. The fortress had grown—now two bunk beds high, reinforced with scavenged beams welded together with Arc Blade heat, a discovery Horacio had made. The energy cost was extreme—but well worth it. Towers now stood at all four corners, offering sightlines over the entire enclosure.

"Open the gate," Romulan barked.

The metallic doors groaned open, swinging on welded hinges sunk deep into the concrete. Once inside, they shut and locked the gate with three iron bars—custom-fit into grooves cut by a blade.

"It's really coming along," Horacio said, wiping grime from his brow. "A far cry from our first hovel."

"And thanks to you," Jessica replied.

He gave a dismissive shrug but couldn't suppress the pride tugging at the corners of his mouth.

The mattresses were piled into the center—cramped, orderly, utilitarian. Survival didn't care about comfort.

Callista approached, brushing dust from her shoulders. Her black hair framed her sharp features, eyes alight with mischief.

"You missed blade practice," Finn said quickly, a little too quickly. His cheeks flushed.

Cojax caught it—Finn's blush, the flicker in his voice. *"He likes her."*

"I was helping raise the top tower," Callista replied, unfazed. "It gives a full view of the dorm. We add another two just like it and you might be able to touch the ceiling."

"What did you see?" Finn asked, stepping closer, interest leaking into every word.

"Adriana's crew is building her a private room."

Cojax's brow tightened. "Are you sure? Their walls aren't even two bunks high."

"Oh, I'm sure," Callista said, amused. "Give her time, she'll be carving a throne."

"What a fool," Cojax muttered.

As the lights dimmed, those who were not on guard duty settled uneasily onto their mattresses. Armor stayed on. Only helmets came off. Blades were drawn but tucked beneath them. Uncomfortable, yes. But exhaustion dulled everything. Sleep came quickly.

An hour later, the alarms screamed.

Three grates blew open—two of them inside Adriana's stronghold. Ankle Biters poured in, fast and low. Reevers came behind, snarling.

From their tower, Jessica watched it unfold. Adriana panicked and gave command to Brutus, who bellowed orders. He organized a three-lined shieldwall—unorthodox, but effective. It was a probing attack—sharp and sudden—but not a full breach.

"They'll hit our side next," Cojax said, already strapping his helmet on. "Make sure everyone is ready."

## THIRTY-SEVEN

Marcus found his way to the Red District quickly. The attendants at the front recognized him on sight—an increasingly common occurrence.

That wasn't a good sign.

Becoming a regular in the Red District meant you were bleeding somewhere deeper, you were Weighted. Marcus didn't like what that said about him.

He tapped a panel on his armor. With a faint *click*, a concealed compartment unfolded along his waist. Inside was a small bag of chits—slender bits of encoded metal currency, barely thicker than a nail. He tucked them into his uniform and kept moving.

He still didn't know why Ion had summoned him here of all places. But if he was going to be dragged into the gutter, he might as well get some Stock while he was down here.

Stock wasn't free.

To buy it, you needed chits—each embedded with a digital signature that self-authenticates when exchanged. There was no forging them, no faking. The only way to earn chits was to work for the Saken Faction directly. Not for points. For *them*.

That meant polishing armor. Cleaning out drains. Replacing hydraulic lifts or reprogramming flickering light circuits in the Saken Faction Hall. Menial work. Tasks beneath most Ninth Tiers. When a Saken did it, the points went to them. When anyone *outside* the Faction did it, the points were awarded to the Saken ledger, and the outsider was paid in chits—disconnected from the system, untraceable.

The most efficient way to earn chits—and perhaps the most humiliating—was to participate in a sham duel. You entered the ring, forfeited the match the moment it started, and your opponent's Score went up while you got paid. Marcus had only done it twice.

Both times, it twisted his stomach.

He wasn't wired to lose on purpose. The moment a duel began, instinct took over. He couldn't help but fight, even when the outcome was fixed. According to the Acadian Code, a duel had to be resolved once initiated—either by shield depletion or formal forfeit. There was rarely a draw.

In this system, the winner gained Score. The loser gained chits. The Saken Faction gained both. It was a masterstroke of corruption. A black market of reputation and influence—hidden in plain sight. And somehow, the Numberless had never shut it down.

Marcus exhaled. "Why do they allow this to stay open?"

He clenched his jaw, pushing deeper into the heart of the District. He had chewed on this question every time he stepped inside this small enclave of lawlessness and disorder.

He pushed the thought aside and entered *Rigor Mortis*. The bar had the same stench as always: hot iron, old blood, and burning synthetic oils. The lighting was low, stained amber by the paned luminaires overhead. The music wasn't music at all—just bassy, rhythmic pulses meant to mimic a heartbeat. Patrons didn't speak much here, and when they did, it was close to the ear or behind a drawn hood.

Marcus spotted Ion immediately.

The stocky man sat at a corner booth, back pressed to the wall, eyes darting every time someone entered. He wore a bulky uniform two sizes too big and had one hand clenched around a cup of steaming Stock he hadn't touched.

Marcus made his way over. He didn't sit at first—just looked down at his old friend, waiting.

Ion cracked a thin smile. "Still got that slow, angry walk. That's good. Means you're still you."

Marcus slid in across from him, not returning the smile. "You asked me to meet here. Out of all places."

"Yeah." Ion scratched at the base of his neck, where a half-finished neural port glinted against his skin—an upgrade that allowed him to interface directly with the Acadian System. "Figured it was the one place no one would be listening. Or caring."

Marcus grunted. "What is this about?"

What followed were awkward pleasantries. Ion mentioned the old Mahghetto trials. Brought up a story about a malfunctioning Arc

Blade. Tried to laugh. Marcus didn't.

Then the questions came.

Innocent at first. Vague hypotheticals about energy transfer. About siphoning small charges from isolated panels. Theoretical vulnerabilities in Acadia's outer grid. Marcus answered cautiously, aware the conversation was skating on something thin and cold.

"You were an ElectraTech once, right?"

"Yeah, it was my Second Stewardship before the Archives. I did it for two years—got pretty good at it too."

"A Golden Orb," he said, smiling like this was casual conversation. "In theory, could it be powered by tapping into city power?"

Marcus had gone still, the cup in his hand tightening until it creaked.

"You want to tap city power to feed a *Golden Orb*? Ion, do you know how difficult that'd be? The feedback surge alone—"

"We'd control the feedback," Ion whispered. "With a splitter, with calibration. It's all theory. I swear."

"Blood and bile, Ion, cut the theory talk. What are you trying to do?"

Ion hesitated, his face shaking. He took another swig. Then another. Each one seemed to make him more nervous. He finally muttered, "Can… I trust you?"

"Trust?" Marcus asked. "We were blood brothers in the Mahghetto—I was the Alpha, you the Beta. If you can't trust me, you can't trust anyone."

"This is big," Ion said.

"You're trying to raise your Score by using a Golden Orb, right?" Marcus said. "What? Second Tier food selection not good enough for you?" This barely passable joke seemed to break Ion's secrecy altogether.

"I'm not cut out for this."

"What?"

"I'm part of a group—an underground movement."

Marcus' tongue caught in his mouth. He knew where this path was going.

"We're trying to *break Acadia*, Marcus. We're trying to take it down from the inside."

Silence fell between them like a blade.

Marcus's heart thudded slowly, each beat dragging like iron through his chest. He stared at the man across from him, the same one who once pulled him from the maw of a Reever in the Mahghetto.

"And you think I'll just help?" Marcus said at last. "You're asking me…" He glanced around carefully, triple-checking that no one was within earshot. "…to commit treason. You think our memories give you the right to ask that? Do you even know what these people want from you? Or what will happen if *you* get caught? This is Acadia—the last human city—and you want to take it down?"

Ion's voice cracked. "I didn't know who else to turn to. You were always the one who—"

"And then what? Once our system breaks? Will you let the Roaches come on in and feast?"

"No," Ion said. "We're just going to change the system. Stop the Riftings, the Releases, the brutality. Haven't you ever wondered how different things would be if there was no more war?"

"The only way the fighting stops is if we drive the Roaches to extinction."

Ion let out a long breath. "Acadia is *not* the last human city, and we don't have to be in this war. It's all lies. I can't tell you more than that—for your own safety. But we need your help. We need to charge a Golden Orb."

"Stealing it from the grid is possible, but not for long. Ion, if you try that, they will eventually trace the leak and you'll be caught. Only an ElectraTech could do something like that. Or find a Nova that's willing to share their charge—still illegal but much less likely to get caught."

"And *you're* a Nova—one of the few in the city."

That stopped Marcus cold. How had Ion found out?

"Please, I need help. Can you charge a Golden Orb for me?"

"Yes…maybe. For how long?"

"A few months."

"A few months," Marcus hissed. "I might as well jump into the Rift. Golden Orbs slowly deteriorate the user—taking more than just energy every time. A few months and I'd be lucky to be a Third Tier."

"It's a matter of life or death."

"So you can do what? Destroy the city?"

"I'm not explaining this well," Ion said, standing abruptly. "This was a mistake. Please…please forget everything I said."

Marcus grabbed him by the arm.

"You came here to solicit me into sedition," he said, voice measured but burning beneath. "Acadia is what keeps us alive, Ion. Don't let them convince you otherwise. Break ties with that group. Never contact them again."

"I just—" Ion shook his head, panic in his eyes. "I didn't mean to do it like this. I'm sorry, Marcus. I'm *sorry*."

He fled.

Marcus slumped back into his seat. Eyes closed. Breathing heavily. Things had been going so well for him lately and now this. He drank for hours after that. Stock—thick, bitter, distilled from the marrow of synthetic cattle—burned through his system like chemical fire. He welcomed it. Anything to chase the numbness gnawing inside him. The Red District faded around him, blurring into lights and movement and sound.

His best friend was a traitor.

And he was now part of it—just for knowing.

He could turn Ion in. Report everything to the Numberless. Walk into the Trinity and purge his conscience with a confession. Or he could pretend he hadn't heard a word. But pretending wouldn't erase the truth. There *was* a group working to bring down the city. And if they'd gotten to Ion—a quiet, loyal, and fiercely dedicated Validated—then it meant things weren't just beginning.

They were already in motion.

*"They aren't planning a rebellion—they're neck-deep in it."*

Marcus took another drink.

# THIRTY-EIGHT

Marcus' head throbbed—remnants of a hangover still echoing behind his eyes. Another night spent drinking Stock, but this time, he'd done it alone. He was in no condition to be on the Wall. But he showed up anyway.

He always did.

He barely made it on time, boots clunking against the stone just as the shift bell echoed across the ramparts. He was a soldier— he'd sooner drag a broken leg than miss his post.

As he paced the length of the Wall, the Validated from his Decuria saluted him in turn. He returned the gestures with far less enthusiasm, his mind spinning too fast to feign composure.

Lately, life had meant more.

He had begun to read again—*truly* read. Strategy texts, philosophy, old works of lost civilizations. He excelled as a Gamma, leading his ten thousand Validated into battle after battle—each engagement sharper, more efficient, more successful—honed by the very ideas he once thought he'd never have time to understand. He'd shared real conversation with Sejanus. Not postured rhetoric or rehearsed praise, but actual discourse. And then there was Aleniana. They were not close, but they were closer now than they'd ever been. In five months, his children would be delivered by the Scolastica Genetica. Not his biologically, perhaps, but it didn't matter. He was going to be a father.

So why did Ion's words still cut so deeply? He couldn't shake them. The edge of them kept turning over in his mind like a blade on a whetstone. He would never support the collapse of Acadia. At least, not before he knew another way might exist.

The AC had always seemed indispensable—brutal, yes, but born of war, of necessity, of the survival of the last human city. But was that really true? Ion didn't seem to think so.

What had he said? *"That the war didn't have to go on? That it was all a lie?"*

Part of Marcus wished he had let his friend explain more. The other part regretted not shutting him down the moment he realized what was being said.

*"Ion is a traitor,"* Marcus thought, *"...or a patriot. Depends on who wins the revolution."*

He shook his head. No, Ion was going to end up dead. The Numberless, the Acadian System, the Mahghetto—it was all too entrenched to simply disappear. Uprooting it wasn't like cracking a code. It was gutting a living organism.

And then there were the Roaches.

*"How would Acadia survive the endless swarm without the structure? Without the Code? Without discipline carved into children and obedience boiled into bone? How could anyone believe there was a future beyond that?"*

Marcus squinted, trying to focus his mind. But there was a cost, as the pain in his head could attest. He was at the Western Parallels—a stretch of wall where, for half a mile, the twin barriers of the city ran side by side before converging at the Western Gate. He was only granted half of his Decuria, a mere five thousand. The Parallels were hardly ever attacked, and if they were, it was always a slaughter, the two walls providing the perfect height advantage to rain down light and brimstone upon the charging army.

Then he was hit hard in the back, his body pitching over and rolling to the side, his circular shield torn from his grip.

"Sir… the… in… now," said a voice through the Comm-Link in his helmet. The words were broken and disjointed. A frustrating rage tore through his body and he turned around, his blade already drawn. He was expecting to see an enemy, perhaps one of those Hellions that tried to pick a fight with him in the Red District.

*"They had spent this time plotting… waiting for the right time to strike…"* When he whipped around, these thoughts evaporated as he took in a horrific sight. Thousands of Roach Fliers were dropping from the skies, each one aimed at a patrolling Acadian with its three-prong stingers.

*"But…how?"* Marcus thought. He did not have time to answer his own question before he was performing the work of death, his Arc Blade cutting creatures in half with each swing, leaving behind a smell like burned onions.

Marcus saw the one that had hit him. It was an ugly, porous creature, its dozen eyes black and beady. At its full height, it was twice as tall as Marcus but it curved around like a larva, making it seem more bulky than tall. Pus and putrid liquid poured out of various orifices, a dozen appendages spread up its body, each one a weapon in its own right. Its primary weapon was the two-foot-long stingers—one on its tail, another on its belly, a third on its head. The object was simple—fall from the sky, smashing the shields of the warriors below and skewering them in one quick movement.

The attack had worked surprisingly well. Almost all of his Validated were already trapped beneath the sudden horde of creatures. Most of their shields had shattered. The rest were overwhelmed by dozens of thrashing appendages. Within minutes, his entire Decuria assigned to him that day would be lost.

"Blood and bile," Marcus said over the Comm-Link. "We have Fourth Class Crashers at the Parallels! Call up the reserve Invictorian!" There should have been an immediate response—or at the very least an acknowledgment that it was received... but... nothing.

"We have Crashers at the Parallels! My Decuria is under attack!" Marcus yelled.

A voice over the Comm-Link crackled back. "We... nothing... sev... eral... posi... tion...."

Marcus narrowed his eyes, trying to parse the garbled words. He was going to try again, but then he saw it, an enormous slug of a creature on the battlement, slowly sliding its way up. It was quivering as if shaking from the cold, a low hum emanating from its body.

*"How did they get a Slug past the sensors?"* He had no time to piece it all together; as long as that slimy thing lived, their Comm-Link would struggle to work. The attack had been perfectly executed, and the Wall was getting overwhelmed, surpassing their best line of defense.

A horde of Crashers flew in low—some fast, some slow—blocking his path to the Slug. Their forms twitched and twisted midair, hovering on membranous wings like stitched-together carrion birds. One dove, claws extended.

Marcus met it midair, cleaving it straight through the thorax.

Another slammed into his shoulder. He stumbled, barely

keeping his footing, the jolt rattling through his helmet like a bell. He retaliated with a wide arc of his blade, the weapon pulsing with energy as it bit through hardened chitin and left half a creature melting on the floor.

Three more surrounded him.

His strikes were still lethal, still precise—but not *clean*. He was too slow. His timing was off. His balance dulled by the Stock.

*"Blood and bile,"* Marcus thought. *"You're fighting half-awake."*

A stinger slammed into his side. His shield flared. Two more insects struck him in quick succession, his shield hemorrhaging light. He was able to kill two before the third struck him in the back. He turned around, separating its head from its body.

He gritted his teeth and pushed forward. *"No time to fight. Push on."* If he didn't reach that Slug, every warrior under his command was going to die from the onslaught. He bellowed a horrific war cry, magnified by the speakers in his armor. The large man surged forward, his size enough to send most enemies reeling. The creatures would pay. They would suffer for attacking Marcus, The First in the Gap at the Battle of Menoch.

He surged down the battlement, deflecting a strike with the hilt of his Arc Blade, then spun low and severed a Crasher's legs from its body. Another came from behind, but he pivoted, letting it drive itself straight into his edge.

His HUD screamed at him—warning lights dancing across the display of his diminishing shield. The Crashers were not agile, but their stingers could deliver a powerful blow. He ignored it all.

One of the creatures had tangled a warrior against the wall, pinning her with its stinger against the rampart. Marcus ripped the thing away in one brutal cleave and pulled the woman up with his free hand.

"Form up!" he barked. "Anyone with a blade, follow me!"

The call pierced the fog of panic. Warriors turned. Some bled. Some limped. But they followed. More were freed as he fought. One by one. Then in twos. Then in clusters. His Decuria began to reform. Twenty. Thirty. Then nearly fifty, rallying behind him, pushing on. *"We have to reach that Slug."*

They moved like a tide through the carnage, cutting toward the gelatinous beast. It was enormous—its bloated body clinging to the battlement wall like a sack of trembling flesh. The hum coming from it had grown deeper, more dissonant. A nauseating drone that buzzed in the molars.

Marcus didn't wait.

He drove his blade into the Slug's center mass, twisting hard. The creature shrieked, the sound sharp and wet, like steam escaping meat. It convulsed violently, ichor spraying in every direction. Its humming died with it. He stabbed it again and again. He repositioned on top of the creature, slicing at a wayward eye before driving his blade into the brain box.

Immediately, his Comm-Link flared back to life.

"...repeat: Gamma Marcus, confirm your position. We've dispatched a Phalanx."

"I'm alive," Marcus growled, still catching his breath. "Western Parallels compromised. Enemy types: Class IV Crashers and a Class V Slug. Repeat, we've reestablished communications. But scratch the Phalanx. We need an Invictorian deployed. This is a full-scale invasion."

"Received. Your orders are to hold the Wall at all costs. Invictorian en route."

But even before he could finish, something slammed behind him. The sound of claws scraping metal.

He turned.

Three hulking forms had landed on the battlements—Class V *Launchers.*

Shell-backed monstrosities, they launched themselves across vast distances by violently dislocating their own spines, converting the whip-crack recoil into raw inertia. Twelve jagged, javelin-like appendages bristled from their carapaces—each one capable of impaling a boar mid-run. Their wide maws hung open at unnatural angles, as if unhinged, gaping with rows of uneven teeth slick with gore. The stench of rotting flesh clung to them, thick and foul, like meat left to sour in the sun.

The first hurled a javelin-sized limb.

Marcus deflected it—but the impact nearly threw him over the edge. Another leapt onto him, claws slashing. His shields flashed with light. The first strike raked across his chestplate. Sparks flew, his shield gave out. He staggered. The creature moved in, its jaw wide. It clamped down on his left arm with a wet *crack*. Pain rippled through his body—but then... nothing. The Launcher's head was already retracting. It had thankfully released its grip almost as soon as it bit down on his flesh.

This gave Marcus the opening he needed.

He drove his Arc Blade upward, ramming it through the creature's chin and into its skull. It spasmed violently, then collapsed. Other Validated joined him, driving toward the other two Launchers. The creatures twisted violently, but they were overcome by the smaller, more agile opponents. Marcus stood there, heaving, blood soaking through the joint of his armor. His left hand felt strangely light.

Too light.

He looked down.

And saw nothing.

Just below the elbow, his arm was gone—bitten clean off. He stared at it for a moment, the pain a distant buzz, unsure whether it was the shock or the blood loss that made the world sway.

Then he collapsed.

## THIRTY-NINE

Cojax and his friends worked themselves to exhaustion each day—first in their sanctioned classes, then again under Jessica's instructions at night. Days blurred. The Rifting loomed closer.

Since the Mahghetto had begun, Cojax had wished time would pass quickly. But now, for the first time, he wanted it to slow down. He had put off this conversation long enough. Tonight, he was determined. After the others had gone, and just before she could follow, he reached out and pulled Jessica gently into the storage room.

"What were you thinking about today?" he asked.

She smirked. "You want the whole playlist or just the general theme?"

"You were more focused than usual—and that's saying something."

Jessica scratched her arm, then locked eyes with him. There was something about the way Cojax asked questions—earnest and without pretense. It made truth feel like a duty.

"My father," she said at last.

Cojax sat on a crate and motioned for her to join him. She hesitated. Tomorrow was too important to waste on distractions—and if this was a distraction, it was a tempting one.

Cojax caught her hesitation and grinned, the boyishness in him flickering through. "If this is my last night alive, then I—"

"—want it to be with me?" she said, raising an eyebrow.

"Well," he replied, his grin softening, "or something like that."

"How often has that line worked before?"

"If you stay," he said, confidence returning, "just once. But it's the one time I really want it to."

Jessica sighed and sat beside him. Her features were drawn from fatigue, but her expression remained warm.

"You were saying… about your father."

"I was only nine when he died," she said. "I don't have a steel trap memory like yours, but I remember some things. That's a compliment, by the way. Be careful—if your head gets any bigger, it might not fit inside your helmet."

"I think that's the first joke I've ever heard you make," Cojax said, feigning shock.

"Who said I was joking?"

He laughed. "That makes two in ten seconds. You keep going, and Finn might have competition."

She shook her head. "I'm not good at this."

"This?"

"Talking. To people."

Cojax laughed. "I once saw you face down over twenty Disciples who wanted your blood, and you didn't even flinch."

"That's different—more familiar."

"Tell me about your father. It seemed like you were going to say something before we got sidetracked by my alleged massive head."

Her voice softened. "He's gone now. He wasn't my real father, not by birth anyway."

"I'm sorry."

"He was a good man. Always found something to laugh about. People liked him—I remember that. We had visitors all the time, especially in winter. Ours was one of the only homes with a fireplace, and I think he felt bad for the ones who didn't have one."

"Fireplace?"

"It's a stone structure. You build a fire inside it and the smoke gets funneled up through a vent in the roof."

"I know what it is," Cojax said, squinting slightly. "I just don't understand why anyone would build one."

"To keep warm."

He shook his head. "Your world… it's strange."

"Oh, come on," Jessica said, a grin tugging at her lips. "You've seen fire. You know it's warm. Using it to heat a home just makes sense."

"We have heaters for that."

"Imagine if you didn't."

He paused. "I see your point."

Jessica inhaled and looked away, her voice quieter now. "Listen… life wasn't easy—before I came here. It was difficult… but in a different way. Food was scarce. Water had to be hoarded. We grew our own crops and guarded them—especially from those who didn't."

"Your food didn't just appear in chutes?" Cojax asked, a grin playing at the corners of his mouth.

Jessica gave him a look. "Now you're messing with me. Do you really think everyone's food comes out of a wall?"

"No, I know people actually have to grow their own food," he admitted.

"It's harder than you think."

Cojax shrugged. "Seeds in the ground, splash a little water, then wait. Unless you mix up the order of those three things, I don't see how it could be complicated. We studied agriculture in school."

"Where is your food grown?"

He hesitated. "Some of it's grown in the Trinity, I think. In hydro-domes or something."

"That might be enough for the Numberless if they weren't mostly in Crono-Stasis. But for ten million?"

Cojax exhaled, rubbing the back of his neck. "Fair point. I guess I don't know. But what were you saying about your father?"

Jessica nodded slowly. "He had a big heart."

"A big heart?"

"It's an expression where I'm from. It means he was kind."

Cojax raised an eyebrow. "The heart's a muscle that circulates blood. How does that mean anything?"

She laughed—his confusion was genuine, and that made it all the funnier. "It's just a saying. No idea where it came from. Your people have sayings, too."

"Yeah, but ours make sense."

Jessica grinned. "Like what? 'Don't get all shiny'?"

"What's wrong with that?"

"You saying I sparkle?"

"In certain light," Cojax said, leaning closer with a wink, "you might."

"You're a fool." She gave him a playful shove, her hand

lingering briefly on his chestplate. The motion was lighthearted—but something shifted. Her touch lingered longer than she intended. Her eyes traced the armor up his torso, then paused. A warmth spread through her, uninvited and unwelcome, yet impossible to ignore. Her fingers twitched with the impulse to reach past the armor, to feel the muscle beneath. She wanted to touch his arms. She wanted to kiss him.

Cojax felt her eyes on him and looked down—drawn to her lips. Full. Soft. His breath caught. Slowly, almost without meaning to, he leaned in and their lips touched. First softly, and then with passion. When the kiss broke, she rested her head on his chest, feeling the warmth of his armor. A warmth that tomorrow might disappear completely. She pushed the thought away.

Cojax's voice fell low. "Whatever happens tomorrow… I hope you know that… I hope you know I'm grateful for having met you. For opening my eyes." He suddenly shifted, remembering something. "I have something for you."

Jessica leaned back slightly, caught off guard. He placed something in her hand—cold, metallic. She brought it closer to the dim light: a necklace of dark leather, set with a curved talon.

"It's beautiful," she whispered.

"It's a Keen-Keen talon," Cojax said. "My father told me they used to be everywhere. He found it on a fallen Damnattii—"

But Jessica's gaze had drifted. Her fingers still held the talon, but her thoughts were clearly elsewhere.

Cojax leaned forward and gently touched her hand. She didn't pull away. Despite a flicker of guilt, the warmth in her touch sent a quiet thrill through him. He suppressed the smile that threatened to rise and focused on her troubled expression.

"What is it?"

Jessica shook her head. "This is all wrong."

"What's wrong?"

"I've heard the word *Keen-Keen* before," Jessica said quietly, "when my father was trading with them…"

"Them?" Cojax asked.

Jessica nodded. "The Damnattii."

He blinked. "Do any of your people speak Acadian?"

She shook her head. "No, we spoke English. That's what I

don't understand."

"What don't you understand?"

Jessica leaned back slightly, her brow furrowed. "The Roaches had several birds caught in one of their machines. It happens sometimes—those things pull in all sorts of flying creatures when they move. They let us clean the birds off and keep them… to eat."

"Ugh," Cojax muttered, recoiling ever so slightly.

"One of the Damnattii pointed to a bird and called it a *Keen-Keen*."

Cojax stared at her. "So?"

"So…" she said, the word lingering in the air. "The Damnattii use the exact same word the Acadians use—for a very specific animal. A bird that barely exists anymore. That's not coincidence, Cojax. That's impossible."

She grew quiet, rifling through memories long buried. She could still hear their guttural language—a series of choking syllables, thick and primal. She had tried back then to make sense of it, but she had been too young, too afraid.

Cojax frowned, gears turning behind his eyes. "What are you saying?"

"I'm saying the Damnattii and the Acadians are connected. There has to be a common past."

He crossed his arms. "That's a leap."

Jessica didn't flinch. "You're the math prodigy. What are the odds that two entirely different civilizations—one alien—would use the *exact* same word for an obscure creature?"

Cojax opened his mouth, then shut it again.

"Not improbable," Jessica said. "Impossible. *Acadian* have must descended from their language—or the other way around."

Cojax stood and paced half a step, his expression hardening. "That makes even less sense. We've fought against the Damnattii and Roaches for centuries."

"I know," she said. "It doesn't make sense. But that's what makes it worth asking. We need to talk to a Damnattii now more than ever."

For a moment, neither of them spoke. Then Cojax stood, stretching his back and offering her a hand.

"Well," he said, pulling her gently to her feet, "my armor's almost charged—and I doubt this little discussion would be sanctioned by our Magisters. So, thanks for upsetting every paradigm in my head. Again."

His voice was dry, but his smirk betrayed him.

Jessica smiled and squeezed his hand. "We'd better get back so you can get some sleep. The plan will work, Cojax. Have faith."

He wanted to protest—to point out how many things still had to go right for his Score to shift so drastically. Tomorrow was the final day before the Rifting, and he remained in the bottom five. But he didn't want to waste their last quiet moment with pragmatism. Not tonight. Not with her. So, he let the argument die on his lips… and kissed her instead.

## FORTY

At lunch, Cojax laughed so loudly and so obnoxiously that nearby Disciples turned to stare, convinced he'd finally lost his mind. Normally, others would've sat with them—but Jessica had warned them off. Today, they needed to appear weak. Isolated. Vulnerable.

The three of them—Cojax, Finn, and Jessica—had deliberately taken the table directly behind Adriana, Brutus, and several other Top Tier Disciples, as had become their routine.

From the moment Cojax sat, the table erupted into a calculated performance: chirping, clanking laughter, inside jokes, and exaggerated cheer. Cojax and Finn—both having perfected their obnoxiously bright, birdlike laughs—led the charge. At the peak of one story, Cojax leapt to his feet and raised a glass mid-toast while Finn regaled them with a tale about swapping Brutus' toothbrush with a neighbor's. At the punchline, Cojax accidentally slipped, splashing cold water across the backs of the Disciples seated behind him.

Adriana calmly wiped her ArmGuard, her expression icy and unreadable. But Brutus bristled.

"Adriana!" Cojax exclaimed with a mock bow. "My sincerest apologies, oh Front Runner. Runner of the Front. The Front that—you—run. But you can't blame me, can you? Did you hear that story? Right from under Brutus' nose."

"Enough!" Brutus barked, his face flushing with fury.

"Easy," Cojax said under his breath, hands raised. "We don't want any trouble."

"Then keep your dimmed laughter down," Adriana said coldly, "or I'll drive my blade through both your skulls."

"We'll tone it down," Finn offered, wagging a finger. "But you can't kill us—that'd be a direct violation of the AC. And nobody's above the Code."

"That includes you, Cojax," Brutus snarled. "Why don't you

just find the Rift and jump? Why drag this out? You think this circus is what your father would've wanted?"

"No, Brutus, I don't," Cojax replied. "I'm just surprised that you're still the Beta, given your analytical mind."

That drew a reaction. Brutus' jaw clenched. The Dining Hall fell eerily silent. Across the chamber, heads turned. First to Brutus. Then to Cojax. The tension had hung in the air for the last three weeks—now, it was at a breaking point. And yet, somehow, the tension deflated. Plates clattered again. Voices resumed.

Finn picked up the rhythm with another tale—this one about the time Cojax showed up to school an entire day early.

"The best part," Finn said theatrically, "is that he stayed there half the day, convinced it was some kind of endurance test."

"That's not how it happened," Cojax countered. "First off, it was thirty minutes. And second—there's nothing wrong with being cautious."

Finn laughed so hard he dropped his fork. Jessica snorted into her sleeve.

Brutus slammed both palms on the table as he stood. "Enough! I've listened to this drivel long enough. Nobody cares about your pathetic little memories. If you had an ounce of honor, you'd stop acting like children."

Finn spun toward him, hands raised. "Come on, brother. It's just a story—one that used to make you laugh."

Then something happened Jessica hadn't predicted.

Adriana stood.

Her hand was on Brutus' arm—not to incite him, but to restrain. Her expression remained severe, but her grip was firm. She wasn't escalating. She was trying to pull him back. The situation had spun past her control, and even Adriana knew it. The situation was becoming unpredictable.

"Well," she said, voice sharp and projecting, "I, for one, won't sit here and listen to you three Rifters debase yourselves." Her tone was commanding, but her eyes betrayed something else—pleading. "Come, Brutus. Let them rot in their own decay."

Brutus stiffly grabbed his tray and turned to follow—but Cojax had one last card to play.

"Funny you speak of honor, Brutus," Cojax said, voice low

and bitter. "When you were the one who left me to die in the Tunnels. You couldn't best me until I had a hole in my leg."

"I'm the Beta. Not you," Brutus snapped. "I shattered you the last time we crossed blades. Or have you forgotten? I've always been better than you."

Cojax raised his voice, loud enough for the entire hall to hear. "Remember when Brutus got sick during the Games? Soiled himself right there on the sands?" He turned slowly, addressing the crowd now. "I went to fetch him clean trousers. But it wasn't me who sat outside the bathroom, warning others it was down for maintenance. That was Hadrian. The same boy Brutus called weak. Hadrian shielded him from shame when he couldn't even stand. And now, Brutus wraps himself in rank and acts like he's above the rest of us."

Brutus' hand went to his sword. Cojax mirrored him. Their blades cleared in the same breath, igniting with a crackle of searing light.

"No!" Adriana barked. "There will be no fighting in the Dining Hall."

Cojax held his ground. "I don't want to fight you, Brutus. Once, I called you a friend. I won't stain that memory."

Brutus scoffed. "A coward to the end."

Adriana's voice cut sharper now. "There will be no fighting."

But Brutus couldn't let it go—not now, not ever again. For weeks, they'd all been conditioned to endure Cojax's laughter: loud, unrestrained, unchallenged. The only time it ever stopped was after a duel—after someone reminded him of his place. Now, staring at him, seeing the smaller frame and that pitiful Score, Brutus wondered how Cojax had ever bested him in anything. It was incomprehensible.

*"He's nothing. He always was."*

Brutus would remind him—remind everyone—why he was the Beta.

"No, Adriana," Brutus said, his gaze never leaving Cojax, "he's Bottom Tier. He's not worth the armor he wears or the sword he carries. And today, I will remind him of that."

"I don't want to fight," Cojax repeated.

"Of course you don't," Brutus sneered. "You have two wins to your name. Weeks old, both of them. Your Score is so low it's almost nonexistent. You're not a threat, you're a relic."

Adriana appeared calm, but Jessica—watching closely—noticed her left hand nervously twisting at her side. The whole hall was watching. Her authority, carefully arranged and reinforced through weeks of psychological manipulation, was beginning to slip. Brutus had never gone against her wishes. She had to act—or lose control.

"Brutus, as soon as we get on the parade grounds, remind him of his place," she announced, framing it in such a way that it sounded like her idea.

Chaos erupted as trays clattered, chairs scraped back, and bodies scrambled. Lunch was cut short by the mere anticipation of the conflict. Within thirty seconds, the chaos resolved into crisp, symmetrical rows. Eyes forward. Backs straight.

As soon as they were in the parade grounds, Brutus' voice filled the room. "I challenge Cojax!"

Minor Magisters lined the walls, caught off guard by the abrupt arrival. But something shifted—whether they sensed the tension or simply read the room, it didn't matter. The combat chamber stirred to life.

Cojax felt the nerves kicking in—his feet restless, fingers twitching on his ArmGuard. He refused to meet Brutus' eyes. Instead, he stepped toward Thea, helmet in hand. Of all the Magisters, Thea was the one he needed. Loud. Bombastic. Pride in her Tier.

Cojax lowered his voice to a whisper. "It's not fair, ma'am. I'm Bottom Tier. Brutus is the Beta. I'll probably be challenged by the Alpha next... maybe the third-ranked after that. Three fights back-to-back? I can't. That isn't proper training—it's just a beating."

Thea was so shocked by these words, she did not have an immediate reply. "Are you a coward?"

"No," Cojax answered, shifting nervously. "I just don't think having three fights back-to-back is fair."

At the word *fair*, Thea jolted—an involuntary, visceral response. It was as if he'd questioned something sacred, something so self-evident it bordered on absurd.

"Acadia is fair, boy. What you have is what you've earned. If they challenge you, it's because they've earned the right. And if ten of them step forward, then you'll face every last one—until your shields break."

Thea, her veins pulsing, addressed the group with a violent tone. She pointed to Adriana, the Alpha, the leader of their group. "He's afraid of you! Afraid that you and your followers will challenge him in turn and defeat him one by one. He says it's not *fair*, not right that the greatest are picking on the least."

Adriana should have answered immediately—every eye in the room was on her. But she hesitated. Indecision flickered across her face, the gears behind her eyes still turning, caught mid-calculation.

Cojax stepped in closer, voice weak and urgent now. "Please, ma'am. I didn't mean disrespect. I'm just trying to survive…"

"Are you afraid of him?" Thea asked. Her words were sharp, deliberate—a stark contrast to Cojax's measured, subservient tone.

Again, Adriana hesitated—long enough for those watching to notice. Disciples began to whisper.

Finally, she replied, her voice sharp but faltering beneath the surface. "He's beneath me. A Rifter. One foot already in the abyss."

Thea's expression darkened. She stepped toward her, jaw clenched so tightly it warped the edges of her profile. "That's not what I asked you."

Adriana stiffened. "No. Of course I'm not afraid of him."

But her grip flexed again—fingers tightening and releasing in rhythm, betraying the storm building within.

Then the boy ranked third stepped forward, his voice mimicking Thea's growl. "Let me have first crack. I doubt there'll be much left for the rest."

A girl followed from the fourth position. Her helmet masked her face, but her voice carried like a thrown spear. "That Rifter couldn't match me on his best day—even if I were bleeding out. Whatever's left, I claim."

It had begun.

They no longer saw Cojax as a man. They saw a placard. A Score. A joke with a chirping laugh. A former Alpha degraded to Bottom Tier. He was no longer a threat in their minds—only a stepping stone. One by one, they began to compete, not to survive, but to humiliate him.

Adriana remained silent. Her body was still, but her hands betrayed her—clenching, unclenching, desperate to maintain composure. The control she once wielded like a blade now slipped between her fingers. She had watched Cojax fight the Roaches night after night—always at the front, always leading. His blade never faltered. But did that kind of battlefield instinct translate to the dueling arena?

She didn't know—and she didn't care to find out. The equation was too complex, the outcome too uncertain. She had never liked stepping into a situation without clear parameters, without control. Too many variables. Too much risk.

The challenges poured in, each more mocking than the last.

Cojax hadn't expected this—hadn't expected so many enemies. Apparently, his laugh had rung louder than he'd realized. For three weeks, he had conditioned them to believe he wouldn't stop unless someone beat the sound out of him. Now they were lining up to try. Finally, in a show of control and confidence, Adriana challenged him last.

As the final challenge was called, Cojax let it all go.

The feigned nerves vanished.

His face settled into something calm, resolved—*dangerous*.

"If we win," Adriana said suddenly, "I want silence from you. Forever. No more noise. No more arrogance. You've disrespected this place, these people—your own legacy. Look at your placard, you filthy Rifter. Look at how far you've fallen."

Cojax said nothing. He snapped his helmet into place and retrieved a falcata blade.

"Agreed."

The third-ranked Disciple—Aeson—stepped into the ring. He was broad across the chest, thick-limbed, a wall of muscle with a face like cracked stone.

Cojax didn't know how good he was.

Didn't matter.

"Begin!" shouted Thea.

Cojax pulsed energy through his blade, igniting it in a burst of blinding white light. Aeson flinched—unguarded.

Cojax struck.

The blade slammed into the side of Aeson's helmet, light exploding as his shields absorbed the blow. The impact launched him through the air, twisting his armored body like a marionette on snapped strings.

There was a tradition of allowing an opponent time to rise, a sign of respect. But Cojax had no respect for those who had called for his blood.

He didn't wait.

He closed the distance in a blur, blade carving streaks through the air. Aeson took hit after hit—each one punctuated by a violent flare from his shielded armor. Desperate, Aeson lashed out with a wide, clumsy swing.

Cojax ducked, stepped in, and kicked with every ounce of force he could generate.

His boot cracked against Aeson's chest, sending him flying backward like a launched crate. He slammed into the far wall with a sound like thunder. The concrete fractured behind him.

His armor flickered—then powered down.

Silence fell.

Every eye in the chamber turned to the heap of armor and dust. Then to Cojax—standing tall, unmoving, aglow with residual charge.

The entire duel had lasted seconds. He had drained Aeson's shield to zero—a feat none had seen done before.

Cojax clenched his fists, jaw tight. Weeks of humiliation boiled to the surface and spilled out—not in shouting, not in gloating, but in radiating power. His very presence forced those near him to step back; light bled from the seams of his armor with every breath.

"Who's next?" he growled.

They came.

One by one.

And one by one, they fell—like students before a master. Each approached with confidence. Each believed the last loss had been a fluke. Each left the ring broken.

Cojax's movements defied expectation. He was faster, stronger, more precise than anyone had remembered. The Disciples had spent their free hours gossiping, sleeping, complaining.

Cojax had been sharpening his blade.

And now, the investment returned in full. But more than discipline, more than technique, something else had awakened—something rare.

Something feared.

He was a Nova.

The energy he radiated pulled the strength from his enemies like a vacuum. With every strike, he drained them. With every breath, he seemed to grow stronger. And yet, he remained focused. He did not let the moment consume him.

Until Brutus.

When Brutus stepped forward, something changed. Heat surged through Cojax's chest, igniting his limbs. His hands tightened until the gauntlets creaked. Brutus loomed ahead, a wall of muscle and armor—a sheer cliff he had once called brother.

Brutus was the last obstacle between him and Adriana.

The once-friends faced off. No more games. No more hesitation. Cojax dropped into his stance.

He was done playing.

He was done hiding.

"Begin," Thea barked.

The room detonated with movement as the two collided, a blast of energy and violence. There would be no mercy—no quarter. Not this time. Cojax struck first—fast, aggressive, a flurry of controlled swings meant to disorient, not kill. Brutus answered with raw strength, but Cojax ducked a wide arc and countered, his blade slicing up into Brutus' chestplate. The hit staggered him. Cojax pressed the attack, driving a punch into Brutus' leg before rising with a vicious uppercut from his sword that smashed against the large boy's helmet. Brutus twisted away, armor flaring with defensive light.

He rolled and rose in one fluid motion, letting out a roar as he launched into a counteroffensive. His skill with the blade was better than Cojax had anticipated—but not enough.

Brutus was not enough.

Cojax struck again. Once in the arm, another time in the leg. Brutus' breath came fast, ragged. Rage tensed every muscle.

"All this time," Brutus growled, "you were playing."

Cojax's voice cracked with something deeper than anger. "Why, Brutus? Why did you turn your back on us?"

Brutus sneered. "You think that matters now? You think friendship survives the Crossing?"

"I would never abandon you."

Brutus' eyes narrowed. "What about five years from now, when we've all got different Scores—when one of us gets Rifted? You put the Aberration's life above mine. That was your choice. Don't pretend otherwise."

He charged—three fast strikes. Cojax parried but didn't return the blows. Brutus took it as weakness. His confidence surged, and his pattern became predictable.

That was his mistake.

Cojax shifted tempo—ducked the next attack and sidestepped. His sword came crashing into Brutus' chest with a blinding surge of light.

Brutus howled.

The rage overwhelmed his footing. Cojax struck again. His blade burned, shedding arcs of molten light as he carved into Brutus' defenses. Hit after hit. Brutus retreated, step by step, until he found himself pinned against the wall. Two slashes to the arm, two more to the chest. Brutus' form faltered. He dropped to one knee.

"I called you brother!" Cojax shouted.

Brutus met his gaze, hatred burning through the visor. "You were never my brother."

Cojax twisted and kicked, the blow thundering into Brutus' chest. He slammed into the fractured wall. Chunks of concrete fell. Brutus' armor flickered—then went dark.

He lay crumpled, sword slipping from his grasp, limbs sluggish. His movements were slow, cautious. He tried to rise but collapsed again. His armor had failed to absorb the full impact. The damage was real. Cojax stood over him, heaving. The fury inside him wavered, replaced with something cold.

*"What am I doing?"*

This was Brutus.

He pulled off his helmet and dropped to one knee. "You're not a puppet," he said softly. "Don't let Adriana use you. You're better than this."

Brutus didn't answer.

"Let's end this, Brutus. Come back with me."

"I would rather die," Brutus spat.

Cojax froze, jaw clenched. He stood slowly. "So be it."

He turned toward the center of the chamber—one match

remained. But his mind wasn't on Adriana. It was still trapped in Brutus' broken words.

Then—

"Cojax, behind you!" Finn shouted.

Cojax spun.

A blade arced toward his head.

Instinct took over. His body moved before thought. He twisted, raised his Arc Blade, and struck upward. His weapon pulsed on contact, surging as it connected with the attacker.

There was a scream.

Cojax stepped back, bracing for another blow. But none came. Brutus collapsed to his knees, clutching his face. His helmet cracked, split open across the front. Cojax's eyes widened in horror; for a heartbeat, he feared he'd killed him.

Then Brutus ripped the helmet from his head. The wound zigzagged across his face, a brutal blistering cut that claimed most of his right cheek and eye. His skin was charred, melted. He looked monstrous. Unrecognizable.

Brutus' scream tore through the chamber—not from pain, but from wrath. "I'll kill you, Cojax! I'll end you!"

"Get that boy out of here!" Thea shouted.

Two Minor Magisters moved at once, seizing Brutus by the arms as he thrashed.

"I will finish this!" he shrieked, voice feral, animalistic.

They dragged him from the room, but his screams echoed long after he'd vanished. Cojax could only watch.

Then he looked down at his blade as though it were a serpent. *"I didn't need to surge energy into the blade."* He gritted his teeth.

He wanted to let go of the weapon—but his training screamed against it. He only wished it had taught him not to let go of people too.

Adriana stepped forward, and the next duel began. Moments into it, Cojax realized the truth—why she had hesitated. She wasn't Alpha because of her skill. She was competent, but not exceptional. She should have been in the Second Tier at best. Her strength was in manipulation, not in wielding a blade or commanding a battlefield.

Cojax didn't even try to intimidate her. He was beyond that. Beyond the pageantry. She attacked. He blocked. She landed a few hits—his focus had waned—but her efforts were wasted. She lacked the control, the weight behind each strike.

It ended quickly.

Another victory.

Another hollow taste.

As the Magisters announced his win, Cojax stood still, staring past the moment. His mind wasn't on Adriana. It wasn't even on the match. It was on Brutus. On the half-destroyed face, the ruined eye, the screams that still echoed in his head.

## FORTY-ONE

Jessica awoke to the news of ten more Disciples being Rifted in the night. She shivered at the thought. As always, there were no warnings—no ceremonies. The Disciples simply vanished.

She bolted upright, panic flaring for a heartbeat that Cojax might be one of them. His bed was *empty*. But then her breathing slowed as she caught sight of him heading her way, a bronzing brush in hand. He sat on the edge of the mattress, his voice heavy.

"Romulan."

"Rifted?" Jessica asked. Another chill crept down her spine.

"Yes."

"How?"

Cojax closed his eyes and looked up. "He was in the $11^{th}$ spot from the bottom—safe from the Rifting. But when I rose, it pushed him down."

"That's not your fault," Jessica said quickly.

Cojax remained silent. His string of duels had saved him from the Rift—and more than that, it had launched him into the Second Tier. One rank below Finn.

But there was no celebration.

No jokes. No laughter.

Not after a Rifting. Not after Romulan had been taken.

They moved mechanically throughout the day, their bodies worn but still alive. At breakfast, Cojax and Jessica were among a crowd of people—the ones he had saved from the Roaches during the first attack, and the others he had protected within the walls thereafter—those who had suffered under Adriana's point manipulation.

"Brutus isn't here," Finn muttered.

Cojax's eyes scanned the room, confirming it. He hadn't wanted to look. He hadn't wanted to face the guilt.

"Where is he?" he asked quietly. "You don't think—"

"—he was Rifted?" Finn finished.

"No," Jessica said quickly. "He was the Beta. He couldn't have fallen that far, that fast."

"He was in worse shape than you realize," Finn said. "It wasn't just the cut. I think he broke something when he hit the wall. His armor absorbed most of the impact—but not all of it."

Cojax felt a weight settle in his chest. A deep, creeping guilt. Emotions had overtaken reason. For weeks, he'd been treated like rot—trampled under bootheels, laughed at, ignored. The rage had built, unrelenting. When it finally came loose, it left nothing but devastation in its wake.

*"He attacked me."*

But the justification rang hollow.

He couldn't meet Finn's eyes. And Finn, sensing it, didn't look up either.

Then Brutus entered.

His steps were slow, deliberate. A white bandage wrapped his left eye. He moved stiffly, posture rigid and unnatural. His usual swagger was gone. He looked like a stranger. Still, he carried himself with forced confidence until he reached the chute. That's when Cojax saw it.

His Score.

Still First Tier… but barely.

Cojax was only five ranks below him.

Then their eyes met.

Brutus' expression was unreadable. Not hatred. Not grief. Just… finality. In that moment, Cojax knew—there would be little chance of making amends. Whatever friendship they once had was gone. Shattered.

But Cojax refused to accept that.

*"No,"* he thought. *"I can fix this."*

He began to rise.

Finn's hand caught his wrist. "Wait."

Cojax hesitated… then slowly sat back down.

Brutus stood beside his usual seat next to Adriana. The air turned heavy. They weren't speaking—but something passed between them. A silent argument. Brutus looked torn—stuck between two directions. His fists clenched so tightly his tray shook. Then, without a word, he turned and walked away.

Cojax watched him go, noting the tension in every step.

"She blames him," Cojax said.

Brutus took a seat at the far end of the Dining Hall—alone. He looked hollow. His movements were sluggish, weighted, mechanical. He didn't eat. He just sat there, staring into his tray, stirring the contents like it was poison.

And then he looked up.

His one good eye locked on Cojax—burning with something raw and wordless.

Pain. Betrayal. Fury.

And something deeper than all of that.

Cojax and Finn had assumed the sword wound had damaged Brutus' mind—that the blow, or perhaps the trauma, had altered something deeper. But that proved false. When questioned by the Magisters, Brutus spoke as clearly as ever. When tested on Roach classifications or tactical theory, his scores remained high.

The only change—one that no amount of intellect could fix—came when he picked up a blade or a Blazer.

Without his eye, his depth perception was gone. His timing was off. His swings lacked precision. He reacted a beat too slow, missed by inches, and overcorrected the next time. The frustration bled through in every motion. The harder he tried, the worse it got.

Soon, the Disciples weren't the ones targeting him—the Magisters were. They saw his decline not as misfortune but as weakness. A lack of adaptability. A flaw that needed to be removed.

So they turned on him.

Each session, they pitted him against multiple opponents. Again and again, Brutus was beaten down. Again and again, he failed to recover. The whispers started quietly at first—that Brutus was *Weighted*. Cojax and Finn didn't want to believe it.

But as the days passed and another week bled away, Brutus' Score kept falling. From the lower First Tier to the mid-Second. Then lower. By the time the rumors reached full volume, he had slumped to the bottom of the Third Tier.

He was Rifted-in-waiting.

Every time Cojax saw him, his chest ached with guilt. Brutus' posture had changed—no longer upright and indomitable, but slumped. Rigid. Burdened.

Cojax longed to reach out, to clasp his arms around his former friend, make some stupid joke, hear Brutus laugh like he used to. He wanted to remind him they were brothers once.

But he knew it was no use.

While Brutus fell, Cojax and Finn rose.

With no reason left to conceal their skill, their ascent was rapid. Their dueling scores surged. Their precision, power, and control set them apart. Whispers followed them now too—but of awe. Of inevitability. Even before the rankings adjusted, the other Disciples began treating them as Alpha and Beta.

That was when Adriana approached.

Her face was still composed, but subdued—less queen, more supplicant. Her power had fractured. Her loyalists remained, but the numbers had thinned. What influence she still held paled next to what Cojax and Finn now carried.

She spoke quietly, almost pleading, her words coated in civility but devoid of command. Cojax wasn't rude, but he didn't indulge her. His answers were short. Controlled. By the end of their exchange, her message had been delivered—Jessica would be left alone.

She didn't say it outright. Instead, she told a strange story about a boy who found a piece of trash on the beach. He became so convinced it was a treasure that his parents let him keep it.

Then she moved closer.

Too close.

Her body brushed against Cojax's chest, soft and deliberate. Her fingers traced his arms, trailing up to his chin. For a moment, he thought she might kiss him—if such things had been allowed.

But she didn't.

She just smiled.

And walked away.

She never spoke to him again for the rest of the Mahghetto.

***

Cojax found Brutus by himself near the showers, in a small room cracked with time. He sat slouched in a chair, head tilted toward the ceiling, eyes fixed on the harsh white glow above. Cojax lingered in the doorway, unsure whether to keep walking or cross the threshold.

"So," Brutus murmured, voice gravel scraping the silence, "you've come to gloat."

"No," Cojax said, his tone just as low.

Brutus growled, snapping upright. "Of course it's you. So predictable. So pathetic."

The chair slammed down. Brutus stood, his one good eye seeping hatred. His vision momentarily focused on Cojax's Placard—he was the Alpha once again and it took him a little less than a month to do it.

"It wouldn't be Finn—he doesn't forget, but he doesn't chase ghosts. And Adriana? She acts like I never existed. The Magisters? They don't even bother to look me in the eye." He scoffed. "I was their Beta. *Their Beta.* And now… nothing. So of course… it would be you."

He stepped forward, half-shadowed, the scar across his face harsh under the flickering light. "Are you here to savor what's left of me? To count the cracks in my face? To see the great Brutus—toppled and broken?"

Cojax said nothing.

Brutus leaned in, voice rising. "Have you come to tell me I earned this? That I broke the Code, betrayed our friendship, and deserve every last bit of rot I'm wallowing in? Is that the glitching story you're here to sell? Save your breath."

Still, Cojax didn't speak.

Brutus' eyes narrowed. "Say something, you dimmed Rifter. That's what you are now, isn't it? A righteous statue carved out of pride. You've always thought yourself the better man."

"I didn't come to belittle you," Cojax said quietly. "And I won't sit here to be abused."

Brutus' jaw twitched. "Then go Rift yourself. But don't pretend you fooled me. You might have duped Finn with your calm and restraint. But not me. *Never me.*"

He pointed to the scar.

"I had no armor. No defense. I was already broken. But you pulsed with an Arc Blade. You *chose* to scar me—chose to maim me when the fight was already over. You had your Score back. You had your standing. But that wasn't enough, was it? You needed to take my face too."

Cojax's gaze dropped, then steadied.

"I deserved to be beaten," Brutus said, voice raw. "I expected it. I earned your wrath. That was justice. But what you gave me… that was vengeance."

"I—"

"*Don't lie to me*," Brutus snapped. "Tomorrow is the end of the month. I know how this works. I'll be Rifted before dawn. My Score is lower now than yours ever was, even when Atlas turned you into a puddle of blood. So do me one favor—don't soil this moment with some polished lie."

The large boy stepped closer, eyes blazing. "*You wanted to kill me*. Admit it."

Cojax's voice was quiet. Steady. "Yes."

Brutus laughed, bitter and hollow. "And now I know the truth. You're no better than I am. You wear your ideals like a shield, but when the power shifted, you did exactly what I would have done. You struck low. You struck hard."

"Did you think mercy was part of the curriculum here?" Cojax said. "This place doesn't reward restraint. Only merit."

Brutus tilted his head. "And you—above all—are winning the game."

Cojax took a breath, deep and deliberate, and stepped forward.

"If that were true," he said, "I wouldn't be here." He looked around at the empty space, the silence. "Your friends are gone. Your Score's a shadow. The Magisters don't say your name. If I were like them, I'd see you as they do: a Weighted, broken Disciple."

He paused.

"But I'm not them. I came because my brother fell. And despite everything—every mistake—we made, I won't let that brother vanish without knowing two things."

Brutus' muscles tensed.

"First," Cojax said quietly, "you don't hold the monopoly on sin. That's something we both share."

He took a breath, eyes steady. "You were right about me. For a moment—I won't deny it—I wanted your head. I wanted to feel your blood on my hands. I wanted to cleave your skull and raise it like a trophy. And I would have... had I not misjudged the distance between us."

His voice dropped further, weighted by memory. "In that moment—blinded by rage—I became something cruel. Something unforgiving."

Brutus' scowl faltered. He stepped back slightly, thrown off by the confession. His expression darkened—not with anger, but with something quieter. Sorrow. Shame.

Cojax looked up, eyes searching the light overhead, as if hoping it would offer clarity.

When he spoke again, his voice was softer.

"I'm not better than you, Brutus. I was forged in the same fire. And when I was placed in hell... I acted like a demon. I don't blame you for what you did. You did what you were taught to do."

Brutus shook his head. "That doesn't change anything."

"It does," Cojax said. He stepped forward, as if to say more—but the words stuck in his throat. He closed his mouth again.

"You like the sound of your own voice too much," Brutus muttered.

Cojax didn't flinch. "Then I'll say only this."

He met Brutus' gaze.

"Second, your Score means nothing to me—whether it's above or below mine. That number doesn't change who you are to me. Not now. Not ever. You are *not* broken. You are not what they say you are."

He paused, then added, "You're still my brother. That was true before this place, and it'll still be true long after we're both thrown into the Rift."

Brutus turned away, his hand resting against the wall. His voice cracked as he spoke. "You won't face the Rift, Cojax. You're too strong. You always were. I wanted that strength—your pull, your presence. Finn idolized you. Hadrian respected you. Even my own blasted father compared me to you like I was some failed prototype."

Cojax lowered his gaze. "I *will* be Rifted. If not now, then later. That's the fate for all of us. Different paths, same end. There's always talk of an Honorable Release—but what's honorable about being torn apart by the same monsters you spent your life killing?"

His voice grew quiet. "So yes. I'll fight. I'll survive. And one day, I'll fall."

Brutus turned, bitterness creeping back into his tone. "Then why does any of this matter? Why are you even here?"

Cojax looked down at his chest—his armor's recorder was still active. So was Brutus'. Already, he'd said more than he should have. He wanted to say something real—something about the storm building beneath the surface. About the coming rebellion. He wanted to offer hope, to tell Brutus that if they succeeded, maybe—just maybe—he could find his way back. But he could not afford it. Not even to give his once friend a sliver of hope.

He didn't answer.

Brutus filled the silence. "Sit with me," he said. "Let's talk of better times."

Cojax took a step back. His fingers drifted instinctively toward the blade at his side. "No, Brutus. I didn't come for nostalgia."

Brutus scoffed. "Even now, you think I'd use our friendship against you. You think I'd strike."

Cojax held his gaze. "Be honest with me. If I did sit down... would you have tried to kill me?"

Brutus smiled, a ghost of something old and cruel. "Maybe... I hadn't decided yet."

Cojax nodded slowly. "Then let this be the end—while we're both still breathing."

He raised his fist and pounded it once against his chest. Then bowed—low and respectful. "Take care of yourself." He stepped back, eyes locked on Brutus' hands, and slipped through the doorway.

Brutus remained motionless, staring at the spot where Cojax had stood—his one good eye burning like an ember, face turned to stone. He didn't move for hours.

## FORTY-TWO

"We will no longer be two factions—broken and divided. We will no longer have two fortresses, but a single structure built at the center of the room, away from the hatches where the Roaches can pour inside," Cojax said, pacing in front of his gathered Phalanx in the large dormitory room.

Ten more had been Rifted—Brutus, chief among them. They were down to two hundred twenty-nine—nearly half their original number—and the trials weren't over yet.

"In the evenings, we will all work. Building, training, developing strategy. At night, everyone will fight the Roaches— whether you are First, Second, or Third Tier." He stopped pacing and turned. "I don't know how many more we will lose to the Rift, but already we've lost forty-three to the Roaches. That ends now."

The Disciples saluted, a few cheered. It was more than he expected, but still underwhelming.

"Disciple Horacio has drafted a new blueprint and has pushed it out to your ArmGuards," Cojax said. "Now let's get moving. We've only got a few hours before the Roaches will be here and we'll need at least the first wall done by then. Horacio will oversee the building."

The shorter Disciple stepped forward. "We're going to begin with the outer wall first—a strong base is key. We need to split up into teams of ten."

Cojax walked away from the center and toward Finn and Jessica. "How'd that go?"

"Good," Finn said. "Direct. Simple. Fair. Pretty refreshing after Adriana's leadership."

"Is Horacio going to divide up Adriana's supporters into different work groups?" Jessica said. "We need to break up any lingering loyalties."

"I wouldn't worry about her anymore," Finn said. "Everyone

now sees through her façade."

"I just don't want old roots to sprout new weeds."

"Yes," Cojax answered. "Callista is also going to make sure they are assigned to different sections to sleep. I'm sure they'll realize what we're doing, but there's not much they can do about it."

Just then, Jessica saw a Magister appear near the entrance to the bathrooms. He didn't enter the room with pomp or pride. Instead, he stayed in the shadows at the threshold, gesturing toward her.

"We have a visitor," Jessica said discreetly, nodding toward the bathrooms.

"A Magister?" Finn asked. "That can't be good. They never show up after we've been dismissed for the day."

"It's Orch," Cojax said, his keen eyes picking out his distinct features. "I think he's gesturing to us."

Orch raised a finger to his jaw, a familiar signal. The one that Elena used to indicate that they needed to be careful what they say. The same one Jessica had taught Cojax and Finn.

"I'll go see what he wants," Jessica said. She turned toward him.

"Wait," Cojax said. "Could be a trap. Does your armor still hold a charge?"

"No," Jessica answered. "I'll be fine."

She pushed past the mess of Disciples as they were disassembling different parts of the old fortresses. They had just started and already the noise was filling the room. As she approached, Orch slipped deeper into the bathroom. She found him in the back standing at one of the VaporSweeps. He had a service panel open and was pretending to do some maintenance. It was a bad ruse as he clearly had no idea what he was doing.

Orch carefully looked her over, making sure her armor had no charge. He gave a second gesture, and she returned a different one, confirming he was indeed part of the uprising.

He waved her inside the small VaporSweep compartment. She stepped inside, and he followed, activating a panel that emitted a low hum to mask their conversation.

"You?" Jessica said.

"Yes, who'd you expect?"

"Out of the three Primary Magisters, not you," Jessica answered. "I would have guessed Octavian."

"But I'm the most charming."

"Charming? You almost got me killed on the first day of Blazer training! Ten against one—what was that?"

"Your Score surged after that, pushing you into the First Tier. Waffles, Jessica. That little point increase made it so you could select waffles for breakfast."

"What about the 1,000 points I got the day we received our armor? Was that your handiwork too?"

"No, that was all you. You ignored everything Elena told you and took the lead—made yourself the perfect target."

Jessica frowned, half-tempted to leave. "Who sent you?"

"Elena."

"Is she alright?"

"It's... well... she wants to talk to you."

"Here? Now?"

"In the Medicus wing. If you go now, you won't run into any Roaches and the cameras are on a loop. But I won't be able to keep it that way for more than an hour."

"What's wrong?"

"She... well... you just need to talk to her. Do you know the way?"

"Yes."

***

To the side of the bed, several metal machines hissed and ticked. One pulsed with a rhythmic beep—likely monitoring a heart. At first, Jessica thought the room was empty, but then she saw the shadow curled beneath the sheets. Her breath caught. It had taken so long to see her because there was so little left to see.

The figure was skeletal—skin stretched tight across bone. Her hair was dry and smelled of rot. Her skin was nearly translucent, lips pale and cracked, and beneath the taut flesh, dark purple veins bloomed like bruises.

Even though the woman was facing away, Jessica knew at once. She rushed forward and took the bony hand between her own. It was ice. She tried to warm it with her youth.

"Elena?"

It had been months since she'd seen her. Months since Elena had appeared on the CityScreens, tearing through Roaches like a goddess of war. Now, she looked like a forgotten child, too frail to sit, barely breathing.

*"Elena is invincible,"* Jessica thought. But the thought died. She felt hollow—like her anchor had snapped loose.

"Who did this to you?" Jessica whispered. "You look like you haven't eaten in a week."

Elena stared at the ceiling. "My life no longer matters. When it leaves me, I will return to my children. I welcome that meeting. I embrace death."

The words hit like ice water. It was so final. So bleak.

"You can't die," Jessica said. A memory surfaced—vivid and stupid and sacred. Jessica had never tasted sausage before. Not before the city. Her food had always been bland, functional—nutritional mush or oversalted soup. She'd eaten every bite because she had to. But one morning, Elena left a single sausage on the table. Not handed to her—just left.

Jessica wouldn't have eaten it—not at first. But Elena had reminded her not to waste food, and then told her to clean the table. The logic had seemed clear.

She ate it. Slowly. Reverently. The salt and grease burst like fireworks on her tongue. She even licked the table afterward. It felt smart at the time.

She'd spent the day panicked, thinking it was a test. The next day, it happened again. Then again. Sometimes sausage. Sometimes steak. Sometimes fruit with a name she didn't know. They never spoke of it. Even when the armor was drained and they were safe to talk. Jessica had been afraid to name it, afraid it would vanish if spoken aloud.

And she had never said thank you.

It wasn't about the food. It was the sacrifice. Elena had been given just enough nutrition to maintain her own Score. Everything was measured. She had broken the Code—not for comfort, but for

Jessica. The Aberration.

Jessica wanted to reach forward, to kiss Elena's forehead. But she didn't. Not for fear of losing points, but because she knew it would disappoint Elena.

Elena must have sensed this. She looked away, her eyes surprisingly dry, absent of tears.

"You've done well," she said. "Beyond anyone's expectations. You've run the race despite the obstacles, conquered the mountain though the winds battered you. In the end, it is I who has failed you."

"Never," Jessica said.

"Tonight, when you return to the storage room, the Orb will not be charged. I don't have the strength to charge it anymore."

"That's ok," Jessica said, forcing her emotions down. "You'll be fine. Rest. Eat. You'll recover."

"I didn't realize how much it would take out of me—the two absorptions a day. I'm so sorry, my child."

"You'll be fine," Jessica said. "Don't worry about me. Just rest. Don't worry about the Golden Orb. I can find my own way."

"We tried to find another... another way, but it... well... it fell through. On the morrow, I will be Released, a right I earned by virtue of once being a First Tier, but it won't be broadcast on the CityScreens as I can't stand. It will be here, at the place of my Second Stewardship, a place where I made a friendship with a girl who had more determination and grit than I've had my entire life."

This broke something inside of Jessica. Elena was the paragon of power, of strength. This woman had carried her through the darkest days of pain and doubt. She was the one that pushed her when she had no more strength inside, when she was broken, when she was too weak to stand.

The tears slipped down Jessica's face. "I need you."

Elena smiled. "I think we needed each other. I'm sorry."

"You can't just quit," Jessica said, her voice tinged with anger.

"I'm not child, but we've been undone."

"I'll find another way."

"Only a Nova has the strength to charge an Orb, and we weren't able to recruit the only other one I know of. But I want you to remember this: I might have failed, but I did not falter. The city may take my life, but they were never able to rob me of my will. My husband was a Fourth Tier. A brilliant engineer. It was an arranged Civil Union, but we found love in time. We applied for children and were approved. Genetically, they weren't mine—but I cared for them. Three litters of quadruplets. Only twelve, I know—below the standard, but they were mine in every way that matters."

She paused, breath catching. "I believed in the city. Defended it. Killed two Acadians for treason. I was praised for it. Rose to the position of a First Tier—almost selected to be a Numberless. My Score soared. His did not. He stayed in the labs, trying to earn points in ways that weren't enough. He was never a warrior—and the battlefield is where rising Scores are made. When the last of our children turned sixteen and subsidies ended, he faltered. He was Weighted. I did nothing."

She swallowed hard.

"He went blind. I didn't even know. I was on the Wall. Three days passed before I saw him again—his mind absent reason, his eyes blank."

Jessica clenched her fists.

"My children followed. Five died in the Mahghetto. Four in battle. Two went blind. One was killed for treason. None were Honored. Not one. They were each perfect to me, and yet, they were weighed, judged, and found lacking in merit."

Her voice shook.

"I knew them. I loved them. They deserved better. That's why I don't leave this city in peace. I leave it drenched in blood—more red than anything the Roaches could offer."

Jessica nodded, fire rising behind her tears. "We'll change it."

Elena smiled again—soft, far away. The kind of smile meant for goodbyes. "It's time for you to go."

Jessica squeezed her hand. "How can I go on?"

Elena looked at her, really looked at her. And for a moment, the old strength returned—flickering through the ruin of her body like the last heat of a dying star.

"You go on because purpose isn't about surviving—it's about choosing what to stand for, even when you're certain it won't save you. You walk forward, not because the path is clear, but because someone behind you might see your footsteps and find the strength to rise. We live by inches, not miles—and some inches are bought with blood. Take them anyway."

***

Jessica collapsed to the floor of the storage room—jaw clenched, hands to the ground. For a moment, she let herself break. Just two breaths. Two miserable, choking breaths.

Then—rage.

It boiled in her chest. It hardened her heart. She stood. Sword drawn, eyes burning, she ran full-force at the wall. The blade howled. Stone cracked. Sparks flew. She did not have the energy to pulse into the weapon, but it still cut deep gouges into the rock. Her cries echoed with every strike. Her heart poured into every swing. It was grief. It was rage. It was everything.

When the fury faded, she dropped to the floor—spent, breathless, and only half alive.

Cojax and Finn found her soon after. They went to her as if she was wounded. But they found her whole, at least physically. Finn had been hefting metal barricades in the dormitory and his shields had been drained. Cojax defaulted to using the Golden Orb. Soon, they could speak.

"What happened?" Cojax asked.

"Elena is dying."

Cojax and Finn exchanged a quick look, each trying to puzzle out what the words meant.

"It's over. She was burning herself too thin recharging the orb, and now she's too weak to stand."

"Doesn't the… rebellion have a different plan?" Finn asked.

"No," Jessica answered. "They tried, but no."

"Don't worry," Cojax answered, his face split with relief. "I can charge the Orb."

"And end up like her? No."

"We only have two more months before the Crossing," Cojax answered. "I can do it. She was doing it for months longer. I'm younger, stronger."

"But… you've worked so hard to be the Alpha."

"That doesn't matter," Cojax answered. "It stopped mattering the moment I knew there was a greater purpose, a greater plan. Our pain here, our suffering, means nothing if we don't change something for the next generation of Disciples. You are what matters. You are the spark of the rebellion. Finn and I can be swallowed by the Rift, but *you* must go on."

"But what of Adriana? The only thing that kept her at bay was you being the Alpha."

"We've dealt with her," Finn answered.

"Besides, Finn will become the Alpha and can make sure to keep her in check," Cojax said. "We're so close, we can't lose hope now."

Jessica's mind recalled Elena—small, frail, vulnerable. She had no idea how much it was affecting her until it was too late. Now, Cojax would be putting his head on the chopping block alongside hers.

"I can't watch you…."

Cojax slid closer, putting his hands on her arms. "Whether you meant to or not, we're part of this now—the three of us. We're part of the revolution."

"You both feel this way?"

Finn did the secret hand gesture, a show of his solidarity—it was completely wrong, and with the incorrect hand. She'd have to teach him the right way later.

"We're all in," Finn added.

"Jessica, you must reach the Crossing," Cojax said. "That's the only thing that matters now. Together, we're going to end the Acadian Code."

# FORTY-THREE

Cojax maintained his Score for three more weeks—a remarkable feat, considering he was draining his armor each night to power the Golden Orb. But he could only endure for so long. He was doing the work of two in a place that demanded everything from just one. When he finally faltered, Finn took his place—but not his voice. Cojax remained the one they looked to when the Roaches shifted tactics. The one they rallied behind when things fell apart. Everyone had their strengths. His was leadership amid chaos.

The Magisters threw everything at them now—laying traps with Roaches along the corridors to the Lecture Hall, releasing Ankle Biters into the showers through the drains, testing the strength of the Disciples' new defenses in the dormitory.

Some days they were sent to rooms and told to wait, only to be ambushed the moment their guard slipped. Other times, Lungers dropped from the ceiling without warning, striking from the shadows. Once, there was a full-scale invasion in the Dining Hall—food and Roach wax smeared across the floor like battlefield gore.

But they endured. Fight after fight, they emerged victorious. Their confidence grew—not in themselves, but in one another. They began taking Roach heads as trophies, hanging them from their parapets like grim medieval lords.

Wherever they went, their shields were linked, blades raised, Arc Spears pointed to the ceiling. The enemy was always near—lurking in unseen tunnels and hidden gates, waiting to strike from the places where the Disciples were weakest. They had seen those tunnels for months, assumed they were relics of the past—never realizing they were arteries for the same creatures that plagued the surface.

But true to Cojax's word—not another Disciple died. He refused to leave anyone behind. Refused to let a shield break. Refused to let a Disciple be dragged behind the walls and made into meat.

Their momentum carried them to the last few days.

They were summoned to the parade grounds, falling into perfect formation. Straight lines. Silent discipline.

"Today," Octavian announced, voice uneven with emotion, "you receive your Sacred Blade—crafted specifically with your talents in mind. Finn, son of Brutian, as Front Runner, you will receive your blade first."

Jessica was so focused, she almost didn't hear her name. The ceremony blurred around her—just another ritual, another checkpoint. Her mind was elsewhere, drifting through memories and dread. It wasn't until the weight settled into her hands that the world snapped back into focus.

It was heavier than she expected—not in mass, but in presence. A pulse ran through her palm. The room quieted around her, though she hadn't realized it was loud before. She stared at the scabbard, hesitant to draw. Around her, steel whispered free of scabbards as others revealed their blades.

Jessica's fingers tensed as she pulled the blade free. It slid out with a sound like breath. She braced herself for disappointment—for something crude or clumsy, marked with the sign of the Aberration.

But what she held was nothing like that.

The blade was elegant—narrow at the hilt, widening near the tip, where it ended in a serrated curve. It was weighted forward, perfect for powerful strikes, but shaped for speed. A predator's weapon. Not a Disciple's.

She shifted her grip. A thin line of golden light shimmered up the flat of the blade.

*"How's this possible?"* It didn't drain her armor.

Her eyes scanned the weapon again, searching for the trick. Then she saw it—so faint she nearly missed it. An inscription etched into the hilt, almost hidden in the metal grain.

*"Choose what you stand for."*

Her breath caught.

*"Elena."*

She had done this. Created it with Jessica's energy signature in mind. Somehow, she had altered the weapon's energy draw. Modified the transfer. Invented and crafted it with her own hands—without permission, without help. Jessica stared at the blade as if seeing it for the first time. Not as a soldier. Not as a survivor. But as a girl who had been given something she didn't deserve.

This wasn't a weapon.

It was a promise.

The thought coiled around her ribs like wire. The weight in her hands felt different now—not just steel, but sacrifice. She felt unworthy. As if touching the blade dulled its edge. As if her doubt could stain it.

She drew in a slow breath. Then another.

She looked at the weapon one last time and took a silent oath. *"For the woman who forged this blade, for the fallen who were never honored, I will not forget. I will not forgive. With this blade, I will carve a wound into this city so deep it will never heal."*

# FORTY-FOUR

"The schedule just went blank," Callista muttered, tapping her ArmGuard as if it owed her an explanation. "I checked it last night—Arc Blade drills first, followed by lecture. The next two days as well—just gone."

They sat in the heart of their improvised stronghold, a half-circle of Disciples lounging on thin mattresses arranged like pseudo-chairs. At a glance, the structure surrounding them looked like a chaotic sculpture—bent metal, jagged angles, jutting lines. But it wasn't chaos.

It was Horacio's design.

Their fortress had been built from everything they could salvage—stacked, welded, and reinforced. Every corner had been planned with obsessive precision. The outer wall rose two bunks high, a shield of groaning steel. Only two sections broke its flow—deliberate gaps Horacio had called the *Killing Pits*. Narrow murder holes lined the edge, just wide enough to slide an Arc Spear through. It was a butcher's dream and a nightmare for anything crawling in.

Behind that stood their Keep: four bunks tall and arranged in a jagged star pattern. Each spire offered overlapping sightlines, letting Disciples defend one angle while covering another. Metal sheets recycled and reborn.

"Mine's blank too," Finn said, looking up from his wrist.

Cojax stood. His hand drifted to the hilt of his blade. "Something's off. No attacks for two nights and now the schedule goes blank. Why now?"

Jessica didn't need to check hers. If two were blank, all of them were. A weight dropped in her chest like lead. "Sound the alarm. Form ranks. Pull everyone back from the showers—now."

"Now?" Finn groaned. "Some of us haven't rotated yet. I'm up next. I've been fantasizing about my not-quite-a-minute shower."

"They've got guards, right?" Callista asked, uncertain.

"Twenty on standard rotation," Cojax said.

He caught Jessica's look and nodded sharply. "Pull everyone. Now."

"Right," Finn said, already pulsing the order. His voice echoed across the Comm-Link: "Disciples, to the wall. Armor on. Blades up."

The transformation was immediate.

Disciples moved without hesitation, without question. They slipped into armor, raised shields, grabbed Arc Spears. Those caught in the bathrooms sprinted back barefoot and soaked, clothes bundled in their arms, soap streaking their bodies. The guards flanked their retreat, weapons drawn, scanning the walls.

Jessica was already moving. She passed through one of the narrow metal doors in the Keep, barely wide enough for one soldier at a time, and climbed a rough ladder to the top. Cojax followed. Together, they reached the ramparts that circled the Keep. The HoverCams embedded in their armor deployed on their own, spreading across the room to cover every angle—never a good sign. The Magisters were watching.

Then the sound hit.

Drums.

Slow. Deep. Primal.

They hadn't heard that rhythm since the Mahghetto began. Suddenly, every wall hatch blew open like triggered traps. The room beyond came alive with motion. Creatures burst from the tunnels in a frenzied wave. The air clicked—like a thousand pairs of scissors snapping open.

Class IV Reever Carriers led the charge, their backs crawling with Ankle Biters. Their limbs spasmed with unnatural energy, their speed jarring. It wasn't hunger—it was obsession. The first wave struck the outer wall like a battering ram. Reinforced bunk frames groaned and bowed under the weight, but they held—barely. Horacio's bracing had bought them more time.

"They're manic," Cojax breathed. He staggered back a step as the first Roaches hurled themselves into the Killing Pits, flailing and snarling. Their twitching bodies jammed into the steel corridors.

Arc Spears responded. The Disciples jabbed through the slots in unison—precise, brutal. Chitin cracked. Fluids sprayed. Still the creatures came, pouring into the gaps like black water.

"Roach fliers inbound!" Jessica called into the Comm-Link. Her voice was steel.

"Class and location," Finn snapped back.

"Vents. Main gate. Class II Skewer Skyhooks."

From above, the creatures looked almost delicate—their wings glassy and veined like insects, catching the light in fractured glints. But the illusion shattered as they folded them back and plummeted. Their bodies were long and gaunt, twisted at unnatural angles, with jagged spines that jutted from stretched flesh. At their fronts extended monstrous skewers, bony lances as long as their torsos, honed by nature for one purpose. They didn't flap or flutter. They dove—silent, deliberate, fatal. The force of their descent alone was sometimes enough to break a warrior's shields and drive their weapons clean through armor and bone alike.

"Eyes up. Shields raised. Formation Eta," Finn ordered. "Break into teams of four—two watch the skies, two the ground."

"Class III Launchers at the bathroom wall!" another voice cut in.

"Cojax," Finn said, already on the move. "I'm transferring battle command to you. I'll take two Spear Lines and deal with the Launchers."

"Received," Cojax replied, his gaze locked on the horizon of creatures. He then switched his Comm-Link so it reached the entire Phalanx. "Disciples! Split into Spear Lines of twenty grouped by location coords. Link shields. Stay together. Push them off the ramparts. Don't let them breach the wall!"

Reever Subjugators and Skitterfangs continued to pour out the grates like an endless wave of black tar. They clawed over their dead, stacking bodies like a macabre ladder. One creature sank its jaws into a fallen comrade's carapace just to gain footing. Another launched from its perch, scraping claws across the metal wall before another clambered upward, slowly stacking higher toward the top of the first wall.

A line of Disciples met them with shield and blade, hacking into them, pushing them back, spears bursting through carapace. Black Roach wax painted the wall, dripping on the creatures being suffocated underneath. It was a massacre. But it didn't seem to matter. The creatures pushed on, relentless, ruthless. One by one, they breached the top, gaining inches of terrain on the battlements, driving wedges between the defending forces.

The air above was thick with Skewers diving down, slicing the air like jagged arrows. Arc Blades hissed. Sparks flew. Disciples screamed.

"They're on the wall!" Callista shouted through the Comm-Link.

A flurry of limbs and screeches tore over the wall just to the right of Cojax, trapping three Disciples. They backpedaled into a corner, instantly overwhelmed, blades and shields failing. In the confusion, they had broken from their Spear Line.

Jessica moved before anyone could stop her.

She vaulted over the edge of the Keep, dropping down the outer support strut. Her Arc Blade flared as she landed. One clean strike took a Reever at the neck. A second severed a leg from another. The third lunged—and she met it shoulder-first, slamming it against the metal frame before driving her blade into its gut.

"Pull back!" Cojax shouted into the Comm-Link.

Jessica pushed hard, chopping off a swinging mandible. The creature bellowed and tried to bite Jessica with its razored teeth. She in turn severed the other mandible and kicked the creature in the head, pitching it back.

This bought just enough time for the three Disciples to slip into a curving hallway and vanish through a hidden door, Jessica only moments behind. A swarm of Reevers and Ankle Biters flooded the passage in pursuit. She barely outran a snapping set of mandibles, their jagged tips clamping shut with a metallic clang that dented the wall beside her. The Ankle Biters, nimble and relentless, weren't hindered by the narrow space. She crushed one underfoot, grabbed another and slammed it against a jagged edge, then spun and cleaved a third clean in half.

The Roaches became even more frantic, their voices screaming an unearthly howl, black wax seeping from their bodies in oozing streams. The battle waged on, Disciples holding their ground against increasingly bad odds.

"Reserve Spear Line Zeta, reinforce the metal corridor!" Cojax growled. "They've been hit hard. Spear Line Theta, rotate left and drive them off the ramparts! Lambda, reinforce the main entrance. We can't let them breach the gate. Hold at all costs."

Cojax studied the HoverCam feed streaming to his ArmGuard, the flickering display offering a sweeping, bird's-eye view of the battlefield. The vantage point was invaluable—every movement, every position laid bare before him. But the clarity came with a cost. What he saw was bleak. They were an island of bronze, isolated and gleaming, completely engulfed by a rising sea of black carapace.

The metal groaned as Roach corpses were shoved aside or crushed underfoot. Blood coated the floor. Shells cracked. The smell of iron and rot was suffocating.

The wall rattled again. An Erupter exploded against the far side—detonating on impact and hurling acid into the Keep. One of the makeshift towers collapsed, dragging two Disciples with it and into a sea of pincers.

"Shields up! Stay close! Do not let them separate you!" Cojax commanded.

He turned—just as a flying Skewer slammed into his side, hurling him over the edge of the Keep and onto the lower ramparts. They hit the steel hard, the impact knocking the air from his lungs. Claws tore across his shoulder, reaching for his throat. He drove his elbow into the creature's twisted face and rolled, narrowly dodging a Reever's lunge as it crashed down where he'd just been. His blade snapped into his hand.

He didn't swing—he carved, his entire body flowing with the momentum. The Arc Blade tore through a Reever from hip to sternum, sending a spray of dark fluid across his chest. Another lunged from behind. He caught its jaws on his forearm and twisted, bones snapping as its mandibles shattered. Without hesitation, he drove the hilt of his blade into its skull, caving it in with a single, brutal strike.

But they were coming faster now. Two. Four. Six. A swarm had broken through a compromised section of the ramparts. They swarmed like rats through a crack, ignoring the spears stabbing from below. Cojax found himself surrounded.

He ducked under a claw, kicked off the wall, and spun. His blade flickered like lightning—too fast for the eye to follow. One dropped. Another. Then a third. But his feet slipped in the blood. A Reever tackled him low, knocking him to a knee. Another leapt.

And then—

"Cojax! Down!" Jessica's voice.

A burst of heat scorched the air above his head as an Arc Spear shot clean through the creature mid-jump. It jerked, spasmed, and slammed into the metal just beside him.

Cojax roared and surged to his feet, blood streaming down his neck and soaking into his collar. He didn't care. Jessica was at his back now—steady, unyielding. Together, they carved a path through the chaos, blades flashing in unison. They reached a twisted hallway below and burst through a narrow door that led into the Keep, slipping inside just moments before the swarm could overtake them.

The air was a blur of energy. Blades flashed. Screams echoed. The Roaches were everywhere. Climbing. Scratching. Tearing. And still—they held their ground.

He screamed over the Comm-Link. "Finn, report!"

Static.

Then a broken voice. "—Launchers neutralized, but they're reforming. Half my Spear Line had to withdraw to the Keep after their shields broke. We're pulling them toward the north wall—stalling as long as we can."

Cojax didn't flinch. "Pull back to the Keep. Regroup with your Spear Lines on the highest ramparts. Focus your attention on the fliers. They're proving to be too much of a distraction."

The sky was a blur of wings and steel. Skewers dove from above, their gaping jaws unhinging mid-air, screeching like tortured metal. They came in waves—arcing, spiraling, striking fast and pulling away faster.

Finn and Callista reached the ramparts of the Keep a minute later, shields raised, eyes scanning for the next threat. Their Shield Line followed, making the creatures pay—cutting down Fliers by the dozens. They were never allowed to take the Blazers from the firing range, so the only answer they had was blade and shield.

Callista's stance was solid, but her shields had already taken a beating from the conflict with the Launchers. She moved boldly, dealing with the creatures like pests. She recklessly felled six of the creatures in quick succession before a seventh plummeted from above—too sudden to track, too low to intercept. Its serrated maw shredded her shield like parchment, the beak spearing through with a shriek of splitting metal and driving clean into her chest.

She gasped—but no sound came.

Then the weight lifted, and her body folded backward—over the edge of the ramparts, gone in an instant.

"Callista!" Finn screamed, but it was already too late. He reached the edge just in time to see her body strike the writhing carapace below, vanishing into the churn of black chitin. The impact had taken her instantly—no chance to be saved, no breath left to scream. Her fair features were swallowed by the swarm. Finn's hands clenched the hilt of his sword until his knuckles turned white. A guttural roar tore from his throat as he plunged into the fray, slashing with reckless fury, each strike fueled by blinding rage.

Cojax's jaw clenched, shouting through his Comm-Link. "Finn, I've got an idea. Keep the fliers busy."

"What are you going to do?" Finn asked.

"We've got to take the pressure off the walls," Cojax answered. He selected proximity orders, recalling one hundred and fifty to the bottom of the Keep. He placed them in formation—three sides of a box. Open at the front. They moved fast and reorganized in only moments. Blades at their sides, Arc Spears bristling forward. Not one was covered in anything but their armor and the work of death.

Cojax cued up his Comm-Link. "This is where we hold them! Front line, draw them in. Flanks, pull back and hide in the shadows. Wait until I give the command to move in."

He keyed the Comm-Link. "Open the gate."

"Sir?" came a confused reply.

"Do it now."

"Front line—death rattle," Cojax growled, slamming his hilt against his shield. The metallic rhythm echoed down the line, a grim, deliberate cadence. It was the Acadian war chant—a call not of fear, but of defiance. A challenge. A promise. The sound rang out like a dare, drawing the Roaches in with its savage allure.

A heartbeat passed. Then the screech of metal rang out. The gate cracked open. The Reevers screamed and surged forward. Dozens. Scores. A stampede of rage and claws, believing victory was in reach. They charged through the breach like floodwaters. Straight into the jaws of Cojax's trap. They bypassed the Disciples concealed on either side, barreling for the noise and the easy prey of the Spear Line in front of them. The two sides clashed in a flash of light and screams.

"Hold!" he shouted, his voice cutting through the chaos like a blade.

More creatures surged forward, spilling into the corridor in a frenzy—clawing, shrieking, trampling over the dead and each other in their desperation to reach the Spear Line. The air grew thick with the stench of blood and bile. The floor trembled beneath the weight of the stampede.

"Hold!" Cojax bellowed again, louder this time, his knuckles white around the hilt of his blade.

The wall of monsters slammed against the formation, a tide of chitin and limbs, so wild they tore their own apart in the madness of the crush.

Cojax let the creature's momentum die before he gave the final command. "Charge!"

The waiting Spear Lines surged forward with a unified roar, weapons leveled, crashing into the horde like a blade cleaving flesh. Disciples bellowed the cries of war as the formation snapped shut, boxing the creatures in on three sides. Arc Spears punched through exposed joints, while blades sank deep into necks and bellies with ruthless precision.

The Reevers thrashed wildly, but there was no escape—only walls of sharpened steel and cold, disciplined fury.

They were slaughtered. One after another, the beasts fell. Dozens dropped. Then more. The frenzy of the swarm gave way to desperation, and desperation turned to collapse. Minutes later, silence returned. The last of them twitched in a spreading pool of ichor.

The gate groaned shut behind them, sealing with a final, echoing clang. The walls held. The sky was empty. The shift was so sudden—from deafening chaos to eerie stillness—it felt unreal. For a moment, no one moved. Then Cojax stepped forward and drove his blade into the twitching skull of a Reever, silencing its final spasms. He turned, blood-slicked and breathless, raised his weapon high— and roared.

The sound ripped from his throat, primal and unrelenting. A heartbeat later, others joined him. Raw. Unfiltered. Victorious. Bloodied fists punched the air. Swords clanged against shields. The silence was shattered by the cry of survivors—wounded, enraged, but still alive.

Jessica did not cheer.

She stood at the edge of the gate, staring out over the field—at the bodies, the blood, the twisted limbs. Her eyes flicked to the tunnels. The vents above. Cojax joined her not long after.

"It's not over yet," she said softly.

Cojax turned toward her. His blade hung loose at his side, dripping black. He wiped it on the metal gate before sliding it into its sheath. His armor was still powered, despite the beating he had received. "How much time do you think we have before the next wave?"

"No way to know," Jessica said. "But we better start clearing the bodies and making repairs. This is only just the beginning."

## FORTY-FIVE

Marcus' chest tightened at the pneumatic hiss of the front door. The sound alone was enough to knot his stomach. He had rehearsed this conversation a thousand times—and now wished he had rehearsed it a thousand more.

The house system announced his presence, but the man who had just come in didn't come straight to the kitchen, where Marcus sat waiting. Titan took his time. First to his quarters. The soft thump of armor plates being set aside. The dull clink of swords against the wall. A fresh uniform sliding over broad shoulders.

Marcus had been waiting for over an hour, his fingers tapping against the table in a slow, patient rhythm. Months ago, wasting time like this would have been unthinkable—an indulgence that would have eaten at his Score. Now, the Score didn't seem to matter. He was already Weighted. Alive, but not far from dead.

This wasn't anxiety—not in the usual sense. It was pressure. The weight of knowing that every triumph, every failure in his life had led to this one conversation. He already knew what his father would say. He already knew the odds. But he still had to ask. It was the last thread of hope he had left.

When Titan finally entered, Marcus rose, saluted, and bowed low. "Numberless present."

Titan returned the salute with so little formality, it made Marcus' stomach sink. A bad omen. Still, Titan gestured for him to sit.

But he didn't sit himself. Instead, Titan tapped a micro-tag in his wrist, went to a locked cabinet, and opened it. From within, he drew a purple bottle and two small glasses, setting them down with deliberate, unhurried care.

He poured both, sliding one toward Marcus. Marcus recognized the drink instantly. *Stock.* He had never imagined Titan keeping a private stash—not after the countless warnings about the

Red District, about how Stock was for Dependents, for those too far gone to climb back up.

Marcus kept his gaze down. Two months since the battle. Two months since he had lost his left arm. Two months of silence between them. He'd avoided his father until now, hoping to stabilize his Score first. Hoping to avoid seeing the look he feared most—not anger, not even loathing, but the absence of pride.

Titan downed his first glass in a single motion, then poured another and did the same. Marcus' glass remained untouched.

"If I'm going to be the only one drinking," Titan said, "this will be a sad conversation."

By the third, Marcus finally lifted his glass and sipped.

"You drink it like that," Titan said with a faint, almost teasing smirk, "and we'll be done here before you finish your first. Come on—you're falling behind."

Marcus gave in, slamming the shot. It wasn't the gutter swill from the Red District, but something richer—stronger, smoother, with spices that lingered on the tongue.

"Horace brews it," Titan said, pouring again. "Numberless. He's in Crono-Stasis, but he'd stashed a bunch before he went into the pod. Thought I didn't know where. He says the secret's in the fermentation. I told him none of that matters to me, just as long as he keeps it brewing."

Marcus was stunned—not just by the drink, but by this glimpse of his father he had never seen before. A man who could smile, if only faintly.

By the fourth glass, Marcus dared to look up. The pride was gone. But it wasn't replaced by disgust. In its place was something heavier—eyes clouded by sorrow, distant yet fixed on him, carrying a weight no one man should bear. He had the look of a man carrying a mountain on his back.

Marcus leaned forward, his stomach tight, and revealed the stump of his left arm for the first time. Titan already knew, of course. But Marcus hadn't had the courage to show him until now.

Silence stretched.

"You fought well," Titan said quietly. "I saw the footage. An altered Slug egg buried under the Wall. Sensors missed it. It waited, growing, until the Roaches timed their strike. Perfect coordination.

Tactical genius. You stopped it. Without you, your Decuria would've been wiped out. The Wall would've fallen. Tens of thousands dead before we could have taken it back."

Marcus swallowed. "I'm… sorry, Father. I failed you." A tear he hadn't felt coming slid down his cheek. He was embarrassed all the more by it.

Titan's voice wavered. "No, boy. I failed you. I should've watched him—Atlas—closer. Seen how he shifted the battle schedules… That twisted Rifter. This is all his fault."

Marcus didn't let the words settle. His voice came in a rush, raw and desperate. "Is there… is there any way forward? To replace my arm? Dad… I'm Weighted. Falling. I won't last a year…"

Titan took a long pull of Stock before answering. "There are ways—mechanical limbs or genetically regrown arms in the vats. But they're reserved for the Numberless. It's a privilege denied to the Validated—even a promising First Tier."

Marcus already knew that. No one came back from a lost limb. But this had been the last ember of hope keeping him from going Blind these past two months. He didn't know exactly how someone went Blind—whether they simply gave up, or if something inside their mind snapped, leaving them unable to process the world around them.

They drank in silence, the minutes passing slow. Then Titan spoke again, voice low.

"You might find… something… in the Red District."

Marcus stared, stunned. His father's words landed like a blow to the chest. The Red District—he understood now why it existed. Why the Numberless tolerated it. Why Titan had always warned him away—until now.

It wasn't a place for salvation. It was where the Weighted went to spend what was left. A last meal on death row. A final comfort before the sands ran out.

Marcus lifted his glass and drained it, the burn doing nothing to warm him.

## FORTY-SIX

It had been three grueling days—no food, little water. Sleep came in stolen moments, and even then, it was haunted. The assaults never stopped for long, only giving them a few hours for repairs or rest in between. Wave after wave crashed against their battered fortress, each as savage as the last. But they had held.

They fought shoulder to shoulder, teeth clenched and blades drawn, until the floor ran slick with Roach wax. They held the lines until no more of the foul creatures emerged from the cavernous walls, until their arms trembled with exhaustion, until their bodies threatened to give out entirely.

Six had fallen—five in the first wave, but only one since. Horacio's defenses had held, stronger than anyone had dared to hope. His planning, his placements, his brutal efficiency—they had made the difference.

Only two hundred and thirteen remained. A shadow of their original number. Once they had been more than four hundred.

Now, they stood on unfamiliar parade grounds near the surface. Their armor gleamed—immaculate, untouched by flaw. Their formation was perfect, not a shoulder out of place, not a gaze unfocused. They were no longer a group of Innocents with fractured thoughts and scattered hearts. Now, they moved as one. The Mahghetto had done its work, forging them between hammer and anvil. And though it had nearly broken them, they had held. This was what was demanded. This was what it cost.

Before them stood their Magisters, cloaked in gleaming armor, weapons polished, expressions unreadable. Atlas stood chief among them, towering and silent. His eyes swept across the formation, meeting each Disciple one by one—an unspoken challenge not to flinch, not to blink. None did. These were the best the BloodBorne had to offer—the ones who had refused to drown in the burning waters of hell.

When Atlas reached Jessica, he did not sneer. He didn't glare. He simply looked past her, as though she didn't exist.

She let out a slow, imperceptible breath.

Their last encounter had ended with her unconscious, the mark of the Aberration carved into her face. She still couldn't bring herself to look in the mirror for more than a few seconds. The sight was a reminder—one she couldn't scrub away. But now, there was nothing. No hatred. No disdain. Just absence.

*"Has he simply accepted that I earned my place?"* Jessica thought. But the idea seemed absurd. And that scared her most of all.

When the inspection was finished, Atlas stepped forward, arms outstretched. "You have descended and come out reborn. By the blood you've spilled, you've made us stronger. As a body cannot survive with infection, so too must we sever the weak, the tempered, the broken. Just as a hand is cut to save the whole, the Dependents must be cut away—for the betterment of our city."

He paused, his voice lowering, growing colder.

"But you are not yet True Validated. One challenge remains." He turned and gestured to the towering doors behind him. "Beyond these gates waits one of the enemies that has plagued our lands. End its life—so that you may begin yours."

With a dramatic turn, his cloak flared behind him.

Octavian stepped forward and called out, "Finn, son of Brutian—enter between the doors of death, and claim your right to live."

Finn drew his sword and slammed it against his shield. The impact rang out like thunder—the IronHorse Rattle—amplified by his armor, echoing across the hall like the tolling of a war bell. He marched forward, the war cry building in his chest until it poured from his mouth in a primal roar. The great doors opened. He disappeared inside.

Silence.

The doors sealed shut behind him.

No sound escaped.

Moments passed. Then the doors opened again, and another name was called. One by one, the Disciples vanished through the iron threshold. Some entered with roars, mimicking Finn's cry. Others went in silence, gripping weapons that felt heavier than ever before.

Each knew what waited.

Before Cojax stepped forward, he met Jessica's gaze—a silent moment of solidarity. Then he walked forward, calm and composed, eyes up, chin down.

And then he was gone.

Slowly, the parade grounds emptied—until Jessica was called.

She stepped forward, steady and silent. No war cry. No performance. She drew her sword. Her shield felt light in her hands, her blade warm with latent power. She was not born of Acadia—but she had survived it. She was a daughter of Eve, a remnant of those who lost the first war. She had bled, suffered, nearly died—again and again.

For four long years, she had prepared. And now, it all led here—to this final battle. She knew what waited beyond the doors. Not just any Reever. Not some mindless drone. If Atlas had any say in the matter, it would be the largest creature they could cram into the city—maybe a Class VI Reever, if such a thing even existed.

And she was ready.

The moment Jessica stepped into darkness, her helmet adapted, casting the world around her in a pale monochrome glow. With a blink, she activated the thermal lens—anything alive, anything radiating heat, would shine in red. She swept her gaze across the room, scanning every corner, every crevice.

The chamber was vast at first, open and still, but it gradually funneled into a narrowing hallway. She advanced slowly, eyes moving in a practiced pattern—left, right, up, down. The Leaper Roach had a reputation for dropping silently from ceilings, its talons severing spines before its victims could scream. She saw nothing, but she didn't trust the silence. Every step was deliberate, her pace dictated by caution rather than time.

The corridor ended in a wide, circular chamber, and she saw the creature immediately. A Razor Side. It was massive—larger than any she'd ever seen. The lower half of its body was a nest of spindly legs, clustered in uneven trios. Its upper body was thick with layered carapace, dull and armored like layered stone. Four hooked arms protruded from its torso, but the most unsettling feature was its head—sunken, positioned low in the chest, peering forward with an unnatural, predatory focus.

It was terrifying—except for one thing.

It was already dead.

Jessica's breath caught in her throat. The thermal lens showed faint residual heat radiating from the corpse. It hadn't been dead long.

The creature's underbelly had been split open—one of its rare weak points. Its organs were strewn in a twisted sprawl across the floor. But the usual acidic blood that should have sizzled stone left only a dull smear, like grease or oil.

She stepped forward slowly, every muscle tense. No alarms, no traps. Nothing stirred. And that, more than anything, unsettled her. Maybe all Disciples faced a dead Razor Side?

*"What is the point of the test?"*

Then—light.

The door in front of her burst open, flooding the room with blinding brilliance. Her helmet darkened instantly to shield her vision. She stepped through the threshold and into the open.

Outside, her unit stood in perfect formation.

"Fall in line," barked a Magister.

Jessica obeyed, slipping into place without hesitation.

Only then did she notice—every Disciple around her was coated head-to-toe in Roach wax: thick, gritty residue from close combat kills. In contrast, her armor gleamed. Immaculate. Polished. Radiant. She looked like a statue of bronze among the ash-covered.

The rest of the Disciples finished the task, all of them surviving, all of them covered in gore except for Jessica.

"You are victorious," Thea declared.

Three simple words—yet they struck with more force than any blade. A thrill surged through Jessica's chest, more powerful than anything she had felt before. Not when she broke the four-minute mile. Not when she first destroyed the shooting simulation. Not when she passed the Mahghetto's opening gauntlet.

This had been her purpose—for four long years.

Elena had given her life for this moment.

And now, it wasn't in vain.

She had succeeded.

Her limbs felt lighter, her thoughts sharper, as if the crushing weight she had carried for years had finally been lifted. She had made it. She was one of them now—one of the Validated. A true daughter of Acadia. Tears threatened the edge of her vision, but she held them back. Crying now might tempt fate.

"All that's left," Magister Octavian continued, "is the Crossing Ceremony. That is when you will be embraced by your Faction. That is when you give up your title as a Disciple—and take on the mantle of the Validated. From this point forward, your fate is your own. Rise, and bring honor to your House and Faction… or falter, and fall."

As before, they were called forth one by one—but this time, they began with her.

"Jessica, adopted daughter of Elena," a Minor Magister called. "Enter into the Faction of BloodBorne and be remade in the city's image."

She obeyed.

The crumbling concrete beneath her boots gave way to smooth marble, and the cracked walls turned into soaring white pillars. The contrast was jarring—almost dreamlike. The world of blood and fire was gone, replaced by something ancient, curated, and imperial. Towering statues lined the expansive corridor, each one carved in the image of great Numberless warriors, frozen in their moments of triumph. Their faces were chiseled in defiance, their weapons raised as if time itself bowed to their glory.

Jessica kept her eyes forward. She dared not linger.

Two fully armored Validated walked beside her for the final stretch, silent as statues, each bearing an ornate Arc Lancer crowned with the crimson standard of the BloodBorne. She passed between them and approached a red curtain—the final threshold. Beyond it, she knew, hundreds of BloodBorne Validated waited. From this moment forward, every movement, every word, would be watched, recorded, and remembered. Elena had prepared her for this. The speech had been drilled into her for over four years. All that work was for this final moment.

She replayed the words in her mind, making sure she had them right. *"I am Jessica of Claymont, a city not far from the walls of Acadia. I am the daughter of James Halworth, the Great Warrior who slew the White Wolf… granddaughter of Emily Halworth, who restored the lost art of agriculture… and great-granddaughter of Eric the Grand, who forged the peace treaty with the Roaches that still holds today."*

She whispered it silently, word for word, as she stepped through the red curtain—and into a cathedral of war.

The chamber beyond defied description. Towering alabaster pillars reached for the domed ceiling, each one etched with heroic figures who seemed less carved than summoned into stone. Banners coiled like serpents along the ribs of the architecture, dipping down from vaulted arches. The whole room gleamed with imperial dominance. And yet—despite its grandeur—it was mostly empty. Despite being designed to hold hundreds, only a few dozen Validated stood present. Their numbers were dwarfed by the vastness of the space, their presence like ghosts in a hollowed temple.

As she entered, they came to attention, saluting her as if she were already one of their own. She mirrored the gesture, her fist striking her chest with a sharp thud. They waited—silent, unwavering—for her to give the command.

She nodded.

At her signal, they relaxed in perfect unison.

Jessica moved forward, nerves tightening with every step. Ahead stretched a narrow bridge arching across a deep chasm. Only as she reached its center did she realize how far the darkness beneath her extended—an abyss without bottom, swallowing sound and thought alike.

Then Atlas stepped forward.

He was resplendent—his armor polished to a mirror sheen, his Numberless Placard glowing with subtle energy. He stood like a statue brought to life, as commanding as the hall around him.

"We, the Validated of Acadia, welcome all those who merit our ranks," he intoned, voice ringing with ritual. "Who now enters our presence?"

"Jessica, of the adopted house of Elena," she said firmly, "the Runner in the Night."

She knew these words. She had rehearsed them with her entire Mahghetto class the day before. But hearing them aloud, in this place, with Atlas looming before her—*it felt different*. Like reciting a script in a play she was only just starting to understand.

"You have passed the Mahghetto. You have proven your worth. You descended into hell and emerged remade—a warrior. The Roach wax upon your body is the mark of your triumph."

Her chest tightened.

She looked down—clean, polished, untouched. Gleaming bronze where there should have been muck and gore. The others were drenched in wax and ash. She shone like a beacon.

For a moment, shame pricked her chest.

*"I will not be embarrassed,"* she told herself. *"Not by him. Not now."* She had passed every trial. Endured every trap. Outlasted the carving he left on her face. She had descended into darkness and returned stronger. He would not take this moment from her.

Atlas turned from her and addressed the crowd.

"We welcome her to our midst. All who sustain her, let me hear you cry the words of war!"

This was the moment.

The moment she had dreamed of—when the crowd would erupt in unified cries, when she would give her speech, when she would be pulled into their ranks not just as a Disciple, but as a sister, a warrior, a true Validated.

But the silence held. Jessica's heart stopped.

Not a single voice.

Not a whisper.

Her fingers curled slightly at her side. Her helmet hid the tremor in her jaw, but it didn't stop the rising sting behind her eyes.

*"Not one? Not one will speak for me?"*

She scanned the crowd from behind her visor. Elena was gone. Orch was missing. Two other Minor Magisters were absent as well. All of them had been there for most of the Mahghetto—where were they now?

Atlas let the silence stretch, cruelly, mercilessly.

Then, at last, he spoke.

"Will no one sustain Jessica of the adopted house of Elena?"

*"What's happening?"* Jessica thought, heart pounding. *"This is all wrong."* Her immaculate armor. The half-empty ceremonial hall. The breaking of a century-old tradition.

By all customs, she should not have gone first; that was an honor reserved for the top-ranked Disciple. Instead, they had called her first, ensuring that the few Disciples who might have sustained her wouldn't have the chance. The order had been changed—it went against custom, but apparently not law.

Atlas stepped toward her, towering, regal, his presence carved from arrogance and centuries of obedience. He wore the authority of a god and expected her to crumble beneath it. To kneel. To beg.

But Jessica didn't kneel. She wouldn't.

Not to him.

She saw him now—not as an untouchable figure of legend, but as a manipulator. A coward hiding behind protocol and power. He had found the one loophole that could defeat her: tradition without merit, spectacle without truth. By the Acadian Code, she had passed. But here, if no one would sustain her, that meant nothing.

*"I will not die on my knees."*

In one breathless motion, she reached for her sword—but Atlas was faster. His blade slashed across her arm, and the force of the blow sent her tumbling backward into the void.

She flipped through the air, the world flashing between light and darkness as her helmet struggled to adjust. Just before the chasm swallowed her, she ignited her Arc Blade and drove it into the concrete wall. The blade sank to the hilt, locking her in place. Her arm screamed in protest, but her grip held. The move had saved her, but it came at the cost of her Repulse Shield, which fell into the depths below.

Dangling in open space, she twisted her body and kicked off the wall, flipping back toward the ledge with a burst of energy-enhanced strength. She soared through the air and landed hard on the edge of the pit, her blade still gripped in her hand. The landing was rough—but impressive. She rose slowly, every movement deliberate. Her breathing steady. Her heart locked in resolve.

She was still on the bridge's near side. Atlas stood between her and the Crossing. But she walked forward anyway, blade raised.

She had been treated like a problem to be erased. As if her life were disposable. As if her accomplishments were a blemish, not a badge. Her thoughts burned with fury—Cojax's broken body, the scar carved into her face.

No more.

"I will not go quietly," she said, her voice low and sharp, every syllable laced with steel.

"You foolish girl," Atlas snarled. "You dare raise a weapon against a Numberless?"

"I have earned the right to the Crossing," she replied, louder now, stronger. "And you cease to be a Numberless the moment you break the Code. By Acadian law, I am one of the Validated. You cannot strip from me what I have earned."

"You have not been sustained. You will not cross this bridge."

"You manipulated them into silence," Jessica said, blade still pointed. "You bent the ceremony to your will. That is not merit!"

"Silence, little girl—"

"Why else change the order? Why else rush me through first?" Her voice cut through the chamber now. "Because you knew someone might speak for me."

Atlas lunged.

He came at her with his full weight, his weapon a streak of light and fury. She met the blow, her Arc Blade locking with his in a flash that lit the entire hall. The shock of impact rattled through her bones.

Then came another strike. And another.

She was forced back step by step, each blow heavier than the last. His strength was monstrous—far beyond anything she had faced. Her helmet rang from a glancing strike. Her shoulder buckled under another. Every impact drained her shielding. Sparks bloomed across her HUD.

She barely managed to deflect a third blow, spinning low and slicing upward in a desperate maneuver. Her blade struck true, slashing across his armored chest in a flare of white light.

Atlas didn't even flinch.

He laughed.

"Pathetic," he spat. "Is that all? That's the strength you bring to our ranks? I will not allow you to stand among the Validated. Your weakness will kill others. I won't let that happen."

Jessica pressed the attack, but her strikes were easily turned aside. Her energy reserves were plummeting. She felt the armor grow heavier, the strength in her limbs beginning to fade.

She wouldn't win a straight fight. Not against him.

Then—an idea.

She retreated toward one of the towering marble pillars. With a single, arcing strike, she carved a deep wedge through its base. It toppled with a thunderous crash, sending tremors through the floor.

Atlas tilted his head. "Reduced to vandalism?" he sneered, unimpressed.

She didn't answer.

Instead, she seized a massive chunk of the broken column and hurled it at him.

He punched through it—stone exploding into a cloud of dust and shrapnel. His helmet flickered, recalibrating between day and thermal vision.

For a split second—he was blind.

Jessica lunged.

With every last ounce of power, she pulsed energy into her shoulder and slammed herself into the giant's chest.

Atlas had braced for another thrown slab of stone, shifting his weight to the back of his heel to absorb the impact—but it was a mistake. Jessica's sudden charge caught him off guard, and the force of her shoulder slammed into his chest. Off balance, he stumbled— then crashed to the ground in a thunderous clatter of armor against marble.

She was on him in an instant.

Her sword flared with energy as she raised it high, then brought it crashing down onto his helmet. Sparks flew. She struck again. And again.

With each blow, she saw a face.

Her father—lost to a war he never chose. Elena—who gave everything for her survival. Cojax—broken by the very man beneath her blade. Her strikes grew more savage, more primal, driven less by precision than by rage. She poured every ounce of her charge into the weapon, channeling grief, fury, and defiance into each arc.

But it wasn't enough.

On the sixth blow, Atlas roared to life.

His hand shot up, seizing her wrist in a grip of iron. Her weapon stopped mid-swing, locked tight in his grasp. With the other hand, he clamped his fingers around her throat. Their shields crackled from the contact.

Jessica choked as he rose, lifting her effortlessly into the air.

Gone was the polished ceremony, the illusion of control. What stood now was something monstrous. Something ancient. Armor hissed as it flexed with each breath from his chest, steam rising in coils from the vents along his spine.

He carried her like a trophy toward the edge of the pit, his voice booming through the hall. She tried to bring her sword to bear, but his grip was too strong.

"Jessica of the adopted house of Elena," he thundered, each word a verdict. "You have dishonored your Faction—and your city. For your crimes, I pronounce you *Rifted!*"

He hurled her downward.

The world spun. Light vanished.

She saw the ceiling for a heartbeat—Atlas framed against the brilliant dome—and then it was gone. Her body tumbled through the air, the walls far beyond reach. She flailed for a grip, a ledge, anything—but the chasm was wide and unyielding. She tried to plunge her blade into the wall but it was too far.

The light above shrank into a distant pinprick as she plunged into the black below. And then—nothing.

Only the fall.

Only the dark.

# FORTY-SEVEN

Cojax stood stoically atop the bridge, his armor hardly visible beneath layers of Roach wax. What remained of the light bars on his chest barely flickered beneath the blackened smear of victory. His voice carried far as he addressed them—measured, composed.

Atlas stepped forward. "You have passed the Mahghetto. You have proven your worth. You descended into hell and emerged remade—a warrior." He gestured broadly to the blood-caked youth before him. "The Roach wax upon your body is the mark of your triumph."

It was true. Cojax was drenched in it. When he had charged the Razor Side, he'd driven his blade straight down its gullet, splitting it open in one feral burst. Reckless, in hindsight—any number of creatures could have lunged from the shadows while his focus was fixed. But it had worked. It was bold, brutal, and undeniably Cojax. The creature had died quickly.

Atlas turned from him then, facing the assembly. "We welcome him into our midst. All who sustain him—cry the words of war!"

Three times the crowd howled in perfect unison. A sound like thunder. From silence to storm in a single breath. It hit Cojax like a wave. Adrenaline surged through him, electrifying his every nerve. For a brief, impossible moment, he felt like he could march alone into the tunnels and face the entire Roach army himself.

Atlas extended his hand.

Cojax took it.

With a pull, the Numberless brought him across the final step of the bridge and into the waiting arms of the crowd. Cheers erupted. Hands clapped against his back, strong and celebratory. Laughter rang out. He had never seen so many grins in one place— never imagined joy could feel this real inside Acadia.

He had thought Jessica's speech would have soured the

moment. At the very least, he expected discomfort, a somber silence. But if it had left an impact, it was buried beneath the revelry. For a moment, he even wondered if she'd softened her words.

*"Jessica."* The thought hit him suddenly. *"Where is she?"*

Most of the Disciples lingered near the bridge, a swelling crowd of noise and elation. She should have been there—should have been close. But she wasn't. A flicker of panic tried to claw its way up, but he pushed it down.

"She's short," he told himself. "Easy to lose track of a shrub in a mess of trees."

He chuckled at his own joke. Everything felt light right now—too light to be dragged down by worry.

One by one, the remaining Disciples crossed the bridge. Each was greeted with the same primal roar, the same war-born welcome. Uproarious joy was a rare thing in the BloodBorne Faction, but tonight it flowed freely.

Then came the feast.

Cojax had no idea where the food came from—only that it materialized in overflowing portions across steel tables lining the wall. Towering platters of fatty meats, charred vegetables, and fire-roasted cuts that fell clean from the bone filled the air with an intoxicating aroma.

He couldn't remember the last time he had eaten something that didn't taste synthesized. Even the Faction's two other ceremonies didn't compare.

Music crackled through the room. Not the inspirational, sterilized harmonics but something older. Fiercer. Recorded war-drums and ancestral chants, remnants of the world before Acadia. Instruments were forbidden now—tools of the Dependent—but the ancient recordings were permitted.

He spotted Finn near one of the food tables, standing still amid the celebration, untouched plate in hand. While the hall swelled with laughter and raised voices, Finn's face told another story—his brow drawn low, his eyes distant and wary.

Cojax approached with a grin. "That despondent face is beneath your Tier," he said lightly. "You're a Validated now. We did it, brother. We made it through—and you, of all people, should be smiling. You're the Alpha. Honestly, I'm a little jealous."

But Finn didn't answer. He stared down at his tray, where roasted meats and vibrant greens sat cooling. He hadn't eaten a bite. When he finally looked up, there was something urgent in his eyes—unspoken, but pressing. Then he lifted one hand and pressed it to the edge of his jaw.

The signal.

Jessica's signal.

The one she had taught them—to speak without speaking, to signal when they were not safe. A cold jolt ran through Cojax. The weight of realization crashed into him like a charged blade.

*"She's gone."*

His eyes narrowed. Finn gave the faintest of nods, confirming what Cojax already feared. The color drained from his face.

*"Gone? No. No, I saw her. She survived. She was the first one called to the Crossing."*

It didn't make sense.

The trial was over. The Mahghetto was finished. There was nothing left. She had earned her place. She had survived what hundreds hadn't.

Cojax opened his mouth to speak, to demand answers, but Finn raised his finger again, firm this time. *"Not here. Not now."*

Cojax's throat tightened. Something in his chest twisted, seethed. His pulse quickened, fury clawing its way up from the pit of his stomach. She had made it. She had endured. And still—they'd taken her.

The meat in his mouth turned bitter. He spat it out, slamming his tray to the floor. It hit with a sharp clatter. Silence rippled outward.

All around him, the laughter died.

Finn grabbed his arm, his whisper tense. "Careful. You can't—"

"Attention!" Atlas' voice thundered across the hall. Instantly, the crowd stilled and the music faded. The Numberless ascended a wide staircase at the front of the room, each step deliberate, purposeful. He reached the marble balcony above and turned, his voice steady as he addressed the assembled Disciples.

"My brothers and sisters—for you *are* worthy of being called such—you've endured what most cannot. Torture. Endless discipline. Loss. You've seen those you cared for fall. You've tasted despair."

He paused, letting the silence stretch.

"These things—what you've seen, what you've done—must never leave your lips. The Mahghetto must remain unspoken, unknown. Its power lies in secrecy. If others prepare for it, it fails its purpose. As Horace teaches: 'Adversity reveals true character; good fortune conceals it.' This is the first of the Acadian Codes."

His voice hardened. "If that Code is broken, your life is forfeit."

The silence was suffocating.

Atlas' tone shifted again, smoother now. "You've all been assigned to units. Your ArmGuard will provide the details. But for tonight—eat, drink, and be merry. Tomorrow, you begin the greatest service of your lives."

The applause returned. Some raised their cups. Others clapped, their joy restored by command.

But not Cojax.

He didn't move. He didn't blink.

He stared up at Atlas as if he had Blazers for eyes, the rage in his heart so hot it seared the inside of his chest.

*"It was him."* The realization pulsed like blood in his temples. *"He's not part of the BloodBorne Faction. He has no business being here. He made sure she was Rifted. He stood there and let it happen—no, he made it happen."*

His hand drifted toward his Blade. He could feel it—he could see himself lunging, slicing, ending it now. Beams of light shimmered faintly along his armor as the energy flared within him.

Only Finn's grip held him back. Firm. Steady. Alive.

His next words were hurried and slurred. "Don't give them the satisfaction of a quick end—instead, live long enough to be their reckoning."

His friend then made the secret sign used to identify members of the rebellion. Cojax ignored it at first, allowing his anger to seethe, but slowly he turned away. His friend was right. A blade in the dark could do more damage than one swung in rage. And Cojax would wait—he would bide his time, and when the city least expected it, he would destroy it all.

# FORTY-EIGHT

Jessica landed hard, but instead of stone, her body sank into something brittle—something that cracked and snapped beneath her weight like dry branches. Her armor absorbed the brunt of the fall, but its charge drained instantly, the impact stealing the breath from her lungs. She lay still for a moment, dazed, the strange texture of the ground gnawing at her senses.

It was soft. Uneven. Hollow in places.

She shifted, one arm pressing down for leverage—and something gave way beneath her elbow with a sickening crunch. She rolled to the side and forced herself upright. As she swung a leg over the mound, something clattered free and tumbled into the dark. She pulsed her blade, casting a beam of light. Her heart seized.

They weren't stones.

They were bones.

Human bones—bleached and brittle, stacked like refuse beneath her. Skulls grinned upward from the dark, ribs curled like snapped branches, femurs and finger bones tangled in heaps. They cracked and shifted with her every breath. Her stomach twisted, but she clenched it down. The realization hit harder than the fall: this was no random grave. This was a burial mound—built by design, and by many deaths. The weight of it—of all those who had come before her—pressed against her like a tombstone sinking into her spine.

She thrashed.

She had to get out.

She shoved upward, slipping on loose fragments, her blade hacking through the tangle of bones just to clear a path. She pulsed her blade again. Ribcages buckled. Teeth scattered. The mound felt endless—like it would swallow her whole and drag her down with the rest of them.

*"Get out. Just get out."*

At last, with one final, agonizing pull, she dragged herself free of the bone pit, collapsing beside it in a heap of gasps and grit. A raw, desperate cry tore from her throat—half fury, half grief, and all exhaustion. She flashed her blade again and looked back, capturing the full breadth of the scene. The bones stretched upward to the vaulted ceiling and outward as far as her light could reach. She turned away, not looking back.

She rose on unsteady legs and began walking—blind, aimless, every step disjointed from the last. Her limbs moved like they didn't belong to her. The darkness felt thicker now, more suffocating, as though it had grown aware of her presence and wanted her back.

Her foot caught on something—stone or bone, she couldn't tell—and she went down hard.

She didn't get up.

She lay there, trembling, fingers clutching at the dirt, the taste of dry marrow still thick in her throat. The scent of rot clung to her like a shroud.

Acadia—proud, perfect, unyielding—rested on a foundation not of stone, but of bone. The city's towers, its laws, its glory... all of it built atop the bodies of the forgotten. This wasn't just a forgotten chamber.

It was truth.

Hidden, rotting, buried beneath centuries of control. And it would remain that way for centuries more. The rebellion was over. Elena's whole plan depended on the Crossing. And now, it would never be.

*"I've failed her."*

She staggered to her feet, a wave of exhaustion threatening to pull her back to the ground—not just from the fall, or even the fight with Atlas, but from something deeper. Something hollow. Heavy.

She pulsed the blade, sending a ripple of light into the dark. The room was endless rubble—twisted metal, shattered columns, scattered trash. A thick haze hung in the air, coating her throat and lungs with every breath. The light sputtered and dimmed again.

She sheathed her blade.

With her hands acting as eyes, she crept forward, feeling her way through the ruins—concrete shards, exposed wires, rusted beams. Occasionally, she drew her blade just long enough to check for anything useful. Nothing. Only more decay. It was an old part of

Acadia. Ancient, maybe even the first district ever built. Long abandoned. Long forgotten. An endless stretch of stone, columns, decayed structures.

*"I failed."*

She replayed the Crossing in her mind. Atlas had appeared equitable—measured, even noble. He had set the stage with precision. He'd made sure she looked unworthy. Her armor was spotless—no blood, no grime, no sign of struggle—and the absence of certain Magisters had been no accident. He had crafted the moment carefully, ensuring that when the time came, no one in the crowd would sustain her.

*"And I fell right into his trap. But what could I have done?"*

She took a deep breath, forcing the guilt back. She couldn't have known Atlas' plan.

Hours passed. She walked without knowing if she made progress or circled the same broken ground. She had assumed the many chambers would eventually become a corridor, a hall—*something.* But they didn't.

Eventually, her body demanded rest. She found a flat spot near a low column and risked another pulse of her blade. The room lit up. This time, something new: clusters of pale, fibrous plants clinging to cracks in the stone. They pulsed faintly with bioluminescence, stretching up from fissures like they were feeding on something deep below.

*"Water."*

She scrambled toward one. Its surface was thorny, but soft, slightly damp to the touch. She removed a gauntlet before tearing the root from the soil. She then pressed her fingers into the space it left behind.

Nothing—just loose grit.

Then something wet splashed on her knuckles. She froze, unsure what it was. She brought her hand to her lips, tasting dirt and water. It was faint, but unmistakable. Possibly clean. Her armor could detect pathogens, but uncharged, it was little more than dead weight.

So she waited. Waited for her stomach to twist, for her lungs to tighten, for the sting of poison to set in. But nothing came.

She positioned herself beneath the source. The first drop struck her eye and she winced, adjusting. The second found her mouth. Then another. Then another.

It was slow—agonizingly slow—but it didn't matter.

She savored it.

For the first time in years, she wasn't rushing. There was no directive. No burden. No battle waiting on the other end of the hallway. She wasn't being scored. Judged. Sorted.

She was… free.

Her shoulders dropped. The muscles in her back released. The tension in her ribs softened. No one barking orders. No Magisters. No Placard. No shame. No Score. Just silence, breath, and the steady drip of water in the dark.

She remained beneath the dripping water for what felt like hours—though she had no way to measure time. At some point, a droplet struck her forehead with a sharper-than-usual sting. It took her several groggy moments to realize she had fallen asleep.

She shifted away from the trickling flow and nestled herself between two collapsed pillars forming a wide L-shape. It was colder now—unnaturally so. Normally, her armor would adjust, automatically raising her core temperature. Without charge, it offered no such comfort. Even its natural heat was fading, leaving her exposed to the slow, creeping bite of the underground chill.

And yet… she slept.

Long, dreamless, blissful sleep—the kind she hadn't known since she was a child. The kind Acadia had stolen.

She had no idea how much time had passed when her eyes finally cracked open. Her limbs felt heavy, her throat parched. She yawned silently and stretched, instinctively reaching for her sword.

But it was gone.

Her fingers brushed stone. Then dust. Then empty air. Her heart seized. She patted the ground rapidly, fingers becoming claws as she scraped across the debris.

*"Where is it? How—"*

"Don't worry, young woman," came a voice from the dark— old, dry, and dust-choked. "We're friends, not enemies."

She surged to her feet in a blink, spinning to protect her blind side, heart pounding in her throat. Her senses snapped awake, every instinct screamed. Then, faint yellow light flickered on about a dozen yards ahead, casting long shadows across the rubble.

Three figures stood there just beyond the reach of the light. She couldn't make out their faces—the glow was angled away, deliberate—but she could see the shape of them, still and watching.

"My sword," she said, voice cutting through the silence with more authority than she expected. "Give it back."

"Here you are," the same voice replied, warm and deliberate. A moment later, the blade clattered to the floor. The sound was heavy, metallic. Jessica lunged for it, snatching it up and taking a sharp step back, raising the weapon as if it were a Blazer primed for fire.

"May I have a seat?" the voice asked gently.

She kept the blade leveled, her body coiled. But the voice— there was something about it. Familiar. It carried a softness she hadn't heard in years. A cadence that reminded her of home. Of her father's voice in the quiet moments before Acadia turned everything cold.

The silence stretched, taut.

"Orch said you were a little paranoid," the voice continued, light-hearted but not mocking. "That's normal for the newly Rifted. Though you… you seem especially wound tight."

There was a pause.

"I'm going to sit down on that concrete block over there," he said. "And when you feel ready, you're welcome to join me."

One of the figures stepped forward, revealing himself to the light. Slowly, deliberately, he raised his hands, turning his body in a slow circle so she could see he was unarmed. No blades. No armor. No visible threat.

The light caught his face.

Jessica's breath caught in her throat.

A lattice of scars crisscrossed his cheeks, his brow, his neck— raised and rigid, as if they'd been burned in, not cut. Though long since healed, they still looked raw, as if his skin remembered the pain. And yet, beneath the wreckage of his face, his features were strangely… kind. His eyes, too clear to belong to a killer. His posture humble, even frail. He was thin. Old. Far older than anyone she'd seen since the villages. But there was power in him. Something hidden. A tension beneath the dust.

When he finished his turn, he arched an eyebrow, lifted his hands higher for emphasis, and eased himself down onto a concrete slab with a tired sigh.

"How can I trust you?" she asked, blade still raised.

"I'm not asking you to, Jessica," he said.

"How many of you are there?"

"Three."

"How do you know my name?"

The old man sighed—an exhausted, rehearsed sound. Like this was a role he'd played many times before. He didn't answer right away. But when he did, his words came with a warmth that unsettled her more than any threat.

"My name is Aias," he said, his voice calm, assured. "And I know your friend Elena well."

Jessica flinched before she could stop herself. She hoped the dim light and her trained expression had masked it.

It hadn't.

"How do you know her?"

"She was my wife."

## FORTY-NINE

Cojax felt the pulse in his ArmGuard. He was the first to stand, the first to grab his helmet. He was not supposed to be on duty, but he had volunteered—so had Finn. The East Wall Grotto had been receiving violent and persistent attacks, and that's where they would be deployed. Factions did not usually allow other Factions to protect their portion of the wall, but the BloodLetters had spent the last two weeks in daily combat, and many of their reserves had been spent.

Now the Bottom Tiers arrived, like mercenaries—unfamiliar with the area, but eager to spill blood. Among them were the fresh Disciples from the Mahghetto interspersed with Validated who needed to increase their Score to avoid being Rifted.

It was dangerous work, mostly because they were working alongside a Faction with slightly different training and expectations. Not being from the commanding Faction, the Tenth Tiers were placed at the heart of every conflict, where the ground becomes saturated with black and red blood.

It had been two months since Jessica had been Rifted, and he had not mentioned her name once, for his own safety and those around him. But if even half of his thoughts forced themselves out, every other word would be her name. He could not quite express what drew him to her. It was more than attraction, more than infatuation. She was simply something more.

Cojax met Finn on the roof just as a CargoLifter landed. They nodded to each other and entered, each one focused on the battle to come. They both held spears and shields, their swords at their sides, and their Blazers attached to their backs. They were already Eighth Tier, a feat that seemed impossible to many. But they had paid the price by spilling Roach blood almost every day.

Finn frowned as the CargoLifter jolted. "So, how many times are we going to volunteer for battle?"

Cojax did not answer.

"A month longer? When we're in Sixth Tier? Come on, clue me in. How long do you think we can push ourselves before a Reever cuts us in half?"

No answer.

"Cojax," Finn said, "you need to let things go. I hate to be the one to tell you this, but charging headlong into pitched battle is not the way to live—in fact, just the opposite is true. Listen, we tried. We did, and I honestly thought we had done it. But we can't change what's done—it was all arranged...,"

His voice slowed as he considered his next words. "She would not want you to live this way."

Cojax felt pure rage rip through his body, spreading out and away from his chest. "I have to do this, Finn. I can't explain why, but I'm driven to it. I won't fault you if you don't want to volunteer with me anymore. But there's a point to all of this, trust me."

Finn frowned. "I know. I just wish I knew what it was."

Just then, the CargoLifter flew over their unit. Cojax leaped out, hurtling fifty feet down to the ground and landing in dramatic fashion. With a sigh, Finn followed, leaving an identical crater next to his friend. The stunt was something few First or Second Tiers would ever do. It was showy and used precious energy. This did not faze Cojax, whose armor had never yet lost its charge in battle.

Finn took his position to the right of his friend while other Acadians began to fall into formation. Cojax was not in charge, but he moved as if he were, and in the chaos of battle, the Validated seemed to be drawn to his decisiveness. Finn looked at his ArmGuard and spotted a flashing light that indicated their position in relation to where they needed to line up.

"We're off by three feet."

"They'll make room for us," Cojax answered. "We're to be the tip of the spear, and with all these Tenth Tiers running around, I doubt anyone will want to take our place."

Finn's body pulsed with adrenaline. "We're always the tip of the spear. Have you ever considered what it might be like if we were, let's say, the back of the spear? That could be fun."

Cojax didn't answer.

"I talk to calm my nerves," Finn muttered.

Cojax let out a low laugh, smiling at his faithful friend. "I hadn't noticed."

Finn pressed on, voice edged with frustration. "Why do you keep volunteering us for the front lines—*right* at the enemy's center? What are you trying to prove? What are you looking for? Still trying to impress the 'big guy'? Listen, you've bumped us up two Tiers, so congrats. But those are the *least* competitive Tiers. If you keep burning this hot, you'll burn out just as fast. You think they'll care when you do? They'll just plug someone else into your slot and keep marching. What's the plan here?"

Cojax glanced over. "Are you finished?"

Finn clicked his helmet into place, raised his shield, and pointed his spear forward like a man accepting his fate. "Yes. Thank you for letting me get that off my chest."

"Sure thing."

Cojax did have a plan—one so reckless, so improbable, he dared not speak it aloud for fear it would crumble the moment he voiced it. He wasn't volunteering for battle to climb the Tiers, though that was a convenient perk. No—his reasons ran deeper. Darker.

He'd almost told Finn—more than once—but the words always withered on his tongue. He blamed the ever-recording armor they wore, but that was just a shield—flimsy and convenient. If he truly wanted to talk, they could spar at one of the nearby Palaestras, let their armor burn out its charge and speak freely.

But he wouldn't.

"*No,*" Cojax thought, guilt washing over him like cold water. "*I can't involve him—too many risks for both of us. It's better this way.*"

Just then, their Alpha arrived.

He was a Fifth Tier—late, as usual—still adjusting his armor as he sauntered in. He looked like someone who had once been a great warrior. The frame was still there, the posture, the remnants of precision. But time or trauma had dulled the edge. Now, he moved with the weary nonchalance of a man who had survived enough to stop trying to impress anyone. Still, he wore the mark of the BloodBorne—one of the most feared and respected Factions in all of Acadia.

Each Alpha received orders from a Kappa, one Tier higher, who managed ten units from hovercrafts stationed just above the Wall. And two ranks above *them*, somewhere behind tinted glass and reinforced plating, sat the Omega—the First Tier Commander of the entire battle. The highest rank a Validated could achieve. Enormous power. Even greater risk.

What made the Acadian war machine so effective—brilliant even—was its speed. Instructions weren't issued as commands. They were received as impressions—raw directives transmitted directly into the mind. A whole army could shift formation in the blink of an eye. A wheel to the right. A sudden charge. A seamless pivot.

An impression hit them.

Advance.

And in perfect unison, fifty thousand soldiers took a synchronized step forward, their boots pounding the earth in a deafening wave. The formation shifted instantly into a forward diamond—standard on the East Wall, though rarely seen on the North side, where they preferred a heavier box formation.

The low hum of engines grew louder as Lancers roared into motion on both flanks, skimming across the field on hoverbikes. Their role was crucial—either to flank or to *prevent* being flanked. Their bikes were tipped with Light Blades, deadly against lower-tier threats, and their Blazers could reinforce the Phalanx line when the tide began to turn. They left the high-level targets to the Phalanx—or the Snipers.

The whole scene was impressive, if a little theatrical. It looked more like an overwhelming display of power than a tactical necessity. The enemy was out there, true—but only a few hundred thousand strong, mostly Reever Skitterfangs—fast but lightly armored. The fight would be short. Brutal. Half an hour, maybe less—unless the enemy decided to run. Roaches sometimes tried to drag out engagements, hoping to tax Acadian resources. It never worked. There were just too many Acadians in rotation.

As they advanced across the field, helmets began scanning— analyzing heat signatures, mapping targets, classifying species and aggression levels. Most soldiers relied on the data. Cojax didn't. He found it distracting—the constant highlighting of enemies, the flickering tags and colors that pulsed in his vision. He kept it off.

Which was why he saw it first.

Something moved.

About fifty yards ahead of the formation. Subtle. Too subtle for the scanners. He glanced at the Alpha, who walked alongside them without concern, adjusting a gauntlet. Either he hadn't seen it— or didn't care.

*"Just nerves,"* Cojax told himself.

But there it was again. A ripple—something unnatural. The earth wasn't shifting. Not exactly. It was *the air.* A shimmer, like heat rising from stone.

He narrowed his eyes.

*"No… it wasn't heat. Or if it was, it didn't belong here. Not on this soil. Not in this temperature. It was… Vapor."*

It wafted upward in slow, warping waves, bending the space around it like a mirage. Not from fire. Not from any enemy tactic he'd seen before. Something was disturbing the ground itself.

*"This isn't right."*

Cojax linked his Comm-Link, isolating the line so only Finn could hear.

"Did you see that?"

"Yes," Finn replied, voice dry. "The enemy looks like they're about to bolt."

"No. Just in front of us." Cojax scanned the haze again. Whatever had been producing the heat waves had suddenly stopped. A trickle of self-doubt crept in.

Finn shook his head. "I don't see anything."

But then it appeared again. This time, from the right. Not just a shimmer, but movement. Subtle, rhythmic. Controlled.

He opened his Comm-Link to include the Alpha. "Sir, something's not right. I'm seeing heat waves just ahead of us."

The Alpha took a slow moment to respond, as if weighing the effort. "It's a mirage. Nothing more."

"Sir… in the Mahghetto, there were reports… Roaches experimenting with thermal interference to scramble our scans."

"Clear the airwaves," the Alpha snapped. "Your nine months in the Mahghetto don't compare to the years of blood caked on my boots."

"Yes, sir," Cojax said.

But even as he complied, his fingers moved. He switched his helmet to thermal vision—rarely used during the day, because most detail was washed out in the sun's blaze. The display turned blinding white. He swept his gaze left, then right, heart thudding as panic shot up his spine.

*"We're walking into a trap."*

He longed to speak again—but the order had been given. To disobey now would just lower his Score. Or worse, it might be considered insubordination. Even a whisper of that charge could mean severe punishment and dishonor. At Eighth Tier, there would be no Honorable Release for the likes of him.

So he kept silent. Jaw clenched. Heart pounding.

They moved forward.

Nothing happened.

They passed through the heat shimmer, uninterrupted. No trap. No ambush. Just empty air and invisible heat rising like the breath of a dying world. He exhaled, slow and long. Part relief. Part shame. Before the Mahghetto, he would've spoken up. Now, he knew better. Obedience earned honor. Honor preserved the Score.

The rhythm of war took over.

The two forces slipped into their all-too-familiar choreography—Acadians locking into an Ion-Phalanx formation, the Roaches erupting from beneath the dirt in predictable numbers.

Shields slammed into place with a thunderous *clang*, forming a wall of seamless defense. The Acadians became a living machine—lines tight, energy shields overlapping, spears ready. An unbreakable wall of flesh, alloy, and nerve.

The Roaches' greatest weapon was mass. They had no tactics, no real command—not this time. Only teeth, claws, and fury.

Two hundred yards away, the creatures began their charge.

"Halt march. First two lines, retrieve Blazers," their Alpha ordered.

Cojax and Finn moved instinctively, slinging their spears to their upper backs and pulling their Blazers from below. They mounted the weapons against their shields, stabilizing their aim. The second line did the same, but attached their shields to their backs—both hands now free for targeting. As they moved, two HoverCams deployed from each of the Acadians' armor.

The Reevers screeched as they ran—a chorus of rusty blades scraping open and closed. That sound... it got under the skin, a metallic shriek that gnawed at sanity. Mixed among them were the

Class V Sliders—tall, glistening creatures that fired acid from ducts in their foreheads—and the Class I Ankle Biters, knee-high nightmares with segmented legs and barbed scorpion tails.

One hundred fifty yards.

Cojax's pulse roared in his ears.

One hundred twenty.

The Roaches' one chance—if they had one at all—was in this first wave. If their momentum broke the Phalanx, they could swarm the formation before reinforcements could close the gap. But with no SataniKahns in sight, it was unlikely. Only Tenth Tier formations had been broken before against this type of charge—and even then, it was rare. The Roaches never seemed to learn.

"Fire!" the Alpha ordered.

The world lit up.

A tidal wave of light-blades screamed across the field. Dozens of Reevers fell instantly, their bodies folding into the dirt. Their carapaces deflected some of the shots, but not all. Weak points were exploited, clean shots taken. It wasn't perfect, but it didn't need to be. The point was to slow them—to break their rhythm.

The Roaches stumbled. Tripped. Collided with each other in snarling frustration. Sometimes the Damnattii would respond with suppressive fire or bombardment, but this time—nothing. The Acadians were free to shred the front line.

Cojax's Blazer sang, firing rapid bursts with unrelenting focus. Finn, beside him, took slower, more precise shots—aiming for joints, necks, the dark seams of exoskeletons. He claimed each of his shots were worth ten of Cojax's.

Forty yards.

"Fix Blazers," the Alpha ordered.

Blazers returned to their magnetic clamps. Spears back in hand. Shields lifted. Stances braced.

Cojax leaned into the coming tide.

Out of the corner of his eye, he noticed other units still using their Blazers. Their Alphas had waited longer. More aggressive. Riskier. Their own Alpha was conservative—perhaps frustratingly so—but effective.

Twenty yards.

Cojax inhaled.

The final seconds stretched. Time elongated. The air thickened.

Then—

An explosion of light.

The charge hit the shieldwall like a tsunami against stone. Each impact staggered the unit, making the ground sway beneath their boots. The Phalanx absorbed it, absorbed *everything*. The creatures howled as they smashed into metal and energy. Limbs flailed. Claws scratched against shields. The wall held.

Then the counterstrike began.

Acadian spears darted out like piston-driven teeth, skewering anything within reach. Carapaces cracked. Black blood sprayed. The Reevers screamed—high and insectile—as they died in waves. The swarm surged, desperate. They clawed. Bit. Waxy bodies dropped one after another, stacking like cordwood. A pile of death was forming— so high the enemy began to *use* it, climbing over their own fallen to leap into the Phalanx.

The Alpha's voice cut through the chaos.

"Prepare to surge."

In the back, the final line of Acadians unlocked their energy link from the formation. The Phalanx rippled as if inhaling—ready to exhale with violence.

"Surge," the Alpha transmitted.

An instant later, the rear line of Acadians launched sixty feet into the air, spears angled downward like falling javelins. They struck the earth with thunderous force just ahead of Cojax, obliterating the creatures beneath their boots. Spears plunged deep. Black blood geysered skyward.

"Surge."

Again, the order came. Again, the rear warriors vaulted, crushing the enemy with merciless rhythm. The sky seemed to churn with iron as the pattern repeated—rise, fall, impale, rise again. By the time Cojax found himself at the rear, the tide of battle was unmistakable: they were winning. No, not just winning; it was an annihilation.

Cojax landed hard, his spear driving through two of the smaller beasts in a single strike. He didn't recognize the species— hadn't seen them in any archive—but they died the same. A wheezing cry escaped their mangled throats before their bodies turned red like overripe fruit and exploded.

Chunks of gore sprayed in every direction, but the Acadians' shield link held firm, absorbing the blast without much effect.

Cojax pressed forward, naming the creatures as he slew them.

*"Slider. Ankle Biter. Reever. Skitterfang. Pit Viper. No idea what that is—but it's glitching ugly."*

Then the Roaches' center line shattered. The Acadians poured through the breach like a released flood.

"Separate," the Alpha ordered, "and clean up."

This was the part Cojax loved—the chaos after the line collapsed, when formations broke and the hunt began. Single combat. Score-building glory.

Their Alpha must have felt it too—he'd broken the link early, likely wanting to carve his own legend before the other Phalanxes followed. And follow they did. One by one, the rigid Acadian phalanxes severed their energy links, peeling off to pursue individual kills. Their precision dissolved into a beautiful, lethal sprawl of motion.

That's when it happened.

The ground quaked.

A low, guttural roar rolled up from the deep.

Finn was the first to stop. Then he grabbed Cojax by the collar and spun him around. In the spot where heatwaves had shimmered minutes before, the earth erupted.

A black, twitching thing ripped from the soil—misshapen and massive, its body slick with blood. It stood nearly as tall as the Wall itself. No eyes. Dozens of mouths—used not for eating but burrowing. Thousands of mismatched legs scuttled underneath it in panicked coordination. Its entire body convulsed with violent tremors.

Cojax knew exactly what it was. A Digger.

*"But that's impossible. They can't breach the inner shield."*

In past battles, Diggers were rendered useless—shredded to ribbons underground by the Outer Shield's resonance fields. They'd become mulch before they got within range.

"Unless...," Cojax's eyes widened. "The heatwaves—they jammed our sensors. The underground resonance fields were never turned up, because the Digger was never detected."

The creature hadn't emerged unscathed though. It bled from deep wounds, several legs missing entirely, gashes torn across its armored body. Then another Digger rose. Then another. Soon, twenty of them littered the battlefield, swaying like dazed giants. The first fell like a collapsing tower, crashing down with enough force to flatten dozens of Roaches. Then the next and the next—burying their own forces beneath their bulk. Acadians were too quick, too nimble to be trapped by one of the falling creatures.

"What are they trying to do?" Finn asked. "Makes no sense."

Cojax laughed, slapping Finn on the shoulder. "Looks like they're trying to teach us a lesson in stupidity."

Finn grinned. "Go easy on them, Cojax. They're trying their best."

And then the Diggers exploded.

The battlefield was painted in flesh and black blood. The ground shimmered as something even worse emerged—creatures pouring from the Diggers' bodies like maggots from a corpse.

Tens of thousands.

SataniKahns—White Maws, Spiners, Primes—each of them enormous and dripping with gore. Then came the Reever packs, the Leapers, and the snarling Clingers. It was the most terrifying concentration of enemy forces Cojax had ever witnessed—and it kept growing.

From every Digger tunnel, more and more swarmed up.

Then came the sound—snip snip snip—like massive scissors slicing through steel.

Cojax turned.

The routed line of Roaches—the ones they had just chased down—hadn't been routed at all. Reinforcements had arrived in silence, outnumbering the first wave. This time, the Roaches were organized. Disciplined. Led by Damnattii.

The entire deployed Acadian Invictorian was now boxed in by two massive enemy forces—one at their back, one at their front.

"Form ranks!" the Alpha's voice crackled in their helmets. "Form ranks! Now!"

Chaos erupted as Acadians scrambled to regroup. A GPS ping hit their ArmGuards—coordinates, orientation, tactical overview. The rally point was far from their position.

Cojax froze.

Not out of fear—but calculation.

Finn turned sharply. "Come on! If we're not in a shieldwall when that wave hits us, we're dead!"

"There's no time," Cojax shouted over the chaos. "I have a better idea."

Finn closed the gap between them, jaw tight, shield braced. "It better involve us living long enough to retire. Preferably somewhere with a view."

Cojax didn't answer. Instead, he widened his Comm-Link to a 200-yard radius. "All those receiving this transmission, belay the Alpha's order and form a shieldwall on me. Stand by for coordinates."

"You're not an Alpha," Finn snapped. "You don't have the authority—no one's going to listen."

As if summoned by fate itself, four Acadians sprinted into place beside Finn.

"Confusion and necessity," Cojax said, "that's all the authority I need."

"Six people a shieldwall does not make," Finn grumbled, but more Validated were already rushing to join.

Finn gave a sharp laugh. "We're going to lose our heads for this."

"We're already dead," Cojax said, eyes scanning the field. "Might as well die having fun."

The formation swelled—ten, twenty, then over a hundred. Then over two. Their phalanx grew too large for traditional structure, warping into a stretched rectangle. There wasn't time to think about the implications.

The earth trembled again.

SataniKahns led the charge—hulking, feral titans who made the ground shudder with every step. Cojax had only seen them in simulations or on the CityScreens. The real thing dwarfed the holograms.

"First three rows, Blazers out!" Cojax ordered. Not regulation—but it made tactical sense.

"First row, kneel. Second and third, file in behind."

It was messy. The spacing was awkward. But eventually, they formed a thick three-tier firing line—more guns per square foot than standard formations allowed.

"Fire as fast as your finger can move!"

Finn shook his head. *"Wrong command. Wrong timing. Wrong everything."* He still fired.

Light poured from their Blazers in blinding arcs, hammering the oncoming wave.

"Concentrate fire on the following coordinates," Cojax commanded.

Finn's HUD lit up. One of the SataniKahns had been tagged. A wall of laser-fire slammed into its bulk, slowing its charge. The Roaches behind it surged forward, unintentionally overtaking the slowed behemoth.

"Change targets," Cojax said again. Another beast. Another hail of fire. Over and over, Cojax pinged fresh coordinates—each time focusing the fire on a new SataniKahn.

To Finn, it seemed pointless. SataniKahns were all but impervious to Blazer fire. Even the large Gouger guns couldn't really damage them too badly. It was like flicking pebbles at a charging dog.

But then the first wave hit.

The Roaches crashed into the shieldwall.

Finn's eyes widened as the truth struck him harder than any enemy blow. Cojax's directed fire was not intended to hurt the creatures, but slow them down, taking away their greatest weapon—momentum. The tactic was unorthodox, but it had bought them a chance to survive.

"Spears!" Cojax yelled.

The first row dropped their Blazers and drew steel. Their formation lit up in a blast of energy—power igniting across hundreds of weapons.

Cojax exhaled. *"We held. They didn't break us."*

The next few minutes descended into madness.

Roaches poured at them in waves, more savage than before—driven by some terrible instinct that the Acadians were trapped. The black blood of the dead formed pools around their boots, sticky and slick. But they held formation, rotating shields, adjusting to attacks from all sides. They became a bronze island in a sea of claws, chitin, and mandibles.

The SataniKahns finally arrived, crushing their own ranks beneath them as they advanced. One beast—its mandibles dripping with blood—lunged at the shieldwall.

It landed right in front of Cojax and Finn.

Its blades came down in rapid succession, followed by an explosion of light. The energy from each blow drained their shields by degrees. Another SataniKahn joined it.

Finn shouted, "We can't take much more! They're going to break through our collective shields!"

Cojax struck forward, his spear driving toward the creature's core. It cut through the carapace but could not reach far enough to do critical damage.

Suddenly, twin beams of light roared across the field— Gouger Cannons fixed on the Wall. The impact shook the beasts, ripping off small limbs and searing flesh. It couldn't kill them, but it certainly proved a good distraction.

"Cojax, we've got reinforcements inbound," Finn reported.

Other streaks of light appeared as several Acadians took to hovercraft, firing their Blazers from the decks. This initially fanned a flame of hope in Cojax's chest, but it was soon snuffed out. There was a reason Acadians rarely used the hovercraft to engage the enemy directly. The Damnattii returned fire in even greater volleys, sending forth so many rounds that the gray sky completely disappeared.

Even though the hovercraft were shielded, they were quickly overwhelmed by the onslaught. They began to fall to the earth, exploding on impact, their drivers and occupants leaping free of the vehicles before they crashed. The Acadians with Unicrafts proved more challenging to hit, but they too succumbed to the intense fire. Within a minute, the only things still firing were the Gouger Cannons and Blazers from the Wall—every other projectile was from the enemy.

"Command," Cojax said, tapping his Comm-Link. "Patch me into the battlefield feed."

The reply came cold and electronic. "What's your Score? You're not registering as Command."

Cojax hesitated.

"My name is Marcus. BloodBorne Faction. Top Tier. My

armor isn't transmitting properly."

"You're not listed for this engagement."

"I answered the reserve call. Just send the feed."

A second later, the image appeared in his helmet HUD. He zoomed in. His breath caught. The battlefield had been wiped clean.

Every phalanx, every formation *gone*—swept away by the tide. Only one formation remained: a black and bronze square... *his*. He panned toward the Wall. One of the Great Gates loomed in view— but instead of opening, it was being reinforced with Phalanxes positioned on the Wall.

They weren't coming.

They had been *abandoned*.

Cojax felt the fear. Not fear of dying—he'd already made peace with that. But fear that *Jessica's sacrifice* had been for nothing. That all of it, *everything*, would be swallowed by this moment of bureaucratic arrogance and strategic cowardice.

*"No. No, I won't die like this."*

He scanned the image again, frantically now. Nothing. He restarted—zooming in closer this time.

*"There!"*

A collapsed Digger.

Its carcass sprawled across the field like an imploded mountain of flesh—torn, twitching, steaming. Beyond it yawned a tunnel, a black maw plunging into the earth. And farther still, he saw it—his chance. Perhaps his only chance to pursue the reckless plan gnawing at him. A cadre of Damnattii had entered the fray, their elite Tumblers grinding across the battlefield. They were positioned beyond the reach of ranged fire, untouchable for now. But if he could close the distance underground... he just might have a chance.

*"Is it possible? I'll have to fool the others."*

He had his HUD measure the distance between his position and the hole, adjusting for terrain and enemy locations. A hundred yards away. A plan began to form—half genius, half madness.

*"I guess we'll find out."*

"On my count," Cojax said, voice broadcast across the Comm-Link, "we break formation and form a marching column on me!"

No response. Just confusion.

Some heads turned. A few hesitated, faltering mid-swing.

Cojax pressed on. "There's a hole not far from here—maybe a hundred… I mean… forty yards. If we can make it, we've got a real chance of surviving. It's that or die out in the open."

"A Roach hole?" someone asked, incredulous.

"Hold the shieldwall until relief comes," another barked.

Cojax heard the hesitation—*felt* it. He was not their Alpha. They all knew it. He had merely seized a moment when fear outweighed obedience. But that moment was vanishing. Their trust, earned in blood and instinct, was now bleeding out just as fast.

"There is no relief!" Cojax shouted, voice crackling through the Comm-Link. "Our ranks are gone—we are the last! You live because you followed me. I'm not your Alpha by Score, but I *am* your Alpha by necessity. Follow me—or be torn apart!"

He didn't wait for permission.

He didn't *need* it.

He sent the impulse through the Comm-Link—and they obeyed. The shield link dissolved in an instant, catching the enemy off guard.

"Collapse formation!" Cojax ordered.

The Acadians pivoted and compressed into a tight wedge, shields raised high, blades drawn. Then they *charged*—not with order or discipline, but with survival blazing in their eyes. They slammed into the Roaches like a tidal wave of bronze and steel. Spears were abandoned for the intimacy of swords. Cojax led the front, his shield crashing forward like a warhammer. As he impacted with the enemy, he sent a pulse through his shield, producing an explosion of energy that flipped Roaches backwards. Though not fatal, this technique proved useful in clearing a path.

They crashed through a gap between two stunned SataniKahns, slipping past in the heartbeat of confusion. Behind them, Reevers poured through—dozens of spined legs tearing into lesser Roaches as they plowed straight into the Acadian column like a living avalanche.

"Keep the momentum!" Cojax roared.

He pulsed again. And again. Roaches flew like dolls thrown by giants. Shields rippled with each blast, light and blood dancing together.

The formation stayed tight, but the Reevers adapted to their tactics. They began leaping *over* the outer flank, targeting the vulnerable center. Acadians spun and slashed, dropping them as fast as they entered, but it slowed the entire column as they did.

"Keep the momentum!" Cojax ordered with greater urgency. Since he had taken command, he could sense everyone in the unit—a privilege reserved only for an Alpha. But now, he did not want it. Several Acadians at the rear of the column had fallen, their bodies severed in half. One after another, shields were failing, bodies were being left behind. Cojax could sense it, feel it happening—as if he were right alongside them.

"Let me take the lead," Finn said, his usual levity gone. "You've pulsed too much already. Your armor can't have much charge."

"Keep the momentum!" was Cojax's only reply. His fear was pushed to the side as an animal instinct overcame him. He was filled by it, made drunk by it. Their survival was in his hands. His heart beat in rhythm to his steps; his hands became extensions of his will, delivering death with each passing second.

"Cojax," Finn said over the Comm, "Skewer Hooktails, Class III inbound, ten o'clock."

This cloud of flying creatures had appeared on their radar earlier, but with so many enemies around them, they had not paid much attention to them. The human-sized flying Roaches were composed of serrated claws, angular features, and two large skewers that protruded from their jaws. They were particularly suited for scouting, not battle, because they were ineffective against a shieldwall. But since the Acadians now ran as a column, they were vulnerable to attacks from above.

"Organize a welcome party," Cojax replied coldly. "We keep moving."

Finn acted without hesitation. He swapped places with two nearby Acadians and opened a proximity command to twenty others mid-column.

"Pincers inbound!" he barked. "Retrieve Blazers!"

Swords were sheathed. Blazers were raised.

Above them, the creatures climbed high into the sky—then dove, wings tucked, bodies rigid, like living arrows of bone and death. Their blade-lined sides caught the light, rippling like a thousand saws.

"*Fire!*" Finn ordered.

A wall of light screamed upward.

The lead Pincers were hit mid-dive—spinning, crashing, dying in arcs. But not all. *Not nearly enough.* The rest plummeted like missiles.

*Impact.*

Shields cracked. Acadians were thrown. Several were skewered mid-run and lifted into the air, their bodies limp on the Pincers' jaw-spears.

"Cojax!" Finn shouted. "We held the first wave—but they're circling back! We won't survive another!"

"Just a little more," Cojax said through clenched teeth.

He pulsed his shield three times in brutal succession—*thud-thud-thud*—launching Roaches from his path like broken marionettes. He gutted one. Caved in another's skull. A third fell, screaming beneath his boots.

Then, he saw it.

The hole.

The mouth of the Digger tunnel, just ahead—twenty yards across, wide and gaping. Roots and rocks spiraled downward like the throat of some ancient beast. The edges shimmered with unnatural dampness, almost beckoning them. He didn't know what waited below. But it had to be better than dying above.

He was about to order the charge into the tunnel when something moved within it. A shadow unfurled—massive, coiled, wrong. From the depths, a hulking creature surged upward, its serrated fangs catching the pale daylight like molten glass. It reared back, chittering with a sound so low it throbbed through the earth itself.

Cojax froze, breath stolen from his lungs.

For a heartbeat, he thought it was another Digger—some massive remnant left behind.

Then he saw the mandibles.

Not tools for burrowing.

*Weapons.*

It was a SataniKahn Line Breaker—the largest he had ever

seen. Easily a Class X. And now it had come to kill them.

Cojax didn't think. He *moved.*

His left hand dropped the shield. His right tightened on the sword. With practiced fluidity, he drew his Blazer, set it to full-auto, and hurled it directly into the beast's face.

A flicker of motion. The SataniKahn snapped with one of its massive pincers, crushing the Blazer into molten debris. But it had taken the bait. Cojax was already airborne. He soared toward the beast's face, blade-forward. With all his weight and momentum, he slammed his sword into its black and red carapace. The blade sank to the hilt. He caught hold with his left hand, bracing inside the wound as the beast howled.

It thrashed violently.

Small limbs—dozens, maybe hundreds—shot out from beneath its chest like stabbing needles, each one striking his armor with the force of a Blazer round. Death pressed close.

Then, just as suddenly—it pulled back. The stabbing stopped.

The monster turned its head.

Someone else had leapt at it—another Acadian, slashing across its forehead, striking one of the creature's exposed nerve clusters. It wasn't a killing blow, but it sent a tremor through the beast's body.

Cojax didn't waste the moment.

With savage precision, he began hacking away at the area he'd already wounded. His blade cut through carapace and then flesh. He tore a chunk away as he continued to bore into the beast. Behind it was glistening tissue, pulsing faintly.

No two SataniKahns had organs in the same place. But the signs were there—temperature, vibration, internal pulse. Cojax trusted his instincts. He wedged himself deeper into the gash. The stench hit him: vinegar, bile, rotting acid. His armor filters strained to keep out the worst of it. He was inside the monster now, crawling through cords of muscle and twitching sinew.

He raised his sword—angled it upward.

*"Please be right."*

He drove the blade into the cavity where the heart *should* be. The creature screamed. Everything convulsed.

Cojax was flung backward as the entire SataniKahn twisted in agony. His sword stayed behind, still buried to the hilt. He felt weightlessness. Then, nothing at all.

He fell into the darkness below.

## FIFTY

What little caution Jessica had bled away with every word Aias spoke. Within four minutes, her sword sagged; within ten, it was back in its sheath. She lowered herself beside him. She wanted to reach out—wrap her arms around him—but whether it was from the Mahghetto's hard lessons or her own reserve, she didn't.

When she spoke of Elena's last words, Aias only nodded. He knew she had died, but it did not dull the weight of her words. Like her, he had been trained in the depths of the Mahghetto; like her, he would not dishonor the dead with tears, at least not while others were present. Only after a long silence did he speak.

"Do you think she was killed because of the plan? Because of what she was doing?"

Jessica's pulse quickened. "What plan? She died trying to get me through the Mahghetto." Her voice grew sharper, heat rising in her chest. "She died for nothing! I didn't even make it past the Crossing."

Aias didn't answer.

Jessica turned, fists clenching. "What was the point? That Golden Orb sucked all the life out of her until she had nothing left to give. Why would she continue to use it once she saw the effect it was having on her?"

"Because she believed in you." His voice never rose, but it carried the weight of command, cutting through her words.

Her tone dropped to a whisper. "Why would that matter?"

"Because you're flawed. Imperfect. A girl from outside the Wall who survived the Mahghetto. If you had defeated their system and revealed the truth they fear most—that humans can live in peace with the Roaches—it would have made others doubt everything."

"What good would that have done?"

"That's when we would have struck."

The voice came from the darkness, light and confident.

Jessica knew it before the man stepped forward. Smaller than most Acadians, but quick on his feet, a Blazer slung across his back alongside an Arc Blade, Spear, and Repulse Shield. No Static Armor. His hair was neat, his face clean—too clean for a place like this.

"Orch," she breathed.

He gave her a smile that was equal parts charm and arrogance. "That's me. And for some reason, I keep coming down here to help in this endeavor. Every trip I make into the Rift, I ask myself at least twenty times *why* I do it. Never once have I given myself an answer I liked. I'm part of the counter-movement—though lately, I'm starting to think it's more hobby than revolution."

Aias shook his head. "You pampered Second Tier. Try living here for six years."

"Some of us have to stay behind to do the dirty work on the surface," Orch said with a wink.

"Six years?" Jessica asked.

"Yes," Aias replied, the word heavy with memory.

"And now it's all wasted," came a third voice.

Another figure stepped forward, broad-shouldered and scarred, his beard woven with bits of bone. His eyes were sharp enough to make Jessica flinch. It was obvious why Aias had spoken to her first and not him.

"Calm yourself, Josiah," Aias said.

"Six years of planning—ruined," Josiah growled.

"It's not her fault."

"Elena is dead because of her—"

"That's enough!" Aias surged to his feet, the air between them tightening. "You're my ally. Don't make me treat you as an enemy."

Josiah's throat corded, but he held his tongue.

Aias faced Jessica again, his calm returning with effort.

"What does he mean?" she asked.

Aias hesitated before speaking. "We meant to start a rebellion with your words at the Crossing—if Atlas had let you speak. The truth, that humans live peacefully with the Roaches beyond these walls, would have been our spark. We would have moved through the streets disguised as Validated, demanding answers. Others would have joined us, believing the AC had made a grave error."

"Just the three of you?"

"Feels like it sometimes," Josiah muttered.

"… and thirty thousand others," Aias corrected.

Jessica blinked. "Where are they? Down here? I thought the Rifted were killed."

"Some are," Aias said. "The rest—those who aren't executed or fed to the Roaches living in the walls of the Mahghetto—are sent here. Forced labor for the surface dwellers."

"Down here?" The scale made her dizzy. "How far down are we?"

"The original Acadian tunnels," Aias said. "Quarter mile beneath the surface."

"If you have thirty thousand, why did you need me?"

"They're not soldiers," Orch cut in, voice dripping with disdain. "Cowardly Dependents in borrowed armor—"

"Careful, pretty boy," Josiah warned. "Down here, people disappear when they talk like that."

"Thirty thousand," Aias said, overriding both. "Against millions of trained Acadians. We've managed to tell a few Validated about the truth of the Rifted, but it wasn't enough. The plan needed your story. Your life with the Roaches. That was the one thing that could have pushed the city to the brink."

"Besides," Orch added, "none of them have their bio-circuitry anymore."

Jessica turned. "Ripped out?"

Josiah's voice dropped. "The scars aren't for decoration. The AC's far less gentle when taking them out. Without bio-circuitry, we can't charge the Static Armor."

"The armor was never the point," Aias said. "The perception was. Numbers in the streets. Questions the AC couldn't ignore."

Josiah laughed bitterly. "Six years of preparation—rotted."

"There's always another way," Aias countered.

"Maybe not before we're all dead," Josiah said.

"I don't like your meathead friend," Orch said, "but he's not wrong. We lost a lot getting her through the Mahghetto—maybe more than we could afford."

"Lost more people?" Jessica's breath caught.

"Don't—" Aias started.

"If people died for me, I want to know."

Silence.

"I deserve to know."

Josiah supplied the number without hesitation. "Twenty-eight."

Aias grimaced. "We have more to discuss—"

Jessica rose, eyes locked on the floor. "*Twenty-eight. Twenty-nine counting Elena.*" Her stomach turned. "I caused this. It's my fault."

Aias stepped forward, gripping her arms. "No. It's the system. It takes everything. They died for the cause you're still fighting for. This is only a setback."

"We might not be finished," Orch said, "but we're close."

***

It took an hour before Jessica and the two men reached their camp. Now and then, a dim light flickered overhead, stretching their shadows into long, shifting shapes across the tunnel walls. As they pressed on, the fixtures became more frequent, their pale glow slowly chasing away the darkness until Aias no longer needed his light stick. He clicked it off, and they walked on beneath the cold, artificial glow.

The landscape never changed—endless forests of concrete columns and yawning caverns of rock, interrupted only by the occasional carcass. Most were creatures she didn't recognize—small, slick things with fur that gleamed like oil, jaundiced yellow eyes, and claws far too long for their paws. Aias called them *Riftlings*.

The longer she walked, the more she began to see the shape of the place—caverns that might have once been markets or barracks, now reduced to crude shelters and fire pits. The wider spaces were broken only by rough-hewn columns, like supports for a forgotten city.

Orch had split off long ago, claiming he had to return to the surface for guard duty. Neither Aias nor Josiah spoke much after that, which suited Jessica just fine. Her thoughts kept circling back to that final moment with Atlas—his hand on her throat, the sickening drop, the world vanishing in darkness.

*"What could I have done differently?"*

Each step replayed the memory, making Elena's death feel smaller, cheaper, as though it had been thrown away.

The camp unfolded from the shadows: tents stitched from scraps, fabrics hanging loose, snapping in unseen drafts. At first glance, it looked like chaos—shacks and shelters scattered in crooked knots with no plan. But when faces flickered into view, she saw the truth. There was order here, brutal and deliberate. The outer ring bristled with the strongest—bodies carved lean by years of labor, muscles stringy but unyielding, eyes sharp as blades.

It was the Mahghetto all over again—her first morning, the stares. Not hatred this time. Not welcome either. Just a distant, cold mistrust.

"There she is!" a voice barked from across the camp. A tall man strode toward them, four others at his back, crude weapons in hand.

Aias raised his palms. "Kane, not now. This is the last thing we need. Put down your weapons."

Kane ignored him, pace quickening. He jabbed a filthy finger toward Jessica, a length of rusted rebar gripped in the other. "You're going to pay for what you cost us! You failed all of us! We spent years—"

Aias stepped between them, but Kane slammed into him, knocking him aside. Two of the men peeled off, wrenching the older man's arms behind him. Josiah didn't help, but he didn't stop it either—he just stepped aside and watched.

Kane raised the rebar.

Jessica moved first.

Maybe they thought the Aberration would be weak. Maybe they didn't realize she'd just spent nine months sharpening her body into a weapon. Either way, they were naïve.

She stepped inside Kane's guard, twisted, and used his momentum against him—executing a clean head-and-arm throw. Kane hit the dirt hard, the air blasting from his lungs. She pinned a knee onto his chest, and in the next instant, a blade kissed his throat, slicing a shallow red line across his skin.

It had happened so fast that only Jessica had kept pace with the movement. Her voice came out tight, low. "You're right. I failed.

And no one knows it better than me. You think beating me will fix it? Think you can pound the hope out of me?" She leaned closer. "You're too late. There's none left."

She slid the blade back and stepped off him. The other Rifters froze, hands raised, weapons clattering to the dirt when they saw the fully functional Arc Blade in her grip.

"You dimmed Rifter," Aias spat at Kane, shaking free from his captors. "Come on, Jessica. Quick."

She followed him, the camp's stares burning into her back with every step. They slipped into a large, makeshift tent. It was dim inside until Aias turned on a small light stick. A crude bedroll, a folded blanket, and a pile of mismatched, hand-stitched clothing lay in the corner.

"This is my tent," Aias said quietly. "You'll stay here."

"Am I in danger?"

"Not here. Not in this camp," Aias said. "There's a bounty on your head—and your armor—but our loyalty's been tested. Kane's from another camp. Usually an ally. I'll post guards. He won't come back without my say."

"There are more camps?"

"More gangs than camps," Aias replied. "Four of them are semi-friendly, all of them located close to ours. There are no laws here—life's cheaper than a bowl of food. We survive by sticking together."

"How many in the Rift?"

"Two hundred thousand, give or take," he said. "Depends on the food supply, the new arrivals… and who dies the night before."

"How do you survive?"

"We're still part of Acadia," Aias said. "The city just doesn't admit it. There's a Tier System here too—segregated, cruel, familiar." He listed them—Elevenths, the Governors, keeping order. Twelfths, food growing and distribution. Thirteenths, combing through surveillance for anything dangerous. Fourteenths, repairing machines the Automata couldn't. Fifteenths, pampered test subjects with short lives. Sixteenths, waste collectors. On and on the list went until the very bottom.

"Twentieth Tier," Aias said. "Hoarders. That's you."

"Can you move up?"

"No. They put you where they need you. If there's no need, and if they didn't feed you to the Roaches, you drop to the bottom."

"What do Hoarders do?"

"Mostly nothing."

"That doesn't sound so bad."

"Until you starve."

"That sounds worse."

Aias laughed. "Elena never mentioned you had a sense of humor. She said you were so focused you often forgot to smile—much like her, I might add."

Jessica tried, but it didn't reach her eyes.

"Hoarders strip the battlefield," Aias continued. "Armor, weapons, anything salvageable. You get food for what you bring in. Feast or famine."

Jessica hesitated. "Can I ask something personal?"

"You want to know why I'm here."

She nodded. "Elena said you went blind."

"That was the plan."

"So you wanted to be Rifted?"

"Yes. Six years ago, after you arrived, people started talking—questioning the system. Those voices were silenced, sent to die. Elena overheard the truth: the Rifted weren't dead. They were here, working. She went to see for herself. The resources were scarce, but the freedom was vast—especially among the Hoarders. The Rift could be organized. It just needed someone to unite it. That was me. Elena stayed above, to get you through the Mahghetto."

Jessica's eyes drifted to the roughspun clothing. It reminded her of life before Acadia, before her father's death—cold winters, lean springs, surviving but never really living.

*"I'm back where I started."*

"When Elena became First Tier," Aias went on, "she learned about the city's power grid. There was a constant draw feeding this place—the abandoned belly of Acadia. She saw what it was. She wanted to change it. Then you walked in from the Killing Fields—proof the outside could be survived. You were meant to be the spark." His voice softened. "I loved her."

The word *love* felt alien here.

"There are at most fifty Numberless awake at a time. How

could they run all this? How come more aren't aware of the Rift?"

"They don't. At most, two Validated are tasked with escorting someone to an elevator and putting them on. They have no idea where that person's going or why. After that, the system handles the Rifting on its own—strips your armor, rips out the bio-circuitry, and drops you down here. Sometimes it's from way up high, other times an elevator takes you down. It's random, really—depends on what they need. The Eleventh Tiers take over from there, making sure you understand your new role."

"So you and Elena started the rebellion?"

"Yes. We seeded rumors. Built resentment. It wasn't enough, so I came down here to grow our numbers. But it was harder than I thought. Every Faction sent their Rifted down here, and many of them have a much different experience in the Mahghetto—most are much less harsh than the BloodBorne. That and other things have made unifying the Rifters much more difficult. But, despite these challenges, the plan progressed. You were phase three."

Jessica barely heard the rest. She sat frozen, mind spinning.

"Best change out of your armor," Aias said, standing. "You'll draw less attention."

She turned to Aias. "How can you survive down here?"

"A few above manage to send us extra supplies—mostly discarded scraps from the Mahghetto's Disciples. People like Orch."

"It didn't seem like he wanted to help."

Aias chuckled as he stepped out, leaving her alone.

Jessica moved slowly, lost in thought. A long while later, she emerged from the tent; the camp was different—darker, the faces lit in fragments of diffused light. Conversations died when she passed. One boy's stare burned with resentment.

*"They blame me."*

She held his gaze, daring him to say it. He looked away.

She stepped back, bumping into someone, muttered an apology, and kept moving—faster now. Her walk became a run, then a sprint. In her mind every face followed, every pair of eyes accusing.

She dove into Aias' tent, the flap closing behind her, shutting out the world. The dark pressed close. Her breath came hard and fast, and she dropped to her hands and knees, eyes clenched shut.

*"And this is how it ends."*

## FIFTY-ONE

It was Finn who leapt onto the SataniKahn, wrenching the monster's full attention away from Cojax. Others tried to follow his lead—brave enough, but not lucky enough. Most were cut down before they could reach the beast.

The opening was all Cojax needed. His blade slid deep, and the giant shuddered. It went down like a tower losing its supports, crashing into the pit floor. The remaining Acadians rode the fall with it—two hundred feet of darkness—slamming into the ground hard enough to rattle teeth.

Cojax hacked himself free of the waxy carcass, his armor slick with its fluids. His energy shield still held. He was on his feet first, his helmet allowing him to see in the darkness.

He pulsed a command to form ranks. Silence.

*"Dead? All of them?"*

His chest tightened. "Get up! All of you on your feet!"

"Give us… a breather," came Finn's voice.

Cojax found him flat on his back, pinned beneath slabs of rock. He swept the debris away in one motion. "You hurt?"

Finn groaned, rubbing the back of his helmet. "Charge is gone. Still breathing though."

"On your feet. Move." The harshness in Cojax's voice surprised even him.

Another pulse for assembly. This time—movement. Figures peeled off of the SataniKahn's corpse. He counted them out: thirty-one… thirty-two… thirty-three. From an entire unit. Cuts. Blood. Two with broken arms. No one had a charge in their armor except Cojax; their world was blind and black.

"Form up on me."

They closed ranks, shoulder to shoulder, following with touch.

"If we stop, we die," Cojax said. "This is their home." Then he plunged into the dark, deliberately steering them away from the Wall—away from the city's safety. The others, disoriented and stripped of their bearings with their armor drained, had no choice but to follow.

Finn slid up beside him, keeping contact by brushing shoulders. "I think you're heading east. The Wall's west, in case you're curious."

No answer.

"Cojax. Why deeper into Roach territory?"

"I have a plan. We need to double back to throw them off our trail."

"That's suspiciously vague. Any chance this plan ends without us being chewed apart?"

No hesitation in Cojax's pace. The city had abandoned them. There was no fighting back through thousands of Roaches to one of the Eight Gates. The only path now was forward—to answers, from the only beings who could give them.

The tunnels bled enemies into their path—wandering Roaches met with a fury like a breaking flood. Cojax cut through them without pause, his blade a constant sweep of steel and light. Even when a dozen blocked the way at a junction, they crumpled under the relentless press.

*"I will get answers."*

The Acadians no longer questioned him. Even when the slope turned upward toward the surface, they followed. Cojax was no longer the Disciple the Mahghetto had tried to shape. Life meant nothing; death had no weight. He would spend both if it meant breaking the AC in half.

Coordinates flashed across his ArmGuard. He adjusted course each time until the blip matched his position. Then he led them into a shallow alcove. They couldn't see him, but he felt their eyes on him. He pulled off his helmet, let the damp earth scent flood in.

He had to choose his words carefully, revealing a mix of half-truths. They followed him for now, but that could change quickly.

"Above us is a Damnattii unit—likely the one commanding this invasion. I marked their position before we fell. If we take them out, we might be able to take out their sensors. They won't be able to track us as we move under the surface. I'm going to cut a path up to them. Once there, we can destroy their sensors and take a few hostages—just for good measure. We cut the head off the snake, and the battle lines will crumble up above."

No one spoke—too shocked to answer.

"They're in Tumblers. Thin, mobile vehicles that we should be able to cut through. We have surprise—they're drunk on victory, probably blind to anything small on their sensors. I'm the only one with a charge; my signature's too minor to notice. I'll cut us to the surface. The rest of you—stand ready."

"Ready? Ready for what?" asked one of the Validated.

"Let's just take them out," said another.

They had followed this young Validated out of necessity, drawn to him because he was the only one with a charge in his armor. He had saved their lives, there was no doubt, killing the Roaches they could not see to fight themselves. Now the boy was talking pure insanity.

"You want to capture a Damnattii?" asked a third. "How does that help us get out of this situation?"

Cojax's mind was racing, desperately grabbing for an answer that would make sense.

It was finally Finn's voice that filled the darkness. "We can force them to withdraw their forces in exchange for their lives. Or at the very least, they or their armor can provide intelligence on the best path back to Acadia." He said these words as if they were so obvious, none of the others seemed to question it.

Cojax did not wait to see if this answer made any sense or not. He slammed his helmet on as he began carving upward—not straight, but on a gradual slope to keep the tunnel stable. The blade cut smoothly, but clearing debris slowed his progress. Others joined in, groping blindly at rock and soil.

"Three charged—myself included," Finn said over the Comm-Link to Cojax. "Won't be long before others start coming online. Once they do, we'll glow like a beacon on the Damnattii's sensor arrays. They'll be coming for us."

"A-firm" was Cojax's only answer. He had made tremendous progress but still had twenty-five feet to go. It had taken twenty minutes; he had minutes left before every suit in their unit lit up their location like the North Star. The Damnattii would send the Roaches in a swarm.

"Finn, I need four shields."

"Alright, Cojax, time to come clean. I might have covered for you down there, but what are you really planning? Why do you really want to capture a Damnattii?"

"Finn, I have to," Cojax answered, all too aware his armor was still recording. "We have to get a Damnattii if there is any chance of survival. This is the only way."

Finn grumbled but did not protest further. Shields scraped and clattered up to his position. The tunnel was cramped, but Cojax wedged two above his shoulders and two at his feet.

"How many are back online?" Cojax asked.

"Ten," Finn answered.

Calm settled in him like a stone in water. "Finn, pull the unit back to the last major intersection. Once I crack this egg open, there's no telling how they will respond. When twenty are charged, tell me."

"You're not going to… You *are* insane."

"It's the only way. We don't have time to dig all the way up. So instead, I'm going to bring them down here."

"Your armor's got maybe a kilowatt left! You can't Pulse with four shields at once. How do you know this will even work?"

"Cut open the Tumblers. Take one of the Damnattii. Then fall back. Don't come looking for me. When they come, it'll be in a flood of creatures. You'll have seconds to get what you need and get out."

"What am I supposed to do with a Damnattii?" Finn asked.

"Talk to it—figure out its motives," Cojax said purposefully, trying to add meaning to his words. He wanted to say more, but it was dangerous, even now.

"And that's what this is all about?" came a third voice, cool and familiar.

"Who's on the line?" Cojax demanded.

"Adriana," she said, her tone dripping contempt. "You want us to ask the Damnattii what motivates them? I know you're pathetic, but are you so lonely you want to strike up a conversation with one of them?"

"How did you get on my channel? What are you doing here?

Doesn't matter—Finn, you get me one of those Damnattii."

"You're delusional, Cojax," Adriana said, unusually direct. "And you're willing to sacrifice all of our lives for that delusion."

"This is more important than any of us," Cojax snapped.

"Why?"

"I don't have time for this—"

"Cojax," Finn broke in, "we just hit twenty-eight—no, twenty-nine. Everyone's coming back online."

"Get that Damnattii!" Cojax barked, severing the Comm-Link.

He braced himself—left arm locked into one shield, right arm into another, feet pressed onto the two below. The angle was awkward, but it would hold. Closing his eyes, he funneled everything into the shields.

He'd never seen this done before. Never even heard of anyone trying it. His gut said it could work; his brain wasn't convinced. It felt like the Mahghetto all over again—transferring his charge to the Golden Orb—but now his energy was being separated into four different objects.

The shields hummed. Blackness shrank before the faint light seeping from them. He pushed harder, driving more power into the metal than he thought his armor could give. For a heartbeat, he almost laughed. He just might be the first Acadian to ever wield four shields at once. Then he pulsed all four simultaneously.

The explosion tore the world open. Dirt and stone blasted upward in an hourglass column, the tunnel vomiting debris like a volcano. Two Tumblers shot into the air, flailing Roaches rolling after them. Two more began to slide toward the fresh wound in the earth.

Cojax's armor went dead.

The shockwave ripped him from his foothold, flinging him into the swirl of collapsing dirt. The weight crushed him from every side, squeezing air from his lungs. His limbs refused to obey. The cold seeped in fast. His vision narrowed to black.

He didn't fight it. Couldn't. He let the earth take him, sinking into the silence. So tired. So utterly, uselessly tired.

***

Numbness. That was all Cojax felt when he surfaced—numbness, and the faint irritation of being woken. His thoughts drifted like smoke in fog, slipping through his grasp. Something jostled him. He was moving—being carried. No more dirt pressing on him. Then darkness claimed him again.

The second time he woke, sound reached him first. Voices—distant, frantic. The irritation returned, sharper now. They were moving again.

"Cojax," someone murmured. Too dark to see. He clung to the voice, letting it pull him through the haze.

"Cojax," Finn said again, urgency cutting through the black.

"Leave him," Adriana's voice snapped. "We can't stay ahead of them if we're dragging dead weight."

"The tunnels end in fifty yards," Finn shot back. "Nowhere else to run."

"Destroy your breastplates," said another voice—low, commanding, eerily like his own. "Destroy your breastplates."

The third time he woke, his mind was clearer. He blinked rapidly, willing sight to return, only to realize it was working—it was just that dark.

"Finn?"

A shift beside him. "You're alive."

"What happened?" Cojax slurred.

"I proved I'm Numberless material and saved your sorry hide. Again. Dug you out of the dirt like a pale-skinned worm. Just in time, too. The Roaches didn't take kindly to your stunt. They came pouring in after us like we'd stolen their eggs. Adriana took point, kept us alive by blasting shields into the tunnels to jam their sensors, but that only bought us minutes at a time."

"Why didn't you lead?"

"I was busy carrying you."

Memory slammed back, sharp and unwelcome. "Did we get a Damnattii? Tell me we did."

"We don't have a Damnattii," Finn said slowly. "We have three."

"Where?"

Finn stood, sliding a hand along the wall. "Follow me. Try not to trip over the bodies."

"Bodies?"

"Yes. Six hours of running has everyone wrecked."

"How many left?"

"Twenty-five. Could've been worse—Adriana pulled some high-Tier tricks. Not quite my brand of bravery, but close."

"Why no night vision?"

"Because of you. You ordered us to destroy our armor. We chopped up our breastplates. Roaches can't track us now, but we can't see a thing. We're so far under the earth, I've forgotten what the sun looks like."

"Don't be dramatic."

Finn snorted. "Me, dramatic? You're the one with the rousing speech—'Let's capture a Damnattii and bury ourselves alive at the same time.' I think I might've cried, if I hadn't been running for my life minutes later."

"Have you spoken to the Damnattii?"

"No. Adriana said we should wait for you."

"Is that you, Cojax?" a voice called from the dark.

His chest tightened. He waited, making sure his voice was steady before answering. "Adriana. So it is you." The blackness made it feel unnervingly close, intimate, despite the company around them.

"The Numberless-in-training lives," she said.

"Where are the Damnattii?"

"A few steps forward and you'll be standing on one," she said. "They're asleep."

"They sleep?"

"They're not machines, Cojax. Just… not people."

"Wake them."

"First," Adriana said, "answer my question."

"There's no time."

She laughed softly. "We have nothing but time. My ArmGuard read the battle was still raging before you had us destroy our breastplates. Now we wait."

"What's your question?"

"No taste for foreplay? Straight to business."

Silence.

"You're no fun anymore," she whispered. "I was hoping for a little… entertainment in the dark before interrogation."

"Your question," Cojax said flatly.

"Why do they speak our language?"

"Jessica knew. There's more going on than either of us understands. And Jessica was the key—while you were trying to kill her, I was trying to keep her alive."

Her tone sharpened, almost dangerous. "If you'd told me like that maybe I would have—"

"—Done exactly the same thing, I'm sure."

"You didn't even give me a chance."

He gave a short, humorless laugh. "If I'd told you, you'd have run straight to Atlas. You forget—when I recovered, you'd already turned everyone against Jessica and me."

"Can you blame me?"

Cojax paused. Given what she'd known, maybe not. But he blamed her anyway. "You manipulated the Mahghetto to decide who lived and who didn't. It's supposed to be about merit—not your ability to pull strings."

"So, taking control of this Phalanx through necessity and basic survival—that's better?" Adriana's voice was edged with acid. "Let me remind you, in doing what you did today, you broke the AC. While I never did. We each have our talents: you can bury yourself under a mountain of dirt; I can survive by bending people's perception."

"Enough rot," Cojax said, venom in his tone. "Wake the Damnattii."

"I'm awake."

The voice was deep, guttural. Familiar words, but shaped by an alien accent—like stone grinding on stone.

Cojax touched his helmet, channeling energy into it as he had with the shields. He'd never tried this before, but night vision flared to life, painting the cave in green clarity. They were in a natural crevice, smooth walls wet with condensation. The sleeping Acadians were in a wider space beyond; here, the three Damnattii were bound at wrists and ankles. Two slumped together, asleep. The third sat upright, eyes fixed on him. Four arms, horned ridges across its face, and black, depthless eyes.

"Leave us," Cojax told Adriana.

Her hands curled into fists. "You don't command me. We're in this together, stuck the same as you. We followed you for freedom—not to play captor. But now that we have them, I will hear what they say."

Her shift in tone caught him off guard. Gone was the sultry edge—now she was all steel and ice. In the dark, he was glad she couldn't see his flicker of surprise. Then it clicked—she was playing her role. Two approaches for the same target. If his failed, she'd strike from another angle. He filed the thought away and fixed on the Damnattii.

"I'm Cojax from the BloodBorne Faction. I have questions."

"A noble banner," the creature said. "Many of mine have fallen before it."

Cojax ignored the bait. "Why do you continue to attack us?" His tone was hard, clipped.

"We fight to maintain our honor, our ranking. We fight to stay alive."

Heat tightened his chest. "You attack us to stay alive? How does that make any glitching sense? We kill Roaches by the tens of thousands." His voice rose into a shout, anger giving him the strength to demand the answer he feared.

"We fight for honor."

"You know *something*. What are you hiding?" His blade lit the cave. "Why have you never offered peace? Or even sent a messenger to discuss terms?"

"Like you, we must obey the Tiers. Merit before all."

Cojax pulled back as if he had been slapped. "How do you know that phrase?"

"They are our words, too," the creature growled.

"How?" Cojax stepped in close. "Tell me, or I'll flay you."

"Your blade would be honored," the Damnattii snarled, "if it ever tasted my blood. Why think yourself greater than us, pink-flesh Dependent? You don't know the extent of my command."

Cojax's grip tightened, but before he could move, Finn's hand found his throat instead of his shoulder. "Calm down," he rasped.

Adriana slid forward, resting a hand lightly on the Damnattii's shoulder. "My friend forgets himself. I'm Adriana, daughter of

Lunitia, First Tier in the Battle of Black Rain. And you are?"

"Release me. I am no Reever to bind."

"Don't," Cojax warned. "He can see in the dark."

"So can you," Adriana said, suspicion dripping from the words. "Your helmet works?"

"I can…" Cojax started.

"What else are you keeping from us?" she pressed, her tone mirroring the creature's cadence, her accent shifting until she sounded almost like him.

"I can charge it," he admitted.

"Fetch me a helmet, charged. I want to see this great warrior for myself."

Three steps away, Cojax nearly cursed himself. She'd taken control without him noticing. He considered dragging her out but left her to it—she was making progress where he hadn't. He found a helmet—oversized, rank with sweat—and another for Finn, plus a spare blade. He charged both and handed the sweaty one to Adriana.

With sight restored, her manipulation bloomed. She cut the Damnattii's wrist bonds, letting him adjust his weight. Then she wove her web—family, honor, hardship, truth tangled with lies. The words mattered less than the way she watched him—tracking every shift in posture, every flicker in his alien eyes.

"My name is Adriana; I am one who is honor-bound."

Cojax almost laughed at the word. He stepped forward to speak—

"I am Qualix," the Damnattii said. "Born of the Son's honor. Undiluted. I speak with ten mouths though I've been given one."

Adriana inclined her head, part bow, part nod. The pace slowed, words spaced like pieces on a game board. Qualix's body eased, his guard lowering.

Adriana slid seamlessly into the questions Cojax had already pushed, her tone softer, almost conversational. The change was enough—Qualix answered without hesitation, the hostility gone from his voice.

His knowledge of Acadia was… unsettling. He spoke of the Tiers, the Factions, the CityScreens, the Mahghetto. Each time Adriana pressed—*how* he knew—his answer was the same: through study.

"How do you get information about Acadia?" she asked.

"From the Acadian System," Qualix said, as if the answer were obvious. "I'm surprised you don't know that."

Adriana sat back, weighing that, then leaned in again. "Who commands you?"

"I am led by GeneriX, Speaker of Fifteen—good warrior, good Damnattii."

"Does he lead in battle?"

"Yes. But he only relays instructions."

"Then who makes the strategy?"

"It changes from battle to battle."

Adriana's voice lowered to a near-whisper. "What about the last large battle at the Northern Gate?"

"The one a month ago?"

Finn and Cojax stiffened.

Adriana caught it but waved them off. "Who planned and organized the battle strategy? Who was the commanding Damnattii?"

"Not Damnattii," Qualix said. "It was a human, of course."

Silence thickened the air.

Both Adriana and Finn turned toward Cojax. His arms were crossed, chest rising and falling in slow, heavy breaths.

"I led a group of Scramblers," Qualix went on. "I remember that battle well. We were commanded by a Numberless named Titan. But he is one of many."

Cojax's head snapped up. "Titan… commanded you?"

"Yes. It was his turn to plan the strategy."

"The same Titan who lives in Acadia?"

"Of course."

Cojax's mind snagged on the name—the words fit together but refused to make sense. "Do you mean Titan, son of Nun? Titan, the Slayer of the Nartic?"

"Yes. Titan, son of Nun. Do you know him?"

Cojax swallowed hard. "He's my father."

"Then be proud," Qualix said simply. "He's a great leader."

Adriana's gaze flicked between Cojax and Finn before returning to the Damnattii. "What do you mean 'his turn' to plan the strategy?"

"The Numberless have overseen every battle since the siege

of Acadia first began. Sometimes Titan leads, sometimes others. But it is always a Numberless who commands."

"Why are you sieging our city in the first place?" Adriana asked.

"This, I do not know," Qualix said. "I have not been gifted with that knowledge."

"How did the Numberless take control of the Damnattii?" Cojax pressed.

"This information has also not been gifted to me."

Finn blew out a breath. "This changes everything. They're not just fighting the war—they're running both sides. Why would they do that?"

"Maybe he's lying," Cojax said.

Adriana's reply was sharp. "You know he's not. He shouldn't know *any* of this."

"Maybe they hacked our systems," Cojax suggested.

Adriana scoffed. "And that's all they'd use it for? Learning about the Numberless? If they could breach the Acadian System, they'd shut down our shields, open the gates, flood the city with propaganda. Do you really think the only thing they'd do is research our society?"

"She's right," Finn said quietly.

Cojax's hands trembled as he stared at Qualix, emotion roiling behind his eyes. For a heartbeat, it looked like he might lunge and crush the creature's throat. But the rage bled away.

He turned toward the exit. "Finn. Don't let him escape."

"Why am I always on guard duty?" Finn muttered.

Cojax didn't answer. He was already gone.

## FIFTY-TWO

Jessica had grown used to the constant grind of each day—the Mahghetto's brutal rhythm, the Magisters' relentless demands, even the fleeting chaos of battle. Down here, the stillness was worse than any of it. Days dragged by, endless stretches of nothing broken only by two meager meals.

She hated mealtimes. If it were up to her, she would have skipped them entirely, but Aias insisted she eat *something*. The rest of the time, she stayed in his tent, trapped with only her memories for company. Occasionally, Aias would speak to her, but never for long, and never with more than a handful of words.

Once in a while, the Hoarders had work—if you could call it that. They would spill into an abandoned battlefield, scavenging weapons from the fallen Validated. It was dangerous; Roaches often lay hidden among the corpses and wreckage, waiting for scavengers to draw close. In those moments, the only option was to run. Hoarders had no Static Armor, no weapons that could pierce a carapace. Jessica still had her Arc Blade—her implants kept it alive—but Aias had made her promise to keep it hidden, to use it only when death was certain.

Turned-in weapons earned small coins that could be exchanged for rations at the distribution center, which was run by Twelfth Tiers. Aias' group received extra food from allies in the city above, but it wasn't much. Jessica suspected that this trickle of supplies was the only reason people stayed loyal to him at all. Even then, it barely kept them alive.

And lately, even that stream was thinning. Aias blamed *technical difficulties*, but Jessica didn't buy it. She saw the truth—support from above was bleeding away. In a few months, there would be nothing left. They'd be just another starving cluster of Hoarders, nameless in the dark.

Days slipped into weeks. Nothing changed, except her body

grew thinner. The will to get off her bedroll drained from her. She felt cornered again—like she had been on the shower floor years ago.

*"She almost killed me."*

But Elena had been teaching her something.

The memory sharpened, and Elena's voice came with it: *"You didn't give in—even when death was near. You chose to live."*

Jessica rolled the words over in her mind. She hadn't given up in the Mahghetto—so why now? She hadn't broken when Elena died. She had stood against a Numberless, an impossible feat, and yet she still stood. Why was she so eager to give up now? Her thoughts drifted to Cojax. She missed him—missed his dramatic flair, his handsome features, his passion. The way he rallied their forces in the Mahghetto and performed a desperate charge.

Then an idea struck her—jolting her to her feet. Ideas started spinning in her mind, fitting together like pieces she should have seen all along. She paced the tent, running variables, refining the plan.

*"Everything's already in place. We just need to push it."*

She went looking for Aias. Her words came out in a rush—jumbled enough that he had to stop her more than once to get her back on track. Jessica was never good with people, and the weight of that felt heavier the longer she spoke. At first, Aias' face was unreadable—then thoughtful—then slowly, with each point she made, his head began to nod.

When she finished, he was smiling. "You just might be on to something. Attacking the one group of people no one would expect."

Jessica's reply came without hesitation. "Then let's do it."

Aias nodded. "I'll gather the leaders. You can explain it to them in detail."

"Me?" Jessica blurted. "I could barely tell you without tripping over my words. Why don't you explain it?"

"It will mean more coming from you." His voice was calm but firm. "Elena spoke highly of you—before and during the Mahghetto. I don't have enemies, but not all the Council Chiefs are my friends. If you want this to succeed, it has to come from you. Just... practice before I bring them together. I will make sure that Orch and Ion are there too."

"Who is Ion?" Jessica asked.

"He's still a Validated, like Orch—but thankfully far less

talkative. He's an exceptionally gifted TechOps, and if we have any hope of success, his involvement will be essential."

Jessica's mouth opened, but no words came. She only nodded.

***

The Council met in a black-walled tent, large enough to hold a small crowd. It was lit up by four glow rods—an incredible use of resources and one that displayed the comparative wealth of the leadership. It took a full day to assemble; none of them seemed eager to gather sooner. Kane and Josiah were there, along with Aias and four others Jessica didn't know.

Orch leaned by the entrance—no official seat, but clearly respected.

Jessica had spent the day running speeches through her head—drafting, discarding, rewriting—before settling on one. Aias had coached her, but even with his encouragement, she'd seen his face falter as she rehearsed. She wasn't Cojax, who could ignite a room with raw conviction. She wasn't Finn, with his humor and charm, or Elena, whose brilliance commanded respect. She wasn't Adriana, weaving words into traps, or Brutus, whose size alone silenced crowds. She had none of their weapons—only the hope that she could channel pieces of all of them.

Introductions came first. Formality lasted only minutes before it dissolved into jokes and bursts of laughter. Jessica sat cross-legged on a pillow at the far end, Orch offering her a single nod in greeting.

To the rest—except Aias—she was invisible.

*"They're not taking this seriously,"* she thought. *"They're not taking me seriously."* It felt like the Mahghetto all over again—dismissed because she was the Aberration, overlooked because of her size and Score. The insecurities faded beneath something sharper, hotter. They laughed and traded stories while Elena's body lay cold, her sacrifice reduced to silence.

Jessica stood. Her hands balled into fists. "I am Jessica of Claymont—"

"We haven't officially started yet," Kane cut in.

Jessica studied the man, recalling their earlier run-in. His eyes slid away before hers.

"We started the moment we were all forced into the Mahghetto," she shot back, her voice hard enough to freeze the air. Rage coursed through her—rage and the memory of Elena's frail hand at the end. *"She will not disappear in vain."*

The tent quieted.

"I am Jessica of Claymont, a city not far from the Wall of Acadia. I am the daughter of James Halworth, the Great Warrior who slew the White Wolf... granddaughter of Emily Halworth, who restored the lost art of agriculture... and great-granddaughter of Eric the Grand, who forged a peace treaty with the Roaches that still holds today."

She hadn't planned to give her Crossing speech, but the words seemed to fit. She let the silence linger, then: "And I know how we can end this war."

The large man she'd heard called Chaucer shifted, skepticism etched into his wide, chubby face. "And how do we do that?" His tone suggested mockery as much as doubt—and the heavy folds of his body suggested he claimed more than his share of rations.

"The truth is simple," Jessica said. "The Numberless control the city."

Kane snorted. "We already know that, girl."

"So, let's remove them from their seat of power."

"How?" Chaucer said, annoyance creeping in. "The entire city is literally at their beck and call."

"Let Jessica speak," Aias said, his voice deep enough to still the room.

Jessica met each set of eyes. "We train the Rifters to fight, raise an army, and when the Numberless are holding an Infinite council, we strike, cutting them all down. There will be confusion, disorder, chaos. And in that confusion, we stand firm, revealing the truth to the entire city. Without the Numberless to counter our argument, everyone will have to believe us."

Josiah leaned forward. "She is mad. Even if we manage to take on the Numberless, there is no telling how many of the First Tiers they will order to attack us."

"Once the Numberless are gone, there will be no need for the

First Tiers to fight us. No one will be left to control and manipulate the narrative. We will have time to share with everyone that there is a better way—that peace with the Roaches is possible, as it was in my village."

Silence.

Kane's voice was careful. "But if even one of them survives, they will order every single last Acadian to wipe us out."

"Then we block their Comm-Link," Jessica said swiftly. "Even if they have a few dozen First Tiers in the room, we should be able to muster thirty thousand Rifters to fight for us—the combined forces of all of your people."

"Impossible," Chaucer declared. "They could easily activate more Numberless from the Crono-Stasis. Only thirty or so are awake now, but if they activate the others—eight thousand of them—we're finished. We don't have time for this nonsense."

"Wait," Orch cut in, his mouth twisting into a grin. "Let the girl finish. For the first time in a long while, I'm halfway interested in what's being said."

Jessica didn't hesitate. "We block their Comm-Links and disable any connection to the Crono-Stasis chambers. They will be isolated, trapped. We hit hard and take out every last one of them."

"Ion, is that even possible?" Kane asked flatly.

Ion's eyes narrowed in thought. "Hmmm... blocking Comm-Links is easy enough for a Validated, at least for half an hour. The Comm-Link system operates on the same data stream as the Camera system, which is something I've disabled a number of times without detection or issue. I've never tried to do it with a Numberless though—might have a different encryption level. But severing the data link to the Crono-Stasis should not be too difficult, as long as I can isolate the data bridge to that section of the Trinity."

Chaucer's voice dripped contempt. "And you're suggesting we send our best on a suicide mission?"

"There are only thirty or so Numberless out of Crono-Stasis," Jessica said, her gaze unwavering. "No one will see it coming. We hit them fast and hard when they are all gathered together. In the confusion, we will have time to spread the truth. We can announce it from all the Major Forums."

"Killing the Numberless is an intriguing idea," Kane said.

"Even if the idea comes from the Aberration's demented brain. But there is too much unknown. When do the Numberless meet? From what I saw when I was Validated, it was random at best. We'd need to recruit a First Tier who regularly sits in on their council. Even then, we'd have to constantly be ready."

"And as soon as thirty thousand Rifters appear, all with swords drawn, don't you think the Numberless will notice?" Chaucer added.

"We don't know what security we'll face," Josiah warned.

"This is mad," Chaucer declared.

"It might be mad enough to work," Aias countered.

Chaucer shook his head. "Our people haven't trained for this. They barely have the strength for the work we already demand."

"They're still Acadians," Kane shot back. "Rusty, but with the right push, they can fight again. We can run an accelerated training program."

Orch stepped closer, drawn to the conversation, a hand massaging his handsome chin. "That's not the real problem. The problem is every Rifter here has had their bio-circuitry torn out. They won't be able to charge their Static Armor—useless in a fight."

"That's why we've never attempted anything like this," Chaucer insisted. "Our warriors would fall like leaves in a violent wind."

Jessica leaned forward. "That's exactly what gave me the idea. In the Mahghetto, my body couldn't charge my armor. I had to use a Golden Orb every day. We can charge the Static Armor."

A slow smile spread across Orch's face. "We have the warriors, we have the armor—we just need them charged. Brilliant."

"Not brilliant," Chaucer snapped. "Only ElectraTechs have access to that kind of equipment, and they're vetted beyond question. Without one, we're dead in the water."

"Cojax's brother was an ElectraTech," Ion said.

Kane's eyes narrowed. "Will he help us?"

"He... knows about the rebellion, and he hasn't turned me in," Ion replied. "So, I guess that's something."

"We ask Cojax first," Orch suggested. "See if his brother can be trusted. I'll talk to him."

"No, let me," Jessica replied. "I'll speak to him."

"You?" Chaucer exploded. "You are the reason the entire plan failed in the first place. I am more inclined to turn you in to the Numberless—maybe we can get some reward from this failed experiment. You're very lucky I haven't done that already."

Jessica tensed at these words but did not move.

"We've already talked about this," Aias said. "If the Numberless get even a whiff that she's alive, they will come down here and slaughter everyone who ever knew or even saw her, of that I have no doubt. You try and contact them, Chaucer, your head will be the first to roll. You're a Rifter, remember? They see you as expendable."

"I was the one that recruited Cojax to the rebellion," Jessica answered. "He trusts me above all else. I should be the one to talk to him, regardless of the risk."

"You don't even know how to get out of the Rift," Orch added.

"I guess you'll have to show me," Jessica shot back.

Orch laughed. "I'm starting to like this girl."

"Cojax is the son of a Numberless!" Chaucer barked. "Am I the only one who sees the danger in sending her to him?"

"He's the only reason I made it as far through the Mahghetto as I did."

"No, too risky," Chaucer said. "We'd all end up dead."

More voices rose, the majority opposing the idea.

Jessica stood up, silencing the crowd, her blade in hand. "Elena started this movement—she gave it everything she had… even her life. Twenty-eight others stood with her, and they paid the same price. If we do nothing now, then they died for nothing.

"But right here, right now, we have a chance to strike—to send a message. And if that means we all end up dead, then so be it—because I, for one, will not die starving in the dark. Let none of us die tearing each other apart for the scraps that fall from the city above. If we die, we die on our feet, not on our knees. And the city will hear us. They will know we chose freedom. Our voices—our defiance—will echo long after they think they've silenced us."

Quiet fell over the group. Those few words seemed to tilt the very air in the tent, forcing a hard truth into focus. They weren't living—not really. They were rotting away, piece by piece, alongside the fading embers of their rebellion.

"I suggest we call a vote," Aias said.

"We need more discussion," Josiah argued.

"All this Council does is discuss," Orch said, folding his arms. "Meanwhile, our agents are picked off every week. It's only a matter of time before they find this little nest under the city. We need to act before we are all discovered."

"Must I remind you," Chaucer sneered, "you're not a voting member?"

Orch's hand settled on his blade. "Must I remind you, Rifter, that I'm Second Tier Validated? You fell from your first estate. I've kept mine. I risk everything by standing here with you."

Chaucer's eyes hardened to black pinpoints. After a long moment, he looked away, sinking into the shadows.

"Let's vote," Aias said. "I'm in favor."

"I vote against," Chaucer replied.

"I also vote against," said Criminion, an older man who had been silent until now. "But I'll admit the idea has merit. We have to do something. I suggest we begin training, just in case the opportunity presents itself."

"I vote against," said a thinner man at the far end.

"I vote against as well," Kane said.

"Then the motion fails," Chaucer said with glum satisfaction.

"But I also would like to put forth a new vote," Kane said quickly. "I vote that we start training our Rifters for combat. At the very least, it will give us protection from the other gangs of Hoarders down in the Rift. But if, by some miracle, this plan does have merit, at least we won't miss our opportunity to move forward."

"They don't have enough calories for something like that," Chaucer answered quickly. "Their energy is a resource we will quickly diminish."

"I vote in favor," Aias said quickly, capitalizing on Kane's unexpected support.

The votes came in one by one and only Chaucer opposed it.

"The motion carries," Aias said. "We can train on the parade grounds in the center of our camps. For now, at least we finally have the framework of a plan."

## FIFTY-THREE

*"My father commands the Roaches? Is that even possible?"*

It seemed so far from reality that Cojax found himself endlessly repeating what the Damnattii had said. The more he said it, the more unreal and unbelievable it seemed. He had left the small cave and was sitting on a large rock. Initially, Cojax thought it was a natural cavity that Adriana had led them into, but as he stepped out, he realized that one side of the entrance had been perfectly sliced by an Arc Blade. He looked up at the roof of the tunnel, his mind far from his present surroundings.

"Can I sit with you?" Adriana's voice came from behind.

"No."

She sat anyway, her posture accenting her perfect form. "I would have never guessed that, but now that I know it, it doesn't surprise me."

Cojax's confusion suddenly turned to anger. "What are you even doing here?"

She let out a long sigh. "Same thing you were doing—carefully volunteering for battles that appeared to be easy victories."

"How could anyone possibly predict which battles are going to be easier?"

"Roaches usually engage in a pattern. They slowly deescalate the conflict throughout the week and then suddenly throw everything they've got."

"Well, you were wrong."

"It's happened twice before," Adriana said. "The first time I was wrong was about you."

"Must be frustrating when someone doesn't fall for your charm."

"I was wrong about why you were helping Jessica—I thought you were just looking to tick off your father. But there's much more to the situation, isn't there?"

Cojax did not answer.

"So, how long will you pursue this obsession?"

He shook his head. "I will find out what happened to her—whether she is dead or alive, even if I have to tear Acadia apart with my bare hands." Then he turned to her, as if noticing her presence for the first time. "And you? Now that we know the truth about the Numberless, what do you plan on doing?"

"What makes you think I'm going to do anything?"

"Because your mind is always considering all the possible variables. You can't pretend that something this important hasn't changed your plans."

"Perhaps."

"Where did you come from?"

She laughed—for the first time, it actually seemed genuine. "What does that mean?"

"You did something I thought was impossible," Cojax said. "You aren't that great with the Arc Blade. You weren't the best leader. You graduated near the middle of your class, despite your lack of skill."

"You really know how to win a girl over, don't you? I can see why Jessica fell for you like a Weighted Tenth Tier. But you're right—I can fight, but I'm no warrior, no battlefield leader. I knew that going into the Mahghetto, and once I was there, it didn't take long to realize I was going to die unless I manipulated the game. So yes, I clawed my way to the top, not out of malice, but because survival demanded it. Unfortunately for Jessica, she was the quickest way to make that happen. What was your plan anyway? Now that we've captured a few Damnattii?"

"Jessica once asked me why we'd never even tried talking to the Damnattii—so I decided to."

"That's the most dimmed thing I've ever heard," Adriana said.

Cojax let out a frustrated sigh. "Well, next time I plan on doing something rash, I'll run it past you first. Is that alright—"

"—You didn't let me finish," Adriana said. "It was dimmed but inspiring. You're keeping your hope alive that there is a solution besides endless war."

"And the war might have ended had Jessica not been Rifted. She's important."

"I know she is."

Cojax shook his head. "I feel like you're trying to manipulate me somehow."

"Me?"

"You had everyone twisted around your finger with perfect calculation in the Mahghetto. You were even manipulating the Magisters' actions. The AC is all about merit—about linking one's ability directly to their rights. But somehow you sidestepped that whole system. How did you learn to do that?"

"Are we really talking about this right now?"

Cojax only stared at her in response.

"You're cute, but that doesn't mean I'm going to tell you my secrets," she continued.

"Let me be direct with you," Cojax said. "How you controlled your situation was disgusting. I thought it dishonorable. I hated you for it. But at the same time… it was amazing. I've never seen anything like it."

"First rule of manipulation, Cojax: never reveal your true self. People will take that and destroy you with it. If people know what you truly value, you have given them a pressure point they can use to cripple you. But, you're pretty dimmed, so I'm sure it doesn't matter much what I tell you. Manipulation is about perception. And perception determines reality. When people believe you're in control, they'll place themselves beneath you. They don't have to like you, they don't even have to respect you, but if they believe you can hurt them, they'll aid you."

"So, is this something you've made a study of?"

"I was the youngest of sixteen siblings. I was the least among them. My father, no doubt in an attempt to toughen us, would beat the weakest—sometimes nearly to death. I was never the strongest, or the fastest, or the best at anything. There was far too much talent and competition in my house. So I could either do what all my other siblings tried—that is, excel at everything possible—or I could change their perception of me…"

Something about her words pulled Cojax's mind from the conversation. She continued to speak, but the words failed to keep his attention.

*"That's the problem with the city. Everyone's perceptions don't line up*

*with reality."*

His mind started working through different variables. And then it hit him. He knew exactly what he needed to do. He stood up, his legs moving faster than his brain could keep up. He stumbled back into the rock cavity, leaving Adriana behind in mid-sentence. He mumbled an apology to her, but he doubted that she cared.

He expected Qualix to have fallen asleep like his companions; on the contrary, the creature was deep in conversation with Finn. Their tones were not bitter, but they were not friendly either.

"Qualix," Cojax said. "I apologize for doubting you. It was… a lot to take in."

"What's wrong?" Finn asked.

Cojax turned to his friend. "Nothing is wrong. In fact, for the first time, I think we have a chance to set things right. Finn, can you grab your ArmGuard?" He turned back to the Damnattii. "Do you know how to use an ArmGuard?"

"Not an Acadian ArmGuard."

"Well, Finn is going to show you how."

"Why?"

Cojax stepped closer. "How would you like to end this war?"

## FIFTY-FOUR

Either from habit or sheer lack of nourishment, the Rifters moved with a sluggishness that grated on Jessica's nerves. They shuffled toward the makeshift parade grounds like sleepwalkers—bodies awake, but more dead than alive. She watched them with a critical eye, her jaw tightening.

*"It doesn't matter how loyal they are. They don't have the strength to fight."*

When the sword drills began, whatever discipline they had dissolved completely. Only a few could keep moving for more than a handful of minutes. Jessica wasn't assigned to train them—that duty belonged to a few hardened veterans—but the sight still felt like her responsibility. This was her plan, after all, at least part of it. If they failed, it would be on her.

She searched her memory for an answer, and one name surfaced—a name she'd heard soon after arriving from one of the Hoarders. At the time, it had disgusted her, but now it returned with unexpected force. It belonged to a boy who worked in food distribution. She broke off and headed in that direction, following the dim array of lights above.

The center was a squat concrete building nearly a mile away, functional and joyless, with a single broad window where Hoarders surrendered armor in exchange for coins or food. Behind that window, a familiar face appeared—one that froze her in place.

*"It was him."*

The crisscross scars of a Rifter were there, but another cut stole the focus—a jagged slash running up his cheek and through his right eye. The Rift had done nothing to soften him. His presence was still heavy, oppressive.

*"Brutus."*

The big boy didn't bother to hide his delight at seeing her down here. His smile was wide, mocking. "All that work, and you and me end up in the same place."

Jessica almost turned away—almost. It would have been safer. But she had already come all this way; it would be a waste to turn back now.

"Did they remove your brain when they Rifted you, girl, or just your tongue?" Brutus laughed.

"I outlasted you in the Mahghetto by a fair margin. I'd be slower to criticize your betters."

It wasn't her sharpest insult, but it landed. Brutus' expression darkened. He began spitting every foul name he could summon. Jessica stayed calm, turned her back, and walked away.

That was enough to send him over the edge.

She drifted from the crowd, making herself look alone—vulnerable. She ducked behind the corner of a building, ensuring that there were no witnesses. The bait worked. Brutus appeared from a side door, a rusted metal pipe clutched in his hand.

"Aberration!" His voice was low, dangerous. "At least I'll have the satisfaction of your death."

Jessica kept walking.

"You dimmed Rifter, I'm going to split your skull!"

He lunged. Jessica spun, Arc Blade flashing. The pipe split in two, the top half clattering across the ground. She stepped in, kicked his leg, then drove a fist into his throat. Each time, she used her bio-circuitry to sync with the movement and increase her power. He dropped to a knee, still clutching the stump of pipe.

"Brutus," she said evenly, "you never learned from your training. This is how Cojax drew you out in the Mahghetto—and here I am, doing the same."

Brutus spat at the sound of Cojax's name.

"You were the one who abandoned him," Jessica said. "Not the other way around."

"He abandoned me the moment he stood up for you."

"None of that matters. Look around. We're in the Rift now—dregs of the dregs. And yet you hate me more than the people who put you here. We're equals, Brutus. Outcasts."

He let out a deep sigh. "Either kill me or let me go. Spending my time with the Aberration isn't how I want to waste my day."

"You don't have to like me or trust me. But you can still

benefit from me." Her blade stayed steady near his throat. "I drew you out here for a reason—one that could help us both."

"What reason?"

"You work in the Twelfth Tier. Food distribution."

He barked a laugh. "You want *me* to help you? I was about to bash your skull in. Still would, if not for that blade."

"And that's why you'll never get more than what's right in front of you. What would killing me accomplish? After all the Mahghetto put you through, am I really the one you want to finish? They did this to you—not me."

Brutus' eyes narrowed. "What do you want?"

"I need food."

Brutus shook his head. "And possibly get in trouble for helping you? Get Rifted."

"I already am," Jessica said, stepping closer. Her Arc Blade hummed with a short pulse of light. "So… is that really the answer you want to give me right now?"

"What do I get out of it?" Brutus asked, his tone shifting from mockery to calculation.

"Now you're starting to think long-term," Jessica said. "I'm planning on leaving the city, and I need a lot of food to do it."

"That's all I'd need to turn you in," Brutus said flatly. "If I told the Eleventh Tiers, they'd string you up and never cut you down."

"Good thing you're not going to tell them."

"And why wouldn't I?"

"Because whatever they offer you—a hot shower, an extra bowl of soup—pales in comparison to what I'm offering."

His good eye narrowed. "Which is?"

"Freedom."

That word made him pause. "What are you talking about?"

"I'm not staying in this hellhole," Jessica said. "And if you help me, you come with me. Dangerous, yes. Worth it, absolutely."

"Is Cojax coming?"

"That doesn't matter."

Brutus' face hardened. "Is… Cojax… coming?"

"No. But even if he was, you'd find he's your friend, not your enemy—same with your brother. Neither of them wanted you Rifted.

You cut yourself off from them, not the other way around."

Brutus stared past her, jaw working. "Maybe you're right. Maybe I do need to widen my gaze. What do you want?"

"Food. Lots of it."

"I've only been here a few months. I'm as low as they come. I can sneak a can or two, but nothing more."

"Then tell me where they store it."

"I can show you."

"Is it shielded?"

"No. Why would it be? No one has sensory implants—Arc Blades are useless." His gaze dropped to the weapon in her hand. His expression darkened. "Why do you still have yours?"

Jessica ignored the question. "What else protects it?"

"Several feet of concrete. And only the Twelfth Tier knows how to get down there."

Jessica's lips curved into a small smile. "A few feet of concrete won't stop my blade."

"If they catch me helping you, I'm finished," Brutus said. "Sweeten the deal."

"Like what?"

"Whatever you're planning, I want in. And don't feed me that you're 'just running away' nonsense. I want the real plan."

"What? Freedom's not enough for you?"

"Do we have a deal?"

"How can I trust you?"

"You don't have a choice."

Jessica weighed him for a long moment. "Alright. But once you show me where the food is, you can't go back to the Twelfth Tier. You'll be a Hoarder like me."

"Right now, I get three meals a day and my own room. That's rare in the Rift."

"Otherwise, no deal. If I tell you more, you can't have a way back to your cushy life. If you want in, you live with us."

A wicked grin spread across his face. "Fine. Meet me here in six hours, after distribution closes. Not a second later."

***

394

Much to Jessica's surprise, Brutus showed early—a small but telling sign of his commitment. He wore the same disheveled rags as before, but this time a coil of rope hung across his chest.

"I was half-sure you'd be too scared to show, little Rifter," he called.

Jessica's nod was curt. "We're both Rifters, remember."

"Come on—if you can keep up."

He plunged into the dark, a thin red beam from a penlight he carried cutting through the gloom. Jessica followed, resisting the urge to use the old flashlight she had borrowed from Aias. The ground was uneven, her footing clumsy, but she noted with quiet satisfaction that Brutus' breath turned ragged long before hers did.

They stopped at a massive pillar. Jessica's instincts screamed ambush—she was alone, far from camp, and Brutus knew this terrain. Her hand found the hilt of her Arc Blade.

*"If he so much as twitches wrong..."*

But Brutus was focused on the wall. What she'd thought was him crouching was, in fact, him prying loose a rock-shaped cover.

"Need a hand?" she asked.

"Stay back," he hissed.

Moments later, the false rock came free, revealing a human-made shaft. Brutus slipped in without hesitation, finding the ladder. Jessica followed, navigating by touch until they dropped into a concrete hallway threaded with pipes.

Brutus scanned the tangle like a puzzle before pointing. "Cut there. No pipes in the way."

"What is this place?"

"Back access to the food storage. Learned it my first week here. How much are you after?"

"Enough to supply thirty thousand—for weeks."

His eyebrow lifted. "Ambitious."

"What is the plan?"

Jessica let out a long sigh but did not answer.

"We don't move until you tell me," Brutus answered.

"I'm not sure if I need you anymore."

"You do if you don't want to trigger any alarms."

Jessica hesitated for several moments longer before finally answering. "We're raising an army of Rifters—enough to corner, attack, and wipe out the Numberless."

"You're serious?" Brutus said, his eyebrows arching in surprise.

"When they are removed, there will be no one to stop the spread of truth. Once they fall, the city will have the freedom to decide its future. Rifters will be able to return to the city."

Brutus nodded, a hint of admiration in his eyes. "That's good enough for me. Right this way, princess."

Using the pipes as footholds, Jessica reached the spot and carved into the wall. Two feet of concrete fell inward with a dull crash, revealing the dark hollow of a warehouse. Inside, crates stretched in endless rows. Jessica scored open a nearby box.

Brutus reached in, hefting a sack. "Beans. I hate beans."

"You don't have to eat them. How long before someone finds this breach?"

"A week, maybe more. This is the back of the warehouse."

"We need three weeks or more."

"Then cut from the back of each crate. They won't realize anything is missing until they actually need it."

"Good idea. This might actually work," she said with a sly smile.

***

She returned two hours later with hundreds of Hoarders in tow. Down in the warehouse, Jessica cut into remote crates while Hoarders swarmed in, carting away sacks in a ceaseless line.

Each bag held more food than most had eaten in a month. This solidified their commitment. There was no going back now— they were no longer bending rules, they were smashing the Acadian Code. When the missing food was eventually discovered, there would be consequences. But for now, even the most hesitant joined in. Brutus carried six sacks at once, chest out in silent challenge; Jessica kept to the flank, eyes sharp.

They returned to camp like conquering heroes, the scent of forbidden food luring everyone from their tents. No more gruel, no more tasteless mush—tonight, it would be beans, corn, salted beef, all washed down with sweet fruit juice.

Aias tried to lecture her for recklessness, but Josiah appeared with a bowl of meat in hand, cutting Aias off with gruff praise. When the two left, Jessica finally had a quiet moment. She watched carefully as, for the first time, the Rifters moved with purpose.

As the food was passed around, Jessica became uncomfortably aware of eyes on her. At first, she ignored it, but the weight of the stares grew until it felt suffocating. Hoarders watched her openly—some even pointed. She had only meant to feed them so they could train and fight, but the looks they gave her now were something else entirely. Gratitude. Awe. As if she had given them more than food.

And now she realized she had.

She had given them hope.

"It's not hope they have—it's just delayed death," Brutus said, settling beside her with a bowl in hand.

Jessica kept her gaze forward.

"You want to know how I knew what was in that broken mind of yours?" Brutus asked.

She didn't answer.

"It's the way you scan every face—trying to read them. There's a longing in your eyes to belong, to fit in, to find a place where you'll be accepted. But you never will. Not here."

"You're quick to assume you're right."

"You dimmed Aberration," he growled. "You know I'm right."

"Why does it matter?"

"You care too much about what people think of you. That makes you weak—vulnerable. The others don't see it, but I do. And if you can't kill that habit, it'll kill you."

His words sank deep. He was right—she had always measured how much people hated her, always calculated how to survive it. Elena had taught her that skill. But no matter how she tried, something in her knew she would never truly be Acadian.

"And when did you become so perceptive?" she asked.

"Cojax threw himself at you like some love-struck Dependent, but the way you looked at him… as if you would wilt if he ever shut it off. Made me sick."

Jessica's frown deepened. She had thought her detachment convincing, but even Brutus—never praised for his insight—had seen through her.

Brutus stood, tossing his empty bowl aside. "Take a page from me—stop caring what anyone thinks."

"Wait." Jessica's voice stopped him. "Why do you hate Cojax?"

His face darkened. "I've only got one eye because of that Dependent. I've got a right."

"That might've pushed you over the edge, but it didn't start there. Even before I knew Cojax well, I could feel the tension between you two."

Brutus stared at the ground. "You don't know him like I do—though you think you do."

"What do you mean?"

"Light and darkness can't share the same room. That's me and Cojax. One has to give way."

"It doesn't have to be like that."

"Just do your part," Brutus said, his gruffness snapping back into place, "and we can leave all this rot behind."

## FIFTY-FIVE

Fourteen hours later—after the battle had ended, after the Roaches had slithered back into their holes—Cojax dragged himself up out of a Digger tunnel. He was coated head to toe in mud and Roach wax.

During the fighting, his unit had hesitated to follow him. Now they insisted he lead the way. He rolled to his side, chest heaving, arms trembling from the climb. The only armor left to him was his helmet. His Arc Blade, still strapped to his side, felt heavier than iron.

"It's… clear," he breathed into his Comm-Link.

"Good," Adriana's voice crackled back. "Now go get some rope or something."

Cojax blinked, not understanding. "Rope? There's no rope up here—"

The whine of an approaching HoverBucket cut him off. The craft blurred against the haze until it touched down just meters away. Cojax pushed himself to his knees and tore off his helmet.

Acadians surged forward with Arc Blades drawn, forming a protective box around him.

"There are still a few down the Roach hole," he said.

"Don't worry about them," one of the soldiers replied, a thin man with a flat voice. "You've got your own problems. Titan's summoned you."

Cojax's pulse kicked into battle rhythm again. He nodded, stepping aboard the HoverBucket.

It carried only him, lifting into the gray air. The battlefield below spread out like a butcher's yard—bodies from both sides littering the Killing Fields in grotesque abundance.

Fifty thousand Acadians dead. The bloodiest fight he had ever seen.

He gave the fallen one last salute before the craft banked toward home.

Within ten minutes, he was standing at attention in his father's living room. He still lived here, although, as an Eighth Tier, he could apply for new housing if he wanted. Mud crusted his uniform, sweat and wax caked his hair. He half-considered showering, but the door slid open and Titan stepped inside.

His father's eyes swept him from helmet to boots. "With a few leaves in your hands, you might pass for a tree."

Cojax wasn't sure if it was a joke or an accusation.

"Boy," Titan said, the faintest curve at his lips, "you're something unexpected. If your mother could see you… she'd yell at you for being reckless, hug you while I pretended not to notice, and then cry under her helmet. She'd think I couldn't tell, but I'd know by the way she fell silent."

The mention of his mother stopped Cojax cold. Titan speaking of her with warmth—pretending she would embrace him—felt like watching the sun rise in the west.

*"Perhaps I misjudged him."* But this thought was quickly put aside. *"No. He's mad. How can he pretend to care for her when he's responsible for her death? How can he pretend to care for me?"*

"You're a Nova," Titan continued. "All Numberless are. I always knew you were, but I didn't think you had the strength to master it. I was wrong. Your energy signature… it was something I haven't seen, even among the Numberless. One moment you were steady, the next—an explosion. What were you thinking when you leapt at that SataniKahn?"

*"Jessica."* Her name was all that had filled his mind.

"I wasn't thinking," Cojax said after a pause.

Titan nodded as though this were wisdom. "You could take a seat on the Infinite Council one day. It would be a rare thing—father and son both Numberless."

"Thank you, sir."

"But don't let it polish your ego. You've a long road ahead. Your Score's been dropped two Tiers for… misunderstanding a direct order. You're back in the Tenth Tier. I'm not worried. You'll rise quickly—Sixth Tier in six months, a command in a year. First a Phalanx, then a Quorum. Four years and you'll be in the Top Tiers. No one else has your ability—they won't keep up."

"Yes, sir."

"The Rifting of the Aberration was the best thing for you."

"Yes, sir."

Titan's voice hardened. "You're becoming a son I can be proud of. Rest. Tend your wounds."

They saluted. Titan stepped toward the door. "Now you understand why I was hard on you."

"Yes, sir. Permission to speak freely?"

"Speak."

"The Aberration was poison. She nearly destroyed me. Sometimes I think I curse her name in my sleep. I just hope it doesn't hurt my Score."

"As long as you sleep here," Titan said, "it won't."

"Thank you."

The door shut behind him. Cojax let out a long, slow breath. He'd feared execution for disobedience. Instead, Titan had been almost… human. Dropping two Tiers was a wound, but not a fatal one.

"One son falls as another rises," a voice rumbled from the kitchen.

Cojax turned.

Marcus sat at the dining table, his face in shadow.

It wasn't until Marcus raised his left arm that Cojax realized half of it was gone—sheared clean just past the elbow.

"Father didn't mention it?" Marcus asked, smiling without humor. "A Launcher took it three months ago, before your Crossing. I can still fight, but they say I weaken the shieldwall so they won't let me. I've been transferred to the Armory, where I work eighteen hours a day in a vain attempt to keep my Score. But—" his eyes softened, "I'm glad you're alive, brother."

Cojax crossed the space in two steps and pulled him into a hug. He squeezed until his own muscles shook, unwilling to let go. Marcus stiffened, then slowly returned the embrace. Tears pricked both their eyes, but training forbade them from falling.

When Cojax stepped back, his voice was quieter. "What happened to your Civil Union?"

"Dissolved," Marcus said, his voice cracking halfway through. "She was reassigned another spouse."

"What about the child application you were going to submit?"

"It was approved at first. Then… this happened." He lifted the stump of his arm. "A few days later, the notice came—unfit to father children. They are now being raised by Aleniana and her new spouse. I'm Weighted and falling fast. My First Tier status won't hold much longer, and when it goes… Well, it seems fortune finds you just as it abandons me."

"No." Cojax's eyes sharpened, glassy with fury. "I will not see another brother broken by the AC."

Marcus' face drained of color. His lips parted but no sound came, only the faint, involuntary shake of his head.

"Don't worry," Cojax said. "We're not being recorded. Privilege of a Numberless' residence."

"How can you be sure?"

"Titan just told me. I asked if speaking Jessica's name in my sleep could hurt my Score. He said, *'Not while you sleep here.'* His armor doesn't just fail to record—it nullifies the recording function of every suit in the room. I wasn't sure if mine would log anything once he left… apparently, no armor can record inside these walls. That's the main reason I haven't moved out yet."

"You mischievous little Rifter," Marcus said with a thin grin. "It was months after my Crossing before I even realized they were recording us. When did you start using your head?"

"It wasn't me," Cojax said. "It was Jessica—the Aberration."

"So what you told Titan about her—just a slab of rot?"

Cojax's tone turned hard. "That's only the beginning. Can I trust you?"

"Of course."

Cojax smiled faintly. "Good. Listen—everything I thought I knew, everything you think you know, is wrong. And I intend to change it. I'm part of a group, and we mean to undo the AC."

Marcus gave a short, disbelieving snort. "Be careful, Cojax. Many have been Rifted for saying far less. You can trust me, but it would be madness to try and change things."

"Maybe. But if I stayed here my whole life, knowing what I know now, that would be true madness. What I know puts my life at risk—and everyone near me. Titan would cut me down if he even guessed what's in my head."

"Then don't give him a reason," Marcus said, his eyes soft but pressing.

"I don't think you understand—" Cojax began.

"—Sure I do," Marcus interrupted, his voice sharpening. "We all lost friends in the Mahghetto. Three of them were my brothers. But throwing yourself into the Rift won't change that, and it won't change the city."

"But I think I *can* change the city," Cojax pressed.

"You can't," Marcus snapped, his voice rising. "Listen, I can barely maintain my Score and I'm Weighted. But you, Cojax—you still have your whole life ahead of you. Father says you're a Nova, like me. You've got the potential to rise as quickly as I did, quicker if what I've heard is true. Don't waste that. Don't fall for the lure of the Red District. Fight on. Leave everyone else behind. Forget me, forget your classmates. Forsake every desire and rise through the Tiers. Within six years, you could be among the Numberless."

"And where will you be by then?" Cojax shot back, anger sharpening his tone. "In the Rift? Swallowed by the very city you think I should spend my life impressing? No, Marcus. I'm not going to lose another brother to the Acadian Code."

Marcus stood, leaning heavily on the table, his words venomous. "I'm already lost." He closed his eyes, forced the rage from his voice, and when he spoke again, it was calm. "I won't betray you, Cojax—not now. You put your trust in me, and I won't turn on you. But if I ever hear you talk like this again, for your sake, I won't let it go. Forget this insane idea of revolution, forget upsetting the system. Forget me, forget all this rot—and live on."

## FIFTY-SIX

Cojax had arranged three meetings since he first spoke to the Damnattii—each one inside his father's apartment. Trust was a rare currency, and they hoarded it. Their circle remained small, slower to grow than Cojax had hoped. Whenever they gathered, they took every precaution to avoid discovery.

Even so, today he was convinced someone was following him—a warrior in full Acadian armor. On paper, Cojax had nothing to fear; he was merely returning home from guard duty. But if the others were spotted entering a Numberless' residence, the explanations would be tricky. One mistake from any of them, and they'd all be dead before sunrise.

He crossed a street, glancing both ways, noting the figure had not followed. Just to be certain, he wound his route into a series of unnecessary stair climbs, feigning a leg workout.

When he reached his residence, the warrior was already there.

Cojax's hand slid toward his sword, muscles tightening. But before he could draw, the figure lifted a single finger and placed it on the edge of their helmet—a silent command for stillness. Had the visor been up, that finger would have been pressed to the edge of their jaw. And then it all hit him at once—the warrior's small stature, the lack of charge in their armor.

A storm of emotions struck him. It took every scrap of discipline not to run toward her like a reckless Reever. The door slid open, and he gestured her inside. No battle had ever filled him with such an unholy mix of fear, excitement, and disbelief. His pulse hammered in his ears, every heartbeat echoing through his armor.

For a moment, he thought it had to be a dream.

*"This can't be real."*

He lifted the helmet. Red hair spilled out like the last light of the sun over the horizon. His armor flared faintly in response. The chin, the nose, the eyes—exactly as he remembered. He had once convinced himself that his memory had exaggerated her beauty, but no—Jessica was every bit as impossible as before.

He went in for a kiss; she went for a hug. They collided somewhere in between, her nose jamming into his shoulder, his lips brushing her ear. Awkward. Perfect. Neither cared. The embrace lingered, long and fierce, the scent of dirt, smoke, and—

"Just so you know," Finn's voice cut in, "you're not alone. We all got here early. Respect for other people's time and all that. I assumed you'd remember since you did leave the door unlocked."

Cojax flushed so deeply he could've passed for a ripened fruit. Jessica colored too, but far less—she had already spotted the others the moment Cojax began his painfully slow, dramatic unmasking.

Cojax pressed his palms together until his knuckles whitened. "Well… let's get started."

"Too bad Finn had to ruin it," Adriana said from the corner. "Looked like it was just about to get interesting."

"Can we—" Jessica began.

"—speak?" Cojax finished. "Yes. My father's rank comes with privileges—we're not being recorded here. You pretty much know everyone already, Havish, Horacio, Finn, and… Adriana."

Jessica's eyes lingered on the only other girl present.

"Play nice," Finn muttered.

"How in the Rift can we trust her?" Jessica whispered.

"Because I'm trustworthy," Adriana replied, flat as stone.

Whether she meant it as a joke or not, the room erupted in laughter. Finn's was the loudest, quick and uneven, like he'd been holding it in for hours.

"Well," Adriana said over the noise, "at least Cojax can trust me." She punctuated it with a wink.

Cojax tilted his head, unsure of the gesture. Jessica, however, understood it perfectly—her fists curled like she was ready to prove a point.

Cojax caught her hand before she could speak. "She's with us—and she's more committed than most would be. Please, just give it a chance. Just listen."

Jessica's gaze flicked between them, sharp but measured. "Alright, but she better not give me an excuse to draw my blade."

Adriana snorted. "How domestic."

Cojax's voice cut through the room like a knife. "We have a lot to catch you up on, Jessica. We've discovered something more dark than any of us would have imagined."

He then gave her the condensed version of the battle, with Finn interjecting at every opportunity to embellish his "heroic" moments. He recounted his interrogation of Qualix, the captured Damnattii, and the revelation that the Numberless were the ones controlling the Roaches. Jessica didn't flinch—not because she knew, but because nothing in this city could surprise her anymore.

Adriana slid in after Cojax, her tone suddenly light and charming—a strange contrast to the brutal tactician she'd been in the Mahghetto. She laid out their plan: hijack scattered city screens, seed Qualix's message in fragments, let it spread underground. It was careful, quiet… and fragile.

Jessica shook her head. "That'll never be enough. They'll crush the rumor before it spreads—telling everyone that the Damnattii had hacked our systems and were spreading false propaganda. And every time you hijack a CityScreen, you risk getting caught."

"She's right," Horacio agreed. "If we have any chance of this working, we'd need to hit every screen in Acadia at once. It has to be so overwhelming that it can't be suppressed."

"That would mean breaking into the Main Control Room in the Trinity," Adriana said, "and that's a fortress. Only Top Tiers get in—and only with clearance coded into their bio-circuitry."

"We have a TechOps who is part of the rebellion," Jessica continued. "With enough time, I bet he could break through the security doors and hack the system."

Finn frowned. "That would take forever."

"What we need," Cojax said, slamming a palm on the table, "is an army to buy us time."

Jessica laughed—light and sudden, breaking the tension like glass.

"Please," Adriana said, leaning forward, "share the joke."

Jessica's smile vanished. "It's not a joke. My guardian, Elena, had been building an army since I first arrived. She planned to use the Rifters to start a protest—but now they have a different purpose.

They're training. They have been for the last four weeks."

She spoke of Aias, who had let himself be Rifted to organize and lead them. She told of the parallel Tier system, the hundreds of thousands laboring in the depths, and the warriors preparing for war. By the time she finished, even Adriana's skepticism had given way to intrigue.

Horacio let out a booming laugh. "This just might be possible, and it's all thanks to Jessica."

Adriana bit her lip. Jessica's cheeks warmed.

"Can we trust them?" Cojax asked.

"There are five friendly camps of Hoarders, two of them are loyal without question," Jessica said. "That should give us at least fifteen thousand warriors, maybe more. But there's just one problem—they can't charge their armor. When someone is Rifted their bio-circuitry gets ripped out."

Finn leaned forward. "Can't we charge them somehow?"

Cojax nodded slowly, considering. "With some creative work, I bet it could be done. We will need the help of an ElectraTech, but I'm sure it's possible to plug their suits into the Acadian main power line, giving them a direct charge. I might be able to figure it out myself…."

Then the front door hissed, sliding open. Everyone stiffened, freezing where they stood. Marcus stepped inside the room, his body armored, his sword hand resting on the hilt of a blade at his side. He first looked confused, then angry. His eyes carefully passed over all the faces present, memorizing each one.

Then he said two words with such cold lethality the others were quick to obey. "Get out."

## FIFTY-SEVEN

Only Cojax and Jessica remained. If this confrontation turned violent, she would not leave—not now, not when she had only just found him again.

"I warned you, Cojax," Marcus said, his voice sounding more wounded than threatening. "I warned you not to go down this path. It holds nothing but death and pain."

Cojax considered a lie—an excuse about why everyone had gathered in his apartment. Social gatherings were rare in Acadia, as they were seen as a Dependent's pastime, but they did happen. Yet the instant Marcus's eyes fixed on Jessica, Cojax knew deceit was impossible. Marcus had never met her, but he was quick enough to know who she was. Her short stature, red hair, and above all, the scar carved in the shape of the sigil of the Aberration gave her away. She had been Rifted. She had no business being here, clad in the armor of the Validated.

Marcus' hand still rested on the hilt of his blade. He had not drawn it yet—not a good sign, but not hopeless either.

Cojax let out a slow breath, abandoning the lie. He lifted his hands, empty of weapons. "Let me show you something—something that changes everything."

"Something she brought you?" Marcus asked, nodding toward Jessica. "It's a lie, Cojax. She's manipulating you."

"I've only spoken the truth," Jessica shot back, her voice steady and fierce.

Marcus drew his blade, anger flashing in his features. "Cojax, she's lied to you this whole time."

Jessica's blade rang free just as quickly. Her armor lacked charge, but the blade could still hold one. "He's beyond convincing, Cojax. Draw your blade. We have no choice."

"No," Cojax said as he stepped closer. One quick strike across his unarmored head could end him, yet he pressed forward into

Marcus' reach. His brother hesitated, and Cojax seized on that hesitation.

"Just watch." Cojax unclasped his ArmGuard and set it on the table, retreating with his hands still raised.

"Did she give this to you?" Marcus growled. "More propaganda from the Aberration?"

"No," Cojax said firmly. "She gave me the idea, but I saw it through. I've been volunteering for battles—not to raise my Score, but to attempt the impossible. And what I found, brother, changed everything. Activate the most recent recording. See for yourself."

Marcus lingered, blade still in hand, reluctant to lower it.

"Jessica, put the sword away," Cojax urged.

"Cojax, we can't trust him. He'll expose us all."

"Put it away. Wait for me in my room. Please. This is my brother. I've trusted him my whole life—I can't stop now."

Jessica hesitated, then sheathed her blade with visible reluctance. "Fine. But if I hear so much as a raised voice, I'll return blade in hand and I won't be stopping to ask questions."

As she vanished down the hall, Marcus finally lowered his weapon. A long moment later, he sheathed it. "Whatever this is, Cojax, it won't change my mind."

"Just watch," Cojax repeated.

So Marcus did. The recording was dim, grainy, but unmistakable. The figure on the screen was no human. It was the captured Damnattii, speaking of things only a Validated should know—Acadia's structure, its endless war. He said most Damnattii had no desire to fight. He revealed their orders came not from their own leaders but from the Numberless themselves—the supposed champions of Acadia.

Marcus watched the first time with eerie calm, as though reviewing a dull field report. Then he rewound, replayed, froze frames, scouring for flaws. For thirty minutes he worked in near silence, muttering fragments under his breath.

At last, Cojax broke his brother's concentration. "The Numberless are playing both sides."

"But why?" Marcus asked, genuinely shaken. "Why perpetuate this war? What is gained by letting Acadians bleed and die by the millions?"

"I don't know," Cojax admitted.

Marcus's suspicion flared again. "Did she give you this? Did the Aberration hand you this video, expecting you to believe it?"

"No, in the last great battle I fought in, we captured three Damnattii. They spoke our language, just as Jessica said they would. We have been lied to."

"This means…," Marcus faltered, his breath tight.

"It means every Rifted, every injury, every death was needless," Cojax said. "Our brothers, our mother, our friends—none of them had to die. The rigid structure of Acadia is not here to protect us, but to keep us wearing chains we never knew existed."

Marcus looked down at the stump of his arm, a new realization dawning. "When I lost this, I asked Father for help. I thought he might pull strings for a replacement. He couldn't, of course; that would be against the AC. But he said something strange—he seemed to blame Atlas, not me. I didn't understand then. But now I do. Atlas must have been the one who commanded the Roach forces that day. He knew I would be on the Wall."

"Yes," Cojax said. "Atlas likely targeted you to weaken Titan's standing. A rising Nova with the potential to be chosen as a Numberless would be a threat to him."

Marcus's voice came out in a sharp, almost breathless whisper. "You're right. This does change everything." He looked up, his eyes blazing with steel. "Tell me what you need me to do. I'm in."

Cojax nodded. "Good." He then picked up his ArmGuard and opened a Comm-Link with the others. "You can all come back in. The situation has been neutralized."

"You had them waiting outside?" Marcus asked.

"Yes," Cojax answered quickly.

"What would have happened if I hadn't decided to join your side?" Marcus asked.

Cojax let out a long sigh. "The important thing is… you did."

## FIFTY-EIGHT

Sweat dripped down Marcus' face, stinging his eyes. He was fast—always had been—but the loss of his left arm dulled his rhythm. Tapping into the main Acadian Power Grid was the easy part; anyone short of an ElectraTech would fry themselves trying it, but Marcus knew what he was doing. The real challenge was rerouting the draw, hiding it in the veins of the city's consumption. A clever trick, one that would buy them cover for a week at most. But they didn't need a week. They needed hours.

He stood in the Rift—the city beneath the city—beside a concrete-bound power line. Cojax had cut open the box earlier, leaving the lines raw and exposed. While Marcus worked, leaders of the Rifters drifted through the shadows: Aias among them, gaunt faces hollowed by hunger and long despair. The rebellion looked fragile in their hands.

Then the Rifters came in droves, dropping off their armor. What they lacked in muscle mass, they made up for in their surreal and silent determination—like a people possessed. A cursory study of these people and he could tell they had suffered, but not in the same way he had in the Mahghetto. It was different somehow, more real. In the Mahghetto one might get Rifted, but no one knew exactly what that meant then. Here, the consequences were much more real—starvation, deprivation, and a slow grinding death. He did not know which suffering was more inhumane—he just knew it was different.

"How's it going?" Cojax asked, his voice carrying a confidence Marcus suspected was part mask, part habit.

Marcus preferred the hum of current, the rhythm of his work. He had already recharged ten thousand suits of armor and still the cords snaked across the floor to waiting piles.

"Tedious," he muttered.

"Since the Rifters had their bio-circuitry removed, how long will a charge last?"

"They will have about twenty percent less charge than a normal Validated."

Cojax nodded. "Not bad. But what about the cameras? Won't someone notice all these feeds waking up? I imagine, only a Numberless could sever that link."

Marcus pulled a cord from one breastplate, slid it into another. "True. But since the armor isn't linked to a user, the feeds have nowhere to transmit. We'll have a window before anyone realizes."

"Then as soon as you're done, we move," Cojax said.

"Have you considered the implications of what you are doing?" Marcus asked, his voice more cutting than he intended.

"Yes."

"Have you really? Have you realized that if we succeed, our father will likely die? He will be blamed with the rest of the Numberless."

Cojax flinched. Somehow, he had not allowed himself to think of Titan as part of the faceless enemy.

"And if we fail," Marcus pressed, "you, me, every Rifter here dies. The rebellion ends in blood, and the Numberless remain."

"I'd rather die than live a lie," Cojax answered. The words came firm, but his mind reeled. Marcus had already traced every implication to its conclusion, while he had charged forward half-blind. It wouldn't change his choice, but the weight of it struck like a slap.

Marcus turned back to his task, wires buzzing in his grip. "And after? When the city falls—what takes its place? Chaos? Disorder? The Roach war may have been manufactured, but it was still a rallying cry. It united us. I don't say you're wrong. I just wish there was time to weigh the variables. To reason with our Father."

"He already knows," Cojax said. "And he still stands with them. When we're on the other side of this, when we have succeeded, we'll have earned the right to discuss all of this. But not now."

Marcus rose, placed his one good hand on his brother's shoulder. "Then let's end it. End the suffering."

"We will," Cojax replied.

"Good," Marcus replied, his voice grim but firm. He then

returned to his work.

Cojax lingered for an hour longer, tried to help, but soon realized he was slowing things more than aiding. He drifted away toward the parade grounds, where Jessica waited among thousands of Rifters. Their armor sat in neat rows, untouched, conserving charge. The men and women gathered in clusters, their voices low, their eyes smoldering with resolve.

"Are they ready?" Cojax asked.

Jessica turned with a smile. His voice steadied her heart, kept the storm inside from breaking. "Yes. They're not the best trained, but you won't find a force that's more committed. Once they reach the surface, they'll fight like dragons. No one fights harder than those who've lost everything, then been given a chance to win it back."

They watched the masses move through the dim light, shadows stirring like a tide.

"There's something you should know," Jessica said finally. "Brutus is here—in the Rift. With us. He's the reason we secured enough food to train."

Cojax stiffened. "Brutus? Alive? How is he?"

Her pause spoke louder than her words. "Bitter. But not broken."

"Will he be a problem?"

"No. Not now. He wants freedom as much as any of us. More than that, he fights like he's chasing redemption. He trains harder than the rest."

Cojax exhaled slowly. "Once this is all over, we'll have to make amends somehow. I'll be sure to tell the others, just so there are no surprises when he pops up on the Comm-Link."

"Here comes Aias," Jessica said, nodding toward a tall, lean figure. His clothes were disheveled, but there was no mistaking the mark of leadership in his eyes.

"Greetings," Aias said, his voice warm, his tone steady.

Cojax saluted, bowing low to honor the man.

Aias blinked, surprised, then returned the gesture with crisp precision. He had not expected such acknowledgment—much less respect. "You honor me."

"As you honor me," Cojax said. "Jessica told me you allowed yourself to be Rifted so you could organize all of this. Without you—or Elena—none of this would exist."

"Yes," Aias said simply. "But it will take more than us to carry it forward. And I bring good news. It took some persuasion, but Kane's forces have agreed to the new plan. They'll fight beside us, bringing our number to twenty thousand."

"Kane?" Jessica frowned. "I thought he hated me."

"Oh, he does," Aias said with a faint smile. "But he hates Acadia far more. His men will bring their armor to Marcus shortly. They had only one condition."

Jessica's voice was cautious. "And what condition is that?"

"That you lead one of the seven units."

"Me?" Her breath caught, the word little more than disbelief.

"Kane opposed it," Aias admitted, "but his soldiers insisted. They want you at the head of one of our forces."

Jessica exhaled slowly, realizing she had been holding her breath. "But I'm... the Aberration."

"To them you are far more," Aias said. "You are strength and fire. You brought them food when they were starving, hope when they had none."

"And Chaucer? Criminion?" she asked.

Aias shook his head. "No. They refused. Their numbers were small, though, so their absence makes little difference. Still, many of their warriors have defected regardless. You've made an impression none of us expected."

"Will they be ready?" Cojax asked.

"The only delay is your brother finishing the charging," Aias said. "How long will it take him?"

"A few hours, even with the addition of Kane's warriors," Cojax answered.

"Good." Aias' tone softened, almost fatherly. "I'll begin gathering everyone. The plan is simple, but nerves can unravel even the simplest of designs."

## FIFTY-NINE

Four hundred feet below the surface, Aias' forces had gathered. Two days of relentless preparation had brought them to this moment. Now, divided into three sections, they stood ready. Jessica commanded one of them.

The steady stream of food had changed them. It had woken something in their muscles, rekindled the Mahghetto training that hunger had dulled. Now, in their ash-covered, freshly charged armor, they looked like soldiers from the CityScreens—crack troops frozen in the midst of some glorious battle. Faces once slack with despair now carried only resolve and hunger for the fight ahead.

In the dim light, something caught Jessica's eye. She slipped on her helmet, letting the night vision bloom into clarity. The first row of warriors bore the sign of the Aberration, scrawled in charcoal across the brows of their helmets. She stepped forward, scanning the lines, realizing it wasn't just the first row—it was all of them.

Brutus emerged from the crowd, his own brow unmarked. "Rifters, all of them. Looks like your little stunt with the food stores gave you a following. Not a soul seems to care—or even notice—that I was the one who led you there. Blazing Rifters... might as well have carved bullseyes into their foreheads."

Jessica turned to her ranks and saluted. The Rifters snapped their salutes back with sharp, disciplined precision. They knew this was the fight for their lives—for their future—and she could feel the anticipation pressing like a storm in the air.

She had no words for them. None were needed. Turning back to the tunnel, she pulsed the command to advance by rank.

*"This is it. We have the element of surprise... but eventually, they'll have the numbers."*

Jessica was the first to step into the newly carved passage, its edges still rough from an Arc Blade's cut. Brutus followed, then the surge of armored bodies behind them. The tunnel gave way to an old stairwell, the space tightening as more Rifters pressed in.

A hundred feet from the surface, Jessica raised her shield and began the Death Rattle—striking the hilt of her blade against the shield's face in a slow, deliberate rhythm. The sound boomed unnaturally loud, amplified through the shield's speakers.

Brutus' voice crackled on her Comm-Link, likely to tell her she was giving away their position. She ignored it. The Rifters needed this. They needed to hear each other, to feel the weight of their combined power. One by one, they joined in. The sound multiplied, the beat quickening until it rattled dirt from the overhead fixtures and set the walls humming. Jessica half-wondered if the structure might collapse under the roar.

The stairway steepened, an old utility access shaft leading toward the surface. Step by step, the chant grew louder. Hearts pounded in rhythm, adrenaline burning through every vein. Jessica reached the storm drain cover, only feet from open air.

Brutus moved to take point, but she shoved him back. "No. I lead the charge."

He growled. "Don't tell me you've caught your boyfriend's taste for drama."

She ignored him and instead looked at the hilt of her blade, its cold steel etched with words that burned hotter than fire:

*Choose what you stand for.*

Her fingers clenched until the metal pulsed with a beam of light. Around her stood an army—not of the proud, but of the condemned: the fallen, the shattered, the castoffs spat out by a world that saw their value as less than dust. She rose to her full height, the weight of their fury gathering behind her.

"Oh, ye Acadians—rise!" she roared above the deafening rattle, each word striking like a war drum. "Stand as one, cast off your chains, and be slaves no more!"

Jessica crouched low, every muscle coiling with stored energy. She could feel the army's strength surging behind her, a tidal wave about to break. Then she sprang upward, blasting through the grate in an eruption of metal and dust.

She landed like a demon loosed from a pit, weapon and shield blazing, concrete cracking beneath her boots. Behind her, a flood of charcoal-colored warriors poured up and out, fanning in every direction.

No hesitation. No quarter.

The Rifters slammed into the guards at Gate One like a living avalanche. Shields shattered within seconds; bodies fell within moments. The enemy line broke apart as Jessica's units split into their assignments—she leading one force, Brutus another.

For a heartbeat, surprise was theirs. Then the Acadians adapted, tightening ranks, forming hardened defensive lines.

And the real fight began.

Only the highest Tiers worked inside the Trinity—elite defenders pitted now against the very lowest. But the Rifters weren't here for glory or pride. They fought like animals, uncaged and burning for revenge. The Validated didn't stand a chance.

Once inside, the Rifters split into surging waves, cutting down anyone in their path. Battle cries collided in the air, filling the once-silent building with a tidal wave of noise. The defenders were bold, but they fell quickly under the onslaught.

"Gate Three and Four secure," a voice crackled over the Comm-Link.

Jessica sheathed her sword and drew her Blazer. Several followed her lead, using the weapon to thin out defenders before the melee swept in. Acadians clung to the honor of steel on flesh—but Jessica wasn't Acadian. That made her unit faster, deadlier, more efficient.

"Gate Six is secure."

"Cojax," Jessica said into the Comm-Link, "are you in?"

"Yes," came the reply. "Marcus just opened the Armory. Any of your Rifters need a Blazer?"

"Yeah," Finn cut in, "we're selling them real cheap."

Switching channels, Jessica addressed the unarmed Rifters still below. "Rifters—head to an armory and claim your weapons."

The sewers swelled again, Rifters emerging from the drains in waves. Slower coming up, but twice as fast once they found their footing. They raced toward Gate One, scooping up charged Blazers from fallen enemies. The armored Rifters held position, parting just enough to let them through.

They poured into the Trinity by the thousands, like a sandstorm in full gale. In the Armory, Marcus handed out freshly charged weapons. Each warrior loaded up, turned, and rejoined the fight.

"Gate Five secure."

"We need help with Gate Two!" another voice shouted. "An entire Phalanx was passing when we arrived—we're outnumbered!"

"I'll handle it," Marcus growled. He pinged a hundred nearby warriors and took direct command. Leading them out of Gate Three, he slammed into the Acadian flank. The enemy had locked shields—but had left their sides exposed.

Marcus roared, swinging his massive blade in a wide arc, sparks spraying with each hit. On his severed arm, he'd strapped a Repulse Shield—awkward to look at but brutal in effect. The Acadians scrambled to reorient their formation, but it was too late. Marcus tore through the line, cleaving three soldiers in a single swing.

Moments later his voice came through, steady and grim. "Gate Two secure."

Cojax opened the channel to all units. "Take defensive positions—hold those Gates! Anyone with a Blazer, move to the upper balconies to provide cover fire."

The Rifters locked shields across the doorways, turning each into a barricade. Cojax switched to a private channel. "Jessica, how's our path?"

"Still clearing," she said, "but I'm almost to the first door of the Main Control Room."

"Excellent. Finn, Ion—meet me at the stairwell. Time to start on the security doors."

"I'll send some Rifters to back you up," Jessica said. "There shouldn't be much resistance, but just in case."

"Don't send more than you can spare," Cojax warned. "Your job's harder than mine."

"Don't worry."

Cojax's tone softened. "Just… be careful."

"Can we stop kissing through the Comm?" Finn cut in. "Some of us are trying to fight."

Cojax, Ion, and Finn converged on the stairwell. They had just reached the base when a fourth figure approached—massive, almost Marcus' size, his armor stained black, twenty more black-dyed warriors followed.

"Who are you?" Finn asked.

"Don't recognize your own brother?"

"Brutus," Cojax said. He'd known Brutus was working with Jessica—but seeing him here wasn't part of the plan. He had deliberately kept them apart. "What are you doing here?"

Brutus gestured to the warriors behind him. "You'll need more soldiers to make it through. I brought extras."

Cojax shook his head. "We'll take them. But you need to get back to your assigned Gate."

"I figured you'd be petty," Brutus said flatly.

"This is not the plan," Finn snapped.

"Plans change," Brutus growled. "Warriors adapt to threats."

"I will not fight alongside—" Finn began, but Cojax cut him off.

"—Now's not the time. You can settle this later."

"He is not coming with us," Finn pressed. "I'd sooner turn my back on a Roach than trust him."

Orch glanced at Brutus. "No time for this. Get back to Gate One—you're needed there."

For a long, tense moment, Brutus held Finn's gaze before breaking it. "Good to see you too, brother. You'd better get going. And don't worry about us Rifters—we'll take the dangerous work." Without waiting for a reply, he turned and disappeared with his warriors.

They took the stairs at a punishing pace. The hallway above had already been cleared—Jessica's work, judging by the bodies strewn across the floor. Reaching the Control Room level, they spilled out of the stairwell, weapons tight in their grips. At the first door, Ion knelt and pulled out a transparent tablet, his fingers tapping until colors flashed across the screen.

"Why not just cut through?" Orch asked.

"Go ahead," Cojax said.

"These are shield-reinforced gates," Ion explained without looking up. "Stab one and it'll overload—maybe explode. Either way, without killing Acadia's grid, you're not getting through."

The gate hissed open.

"That was quick," Finn said.

The second opened faster still. For a moment, their urgency

dulled—it felt too easy. Then the Comm-Link filled with overlapping voices:

"The Acadians are locking shields at Gate One!"

"And Gate Two!"

"Same at Six!"

"We're taking heavy fire!"

An explosion shook the building, rattling every pane of glass. Another hit moments later. From where Cojax stood, the night sky was fractured with beams of light from both sides. Rifter snipers held the high ground, but the Acadians had numbers. Any Acadian who tried to climb nearby buildings was cut down. Debris and bodies fell, turning the streets into a killing ground.

The Trinity's reinforced walls held, forcing the enemy to shift tactics—hovercraft and jetpacks swooping in to strafe the balconies. Within moments, the Rifters' height advantage vanished.

"They've locked shields and are advancing at Gate Five!"

Cojax's chest tightened. He looked to Ion, willing him to move faster. But with each door, the process took longer. Most opened into small control rooms guarded by a handful of soldiers— enough to slow them, not stop them.

Until the fifth gate.

Standing in the center of the room was a figure with no weapon drawn—but far from unarmed. His armor was the kind reserved for the Numberless. Cojax had seen it only once before, at the Wall.

Cojax switched to a private channel. "Keep moving. I'll handle this." His blade pulsed with a sharp beam of light. Finn took the lead toward the far gate. The Numberless didn't move to stop them.

"What are you doing, Cojax?" Titan's voice was low, dangerous.

"Ending this," Cojax said. Behind him, the gate hissed open and the Rifters slipped through.

"You could have been among the greatest," Titan said.

Cojax gave a bitter laugh. "There's nothing great in what you do—or what you represent."

"You know nothing, boy."

"I know you command the Roaches against our own warriors.

I know you keep this war alive so you can rule over everyone in this city. I know you're the reason my mother is dead."

Titan sighed and turned away, rubbing his chin before finally removing his helmet. His features were as sharp as ever, but there was a new weight to them—a sadness that made Cojax lower his blade a fraction.

"I loved your mother more than anything," Titan said. "Not at first—the Acadian way doesn't allow it—but it grew. She was charitable. Loving. Things I didn't think could exist in this nightmare. When she was Released, it nearly destroyed me. Would have, if not for you and Marcus. You're both talented—Novas. I thought if you could rise, maybe her sacrifice would mean something."

Cojax's anger flared. "Why? Why serve the AC? Why let your own family rot in this hell? I've lost brothers and sisters to Acadia— and every one of them was your child."

Titan's eyes narrowed. "The Roaches invaded two hundred years ago—but the greatest lie you've been told is that humanity ever stood a chance. They descended like a plague, crushing our armies, shattering our cities, and driving us into the earth like frightened barbarians. The war wasn't lost during the fighting—it was lost before the first shot was fired."

"What about Acadia?"

"It was built by the Damnattii after they seized the planet. We were placed here a few years later."

Cojax lowered his sword, disbelief pulling at his features. "The Damnattii control all of this?"

"No. They're just another tool."

"Then who?"

Titan's gaze hardened. "The Decamont—they're the ones in command."

"Who?"

"I don't know. That information isn't given, even to the Numberless."

"I thought Acadia was the last refuge."

Titan shook his head. "We fought them with sticks compared to their starships. We never had a chance. After near extinction, we surrendered unconditionally. One term of surrender—live under their rule in Acadia."

"Why?"

"To create the perfect weapon," Titan said simply. "The Roaches were their blade, but we had the potential to become an even better one. They admired our adaptability, our tenacity—and more than anything, our ability to generate energy. That's when this two-hundred-year experiment began. Every generation was altered—quicker, stronger, more durable. We started like Jessica. They made us into gods."

"And what do they want with us?"

"I don't know," Titan admitted. "Our task is to give them the best warriors humanity can produce—the Numberless. In return, they promised to eventually leave, letting the rest of us stay."

"They've done all this for eight thousand Numberless?"

"No. Eight thousand is just this city. There are thousands of other cities. The closest is less than forty miles from here. That's why the fog exists—to keep us blind to them, and them to us."

"Our sensors should see through that."

Titan smirked. "Who built the sensors? Decamont tech. They show what they want you to see."

"So this is about building an army?"

"It was," Titan said. "Until you. The Decamont won't tolerate one of their White Diamonds falling into rebellion. I've severed their system's link—they can't shut us down remotely—but that only buys time. They'll come for us, tear down the Wall, and salt the earth with our dead. They will not stand for this."

He stepped closer, voice lowering. "Yes, I commanded Roach armies—but to sift the wheat from the chaff. Pressure makes diamonds, Cojax. I believed if we could forge their perfect army faster, they'd leave sooner. And when they left, we'd be stronger than ever."

Cojax weighed the words. They rang true—there was no point in Titan lying now. But one thing stuck. "Why cut the Decamont's control at all?"

Titan laughed bitterly. "You don't know me. I'm not Atlas, and I'm not like most of the Numberless. I don't consider lives meaningless. That flaw is why Jessica is still alive. If I hadn't severed the Decamont's control, everyone here would be dead within a month. We depend on machines for power and shields. Without them, we're nothing."

"So—you'll fight with us?" Cojax pressed.

Titan's gaze drifted upward.

"Cojax," Finn's voice crackled over the Comm-Link, "we're in the Main Control Room. Took some fighting, but we're through. You good?"

"I'm fine." Cojax turned back to Titan. "Fight with us, father. You said it yourself—they've been shaping us into an army. This is our home, not theirs. Did you ever think it was possible for Rifters, the lowest in Acadia, to take and hold the Trinity? Yet here they are. Let's show the Decamont just how well they've trained us. I'll be their slave no more."

Before Titan could answer, Jessica's voice cut in, tight with urgency. "We've got trouble. About thirty Numberless just entered through the top of the Trinity. They're heading for the Crono-Stasis Pods."

"Thirty?" Cojax's voice betrayed his fear. "How many warriors are with you?"

"Two hundred—but I don't think we can hold them."

"I'm on my way," Cojax said.

Titan stepped forward. "What happened?"

"Jessica was securing the Crono-Stasis Pods to keep the Numberless inside from waking. Somehow, the other Numberless got in."

"There's a docking bay on top of the Trinity only a Numberless can access."

"She has two hundred warriors," Cojax said.

Titan's jaw tightened. "Enough for one Numberless—not thirty."

The two locked eyes, unspoken calculations passing between them. Titan broke first. "I'll protect her."

"You're a Numberless—tell them to stand down until—"

"I am no longer a Numberless," Titan cut in. "I lost that the moment I severed the link. And even if I ordered them to stop, Atlas would counter it. Get to the Main Control Room and finish what you came for. Patch me into your Comm-Link."

"Please…" Cojax said.

"She'll be fine," Titan promised, already moving. "If I get

there in time."

## SIXTY

Jessica had severed three of the nine connections, but each one took precious time. The device fought her with every step, layers of Acadian encryption clawing back at her work.

Her ArmGuard's scanner suddenly flared—a solid white spike screaming across the display. Jessica's gut tightened. Only one thing puts out a signature like that.

"Numberless incoming—fast! Link shields and hold that door!"

Her voice carried through the Comm-Link, snapping the two hundred Rifters under her command into motion. She sent them to the main stairwell, the best chokepoint they had. There were other routes the enemy could take, but she knew they wouldn't— Numberless preferred the most direct path, and she was right.

The first clash came moments later, a deep, metallic thunder of shieldwalls slamming together. Roars and battle cries rattled the stairwell, echoing back into the chamber like the heartbeat of war.

Jessica forced her focus back to the terminal Marcus had given her. Two Rifters hunched over the device beside her, their fingers a blur over the controls. She let them work—speed mattered more than pride. The fourth connection was severed just as a massive shadow fell across her.

She looked up.

A towering figure stood in the doorway, clad in Numberless battle armor, a long sword burning white in his grip. Every instinct screamed to raise her shield, but instead of charging, he strode past her—straight to the Crono-Stasis Pods.

With brutal precision, he sliced open pods, releasing Numberless in awkward, stumbling heaps. Shields flickered as bodies collapsed to the floor. His hands flew across a nearby terminal, cycling the pods until he found the ones he wanted, then cutting them free as well.

Horror clawed at her throat. He was waking the Numberless—and he was doing it without a data connection. Everything they'd been fighting for could be undone in minutes.

Jessica's hand tightened around her blade. She'd fought a Numberless once before. She could do it again.

Then his voice came over the Comm-Link, deep and unfamiliar. "Jessica. It's me—Titan. Cojax's father. I'm here to help."

Her eyes narrowed. "Then why are you freeing them?"

"We need to even the odds," Titan replied. "These are a few of my old drinking buddies."

Jessica scanned the room—twenty bodies. Nowhere near the force bearing down on them. "Is that enough?"

"Call your troops to the level above us," Titan said. "It's a training floor. The walls are shielded—they'll have to face us there."

"Yes, sir."

Titan smirked. "My boy must think you're something special. I hear you've got a real talent with the Blazer."

"I can trim your eyebrows at two hundred yards," she shot back.

Titan laughed, a short, genuine rumble. "I can see why he likes you."

He turned to the Numberless gathering their footing. "My friends… to you, it's been seconds since we last spoke. For me, four long years. In that time, Atlas has only gotten worse."

A few chuckles rippled through the group.

"My son has led a rebellion against the AC. I've joined him. Every one of you has voiced dissent before. We dreamed about this moment, but never acted. It took the resolve of the Aberration to make it real. I will see to it we don't waste it."

Silence, heavy and electric.

A short, broad man stepped forward. "No need to tell us how many—just where they are."

"Let's end it," another growled.

Titan nodded once. "On me."

They stormed the stairwell, boots hammering steel, and burst into the training hall above. The first wave of retreating Rifters stumbled in—bloodied, armor cracked, eyes wide from the slaughter above.

Jessica moved fast, pulling them into order, forming a second line just off Titan's flank. There were only sixty of them left—many had no charge to their shields.

"Jessica, my girl," Titan said, "this is about to get intense. Have your Rifters line the perimeter with their Blazers. Strongest shots, aim for the head and arms—throw them off balance. Your swords will be worthless against this foe."

She relayed the order, and relief washed over her troops. They moved fast, taking cover along the obstacle course circling the room. Jessica crouched behind a barricade, Blazer trained on the door, finger feathering the trigger.

The silence was short-lived.

A crash tore through the upper wall—metal, dust, and debris exploding inward. The Numberless dropped into the training floor, landing hard enough to rattle the steel beneath them. They hadn't blundered into a trap—they'd crashed straight into it.

Atlas emerged from the breach, towering above the others. His circular shield gleamed under the training lights, his massive sword already in hand. He sheathed it, laughing, and stripped off his helmet. Scarred skin and black tattoos marked his face like a map of violence.

But it wasn't Atlas who spoke first—it was Akirian. "What are you doing, Titan? You've overstepped this time."

Titan's reply came low, steady. "I'm doing what I should have done years ago—before I let you take my wife from me. I will not ignore our people's suffering any longer."

"You'll die for this!" Canik barked from the flank.

"Enough," Akirian snapped, stepping forward until she stood just behind Atlas, weapon drawn. "We can still end this without spilling Numberless blood. Put down your sword, and we'll restore your status."

"No," Atlas growled, voice rumbling through the training room. "Titan has broken our most sacred law. He has ignored the god of *necessity* and instead elevated the weak. He can't hold up the AC one day and discard it the next."

"We can fix this," Akirian pressed.

"Not now," Titan cut her off. "I've severed the link to the Decamont. There's no going back. The city must change—and we must change with it. Join me. For once, fight for our people instead of against them."

Atlas gave a cold laugh. "You were supposed to raise Cojax to your level, not stoop to his. Tell me, Titan—have you been part of this movement all along?"

Titan didn't lower his blade. "It's over, Atlas. No need for more blood."

Atlas' tone flattened to steel. "Your son's life is over along with the rest of these traitors. Surrender your sword, and I might let you live."

Titan's eyes narrowed, his voice a hiss. "If you want my sword… then come and claim it."

Atlas slid his helmet into place. "So be it… old friend."

The collision was instant—an eruption of light and sound. Jessica had thought she'd seen power before, but this was something else. The Numberless didn't link shields or march in formation. They fought like dueling champions from another age, weapons thrumming with blinding energy. Even through her helmet's filter, the glare made her eyes ache. Each one carried the force of an entire linked Phalanx.

*"They're like gods,"* she thought.

Titan moved like the room was his. He slipped under a cleaving strike, his counter sending his opponent flipping over a training post. His next blow shattered a knee with a sound like thunder.

The third came from the side, blade aimed for Titan's chestplate—Jessica's shot took the attacker in the head. The explosive round snapped his neck back, but he kept his feet.

She fired again. And again. Speed over power, driving two more away from Titan before her Blazer was fried by a wild shot. Her eyes locked on a dead Rifter—Blazer still clutched in rigid fingers. But a Numberless stood between her and it.

She didn't hesitate.

Sword in hand, she charged. The Numberless turned toward her, sensors pinging. Her pulsed blade met his, and light exploded from the contact. The weapon shot from her grip and rolled across the floor. She barely had time to register the impossibility before another strike came.

He expected her to duck. She vaulted instead, twisting high over him, driving her fist down with every ounce of strength. It barely staggered him. She landed off balance, the ground rolling beneath her boots. He was on her instantly, knocking her to the floor. Jessica shoved back, terror and adrenaline burning in her veins. She was trapped.

She raised one hand, feigning surrender—while the other stretched for the fallen Blazer. Her fingers locked on the grip. She poured everything she had into it. The round blew the barrel apart, catching the Numberless under the chin and flinging him backward. The shot sapped all the energy from her shields, and her armor lost its charge.

He recovered fast, lunging—only to be split in two mid-stride. His shields cracked apart, armor falling in molten shards. Titan stood over her, sword dripping light, hand extended.

"Get out of here!" he barked. "There's nothing more you can do."

The behemoth didn't wait to see if she obeyed. Titan spun and plunged back into the fray.

The fight was shifting. The Numberless were finally beginning to fall, shields collapsing after the prolonged clash. Blood pooled under their bodies, red mixing on the training floor. Though Titan's side had fewer warriors, they were taking more lives— precision replacing spectacle. The enemy adapted, pairing off to isolate and overwhelm Titan's fighters before help could reach them. It might have worked—if Titan hadn't been there. Each time his allies neared collapse, his fury broke their attackers apart. He was, without question, the deadliest warrior in the room.

Jessica ignored Titan's order and scavenged a new Blazer— only one shot in the cell.

*"Blood and bile... I need a power source."*

That hollow, suffocating helplessness returned—just like when Elena had nearly drowned her in the shower. The tide turned again. Six against two. Titan now fought with a second sword, deflecting from one side while striking from the other.

*"He can't keep this up,"* she thought. *"I've got to do something."*

Her gaze darted across the floor. All her Rifters were gone— dead or retreated. Then she spotted it: a discarded Numberless shield, still humming with power. Two more glowed nearby.

*"I will not watch him die."*

She dragged the shields across the battlefield, slipping in behind Titan. He was slowing now, a faint hitch in his strikes. Two more foes fell beneath him—but then his last remaining ally lost a leg and crumpled into his own blood. Four against one. Titan's shields were moments from collapse.

Jessica jammed her Blazer's power cord into the shields, praying the connection would take. It did. Energy surged into the weapon. She fired instantly, her first shot slicing past Titan's helmet to hit Atlas square between the eyes. The giant staggered, disoriented. She fired again, each round timed to clear space for Titan's blades. Working in tandem, they cut two more down.

"Kill the girl!" Atlas roared.

One of the last broke away, charging for her. Titan and Atlas were left circling—two predators in the final coil. Atlas cast aside his shield and armed himself with a second sword. Their words were lost to her, but the tension was palpable. Then they lunged, blades colliding in a shower of light.

Jessica's attention snapped to her own threat. Two headshots barely slowed him. She fell back, firing between dodges, each round buying inches. A low swing—she rolled under it and came up shooting, rounds slamming into his chestplate to no effect.

In the center of the room, Titan proved himself the superior fighter. One blade cut, the other blocked; step by step, he drove Atlas to his knees.

Jessica wasn't as lucky. Her opponent caught her mid-step, leapt high, and stomped her into the floor. She raised her Blazer, but his boot crushed her wrist, forcing the weapon down.

It would be over in seconds.

Then—a grunt. The weight shifted. The Numberless toppled sideways, a sword buried in his heart.

Titan had thrown it—but the distraction cost him. Atlas surged up, driving an Arc Dagger into the seam beneath Titan's arm. Shields shattered. Steel met flesh. The blade pulsed, then twisted, tearing a deep, jagged wound.

Jessica saw it all in slow motion.

Her hand clenched the Blazer, knuckles white, blood seeping

from her grip. Her heart pounded as she leveled her sights on Atlas' head. Every crime, every wound he had dealt—to her, to Cojax, to Elena—boiled down to this single moment.

The shot took him cleanly. Atlas crumpled, head severed from his body.

Jessica shoved the dead warrior off her and sprinted to Titan. He was on his knees, then his back. The armor adjusted, slowing the bleeding, but it was not enough.

She opened her Comm-Link. "I need help! I need a Medicus!" She pressed hard on the wound, but crimson kept spilling through her fingers. "You're going to be alright."

"I don't have much time," Titan said, his voice still steady. "I've arranged for a few friends to guide him on his way. But I need you to do something for me—give Cojax my blade."

"Of course."

"I've done all I can for him, Jessica… but it may not be enough. The true enemy is coming—swift and merciless. When it strikes, he'll need you. Our people will need you. If there's any hope of survival, it will be with you at his side."

## SIXTY-ONE

Cojax found Finn, Orch, and Ion hunched over the controls, the room dim except for the glow of shifting code and schematic overlays across three terminals. Lines of data cascaded down Ion's screen while holo-diagrams of the CityScreen network pulsed and shifted on the others. The rest of the Rifters lingered at the edges, watching but unsure how to contribute.

"Go help those on the first level," Cojax ordered. The Rifters saluted and filed out, boots thudding against metal as they vanished down the stairs.

Cojax approached Ion, forcing his scattered thoughts into focus. "What do you need from me?"

Without looking up, Ion tapped a string of rapid commands into the terminal. "Hold the door. I can't afford interruptions."

Finn and Orch were both at separate terminals, their eyes darting across the screens. Finn's station displayed a swarm of security subroutines—shifting walls of color-coded firewalls. His job was to flag and isolate anything that tried to overwrite Ion's access.

"Orange spike, left sector," he called out, hands flying over the keys as he injected false packet headers to mask their intrusion.

Orch's display was raw encryption streams, constantly re-scrambling. His fingers danced over the console as he spotted patterns. "Cipher block thirteen repeating… switching to brute-cycle on channels seven, four, and sixteen," he reported.

Ion's voice stayed calm but clipped. "Keep seven open. Flood four with junk data. We're inside the outer shell, but the inner gate will hit back hard."

Cojax felt useless—watching them tear through digital defenses with the precision of battlefield surgeons. He paced, eyes locked on the door, every muscle tensed for the sound of boots in the hall.

"Red is back in sector three," Finn warned, rerouting a packet stream.

"I see it. Orch—when fourteen, seven, four appear in that order, tell me immediately. That's the key rotation window."

Cojax knew Ion was punching into the CityScreens—something only a Numberless could normally do—but the teamwork looked less like random button-mashing and more like a coordinated strike in a different kind of war.

"Almost there," Ion said, code flickering faster across his display. "Qualix ready to broadcast?"

Finn scanned his feed and nodded. "Signal's clean and strong."

"Two more minutes," Ion muttered, hands blurring over the keys.

The Comm-Link crackled. "We're getting overrun at Gate One!"

Cojax's muscles knotted. Another explosion shook the room, dust sifting down from the ceiling.

"They've almost broken our shields!" the voice cried.

Cojax looked between Ion and Finn.

"You're not about to do something stupid, are you?" Finn said, fingers still typing.

"If that Gate falls, the Rifters will be flanked everywhere else. It's over."

"And what exactly do you plan on doing about it?"

"Ion—open the north side balconies in ten seconds."

Finn half-rose, hand on his sword. "I'm coming with you—"

"Sit down," Ion snapped. "If you leave, the hack fails."

Finn clenched his jaw, but turned back to the terminal. When he glanced toward Cojax again, his friend was already gone.

Finn's jaw tightened as he shouted at Cojax. "Hey, if you leave, who is going to protect us while we push these buttons?"

Cojax didn't answer—he ran faster, his body already pulsing with energy. He snatched up two Repulse Shields from a heap of bodies, sprinted down a hallway, and burst through the balcony entrance as it hissed open.

Blinding chaos swallowed him. Rails of light whipped back and forth. Acadians and Rifters screamed far below. Bodies crashed to the floor, blood painting it crimson. He stepped over the dying, narrowly avoiding a jet of light that tore into the wall behind him. Then he was in a full sprint again, pounding past a knot of Rifters locked in a firefight with a CargoLifter.

His thoughts burned away. Noise, chaos—gone. Only his feet slamming the ground, only the bloody path ahead. He channeled energy into his legs; trails of light coursed through them. Then he leapt, clearing the railing. For an instant he hung in the air before plunging down, faster and faster past the balconies.

Below, an Acadian Phalanx pressed forward in perfect formation. Cojax poured power into the Repulse Shields until they blazed white. A heartbeat later, he struck. The impact detonated outward in a surge of energy. The Phalanx shattered, their shared shieldwall ripped apart. Warriors were hurled back in all directions like ripples from a stone cast into water.

The Acadians recoiled, stunned by what they faced. Cojax drew his sword, sending a flash of light racing along its edge. Then they charged. He met them head-on—ducking beneath the first strike, severing an arm, piercing a leg, then kicking another soldier into his comrades. Blades slammed into his back, driving him sideways, but he twisted low and carved upward, felling two in a single sweep. He was light and steel combined, bodies falling around him in rapid succession.

Their armor's charge was nearly gone, leaving them weak. Each pulse of his Arc Blade ripped away the last sparks of energy, cleaving through flesh and plating alike. The Acadian line buckled, then collapsed, retreating before him.

*"I pushed them back. I did it."*

***

Now's your chance. His back is turned.

Brutus' grip on his sword tightened, each step closing the gap between them. This wasn't the plan, but the temptation was a living thing in his veins. Adrenaline surged, thundering through his chest. He could almost taste the iron tang of Cojax's blood.

Years of being the Beta—of losing to the one who should

have been weaker—boiled inside him. Years of living in the long shadow of Cojax's name, his victories, his ego. Brutus' lips peeled back in a grimace that merged with the deep scars cutting across his face.

*"I am still strong. And you will fall before me."*

Only yards now. His blade rose. Cojax had just driven the enemy back, but the effort had drained him. One strike to break what's left of his shields. The next to take his head. He could see it already—Cojax's too-slow guard, Brutus' relentless assault, the clean arc of steel through flesh and bone. The vision thrilled him.

And then—he stopped.

*"Shortsighted."*

Always shortsighted. Jessica's words hit him like a punch. He was about to prove her right again. Always grabbing for the nearest prize. Always chasing the immediate kill. And that was why Cojax had reached the Crossing… and why Brutus had not.

Not now.

To strike now would be weakness masquerading as strength. He let the blade lower, his body dissolving into stillness. Then, without a word, he slid back into the chaos, vanishing like a shadow swallowed by the light.

***

Cojax's relief vanished as quickly as it had come. The first Phalanx lay broken, but another marched in to take its place, shields interlocked, pace relentless. He set his stance, forcing his breathing to steady even as unease gnawed at him. He pulsed more power into his Repulse Shield. *"We have to hold this Gate. I have to hold this Gate."*

Only now did he feel the weight of how alone he truly was.

Then—movement at his side. A Rifter no bigger than a boy stepped into formation. Cojax gave him a nod, and soon several more joined, battered and limping, their armor long since drained of charge. They wouldn't last long, and they knew it. Still, they stood.

Another wave of Rifters arrived, and this time, Cojax caught faint arcs of light flickering over their plating. A few still had energy left.

He opened the Comm-Link to those around him. "We hold until the last. Hold this line! We may fall, but we cannot yield!"

A guttural roar of affirmation rose from the line.

And then—silence.

The Acadians' advance slowed… stopped. The air hung thick and still. Cojax straightened, his gaze narrowing. The Rifters around him held their stance, confused. Across the line, every Acadian warrior tilted their head upward.

Cojax followed their gaze—and froze.

High above, the massive screens of the Trinity flared to life, each projecting the image of a single Damnattii. All across the city, other CityScreens mirrored the broadcast.

A slow smile broke across his face. *"They did it. It's going out to the whole city."*

The screens flickered, momentarily plunging into static before stabilizing. The image sharpened—Qualix stood under dim light, unmoving.

Cojax keyed his Comm-Link. "Finn, tell him he's live. He's just staring at the camera."

"On it," Finn replied.

The sound began low but swelled until it dominated the entire square.

"I am Qualix, born of the Son's honor," the Damnattii began, his voice resonating over every street. "I am one who has never been diluted. I speak with ten mouths, though I have been given one. I am of the Damnattii, and I come before you with an offer of peace."

A ripple of murmurs passed through the Acadians' ranks.

"Acadians and Damnattii are two peoples, but we serve the same master. The Numberless are responsible for the carnage. They controlled us. Forced us to wage this perpetual war. And they would shed the blood of their own to keep this truth from you."

A chorus of beeps cut through the moment—every Acadian's ArmGuard activating at once.

Cojax tapped his own. The display filled with file names: *The Rift, Roach Control, Dealing with Sedition.* Each bore a red banner: Numberless Only—and then, almost instantly, the restriction dissolved. Data spilled across his screen—lists of Rift prisoners, their

Tiers, their labor details, casualty rates from starvation, schematics of the Rift itself.

"Finn," Cojax said into the Comm-Link, "are you seeing this?"

"Yeah," Finn replied. "Ion cracked into the CityScreen systems. Once he bypassed their security, the rest was wide open. He's pulling files that should only exist in the Numberless archives."

"Titan," Cojax muttered. "He must have granted full access to all Validated."

He opened *Roach Control.* What stared back at him froze the air in his lungs—complete battle doctrine for commanding Roach swarms. How to drive them into frenzy. How to force a charge. How to pick apart specific Acadian formations with surgical precision.

It was all there, in writing.

And there could only be one conclusion. The Numberless weren't fighting a war against the Roaches... they were leading it.

As more Acadians bent over their ArmGuards, Qualix's voice only sharpened, each word hammering cracks deeper into the Numberless' control.

"The Numberless prolonged this war—*not us.* We believed there was no other way... until now. Those you fight today are not traitors, but liberators. They have not brought you turmoil; they have delivered you from ignorance. Now you have the truth. Now you can decide for yourself. End the rule of the Numberless, and you end this war!"

"Well, if that doesn't do it," Finn said over the Comm-Link, "then nothing will."

"It's working," Cojax whispered.

He turned, scanning the Acadians around him. Confusion. Disbelief. Blades lowering. Whole ranks fracturing into smaller circles as soldiers argued in hushed tones. Many hunched over their ArmGuards, scrolling feverishly, searching for the truth in the data now laid bare.

The battle had dissolved into uneasy conversation. A few commanders still barked orders, trying to raise one of the Numberless on their links—but no answer came. The Numberless had simply vanished.

Cojax's gaze shifted to Gate One. The once-bright alloy was

charred black, smoke curling from the ruined frame. Bodies from both sides lay heaped around the entrance. He swallowed hard against the bile rising in his throat. Death he had seen before—but this... this was senseless.

On the Killing Field, soldiers had died, locked in battle against a common enemy. Here, they had butchered each other in ignorance.

He shook his head, grief settling like lead in his chest.

Jessica's voice cut through the Comm-Link, high and urgent, "I need help! I need a Medicus!"

"Jessica, are you all right?" Cojax snapped. "I'm on my way."

*****

Brutus lingered in the shadows of the Trinity, his blade resting in its scabbard. Watching Cojax's face tighten in panic as he sprinted past was almost enough to tempt him to draw steel.

But no—he'd learned that lesson. The hard way.

He keyed his Comm-Link. "Hellish."

"Go ahead," came the reply.

"Start moving the food out. No one's going to stop you now."

"Yes, sir."

"And get some Rifters up here. I want every discarded weapon collected. Make it look like they are cleaning up, not looting."

"Yes, sir."

Brutus severed the link and allowed himself a slow, genuine smile—something he hadn't felt in months.

*"Now, we'll see who's really shortsighted."*

## SIXTY-TWO

Cojax, Finn, and Marcus found Jessica in the Medicus wing in the Trinity. Cojax's heart clenched at the sight of her—until he realized, after a quick sweep of her figure, that her injuries were little more than shallow cuts.

"Cojax… Marcus," she whispered, her eyes distant and glassy. "Titan is dead."

It was as if the Golden Orb had drained Cojax again, pulling every ounce of strength from his body. His back went to the wall, but Finn caught him before he could stumble. Cojax raised a hand. "I'm fine… really." He shut his eyes. For several long moments, the room faded away.

Marcus' shoulders sagged, his frame seeming to collapse in on itself. The words he had once spoken now echoed back as a grim prophecy fulfilled—his father was gone. At last, he found his voice, heavy and low. "Jessica… take us to him."

She led the way through the crowded wing. The air was thick with the metallic tang of blood and the muted groans of the wounded. Most injuries were amputations—arms and legs severed—but here and there were the deeper wounds: stomachs, chests, sides, punctured clean through. The silence of the injured struck Cojax in a way he couldn't shake; it was the same silence he remembered from his childhood. It brought his father's image to mind—immortal, unshakable, flawless. The man who could not die.

And yet.

He spotted Titan across the room. The massive frame lay rigid on a table, white sheet drawn to the collarbone. A dark bloom of blood spread from his left side, seeping down to the floor.

"Even now," Cojax murmured, "he looks strong. I half believe he'll sit up any second and scold me for standing idle." His voice caught, the words fracturing as moisture brimmed in his eyes. "Just when I finally see him—when he finally shows me who he really is—he's taken."

He forced a breath through his lungs, pressing the grief deep where it couldn't be seen. He would not dishonor Titan's memory with weakness. Marcus stepped to his father's side, resting a steady hand on his shoulder. He leaned close and whispered a few words, soft and reverent. The cadence carried the shape of Latin, though too quiet to fully discern.

Jessica took Cojax's hand. "He saved me, Cojax. He didn't have to die. He threw his sword to kill the one who was about to cut me down—but that left him unarmed…" Her words broke apart. The tears came hot and fast, pooling at her chin.

Cojax drew her into his arms, running his hand gently through her red hair. "Tell me everything. From the start."

She wiped her face and told it again, this time without the breaks. When she finished, Cojax spoke of the words Titan had given him before charging into battle.

"Now it all makes sense," Marcus whispered. "He was not fighting to keep us trapped, but to hold a greater enemy at bay. Hostem maiorem arcere—to ward off a greater enemy."

Jessica pulled Cojax close, clinging to him as she had in the Mahghetto—wanting, in that moment, to hold him for all time. Then she kissed him, pouring every ounce of feeling into it.

She hated Acadia. Always had. And Acadia had returned the sentiment without hesitation. She owed it nothing, and it would not miss her. She could vanish—be gone before the Decamont attacked, long before the next tide of blood and betrayal. The thought was intoxicating. *"I could be free."*

She saw it in her mind's eye—snow-capped mountains, wild green meadows, rivers twining through endless forests. But Cojax would never leave. And she could never leave Cojax.

She swallowed the temptation and kissed him again, softer this time. His lips carried the taste of sorrow and duty.

Then she drew back, urgency flashing in her eyes. "Titan saved you—saved all of us. His memory can't just… disappear. We should honor him in the old way. Broadcast it to the city."

"A funeral?" Finn's voice came from behind. "That's against the AC."

"So was storming the Trinity," Cojax said with a grim smile.

"But she's right. My father deserves more than a sheet and a hidden cremation."

"Now?" Finn asked.

"No. We can't rush this." Cojax looked at Jessica. "Tomorrow. And I want you to be the one to tell them."

"Me?"

"You were the last with him. It should come from you."

She nodded.

"Come on," he said, leading the way back to the Main Control Room. The pace was slow, deliberate—enough for Jessica to gather her thoughts.

When Ion nodded to her at the console, she was ready.

Her face filled the CityScreens across Acadia. She let the silence hold for a moment before speaking, weighing each word.

"Tonight, we have bathed in the blood of our own. But we fought not to keep the enemy out—only to let the truth in. We have been lied to. Deceived. But one Numberless would not have us blind like the rest. Titan, son of Nun, now lies dead—because he defended me from those who would keep us in the dark."

Her voice faltered, just for a breath.

"Tomorrow, at first light, we will hold a ceremony in the Major Forum closest to the Trinity. And all will hear of him."

## SIXTY-THREE

The next morning, Titan's body was prepared in his finest ceremonial armor—polished until the bronze and crimson caught the rising sun. He was laid upon a marble bier at the top of the Trinity's grand steps, the highest place of honor in the city. The destruction from the night before had been swept away, though blackened scorch marks still clung to the stone—silent witnesses to the cost of truth.

Banners of the BloodBorne Faction hung from every tier of the Trinity, their crimson threads stirring faintly in the morning breeze. Every BloodBorne of the First Tier was present, their armor flawless, shields gleaming. They lined the balconies in rigid rows, a wall of steel and discipline.

The sight struck something deep in Cojax's memory. He had seen a gathering like this before—on the day his mother was Honorably Released. He could still see her face on the broadcast: weary, but unbroken, her gaze lifted toward the camera as if staring through the city itself. She had been the only one Released that day, stepping into the Killing Field with a strange, quiet defiance. He had not understood her defiance then. He did now.

By first light, the Major Forum was swollen with people. Tens of thousands, packed so tightly there was no room to move. Windows were crammed with onlookers; rooftops sagged under the weight of bodies leaning for a glimpse. Those too far to see gathered around CityScreens, faces tilted toward the flickering light, waiting.

As the sun climbed higher, a slow, haunting dirge began to play—its low notes rolling across the stone like distant thunder. One by one, soldiers approached the bier to leave tokens of respect: a dagger, a BloodBorne insignia, a strand of braided hair. Marcus stepped forward first and laid a book at his father's feet—an offering of immense worth. He was clad in his finest armor, polished to a perfect sheen. His gaze was steady, carved in somber resolve, carrying both the strength of his father and the burden of his people.

Cojax was last. In his hands, he carried a blazing torch. He stepped forward, saluted once—a sharp, perfect movement—and lowered the flame. Fire licked the edges of Titan's armor, growing until the whole bier was a tower of light. He looked up to find Adriana, Finn, and Orch assembled at his right, while Aias, Kane, Horacio, and Havish stood firm at his left.

Every camera turned to Cojax. He did not speak immediately. He let the fire frame him, the heat against his back, the weight of the moment in his eyes.

When he spoke, his voice carried like the toll of a great bell.

"I am Cojax, son of Titan. I speak for the man who died so that you might stand here free. His vision is now my own. Today, we choose our truth—not as pawns, but as a people. The path ahead will be hard. We will stumble. But if we endure, we will rise stronger than we have ever been."

He told them of the Decamont—the Roach invasion that had once brought humanity to its knees, the long war that had drained their spirit. He reminded them that the victory of the night before was but a single step in a long ascent.

"The Decamont will try to destroy us before our ideas spread. There is no time for discord. No time for divided Factions. If you value the lives of your children—if you value the freedom we have just won—then we must stand as one."

His gaze swept the crowd.

"As of this moment, the Acadian Code is abolished. The Tiers are no more. We will no longer be measured by Score, but by our unity and strength. No one else will be Rifted. All those already in the Rift are pardoned—unconditionally. Never again will you be forced to choose between your standing and your conscience. Never again will you have to swallow the truth for fear of your own survival."

He paused, letting the weight of his next words settle.

"This city will no longer be called Acadia. That was the name of our bondage. From this day forward, it will be known as Titan—in honor of the man who died for our freedom."

A murmur rippled through the crowd, swelling into a roar.

Cojax lifted his voice above it.

"The Decamont believe we will break when they come. They

will come with armies. They will come with chains. They think we are small, fragile, weak. They think we are but mere mortals. But they are wrong, my brothers and sisters, for we are Titans."

# ACADIA BASIC STATIC ARMOR

Static Armor is worn by **Validated** who have survived the rigors of the **Mahghetto**. It functions best when the wearer has been infused with bio-circuitry, allowing for a stronger and more responsive link. The armor is charged by the wearer and adjusts to allow greater freedom of movement. It also enhances strength, speed, vision, and agility.

While charged, the Static Armor projects a nearly imperceptible shield along its surface, rendering the wearer almost impervious to attack until the energy is depleted.

**Static Helmet**
Contains the HUD display and Comms-Link, and can switch to thermal or night vision. The metal fillet on the helmet links shields within a formation, allowing an **Ion-Phalanx**.

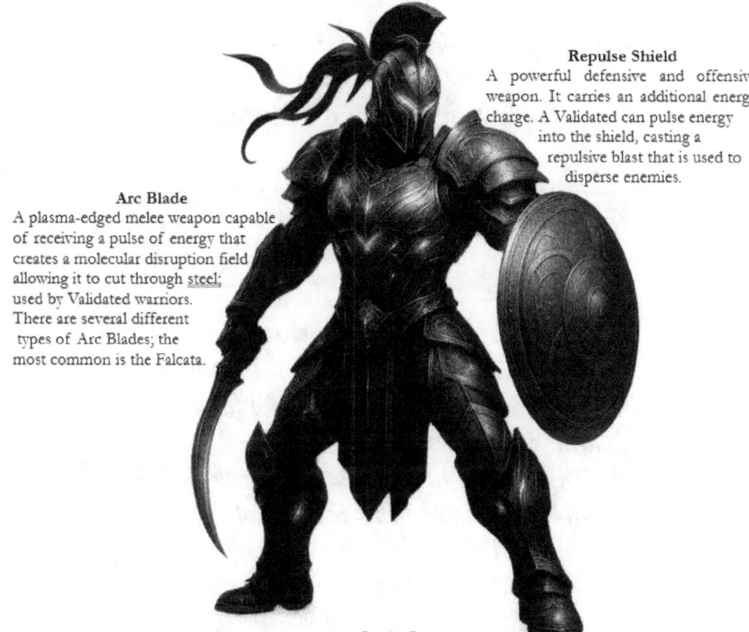

**Repulse Shield**
A powerful defensive and offensive weapon. It carries an additional energy charge. A Validated can pulse energy into the shield, casting a repulsive blast that is used to disperse enemies.

**Arc Blade**
A plasma-edged melee weapon capable of receiving a pulse of energy that creates a molecular disruption field allowing it to cut through steel; used by Validated warriors. There are several different types of Arc Blades; the most common is the Falcata.

**Static Greaves**
When energy is channeled into the greaves and synced to a Validated's bio-circuitry, it can give the user enhanced strength, speed, and jumping range.

## A Note from the Author

Sterling always enjoys hearing from his readers. Whether you have questions, comments, critiques, or just want to say hello, feel free to visit him at <u>sterlingnixon.com</u>. There, you can also find updates on upcoming releases, behind-the-scenes content, merchandise, and details about future projects.

If you enjoyed this novel and would like to see more of Sterling's work, *please leave a review on other major platforms.* Your feedback and support make a tremendous difference.

Other Books Written by Sterling Nixon

### Dystopia/Science Fiction:
*Acadia*
*Acadia Field Manual (Lore Book)*
*Titan*
*Charron*

### Young Adult Fiction:
*Nickle Brickle'Bee: In the Heart of EarthWorks*
*Nickle Brickle'Bee: In the Halls of Harbordeen*
*Nickle Brickle'Bee: In the Home of Atlantia*
*Nickle Brickle'Bee: In the Floating Isles of Balinbar*
*Nickle Brickle'Bee: In the Throne Room of StormHaven*
*Nickle Brickle'Bee: In the Caves of the Goblin King*
*Nickle Brickle'Bee: In the Streets of Ethereal*

### Historical Fiction:
*Gladiators of the Naumachia*

### Non-Fiction:
*Twenty-Two Manly Stories to Inspire Men with Manliness*